CHANGED FOR DESIRE

A WARLOCK OF
KAMVASANA
STORY

CHANGED FOR DESIRE

A WARLOCK OF
KAMVASANA
STORY

CLEA SALAR & TALLIS SALAR

CHANGED FOR DESIRE
First Edition.
October 31, 2025

Copyright © 2025 Clea Salar & Tallis Salar
Printed by Charming Fetish, an imprint of Periapt Press

Periapt Press
PO Box 25693
Colorado Springs, CO 80936
www.periaptpress.com

ISBN: 979-8-9903639-8-4

To the bi babes. Ignore the haters. Keep being you.

Content Notes:

Changed for Desire, much like its predecessor, continues to be inspired by familiar TTRPG settings and is full of open door descriptive encounters between our pansexual heroine, three strapping men of various fantasy races, a primordial deity who defies gender and likes to watch, and a handful of assertive women, also of various fantasy races. There may also be feelings and some hand holding. Be prepared, we don't hold back.

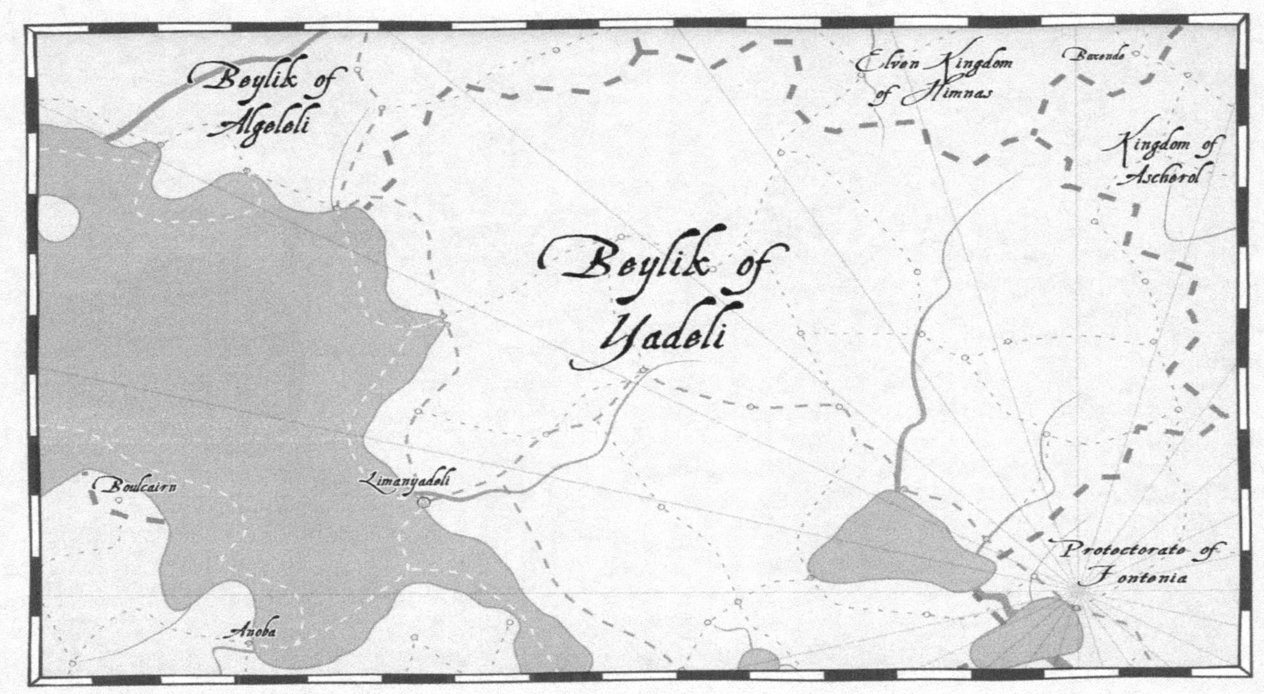

Beylik of Algeleli
Beylik of Yadeli
Elven Kingdom of Himnas
Bazenda
Kingdom of Ascherol
Protectorate of Fontenia
Boulcairn
Limanyadeli
Anoba

ONE

Wagon wheels, tromping feet, and the hooves and claws of various creatures—overlaid with a fluctuating wave of chatter—filled the ears as throngs of people crossed the Ayunt River heading into Limanyadeli, capital port city of the Beylik of Yadeli. It sat on the shore of Lake Sizhou, a massive body of water surrounded by the Beylik of Yadeli on the east and south, and the Beylik of Algeleli to the north and west. Along its rivers and tributaries, one could get to nearly every kingdom and province on the continent from the lake.

They were in the last bits of summer, with fall fast approaching, a cold breeze countering the warm sun above. The wind over the Ayunt whipped through Octavia's curls, swirling them up into a silver blond cloud. She felt like something out of nature for a moment; a lovely woman with a generous figure astride a massive elk, the blues and grays of her clothing reflecting the colors of the water. Then the wind died down, her hair falling down her shoulders and back in a pretty mess. The elk, Nutmeg, shook his great head and made a strange sound between a sneeze and a snort, further ruining the illusion.

It was three weeks since Octavia and her companions left Boxende, well celebrated as the heroes who defeated the Black Crag Clan and freed the townsfolk who had been kidnapped. Four weeks since they'd survived the horrors of Drukankor's Tower and made off with enough arcane knowledge to occupy a cabal of mages for a year or more.

The dragonkin leading their little group, Alces, Knight of the Spree Spirits, grinned broadly as they reached the arch of the bridge and saw the sprawling, bustling city on the other side. "We'll be staying here for a few days, I'd imagine," he announced, looking back to the rest of the group. "Let's try not to get in trouble with the guard too quickly." Alces bellowed out a laugh which left her other two companions, Durante and Sumner, laughing quietly and shaking their heads.

"Give me a day or two to figure out the town," Durante said, lifting a pale hand to push his raven hair back. "By then I should know where I can find what I need, or if they even have it."

"Strix blood and liver, right?" Octavia asked, glancing down at him, and he nodded. She'd been the one combing through manuscripts with him every night—he needed her magical ability to translate the various scrolls and books.

"I'll try to rustle up some work or something," Sumner said, absently rolling a glass ball from his palm to the tops of his fingers and back as they walked. "Funds are getting a little tight after a trip like that." Sumner was a contrast to Durante, with golden hair instead of black and warm fawn skin instead of alabaster.

"Oh, I have some things to sell," Octavia chimed in, "and we might finally be in a city large enough to unload some of the… more interesting items we got from the mausoleum in Gravemont." She smiled wryly, remembering the cabinet of strange objects they'd uncovered. Sumner glanced up at her. His almond shaped, jade green eyes gave the impression of a cat, and were as mischievous.

"Relics from Gravemont, yes," Sumner said, "but more of your own belongings, no. You've contributed enough with your tent and what you used to update the tent."

Alces nodded. "We will earn our way, generous Octavia," he said, clasping a fist against the chest of his vine-inlaid plate armor. The midday sun gleamed off of him—in addition to the plate, Alces was a wall of muscle nearly seven feet tall covered in silver scales that glittered in the sunlight.

"Then help me sell them, take a fence's fee for the purse, and give me the rest," Octavia said, pragmatically. "I need to sell them anyway. I haven't been somewhere sufficiently populated since before I landed in Gravemont."

She appreciated they didn't want to take advantage of her, but she was hardly selfless. Sumner didn't let her buy anything now that they were all traveling together. He kept the purse, as both Alces and Durante were bad with money, and since she was now part of the group, her expenses were theirs.

"Lady, you drive a hard bargain, but I accept your terms," Sumner said with a toothy smirk.

She smiled, glad the matter was settled. "I knew you would." Though speaking of Gravemont. "That reminds me, I still haven't gotten around to looking at that book. The weeks have been… busy."

"Yes, and I can't thank you enough," Durante said, nodding his head to her. "It would have taken me years to decipher that wizard's script."

"I'm glad I could help," she said, smiling again.

Limanyadeli loomed ahead of them, larger by the moment—whatever they were looking for, this should be the place to find it. Beyond the scattered homes and businesses outside the city proper, they could see the Chargate, one of the primary entrances into the city. The scorched, soot-covered wooden gate had been reinforced with metal and stone, a memorial to a time when raiders had attempted to take the city but had been driven off. Those gates were thrown open at this time of day, traffic passing freely through.

It had been a long trip on the road, starting with a rather tense border crossing shortly after Boxende, and then several towns with passable but cheap inns. More than once they had paid a local farmer a couple coins to pitch their tent in a fallow field overnight after discovering the inn didn't have a bed that could support Alces, or didn't have enough rooms for the four of them. They'd reached the Amethyst Road, the major trade route into Limanyadeli, about a week ago. The quality of the inns had increased, and also the size of the crowds.

Octavia reflected that it was certainly the least accosted she'd ever been on a longer journey. No bandits, no highwaymen, and not a single unwanted advance in any tavern or inn they had patronized. Having Alces out front discouraged a lot of people from thinking they had a chance at an easy mark. Having three somewhat dangerous looking men as her steady companions also kept away less dangerous looking men who had ideas about what Octavia was there for.

As they finally left the bridge, she reached forward and rubbed Nutmeg between the ears. "It's probably time to let me down, big boy. You're not going to like the city anyway."

Nutmeg bugled and chuffed and Alces tsked. "Of course they would be, but that's no excuse. Now then," the dragonkin said as he reached up and lifted Octavia off the elk and set her down gently on the brick road, "consider this a vacation."

Nutmug chuffed one more time, nuzzled against Octavia's chest, then wandered off the path and into the field beyond. Soon, the great elk disappeared in a swirl of sparkling purple smoke, and all trace of the creature was gone.

Octavia stretched and adjusted her satchel. Fishing a tie out of her pocket, she pulled back her voluminous curls. "Have any of you been here before? I haven't. Looks a bit like Rupaiya, but less humid."

"I haven't," Sumner said, tossing the glass orb back and forth in his hands. "I think this is the furthest west we've been. I'm from Fontenia."

"Really?" She looked over at him, surprised. While the accent suggested as much, he looked like he was from Amyeol or the Empire of Salt.

"We'd mostly been travelling around Ascherol and just a bit into Ceresia," Durante said. Like Octavia, he was from the Kingdom of Asherol. It was sizable, so the thought of people roaming around it for a few years was reasonable.

"I've been to Yadeli," Alces said as they continued on the road towards the gate. "But never to the capital. New experiences for all of us. Huzzah!" He grinned, his enthusiasm was always genuine.

"More adventure, then," she said with a faint smile. In truth, she was a little nervous. They had joked about not upsetting the guard, but she'd seen what the three of them could do to a tavern. She also usually put more work into researching an area before rolling in.

"Well, first, I assume?" She looked over at Duranted then. It was technically his "quest," as Alces would put it, and so he was currently in charge of their direction.

"Yeah, preferably one near the marketplace," Durante said, tapping his fingers on his bag as he thought about it.

Sumner sighed. "That's probably going to be pretty pricey," he said, more to himself.

"Worth the price," Alces said over his shoulder. "Worry not, I can find work to help. It won't be forever, just a few days."

"I guess I can share a room with someone, if it'll save us some money," she offered with a wry smile.

"So, do we need to ram-gate-blade for who gets to room with you," Sumner said, smiling right back.

"Let us see what options are first," Alces said and continued to lead the way into town.

Limanyadeli was a bright city, with most of the buildings being white plaster with red clay-shingle roofs. The odd religious temple had domed ceilings and high spires on the edges of the land reaching high into the sky. The capital itself, a grand palace in the center of town, could be seen from the bridge, its structure made of layered domes, tiered off in the center, and soaring towers flanking its northern and southern sides. The sides seemed to glitter like the surface of the lake, either by some special paint against the plaster or magic weaved into the architecture.

They finally passed through the Chargate, the blackened reinforced wood stark against the white walls flanking it. People were bustling about with colorful garb; it flowed around them in draped cloth and scarves. Certainly different from Ascherolean attire but very similar to Rupaiyan fashions. A bit more movement in the cloth, the skirts were fuller. Octavia found herself rather enchanted.

"Ohhh, it's gonna be so hard not to spend money here," Octavia murmured under her breath.

"You know, you do have a bit of an advantage," Durante said, following her eyes and close enough to hear her mutter. Over the weeks, Octavia's demeanor and attentions had certainly drawn Durante out. "Not only would you make anything you wear look good, but your gift makes it happen regardless. If anyone needs a new wardrobe, it's me." Glancing over to her, he gave her a playful grin.

"We might want to find you something that doesn't scream Asherolean noble," she agreed quietly, and leaned into him a little as she did. "Or at least find someone to take your shirts in." She looked up at him and smiled. He got that semi-shy look he'd get when she complimented him, but nodded in agreement.

It took them nearly two hours to get to the market square. Limanyadeli was a large city, and the streets were bustling as they threaded their way towards the market. However, what delayed their journey the most was the two times Alces and Sumner caught pickpockets trying to rob them. The footpads were given a stern, but understanding, talking to. One young man seemed receptive to Alces' words. The second was just happy to have lived through it.

Finally they made it. The market was called Stone Cross, an immense courtyard split off in the four cardinal directions, giving it its cross shape, and the ground was made up of a mix of crushed limestone and some local rock, making it white with speckles of green coloring. It had been months, closer to a year, since Octavia had been to a bazaar of this size. The possibilities were thrilling.

"We should look for a place on the north or west side," Sumner said, craning his head to try and see above the crowds and stalls. Unfortunately, he was as short as Octavia—they'd have to rely on Alces. "North for the traders coming in, west for the sea merchants."

"Maybe west? More likely to have a higher variety of strange things," she offered, looking around. She kept her satchel in front of her while in the market, and her purse was actually hung between her breasts. She felt eyes on her, but most likely not thieves or opportunists. It was not unusual for her to draw attention.

"West it is," Alces said, and the crowd parted as he walked in that direction, the other three following in his wake. It was helpful that while Octavia was certainly being looked at, the number of unwelcomed approaches had diminished due to her escorts.

Surprisingly, it was Durante that took the lead in finding a nicer inn. Perhaps less surprising as he and Octavia looked more like nobility or merchants—Alces looked every bit a knight, but had no livery, and Sumner looked like he was casing the place. It took a few attempts, but Durante was able to convince an innkeeper that not only was Octavia a visiting dignitary, which wasn't exactly inaccurate, but with Alces around the security of his inn was all but assured. Once Octavia understood what Durante was trying, it was easy enough to weave a minor charm spell into the negotiation. There was, unfortunately, also a good chance the innkeeper now wanted to sleep with her—many of her spells had that side effect—but the boys would deter any of those ideas. Thus, they ended up with a relatively nice set of rooms overlooking the marketplace for a discounted rate.

The inn also had a sizable dining area, a courtyard with a fountain which would certainly keep the guests cool in the summer heat with its shading foliage and running water. That was something Octavia had also noticed; the city was scattered with trees. Nearly every empty area had some sort of shade tree growing. Here in the early days of fall, shade was still appreciated.

Passing by the courtyard to the stairs, they headed up to their rooms. They got two rooms, each a roomy suite with a pair of large beds. They'd still have to figure out who was bunking with who. The rooms were lovely—heavy carpets with beautiful, elaborate patterns covered the floors and similar tapestries hung on the inward walls to help muffle sounds. The beds were at opposite corners of the room, hung with sheer curtains which Octavia knew, from her time in Rupaiya, would be drawn in the high summer to keep insects off the bed while allowing the windows to remain open. A pair of divans flanked a low table in the center, appropriate for morning tea or late night drinks. There were also pillows large enough for lounging on—well, large enough for everyone other than Alces. There was one basin and wash stand, and a large wardrobe which had been left empty and open by the inn staff, so guests could clearly see it was available.

"Okay, who goes where?" Octavia asked, looking into the two rooms.

"Gentleman," Sumner said, turning to the other three and holding out a fist.

"Very well," Durante said and did the same. Alces laughed and joined in.

Leaning back against the doorframe, Octavia crossed her arms over her chest and watched the three of them with amusement. This was the first time this particular issue had come up - they'd been traveling together for a while, true, but Octavia's magic tent had separate rooms for each of them, and the other inns they'd stayed in had been… well, cheaper. And any time the inn didn't have enough room, they stayed in the tent.

"Raiders hit a wall and fall," they all said in unison as they pumped their fists to the rhythm of the words. Alces and Sumner both held out two fingers held together while Durante kept his a fist. Durante grunted in disappointment while Alces and Sumner turned toward each other and repeated the process. This time Alces held out a flat hand which he raised up vertically while Sumner kept his as the two fingers. Alces grinned and bumped Sumner's fingers.

"It's best this way," the dragonkin said. It seemed Alces had won the little competition to find out who was rooming with Octavia. "Keep up appearances that I am the lady dignitary's loyal knight."

"Congratulations, Ser Knight," Octavia said with a grin. Pushing off the frame, she motioned to the rooms. "Take your pick."

Shrugging, he opened the door closest to them and motioned for her to enter. "I don't feel it matters. After you, fairest Octavia."

As Octavia thought about it, there was a certain fairness in Alces being the one she shared a room with. During their journey, Durante had ended up staying with Octavia the most, primarily because at the end of each day travelling they would work on deciphering and sorting the great piles of notes and books they had liberated from the wizard's tower. When it wasn't Durante, it was Sumner, who simply always desired

Octavia. Alces seemed fine with only approaching her when he felt she needed cheering up over something, or was asked. Whatever oaths his order followed, he seemed nearly as happy knowing his companions were enjoying each other.

Of course, the nights with Durante were as likely to end with exhausted snuggling once they'd stayed up too late translating and comparing notes. Nights with Sumner were always physical, no matter how tired they both were. It was rather flattering, in a way—Sumner was always as excited to be with her as he had been the first time.

Drifting through the room, Octavia sighed happily and set down her bag by the far bed, furthest from the door. She suspected Alces would want the other as her "guard." And also likely on principle.

"I know one day you will live in a hall of luxury, but hopefully this is a satisfying taste for now. I can imagine traveling with us, even with a tent as marvelous as yours, is not quite what you hoped for," Alces said, looking over the room and moving towards the windows to look at the marketplace. It was getting late in the afternoon and night would be falling soon. "Make no mistake, however. We adore your company. and you bless us every day with your presence."

Smiling softly, Octavia wandered over to Alces and took his hand in both of hers. "Ser Knight," she said, lifting up his massive clawed appendage and kissing the back of it, "the only reason I never hoped for this time traveling with you all is because I was incapable of imagining it."

Smiling broadly, Alces caressed her cheek with the back of his claw. "Sweetest Octavia." He gave her two hands a squeeze then stepped back. "We should eat and then take a walk through the market. Things can shift when the sun sets. Hmm, should we walk first?"

"We should probably go for a walk first before the market changes over," Octavia said, letting Alces go and looking out the window herself. "Once the stalls start to close up, we can get dinner, and take our time with it. Then go see if the night market has something more interesting to offer."

Her eyes flicked across the brightly curtained stalls and larger side shops. The Stone Cross was enormous and cacophonous in a way that made Octavia smile. It was teeming with life and people, and she loved that.

The market was not a location Alces likely needed to be wandering clad in blessed steel. He sat at the foot of his bed and started the lengthy process of unstrapping his plate armor so they could be more casual among the crowds.

"We probably won't buy much right now, but we'll at least be able to get a feel for the place," she said, walking back up to Alces. "It's a large market, it'll probably take us a minute to even find the types of vendors Durante is looking for."

Alces smiled up at her as he dropped his pauldrons off his broad shoulders. At first, it seemed Alces was generally pleased with anyone that showed kindness. However, after being with them for over a month and seeing their interactions with others, she could tell his smile was different for her. A little softer, with more meaning than a simple joy of knowing a nice person.

"I will disarm as quickly as I can," he said, now working on the straps along the edges of his chest and back plate.

Octavia helped. She had nimble fingers, but was also a bit stronger than she looked. Not enough to carry any of Alces's plate—she was still a little amazed Durante could easily heft all of it—but enough to pull free his straps. Some of the plates weren't so bad. Namely the ones around his lower legs that formed a boot-like shell around his clawed feet, his wrists, and his upper arms. It took far less time with her help, and soon Alces was in his padding and under clothes. He stripped down to his skivvies, and applied Durante's cleansing fluid over his body to clear off the dirt of the road.

Rummaging through his magic bag, Alces started pulling out his tunic and kilt. As Alces dressed, Octavia examined his padding, casting small spells to mend a tear here and take out a stain there. They cost her nothing, and it was something to do while she waited. She was often surprised by the urge to take care of Alces, simply because it seemed to pop up with a force at times. Maybe because it felt like a way to repay him for all the times he put himself between her and anything potentially dangerous. Granted, they'd only been traveling together for about two months, but still.

"Ready?" she asked as he adjusted his kilt. She set down the padding.

"If I am presentable, then I am ready," he said with another grin, standing before her with a puffed out chest and his fists on his hips.

She giggled. "Always, my knight. I like the kilt, I don't think I've seen you in it yet." She headed towards the door, expecting to find Sumner and Durante waiting.

Sumner was alone in the hallway, leaning against the wall and sighing.

He rolled his head to look over at them. "My lord is getting dressed," he said with a smirk, then lowered his voice a little. "I'm not going to blame you, but I think you gave him a brain nit over his appearance. He's rummaging."

Octavia groaned. "Oh, that's so not fair. I just said we could take his shirts in, it was supposed to be a compliment."

"Oh, no, not about that," Sumner laughed. "No, it was about not looking like an Ascherolean noble."

"Oh." Octavia blinked. "Well, he does. Look like one, I mean. I wasn't trying to imply it was bad, but he said he might need a new wardrobe, and I said looking less obviously like an Ascherolean noble might be a start." She wrinkled her nose. She wasn't good at this, at measuring what she said to people.

Sumner dismissed her concern with a wave of his hand. "It's fine. But I did notice a couple of people giving him looks. Which is certainly different because usually everyone is looking at you," he said with a wink, and she rolled her eyes, "so maybe it wasn't such a bad idea."

"We could probably find a tailor easily enough." Octavia looked thoughtful for a moment. "Shouldn't be expensive either. Take the shirts in, take off the lace or ruffled collars. Should be able to do it in the time we need here, especially if we pay to have it rushed."

"Yeah, probably," Sumner said, then thumped on the door with his foot. "Come on, D! We're burning daylight!"

There were sounds of some scuffling and something being knocked over, hitting the floor with a thump, then Durante arrived with a dramatic opening of the door. He looked out of sorts, but he was dressed in his simplest pants and a laced shirt. It was certainly the least she'd seen him wear when he was planning on actually going out.

"Nice entrance, Kitten," Octavia said with a smile.

"Casual. Good choice, wise Durante," Alces said with a grin.

"So," she began, getting back to the evening ahead of them, "I proposed to Alces that we should walk the market first, get a feel for it, and then have a leisurely dinner before returning to check out the night market. What do you all think?"

"Works for me," Sumner said, out of his leathers but still wearing rather dark clothing. A gray lace-up shirt with matching ties along his forearms and pants of a similar style. "I'll split off, try to hear things and see what they might not have in the open."

"Yeah, that's fine," Durante added.

Nodding, Octavia headed towards the stairs. She subtly patted herself down to make sure everything was tucked away. She didn't think Limanyadeli had a particularly sinister reputation, but as the walk in had proven, busy cities meant pickpockets.

The group headed out of the inn, with the keeper wishing Octavia a pleasant night and to be sure to ask him if she needed anything at all. She smiled politely and thanked him. Sumner snickered quietly, then disappeared shortly after they stepped outside.

The Stone Cross was an immense marketplace, and as they wandered the unique paths, they encountered stores and booths selling a wide array of things. Spices by the pound, pets of unique breeds, fashion appropriate for everything from grand balls to casual gatherings, and all of them being hocked by well-practiced callers. They could smell meats and street foods of all sorts wafting from the center of the market. It was crowded, but with a combination of Alces leading the way and the evening getting on, it wasn't impossible to move around.

It did not take long before Octavia became unreasonably excited about the market. For all that she came across as very worldly and knowing, the truth was she really only knew her corner of the world. Now, she understood people well enough, and she knew when she was being conned, but she'd really never been outside Rupaiya and Ascherol. And as such, was not doing a good job hiding her fascination with some of the new clothing and jewelry and shoes they passed at different shops. It was similar to Rupaiyan clothing, but with an additional flounce and flair. True to her original proposal, though, she didn't try to buy anything. Simply noted where it could be found again.

Durante was a little more obvious as he looked upon shops that seemed, to the untrained eye, to be selling junk. More than once he'd start to ask Sumner for money, then cut himself off as he remembered he wasn't there, and sighed. Alces would just chuckle and pat him on the shoulder, but it seemed both of them were making note of the locations.

They found a little shop selling reagents set in the shade of a tree. Durante examined it with a careful eye, but toned his expectations. As they walked away, he tilted his head back and forth. "They have a lot of things I could use, but nothing I'd consider particularly rare or unique."

"I'm sure there's something else to be found," Octavia said, carefully side stepping a man who looked like he was going to "accidentally" bump into her. "This place is too big for there not to be more."

"Oh, I'm sure," he replied, "especially once the sun goes down and the market turns over."

Alces resumed his spot in front and looked over his shoulder. "Back to the inn for dinner? I say we explore the food stalls tomorrow."

"Sure, back to the inn." She hoped Sumner found a good spot to sell some of the things they found. She was going to spend entirely too much of her remaining coin tomorrow.

TWO

Arriving back at the inn, they lingered for a moment until Sumner trotted up. Tucking his hands into his pockets, he gave them a toothy grin as he walked up to them.

"Good evening, fellow adventurers. Were you able to find what you were looking for?" he asked. "I shopped around, heard a few things, might have some ideas."

"We were all the picture of restraint," she returned, opting not to point out Durante was only restrained because Sumner had left with the purse. "Dinner and discussion, then?"

"Perfect," Sumner responded and gestured in.

"The food stalls smelled particularly good. I am looking forward to trying them out tomorrow," Alces mentioned as they made their way into the dining hall. Unlike the previous inns they'd been staying at in their travels, this one had a fully staffed kitchen and servers, and there was a good chance they weren't all directly related to the keeper.

"Well, first thing I should note is you were correct, we do need to dress D in something more... regionally appropriate," Sumner said after they'd settled at a table.

Octavia's brows rose. "Oh? Are there tensions here? I just made the observation generally, something to make him feel more approachable."

"I guess Yadeli isn't really a fan of any of their neighbors. Particularly elves from the north. Thankfully, none of us are elves," Sumner said, glancing around a little before leaning back.

"Well, that is rather disappointing for such a colorful country," Alces said, narrowing his eyes a bit.

"This curse has made my ears a little... pointier than normal," Durante said, slumping in his chair a bit. "Maybe I should get a hat or a head wrap or something."

"I'm not sure you need it," she mused, tipping her head to the side and looking him over. "Slight point to the ears aside, you don't look anything like an elf. Your coloring is all wrong. Still, getting you some clothes a little more local might help. We'll work on it tomorrow. Shouldn't be too hard. Different shirts and a sash instead of a belt would go a long way."

"Okay," he said, but remained slumped for the moment.

"Does this mean I get to dress you up?" she asked. She was admittedly excited by the prospect and was sure it showed in her smile.

"I rather think it does," Durante replied, smiling a little in spite of himself.

"Aside from that," Sumner said, calling attention back to him, "might have found a few shops to sell our stuff at. Some of the merchants were trying to rob me, thinking I had no idea what I was carrying."

"They'll do that," Octavia commented dryly.

The dinner was a lovely spread. Bumpy red fritters spotted with herbs and served with lettuce leaves and lemon slices. Thin slices of meat smothered in a tomato and butter sauce with a side of yoghurt and accompanied by a pile of flat bread. Lastly, what looked like a pie made entirely out of carefully layered small fish, although the smell was rich with onions, butter, and spices.

"Let's not worry about all that now," Alces said, taking a careful portion so everyone else could get a healthy taste. "For now, we enjoy the food and the company."

The meal was delicious and heavily spiced, making for quite the contrast from the relatively simple yet homey foods they had been enjoying. Since Alces' usual ravenous consumption was slowed by his fascination with the new flavors, Octavia did take a little more of the sauced meat and flatbread. Sitting back, finally done, she sipped on a tart juice the innkeeper had brought out with dinner and looked around the room as she waited for the boys to finish.

The dining room was a formal affair, with nice tables and chairs, tablecloths, and well-made cutlery. It also looked like the establishment was made for more than the guests at the inn, given its size relative to the number of rooms Octavia could guess they had. The clientele seemed a little more sophisticated than the inns they were accustomed to, but not so much that her little group would seem wildly out of place. Well, no more so than usual. Octavia and Durante knew which fork to use and, quite frankly, looked like they belonged anywhere they wished to. Octavia's manner of dress was more eclectic than Durante's, making it less obvious she was also from Ascherol, but they were both well dressed and their upbringing showed in their mannerisms. In this room, Alces and Sumner were more interesting to the gathered diners.

They didn't linger overly long. As they rose to leave, Octavia smoothed the fabric over her hips and made sure to let Alces go ahead of her. Back into the streets they went, this time with the sun set and the shift in stalls.

There was more to be found as the night bloomed. Music could be heard coming from various areas of the Stone Cross, something that would have been drowned out in the bustle of the day. The food carts continued to fill the air with delightful smells. Colored glass was used to tint lanterns and there were definitely a few mages in the area using parlor spells to create wisps of light and signs that glowed and could be read from a distance.

It was amusing to see some of the fashion shops just rotated bits of their inventory and traded out staff. Maybe Octavia would see if anyone had a barely appropriate dress she could swan about in and get one of her companions to pass out from lack of blood to the brain. The idea made her grin. Not everything in the market was so harmless as risque clothing. Look in the right dark corners, and one could find weapons of a more subtle and grisly nature and a few unsavory items the general public would turn their nose up at.

With the reduced crowd, Alces was more casually looking around. Pickpockets would be less active at night, because it would be harder to disappear into the throng with one not fully existing. Sumner was checking out more of the oddity stalls, bartering a little with what they had to sell. As they walked through, she murmured an incantation under her breath, and her eyes shifted, looking purple from a distance, but upon closer inspection, filled with shifting violet runes. One of her favorite and most useful invocations, it allowed her to read anything, and she felt like it might come in handy on this expedition.

The invocation appeared to be the right idea. Some of those illusionary signs had hidden glyphs most people would not have been able to notice, much less comprehend. Added words to the offerings included such things as demonology, hermetics, and rare elements. Moving along with Durante, she looped her arm through his and murmured to him the words she could see in the signs. To an outsider she looked like an attentive lover.

"Let's try the hermetics," he said, patting the hand that hung onto his arm. "Demonology is most likely a scam, most people would be afraid to bring anything like that into a city, if it's real, much less advertise it. If they have to state their ingredients are rare, they're either lying or charging too much."

"As you wish," Octavia murmured, and rose up on her toes to kiss the base of Durante's neck where the collar of his shirt had fallen loose. "This way."

"I could wish for a lot of things," he said with a soft smile. She giggled and gently tugged him towards the sign in question.

Underneath the sign was a little stall manned by a surprisingly studious looking ork. While certainly some existed, neither of them could have imagined an ork this delicate. Instead of a brutish barbarian, they had a green-skinned gentlewoman studying a tome with a small pair of reading glasses balanced on the tip of her nose. She was still tall, but her shoulders were about as broad as a human's, and she was not overtly muscled. Her clothing was made up of a light robe over wraps of fabric which matched the style of the region, and her ears were pierced several times over with small, glittering gems and about half of them connected by chains.

The stall itself was three walls with shelves of small bottles, jars, bins of powders, and small creatures pressed in glass or mounted in shadow boxes. This did look like a place they might find items for Durante's experiments.

Setting a ribbon to hold her place in the book, she folded it up and looked up at the two of them, smiling with a gentleness a mouth full of sharp teeth wouldn't normally suggest. "Good evening, you two," she said with an accent Octavia couldn't place. It was heavy, but it was clear she had spent time trying to tone it down to fit the common tongue of the area. "I feel you may be lost."

"No, madam, I don't believe we are," Octavia said, lifting her chin almost defiantly as she looked at the proprietress. She knew what she looked like, and she didn't enjoy being judged for it—something she would think an ork understood. "My companion is seeking some particular and difficult to obtain ingredients for complex alchemical studies."

"Alright, no need to get huffy," she said, putting her book aside. "Lovely couples such as yourselves don't typically need base ingredients. They ask for completed potions for... well, you can probably guess." Sitting up a little straighter, she looked Durante over and raised a brow. Sure, Octavia was gorgeous, full of figure, and her clothes were always just a little provocative but Durante was unusual.

"Um, yes, good evening," Durante said, clearing his throat and pushing his shoulders back to match. "During my travels I've come across some recipes that call for rare reagents. Specifically, parts of a strix. Do you carry anything like that?"

The proprietress looked him over once more and got a slight smirk on her face, then glanced back at Octavia and gave her a little lift of her brows. "Strix. That is rare. Not native to this area, annoying as hell to capture. Not sure I have any."

Now that night had fallen, the runes dancing in Octavia's eyes had a faint glow. "I appreciate it's the wrong region, but there's always a chance a market this large has something," she said, and shrugged. "It seems a good place to seek out something unusual."

"A little razzle dazzle in the eyes, there, sweetie," she said with a smirk, but got up to look around her shop. She was certainly tall, possibly even a little more than Durante but it was hard to tell, the base of the stall may have been lifted from the stone.

"Any particular reason you're looking for strix bits?" the ork said as she lifted bottles and examined their labels.

"Personal experiment," Durante said, glancing around.

"Aww," she said with a bit of a pout. Clearly, she wanted to know more.

"Nothing wicked," Octavia said with sincerity. She looked over at Durante with another smile, easy and affectionate.

"Okay," the ork said, stretching the word out as she looked between the two of them. After another series of bottles, she sighed and shook her head. "Best I have is a strix proboscis. Will that do?"

"Um, no," Durante said, a little defeated.

"Well, I tell ya what, I'll check in with some of my, um, contacts and see what I can find," she said, putting her hands on her hips and cocking it a little to the side. "You'll be in town for a couple of days?"

Octavia nodded, leaning forward onto the edge of the stall. "Yes, I'm pretty sure that was our intention. We have other things to look into while we're in the city, we can take a little longer."

The ork smirked and looked at the décolletage Octavia was displaying, and what was threatening to spill out of it, briefly before snapping back to her eyes. "Then I'll see what I can do. If you want to negotiate later sometime, I can see if I can drop the price a little as well," she said.

Oh, she was interested. Octavia grinned. "We'll check back in, then, in a couple days." Her tone was maybe a little more honeyed than it had been. Straightening up, she tossed her hair back. "Thank you. We'll see you soon."

"See you then," the green-skinned woman said, settling back into her chair and picking up her book.

As they stepped away, Durante blinked for a moment and turned to Octavia. "Was she hinting at what I think she was hinting at," he whispered as they moved back into the market.

Octavia took Durante's arm again and steered him back towards where she'd last seen Alces. "That she might drop the price if I spend some alone time with her? Absolutely." She giggled. "Could be fun. I've never been with an ork."

"Well, um, huh," he said, pondering and slightly flustered. "I mean, if you want to, you are your own woman, but don't think I'd ever ask you to... you know, just to give me a better price or something, okay?"

"Oh, Kitten." Octavia laughed again, then stopped and pulled him in for a kiss. As they parted, she smiled. "I would never do anything just for a better price or preferential treatment. I might say yes to a date and see how it goes because I'm intrigued by an educated ork. And I know you would never ask such a thing of me. You're too much of a gentleman, I doubt it would even occur to you." She giggled again. "Besides, you can barely ask me for the things you know I'm willing to give you!"

Sighing, Durante shook his head and shrugged. "It's true. But still, just because this is important to me, I don't want you to feel obligated," he said, then stammered a little. "B-But, of course, if you want to, then go have fun. She seems... nice?"

"We'll see," she said, and took his arm again. "Would it bother you if something did happen?" The relationship the four of them shared was still largely undefined. They were friends. Companions in arms. She had been accepted into their coterie, which seemed more like a family. But their relationship with her was... well, different.

He thought for a moment, then shook his head. "No, I don't think it would," he said. "As long as it was something you wanted to do, then you should do it. I mean, I'd probably be sad if you decided to run off and be an assistant to an orkish alchemist instead of travelling with us, though."

She giggled again and squeezed his arm. "Never."

"Well, then," he said with a smile, reaching over to squeeze her hand, "I suppose my little trip is done for the evening. Is there anything you wanted to look at?"

She shook her head. "Not tonight. Though we should plan on finding a tailor in the morning. Give me one of your shirts tonight, I can get Comicha to alter it. She's not bad, but don't give me your best shirt."

"Whatever you need," he said, leaning in and kissing her cheek. It wasn't much, but it was taking him a while to get used to casual affection.

Alces and Sumner had mostly disappeared at this point, although she could easily pick up Alces' voice whenever he spoke, booming over the much quieter market, so he wouldn't be too hard to track down.

Her blood was racing a little. The flirting at the hermetics shop was part of it, the nice evening strolling with Durante was part of it. She wished Durante was the type to pin her against a wall and take advantage of the shadows, but that was Sumner. She might have pinned him against a wall, but she wasn't sure if he'd be too embarrassed. She just leaned into him, and they wove through the stalls until they found Alces again.

They found Alces at one of the metal working booths, talking to the smith about cutlery and cookware. The smith was equal parts amused and confused by this hulking dragonkin talking rather animatedly about cooking. But, the stall looked to have good wares and it seemed the silver knight was setting aside a potential purchase.

"Was your hunt successful, Ser Knight?" Octavia asked as they stepped up beside him. She continued to hold onto Durante for the moment—she saw no reason not to.

"More along the lines of happy happenstance, praise the Spirits," Alces said, turning to look at the two of them. "With these dishes, I could make proper cakes and breads. Pies! Nice, solid pie pans."

Durante raised a brow and looked at Octavia. "I do like pies. Well, I liked pies. Pretty sure I still do."

"I love pies and tarts," Octavia said, nodding in agreement. "Anything involving baked fruit and a crust, really. Extra points for beaten cream."

"I do remember your joy of tarts, dear Octavia, but I will make note of the beaten cream. This is a thing that is plausible now," Alces said, then turned back to the smith. "Set them aside, good man, and I will be by on the morrow to collect my wares and pay you in kind."

"You got it," the smith said, gathering up the supplies and finding a small crate that had hay in it to keep the dishes from clattering around. "They'll be here when you're ready."

"Excellent! Now, how have you two fared?" Alces said, turning to the two of them and stepping away from the stall.

"We may have a lead," Durante said, also seeing no reason to stop holding Octavia's arm.

"We need to check back in a couple days," Octavia added. "Also, we should return to the market tomorrow morning to find a tailor and see about getting Durante's shirts altered. I can do that with just Durante if you and Sumner wish to see to other tasks."

"I should find work," Alces said, looking around. "If nothing else, I must find a way to pay for the spices I plan on experimenting with. And I must find a source for cream, as well." The knight gave Octavia a wink.

"Guess you're stuck shopping with me for another day," Durante said, squeezing her arm.

"Oh no, such a terrible chore," she said playfully, bringing up his hand and kissing the back of it. "I'll try not to be insufferable or make you try on too many things."

Durante got that look on his face that suggested he'd blush if he could. But he did squeeze her hand and give her a light smile. She knew even if she played dress-up with him for all of tomorrow, he'd probably be happy.

She looked back over to Alces. "Are we ready to go back to the inn?"

"Some snacks first, then we should retire. It has been a very long day," Alces said, and it had been. "The smell is too much. I cannot sleep until I have sampled."

"I did see a few pastries I was curious about," Octavia said, following Alces as he began to move towards the food stalls, still on Durante's arm. "There was one that looked like a small, flat haystack that I think was a dessert. And there was something that looked like… I dunno, almost like candles on ropes but I think it was candy?"

"We shall eat it all," Alces announced, grandly and with volume. If his voice hadn't been so full of joy it might have come across as threatening.

Most of the smells had, indeed, been meat. As they approached the food stalls, Sumner appeared out of nowhere and bumped gently into Octavia. "Success?"

"Perhaps," she said, and took Sumner's arm as well. "We have a lead and need to check back in a couple days. And I'm going to take Durante shopping tomorrow while Alces looks for work and I assume you talk to the fence."

"Sounds like our days are fairly busy," he said, adjusting his arm so she could hold it properly and falling into step with the two of them. "I've talked to a few more, sold a couple of things just to give them a taste, so we have a little bit of money, but I think I know the two or three places I'll sell to tomorrow, then join Alces in finding work."

They'd found the main cluster of food stalls, and the smell was almost intoxicating. Spice in Yadeli wasn't just a compliment to the food, it was a requirement. Alces was already ordering many things from several stalls. Octavia released Sumner to go follow Alces and pay for everything, but gave him a kiss first.

This was… nice. Very nice. She felt that flutter just under her ribs. She also felt something further down as she watched Sumner slip through the crowd with his singular grace. She leaned into Durante again. The two of them were sharing a room. Maybe she might sneak over before they left the city and see if they might be willing to share her as well…

She absently started to caress Durante's arm as her mind wandered. Durante may have been altered by his cursed experiment, but he wasn't dead, and he smiled at Octavia as she touched him. Pulling up her hand, he kissed it as she had kissed his, but opened his mouth just enough so she could feel his sharp fangs brush against the tender flesh. They'd been together more than enough for him to know she rather enjoyed being bitten by him.

Octavia turned her head into his shoulder and let out a little whimper. "Kitten, are you *teasing* me?" she asked him, low and throaty.

"Am I?" he asked, feigning innocence.

Alces and Sumner had finished their little jaunt and the dragonkin held a pair of large palm fronds full of food. She managed to compose herself quickly as Sumner and Alces returned, though her cheeks were just a touch flushed. There was grilled meat on sticks; a collection of dark green leafy rolls that didn't look terribly good but smelled wonderful; a pile of small, white dough pouches that were covered in a yoghurt sauce that was dusted with deep red and green herbs; and a little pile of those pastries Octavia had been looking for.

"There is more, but we shouldn't have too many at once, or our tongues may get confused," Alces said, offering the collection to the lot of them.

The little flat haystacks turned out to be a shredded dough that was fried, filled with sweetened cheese, and then soaked in a honey syrup before being topped with crushed nuts. Sumner really enjoyed the meat on a stick. Durante, even with his more tender palette, liked the rolls which turned out to be stuffed leaves full of rice and herbs.

Alces, of course, had at least one of each but sampled them slowly as they walked back to the inn, trying to derive the flavors from each item. Between this and dinner, everyone was quite satisfied. Octavia was licking the last of the syrup from her fingertips as they made it back. She was full and happy and reflective as they climbed the stairs to their rooms. She was also absurdly turned on. Significantly more than she thought she should be. Though it seemed that was happening a lot. She'd never traveled with anyone before, let alone three healthy men who were all eagerly available to her. Was it almost her moon time? That might be it. Or maybe she'd just never had such consistent physical relationships with people she cared about.

"Well, good night, you two," Sumner said with a smirk, "try not to stay up too late. Big day tomorrow."

"Like you wouldn't be up half the night in his place," Octavia murmured with a smile, before kissing him goodnight. It had become a bit of a tradition in their short time, the goodnight kisses—whomever wasn't intending to ask for her time that evening would kiss her goodnight and head off.

"So much sun," Durante sighed, "I am looking forward to sleeping. Tavi, you are under no obligation to get me up early."

"If Alces lets me sleep, I'll let you sleep," she said with a wry smile before kissing him as well.

"Good night, shrewd Sumner, prudent Durante. Sleep well," Alces said with a grin.

"Good night," she said finally, heading into the room. Alces followed Octavia into their room and divested himself of the leftovers from the snack trip.

"Fair Octavia, I feel a need to wash off the road. Shall we explore the inn's bath or should I leave you to sleep. I don't wish to keep you up if you are tired," he said, brushing off his arms.

"I'm not ready to sleep just yet," Octavia said with a smile. "Let's explore the baths. Oh! One moment."

With a twist of her hand, Octavia summoned Comicha, her unusual familiar. A little tall for an imp, and a little human looking, with exaggerated feminine proportions, blue skin that shaded to indigo at her hands, feet, and the tips of her ornamented horns, and skin too smooth to be from the infernal plane.

"Mistress!" The imp cried out happily and clung to Octavia's leg. "It's been forever!"

"It's been two days," Octavia noted with dry amusement.

"Forever!"

Octavia smiled. "Comicha, I need you to go get a shirt from Durante and alter it. Take off anything excessive around the collar, refinish the neck. Just make it look a little less like a poncy noble would wear it."

"Oh! Sure!" The imp smiled. "I haven't done anything like that in a while! It'll be different!"

The imp zipped out the window, and Octavia turned back to Alces. "Now we can explore the baths."

Alces and Octavia headed down and were instructed that they had both a large public bath and smaller private baths that the keeper was willing to provide the first time for free, since they were planning on staying a couple of days. The choice was obvious, and he gave them a key, instructing them where to go. The baths were located on the back side of the inn, away from the market. The set up was a front common area, heated by the steam of the thermals, that led to the changing rooms, which were segregated by gender. They parted ways long enough to undress.

Octavia carefully removed her clothing and folded it up, leaving it one of the cupboards in the changing room. There was an attendant present to keep an eye on everyone's belongings. She suspected one of the inn keeper's children or nieces. She bound her hair up as much as she could (curls always escaped, no matter what she did) and met up with Alces to head into the private bath.

Bare and barely wrapped in a pair of towels, Alces was waiting as Octavia emerged. Beyond the changing rooms, the path led to the large public bath in a semi-open courtyard, which was a shallow, rectangular pool that was tiled in shimmering bluish-green with flanking trees to keep the place shaded during the day. From there, several doors on either side led to the private baths. Each one locked with a number on it.

Alces unlocked the door and motioned for Octavia to enter ahead of him. It was a smaller version of the main bath, but still large enough to fit several people. Hot water constantly flowed in from a rill jutting out of the wall. It, too, was open to the sky by way of a heavily vined pergola but otherwise completely enclosed by thick stucco walls. A wooden slat deck surrounded the pool, ensuring the area around it was not slippery or rough on the feet.

She let out a soft sound of surprise and approval. "This is lovely," she said, moving over to the small area to the side where they were supposed to scrub down before getting in the bath. "Shall I get you scrubbed, my knight?"

"As long as I may do the same to you, my lovely Octavia," Alces said, discarding his towels once the door was closed. Alces didn't have much modesty to begin with anyway.

Smiling, Octavia set her own towel aside. The two of them were a study in opposites. Alces was a mass of muscle covered in scales, near seven feet in height, with clawed hands and feet. She was just barely five and a half feet tall, soft in figure with large breasts and hips, and a butt that was bigger than she felt strictly necessary.

Looking at what was available, she fished out soap and a soft brush for scrubbing. "Have a seat on the stool, and I'll take care of you."

"As you wish," he said. He pondered the stool for a moment, thought better of it, and just sat on the ground with his legs crossed before him. "I don't believe I've been to a bath like this before."

Octavia giggled, and picked up a bucket, filling it with water from the heated tub. "I have. You don't want to actually get in the bath dirty. So, you clean yourself first and then relax in the water afterwards." She gently poured the water over Alces' shoulders, allowing it to run down over the rest of him, and then picked up the soap and brush and got to work.

While she had been to this kind of bath before, she had never been to one with a… well, a romantic partner. She still wasn't sure how to define Alces or the others in that sense. She gently used the brush to scrub his back, over his shoulders, down his arms, allowing herself to press against him from time to time and get soapy with him.

"It is a nice sensation," he said, stretching out his arms when she got to them, but otherwise being an accommodating patient in her care. "I can think of no one I would rather enjoy this with."

Every now and then, when she moved close to the front of him, he'd reach up and slide his hand along her thigh or rest it on her hip as she continued to clean the days of travel out of his scales. Once his back was done, she moved around him and started on his head, mindful of his horns and careful to keep the soap far from his eyes. She kissed him softly, then moved down to his chest.

"I don't think you and I have had a moment alone since Boxende," she said, feeling inexplicably shy all of the sudden. Not because of what they were doing, but she always felt a little awkward in these softer, more tender moments.

"It is true," he said, looking up at her when he could with those vibrant purple eyes of his. "But I carry your light with me always. I do wish for more time with you, however my connection with the Spirits lets me feel a connection with you and the others when you are with each other. That makes me happy."

Alces couldn't sit still, despite his best efforts, and continued to softly caress her thighs and hips as she washed his front, sometimes brushing his claws against her soft and delicate skin.

"You could always ask, my knight," Octavia pointed out with a wry smile as she dropped carefully to her knees before him, getting more soap on the brush and starting on his left leg. "Durante and I have shared a bed so much lately because we both stay up too late working and then fall asleep exhausted. And Sumner is… the right amount of demanding." She scrubbed his massive thighs and followed the brush with a slow caress of her hand. "But you are allowed to have wants, my knight. And I might enjoy hearing that you want time with me."

Given her position and proximity with her hands, she was already starting to stir things for the large dragonkin. Down where she was, his hands had moved to her shoulders, sometimes caressing a cheek. He wasn't so uncouth as to undo her careful wrap on her hair just to touch it.

"I will try to express myself more," he said, still smiling at her. "By my oath and order, I want to make sure everyone I am with or around is happy and taken care of, to be their light, and I do not always consider it for myself. So do not mistake my lack of saying as much as a lack of wanting, my enticing Octavia."

She smiled at him again, a softer smile this time, and scooted back a bit to clean the road dust from his feet. "We should get some oil for the skin around your claws," she remarked, examining him as she worked. "Something to apply at night, so you don't get gritty during the day. I will look around the market tomorrow. All right, let's get your rinsed."

She got up and got another bucket, again pouring it gently over his back, saving enough to have him tip back his head and rinse off his horns. Then she kissed his cheek. "Better?"

"Always with you," he said, another broad smile as he looked back at her. Sitting upright, he shook his head to get the water off then stood up. Giggling, Octavia held up the bucket as Alces shook so she didn't get splashed in the face. "I believe I know how it works now. Take a seat, and I will return the favor."

"Let's leave my hair for tonight," she said as she got situated on the stool. "I didn't bring down everything I need to properly wash it."

"I have a feeling I would need an extensive set of directions," he said, taking the bucket and getting some fresh water from the rill. Steam was rising off of it as he carried it back, and presented it to her. "How's the temperature?"

She tested the water with her wrist. "A bit hot for sluicing."

Alces nodded and inhaled, then breathed gently onto the bucket, swirling the water as he did. Frosty air accompanied his breath, and it tickled her skin as he did so. The touch of frost was a sharp contrast from the warm room. She didn't shiver, but her nipples immediately tightened in response. Not wanting to overdo it, he cleared his throat and offered it to her again.

"How's this?"

She set her wrist into the water again. "That's perfect. Thank you."

Smiling, he kissed her cheek, then stood up and gently poured the water over her, doing an admirable job of making sure her body had been covered in the warm water without getting her hair wet. Setting the bucket down, he crouched next to her and started to lather up the brush. Once a good foam had been generated, he started to scrub her back and shoulders while keeping one hand on her thigh.

"Did you find anything to your liking in the market today?" he asked as he gently washed her.

"A few things," Octavia admitted, and obligingly tilted her head to one side then the other and lifted her arms in turn. "I would like some leathers for the road, and I think I found a good place. We travel more than I've been used to and I could use some… well, less fragile fabrics."

"While a wise idea, I can always mend them if some of your clothes start to get worn," he said, holding her arm gently and scrubbing it down, then moving to the other as he shifted in front of her. "It does seem this place has a little bit of everything. I have not been to such a place since I traveled to Sargo," Alces added, speaking of the capital of Ascherol. Octavia had been there before, as it was less than a week away from Driscoll's Rest by carriage.

"It's also the feel of it," Octavia explained, smiling. "I have a similar spell available to me, but… well, heading through the canyon I had to repair my shirts every night, and my skin gets abraded." She shrugged a bit sheepishly.

Alces shuffled closer, on one knee that rested between her legs, the other leg on his foot, canted off to the side. He gently started to scrub her legs and feet, picking them up slowly so as not to topple her over. She bit her lip as he moved her legs. It was touching how gentle he was with her, but also easy to feel how strong he was as well.

"It seems silly to use a brush at this point," he said with a smile and started to rub the soap into his hands. "I assume you will not mind if I finish washing you this way?"

"Not at all," she answered, trying not to get excited. Not yet, at least.

Resting the bar of soap in one hand, he reached forward and placed his palms against her tummy. Slowly he caressed and rubbed in the soap, moving his way up as he went until he was lifting and cupping her breasts, kneading them and getting them slick and soapy.

"Let me know if I, or my scales, are too rough. I do not wish to abrade your soft skin, flawless as it is," Alces said with a wink.

"You've never been before, my knight," she said softly, looking up at him with flushed cheeks and a bit starry-eyed. Of the three of her companions, Alces was the romantic, and there was something very charming about how he always addressed her like she was a princess in a story.

Alces drew his hands up, caressing the sides of her neck with his fingertips, the claws barely touching her skin, then traveled back down. Over her chest, around her full, heavy breasts, and down her sides and hips. Leaning in, he pressed his forehead against hers and drew his hands down to her inner thighs, squeezing them gently.

"Shall I rinse you now?" he asked quietly.

"Yes," she breathed, trembling a little at his hands on her thighs.

He kissed her forehead then stood up to fetch the bucket. She was not the only one enjoying this moment, as he was nearly at full mast. Collecting the bucket, he got more fresh water, cooled it down a little, then started to slowly pour it over her so she could rinse the soap off her skin.

THREE

Once she was soap free, she stood and looked from Alces to the bath. "Um, are you ready?"

"For anything," Alces said with a grin, "or did you mean something in particular? If you were referring to lounging with you in the bath, I am more than."

She laughed. "I did mean lounging in the bath, though you do have me… a little distracted." She walked over and sat down on the edge of the platform, letting her legs drop in and get used to the heat.

Following suit, he walked over and sat down next to her, his hand sliding behind her to cup her body where her hip and butt met. "Is it a distraction if it's your goal," he said with a glance towards her, "because I am not distracted at all, but thoroughly focused on you, my treasure."

Her cheeks turned pink, and she leaned into him. "Perhaps distracted was the wrong word. I just mean to say, well, I think we both desire more from each other tonight than a bath. And I am trying not to be too focused on that." She turned her head in and kissed his chest.

"As you wish my intentions to be spoken, my delightful Octavia, I desire you and want you this evening, here in this bath or later in the bedroom, or both," he said, laying his head gently upon hers. "So, with that out there, you are welcome to focus on that."

"Yes," she murmured, sliding a hand over his thigh. "I want you here in the bath and likely again in our room. I want us to be lost in each other tonight." She looked up at him again, eyes shining. "My knight."

"I am all yours, my treasure," he said, sliding into the water and moving to face her. The pool wasn't very deep, only a few feet, so he was on his knees but still even height with her as she sat on the edge. His hands moved back to her thighs, and he leaned in, placing his head against hers once more. "Join me in the water, or should I start here?"

"Perhaps we start here," she said, reaching up to caress his face before sliding her hands down the sides of his neck to his massive shoulders.

Leaning in and tilting his head to the side, he started to nip softly at her neck. His lips were thick and scaled, making them a little rougher than your average person, but they were supple. Alces' large hands moved up to hold her body, holding her sides as the claws from his thumbs grazed gently against the underside of her breasts.

Octavia whimpered. While Alces had been with other women—and a number of them, from the stories the three told—this was Octavia's second time with the dragonkin, and dragonkin were exceptionally rare. Alces was the first she had heard of outside of stories. He was a flood of sensation, from his firm kisses to the claws that could rend a man creating fine points of sensation against her skin.

"Yes," she murmured, encouraging. Alces would do nothing he wasn't certain she wanted, so she needed to make sure he knew she wanted everything.

Alces continued his tender nipping at her skin, his flexible tongue gliding across her now and then. Continuing his progress farther down, he pulled her close, one hand on her back and the other sliding underneath her to lift her up slightly in his arms, presenting those enticing breasts of hers to him. Smiling, he kissed along the tops of the large globes. She was secure in his arms but could move freely as his strength supported her. She moaned softly and slid her hands over his chest before running them back up to caress over his horns, which resulted in happy, quiet growls. While Octavia was not the tallest or broadest of women, Alces had a gift for making her feel delicate, small, a toy he could toss about at will. And yet he was so careful with her. The combination was intoxicating.

He brought her up just that little bit farther so he could take one of her hard nipples into his mouth, his dexterous tongue wrapping around it and licking it as his arms held her close. She moaned and did her best not to squirm. So tenderly, she felt his teeth against the swells of her breast before he released her, his tongue unraveling from around her nipple to slip back into his mouth.

"You are such a buffet of delight, my treasure," he muttered between kisses across to her other bosom.

She let out a soft, gasping laugh, blushing at his compliments again. She had never blushed before she met the three of them, and Alces, in particular, could make her pink cheeked so easily. "Am I?"

The question escaped before realized she'd asked it. Her fingertips massaged lightly at the base of his horns, testing. His response was another happy growl, and he hungrily sucked her breast into his mouth, teasing her nipple with a thorough lashing of his tongue. She let out a cry and her hands dropped to his shoulders again, holding tight to him. His hands squeezed her, his tongue and mouth teased her, and his actions answered her question.

"Yes, my knight," she moaned. Her hands moved over his shoulders and chest, eagerly caressing, though he held her so firmly she couldn't reach much more of him. Yet.

The hand that had been holding her up by her butt slid down a little farther until the tip of his finger was able to softly caress her sex. Given he was still holding her, he couldn't do more than exploratory petting with a single finger, but it was certainly stimulating. A teasing twirl of his tongue and a firm suckle and Alces extracted his mouth from her tit and looked up at her. "What do you wish of me, my Octavia," he said, his breathing getting deeper.

Another whimper, and Octavia squirmed in his hands. "Please, Alces, my knight," her voice trembled with want, "go down on me, make me ready for you, then bury yourself in me before bringing me into the water with you. Please?"

"With pleasure," he said, then moved his hands to hoist her up by her rump, lifting her body so that her spread legs were before his maw. While Alces could certainly hold all of her up, Octavia didn't really want to deal with keeping her balance, so she let herself fall back carefully as he lifted her hips, her shoulders against the slats of the platform as Alces raised her to his mouth. Leaning in, he slathered his tongue over the lips of her sex and dragged it over her clit. His breath was just a little cool, contrasting with the warm steam surrounding them. After getting his taste, he pulled her close and drove his tongue into her, snaking it around to lap at every inch of her vessel he could. She let her legs slide over his shoulders and moaned as his tongue slipped into her. Like so much of Alces, the sensation was unique. She'd never felt anything like him.

Legs mounted on his shoulders, Alces had more leeway with his hands. Still holding her up with one, he let the other roam over her body, teasing her breasts with an alteration between kneading and gently raking with his claws. If the growls that rumbled through his chest and along his tongue were any indication, he enjoyed this almost as much as she did.

"Gods, yes," she moaned, hands splayed against the wood beneath her. "Alces… my knight, my dragon…" She had wanted to savor it, but she was racing towards her orgasm faster than she'd anticipated. The legs around his shoulders tightened. She was right there.

Feeling her quiver, Alces braced her body against his hands and stood, taking her with him. In one motion he lowered her down, lined her up, and impaled her on his cock. Used to other women, he didn't fully sink into her, but he did plunge about half of his impressive length into her pussy and chuffed with blissful content.

"The Spirits have blessed you so completely," he muttered, groaning as her tightness clamped around him.

Moaning loudly, Octavia just shuddered against him for a long moment. Like the rest of him, Alces's cock was huge and a lot to take. Octavia had prayed for a boon the first time in order to take all of him—it shouldn't actually be possible for a woman her size. Would she be able to again?

You are fast becoming my most favorite warlock ever, the Incarnation of Desire purred into Octavia's mind. *So long as you desire this beast, and you can inspire lust within him, you will be able to take all he gives.*

Panting, Octavia lifted her head and looked up into his eyes. "All of it, my knight. Hilt yourself in me."

Leaning in, Alces ran his tongue along the side of her neck and slowly released his hold on her. Not letting her fall away, but letting gravity pull her down along his length. His breathing got heavier and when she finally settled against him, his length completely engulfed in her heat, did he let out a long and low groan.

"You are perfection, my treasure," he muttered, slowly walking back into the pool, holding her close. "Light fills me when I am with you."

Another loud moan, and she held tight to him, lightheaded with the intensity of their joining. Kamvasana might have blessed Octavia with the ability to receive Alces, but it didn't take away from the sensations of it, the stretch that almost hurt at first before becoming the most full feeling she'd ever known.

"You're… you're incredible," she finally gasped out, panting hard against him. She wanted to say more, but she couldn't, she just whimpered and felt herself tighten around him as they moved back into the water.

Moving into the center, he slowly sank in, until he was seated in the pool with Octavia firmly joined with him. Her head swam with the sensations combined with the hot steam. Alces only gave her a moment to enjoy her seat before slowly lifting and easing her body down, rolling her hips in his hands. His lips and tongue returned to her neck and shoulder, the cool sensations from his mouth a sharp but welcome contrast.

She moaned again, going soft against him for a moment. The penetrating heat of the water, the feel of him buried inside her, his mouth moving over her skin, it was all just so much to take. She could feel the ridges of his cock as he moved her slowly, and they rubbed at that spot deep inside her that sent a pulse of sensation through her pussy. She turned her head and licked at his chest.

Kissing up her neck, Alces nipped playfully at her ear, which got a sweet whimper, then leaned back to gaze upon her. "You are such a gift," he muttered. He slid one hand up her back, coming up to cup her head. The other continued to roll and pump her body against his. Alces blinked slowly, engrossed in the feeling of her softness just calling to him, enchanting him.

She let Alces move her, resting in his hands so that she could meet his gaze. "A gift?" She felt herself blushing again, though she imagined she was already flushed enough from the heat and what they were doing. Her hands caressed over the parts of him she could reach. She felt a little guilty that she wasn't able to utilize more of her skills in bed with Alces, but being with him just shorted out her brain a little. Maybe in time he would become less all consuming. She could also already feel the pleasure building in her pelvis. The way his giant cock rubbed her inside. She was going to come again. Soon.

"Aren't you?" he asked in a mutter, starting to move a little more. "To have found you, to bond with you like this, to hold and kiss you. I could think of nothing better."

He still supported her head and back, but now instead of lifting her, he planted his other hand behind himself and started to thrust his hips up, bouncing her in hip lap as the water splashed and churned at their efforts. She whimpered, feeling that squeezing around her heart again, and then the whimper rose into a cry as she came for him, squeezing down on him as she shook in his arms. Her clamping tightness and cries were all it took for him to hit his peak as well. Grunting, Alces held her fast and thrusted into her with pounding strokes until he couldn't take it any more. His feet braced and with one hand holding him up behind him, he lifted her out of the water with his hips, completely impaling her as he roared up into the sky. Octavia felt that cool, rushing sensation as he came deep inside her.

Between his frosty breath and the steam surrounding them, there was a sudden soft snowfall coming down upon them. Slowly, he eased himself back down into the water, one hand gently on the small of her back while he rested on his elbow, keeping his head above the water. "Spree Spirits be honored, you are amazing," he said with a grin, his chest rising and falling with deep breaths.

Looking up, Octavia let out a soft, amazed laugh and just let herself lay against his chest. "Amazing? Compared to you? I don't see how," she murmured, smiling and content.

"Your discounting is absurd," he smiled, scooting back and taking her with him until his back was against a wall so they could rest more comfortably. Settled in, he softly stroked his claws up and down her back.

"You are an amazing and singular woman, Octavia. Even without your patron's blessing you would be so," he said, tilting his head down to kiss her forehead. "All Kamvasana has done is accentuated the beauty within to radiate out. Your light is glorious."

She felt blood rush to her cheeks again. "I… I was nothing special. Pretty but not stunning. Smart and educated but not particularly skilled. I was raised to be a socialite, a good trophy wife." She nuzzled at him and tensed around the cock still buried inside her.

"It was an ember then," he said as he rubbed her back. "It just needed kindling. And now, you are a beacon of light. Beautiful, intelligent, creative, and powerful. I will help you see that if you need."

"I love being like this with you, but I'm starting to prune," she said with a sheepish smile. "Maybe we should head back to the room?"

"Can you prune?" he asked with a chuckle. "Given your gift, I figured you'd look soft and flawless regardless. It has been a lovely bath but we have more to do, yes?" He accentuated his question by throbbing hard inside her. They would need a moment for him to calm down after they got out before wandering into the public space.

She moaned softly at the promise in his words. "Um, yes, I can still prune. Kamvasana's alterations do not change the fact that I still have human skin." She smiled and kissed his chest. "Lift me out before you set me down, so we don't make a mess in the pool." She said, giggling a little. "And grab another bucket so I can rinse myself off."

"As you wish, my treasure," he smiled and rolled forward onto his knees before standing up, holding her tight to him and keeping them well joined. He walked to the edge of the pool and stepped out until he was back by where the stool was. Alces kissed her softly, then lifted her off his shaft, groaning as he did so. There was even a shudder that ran through his frame once he was released from her depths, and he set her on her feet, holding her to make sure she was steady.

As soon as she was on her feet, she could feel the cum start to slide down her thighs. Compared to a human or elf, Alces' emissions were substantial. They both got rinsed off and wrapped back in towels. She was relaxed, and her body was humming. As they headed out, she hoped she wasn't too obvious.

When the two of them entered the public area of the pool, they noticed the current bathers were looking worried up into the sky. Their eyes then turned towards the two of them and a couple in one corner started clapping. Soon they were getting an amused round of applause. Their activity, it seemed, had not gone unnoticed. Alces' roar had made the bathers concerned there was a drake nearby. The now obvious reason for it brought an immediate amusement and lightness. Octavia looked a bit sheepish but not ashamed as she and Alces made their way back to the changing area.

Octavia redressed in her lounge clothing and let her hair back down. Even bound up, the humidity had done its thing on Octavia's hair, and now that it was free again it was very full and a little wild. She sighed at her reflection.

Outside the changing area, Alces was waiting for Octavia and offered his arm to her. "Do you need anything before we retire? Food or drink?" he asked. A cold drink might not be a bad idea after heated activity in a steamy bath, but one they could take back to their room.

"Something cold to drink, I think," she said, tossing her hair back. "Something we can take with us, perhaps, or have delivered to the room."

"Perfect," he said and parted from her long enough to place an order with the keeper. With that set up, they retired back to their room and as soon as the door closed, Alces reached out and scooped up Octavia, smiling and placing his forehead against hers as he carried her.

"We should wait for them to bring the drinks before we continue our bonding," he suggested.

She giggled. "We should." She reached up and caressed his cheek and the line of his jaw. "I can't get over how strong you are. It astounds me every time. I mean, I've seen you in battle and yet I'm still so surprised when you just… sweep me up like that."

"You weigh nothing," he laughed, walking towards her bed.

"I do not weigh nothing," she protested, also laughing. "In Driscoll's Rest I'm considered fat!"

"The people of Driscoll's Rest are clearly blind and only attracted to saplings," he said. "It is my gift, my duty. I am the shield of light, the Sentinel of the Spree Spirits. I could not fulfill my oath if I were not so strong. But my strength is yours, and I shall use it to please you."

She pulled his head a little closer. "And so much of you pleases me, my knight," she murmured, then kissed him, and was somewhat determined to just keep kissing him until their drinks arrived.

It seemed they did exactly that, kissing until a knock came to their door. Alces untangled his tongue from hers and set her down, having held her the entire time, and went to retrieve the drinks from the attendant. Curious as the young man had been, he only got the barest glimpse of Octavia before Alces sent him on his way and closed the door.

"Here we are, my treasure," Alces said and set the tray down on the low table between the divans. "I understand this is a common nightcap in this country."

There were a pair of iron pitchers that smelled of sweet fruit while a small carafe that contained a turquoise liquid that was no doubt a local liqueur.

Drifting over, Octavia slid a hand over Alces' back, nuzzling into him again. "Should we have a nightcap, and then follow it with one of the juices?" She caressed over his hip, squeezing his leg.

"Do as you wish," he said, giving her a squeeze back. "I shall get comfortable." Moving to his own bed, he divested himself of his clothing, folding them up and placing them on the bench at the foot of the bed. Stretching, he walked back into the main area and laid himself down on a divan to watch her.

Arching an eyebrow, she poured herself a short glass of the liqueur and took a delicate sip. It was sweet, with a tang to the finish, and one of those alcohols you could easily drink too much of.

"I like that, actually," she murmured and glanced over at Alces. "Can I get you anything?" She undid her top and set it aside.

"My wish this evening is simply you," he said. The way Alces lounged, he certainly looked like he might be a comfortable place to sit. "But I will take some juice. I should also sample that liquor, but juice would be excellent right now."

She poured a glass of juice for Alces and paused to wiggle out of her pants before coming over and perching on the massive dragonkin, handing him the glass. "And how might I satisfy you, my knight?" she asked with a playful smile.

"For now, I wish for you to drink, and touch me to your content as I will do the same to you, then to climb on when you are ready to resume as we were downstairs," he said, being more direct as she had requested the last time they were together.

"After that, I think I have some ideas for you, my treasure, to saturate you in light and leave you glowing," Alces said with a smile.

"I am very excited to discover these ideas," she said with a brighter smile, and sipped her drink as she caressed his thigh.

Taking the glass of juice that was offered, he smiled and blew on it, continuing to do so until frost had covered the vessel. "Would you like me to do the same to yours?" he asked as he drank half of it in one sip, rolling it around on his tongue.

"Oh! Yes, thank you." She handed Alces her glass and occupied her free hand with touching more of him.

Taking the glass, Alces repeated the little trick, chilling her juice to near-freezing. He made happy little rumbles in his chest as she touched him, and she could already see him starting to stiffen and twitch.

Taking back the glass, she looked him over and bit her lip, then calmly took a sip as her hand traveled up his thigh to lightly stroke his shaft with her fingertips.

Alces was returning the favor, his hand stroking up her thigh then sliding down with a tingling rake of his claws, then he'd rub her thigh a little more firmly before repeating the process. When her hand stroked him, the cock bounced in her hand, quite happy with the attention.

"May I assume you have enjoyed travelling with us these fair weeks?" he asked. "Is there anything you'd want to change?"

"I have very much enjoyed traveling with you," she said with a soft smile as she continued to tease him, her hand sliding down to massage his thighs for a moment before moving back up to stroke his monster of a cock. "I really can't think of what I would change. And I… well, there's still an adjustment. I've been on my own for so long. I get nervous. That I've said the wrong thing or done something that might bother one of you."

"We all say the wrong things sometimes," he responded, his hand moving farther up her thigh with each caress, getting closer to the apex of her legs. "But short of outright betrayal, which I know you would never do, you have nothing to worry about. We all care for you quite a bit."

Alces finished his juice and set the glass on the table, then went back to petting her. Slow and casual as this was, Octavia had Alces nearly at full mast at this point. That fit, however, given how enthusiastic and reactive the dragonkin was, why would he not be in intimate moments as well? Ready and willing at a moment's notice.

"I care for you all as well," she said, her gaze dropping, suddenly shy. She finished her drink and set it aside. "It's honestly a little strange." She climbed up onto him, pressing him back against the divan so she could straddle his hips, his cock trapped between them. He rolled to her touch easily, ever accommodating to her, and smiled up at her. "I have had many lovers. And friends. But none that made me feel the way you do."

This time, he had both hands free and could caress her hips, sides, and even a light brush over her breasts. "But of course," he grinned, "we're special, as are you."

She laughed again. "You are certainly delightfully confident." She looked up into his eyes again, and her gaze softened. "But you are also kind, charming, and you say such sweet things to me that it's sometimes hard to believe."

"I would not say them if they weren't true, beautiful Octavia, caring Octavia, sexy and sultry Octavia," he said with a wink and she felt him jump underneath her. "Powerful Octavia, clever Octavia, my wonderful Octavia."

Laughing again, she leaned in and kissed him. "You ridiculous, bombastic, beautiful dragon." She kissed him again, twisting her body against his as she did. His arms wrapped around her, and he held her tight and close against him.

The kiss broke, and she smiled at him again. "So, do I get to know what your plans were?"

He tilted his head slightly to the side. "I could tell you, if you wish, or you could just find out when the time comes."

"I guess I'll just find out." She wiggled her hips a little. "So then, does this mean I should lift up my hips and take you again?"

"Absolutely," he said, moving his hands to her hips so he could assist with the lifting. "You can take as much time as you like up there."

She shifted her body, drawing her legs up before pushing herself back into a kneeling position. She knelt on his wide thighs to give herself the height she needed—she could barely straddle him to begin with and certainly didn't have the clearance to ease him into her otherwise. Besides, she wanted him to see it.

Rising up on her knees, easily balanced, she reached for Alces' cock and stroked him lightly before setting him in place. Then she looked up so she could watch his reaction as she slowly and steadily sank back down. Alces smiled up at her, moving a hand up to stroke her cheek as she sheathed his length into her body. His purple eyes twinkled in the light as he watched her through lowered lids, that deep rumbling growl of pleasure quaking in his chest as she did so.

"Exquisite," he murmured.

Once she was far enough down, she let herself slide off his thighs to fully straddle him once more and bury him completely. She paused there for a moment, panting, adjusting to the overwhelm of sensation.

"Gods," she moaned, and let out another little laugh. "I don't think I will ever get used to this."

"Nor will I," Alces said, his claws gently running down her legs before walking back up to her hips. "I could just watch you, and feel you, just like this, for a very long time."

Biting her lip, she slid her hands up his abdomen and over his chest as far as she could reach, laying out across him even as he remained firmly within her. Her hands roamed his scales, she kissed and licked at him and reveled in the feel of them together, then slowly drew herself back up. She moved her legs again, setting her feet down on either side of his hips, and leaned back enough to brace herself on his thighs. She then began to ride him, slowly at first, and the way she was positioned meant that he could see everything—the ecstasy on her face, the way her body flushed, the way the muscles in her legs tensed, and the way his gleaming cock slid in and out of her dripping pussy.

"My luminous Octavia," he said, his voice low and soft, "you feel exquisite. Never have I experienced anyone like you."

"Nor I, you," she gasped, reaching up with one hand to caress his face.

"Are you ready?" he asked, pressing his forehead against hers. "Shall I show you what I have in store for you?"

She shivered in anticipation. "Yes."

What followed was a test of Octavia's endurance as Alces proved his strength and stamina. In some ways it was like when she had to pay the forfeit of her pact to Kamvasana, only unlike her fickle patron Alces was far more focused on Octavia's pleasure than his own. He cradled her in his hands, had her against every surface that could take them (and one table that couldn't), even carrying her out to the balcony to bring her to climax under the stars.

They ended in the bed, with him above her. His body towering and shielding, seeming to block out the world around her save the covers below her, the pillow at her head, and the muscled form of the knight around, and in, her. He was her world, and her body was his. Alces was overwhelming. Engulfing. Surrounding. She lost herself in him, much as she had the first time they were together. She couldn't count how many times she came. By the time Alces let out his final roar, filling her one more time, she could do nothing but lay there, trembling and spent, soft and vulnerable.

Gently sliding up to sit on his heels, he withdrew himself from her body and ran his hands along her thighs. "You are so amazing, Octavia. Thank you for sharing yourself with me once more," he said, leaning down to kiss her gently. She moaned softly, not able to speak just yet.

Alces then got off the bed and went to see another bottle of Durante's cleaning salve. They had made quite a mess, given how full he'd filled her. She loved the feel of him pouring out of her, but also appreciated the easy clean up. The solution cleaned up their mixed essence and left her, Alces, and the bed clean as it had been when they first entered the room.

Laying on his side next to her, he gently traced his finger along her curves, swirling it around her hip, tummy, and breast as he made gentle loops. "Do you wish for me to stay with you tonight?"

"Mmm-hmmm." She turned in towards him, nuzzling at his chest again. "Stay," she murmured, her voice soft, "please."

Alces moved to settle himself next to her, pulling the covers up around them and pulling her in close. Cradling her in one arm, hand cupping her rump, he caressed her absently with his free hand. Kissing her forehead, he smiled. "Sleep sweet, and if you desire anything when you wake, I will be here," he said softly.

She murmured something and snuggled into him. She wasn't even sure what she said.

FOUR

Morning came with a surprising slowness. She found herself wrapped around Alces with one leg draped over his and her arms encircling his own. Birds could be heard outside along with the growing sounds of the market. She felt a gentle, cool breeze upon her face that was just chilled enough to be refreshing.

"Adorable Octavia, it's time to wake up," Alces said softly.

"Nooooo," she protested sleepily and snuggled into him, attempting to bury her face between his shoulder and the bed. A soft laugh rumbled out of him

Alces reached over with his other hand and brushed her hair out of her face and caressed her cheek. "Come now, we have a full day ahead of us," he said, still gently but more amused.

"But it's so comfy," she said, her voice a little muffled. Her arms and legs tightened around him, as if it mattered - he could get up and walk around with her attached and probably not notice.

"You are very comfy to sleep with, sonsy Octavia, but I need to go with Sumner to find work, and you need to go with Durante to dress him properly," he said, his hand now caressing her shoulder. It was a little awkward, but he was doing his best not to move his body while she was wrapped around him.

She grumbled and nuzzled into him again, then sighed and unwound from Alces, yawning and stretching. "Okay," she muttered, and yawned again before pushing herself up out of bed. Her thighs ached from last night, but walking around with Durante would help with that.

Alces laughed and moved out of bed. He stretched and flexed his arms so his shoulders and back muscles tightened, holding it there until he let out a relaxed sigh. "I would have gotten up, but you were so wrapped around me I feared I would wake you, so I let you sleep in," he said with a smile before walking to his side of the room to find clothes for the day.

"I'm sorry I kept you from getting up," Octavia said as she moved towards her things. "Well, not entirely, but I know you wake early, and I don't imagine it's fun to be stuck in bed when you're ready to be up."

"But I was stuck with you, sweet Octavia, so it was worth it," he responded and started to put on his padding. She smiled softly at him.

She considered her clothing for a moment, then fished out one of her nicer outfits from Rupaiya. Soft pants with just a touch of billow to them that sat low on her hips, a cropped top with elbow sleeves and light embroidery around the collar, and a sheer shawl to drape around herself and over one shoulder. It made the ensemble a touch more modest, though just a touch. Sturdy slippers, a little jewelry. She looked… not rich, but at least a bit successful. And more importantly, she didn't look like she'd come straight from Ascherol.

"Striking as always," Alces said, gazing upon her as he finished donning his undergarments and padding. "I shan't keep you. By all means, send in Sumner to help get me armored up and we shall meet you and Durante for breakfast."

Smiling, she walked over and kissed him lightly. "As you wish, my knight. See you at breakfast."

She headed out into the hall and crossed to the other door, knocking. "Gentlemen? How are we?"

A few steps and the door opened to Sumner, wearing his leathers now. Smiling, he looked her over. "Well, good morning, gorgeous. Come here often?" he asked with a wink. "His lordship is currently still trying to wake up."

"I mean, almost every time," she said with a grin.

"Almost," Sumner said, feigning offense, "guess I'll need to up my game."

She stepped into the room and pressed herself against Sumner, giving him a light kiss. "I'll take over waking up Durante. Alces told me to send you over to help him finish suiting up."

Chuckling he gave her a playful swat on the ass as she slid by him. "Ah, armor duty. Guess we'll see you downstairs?"

"Yes. See you at breakfast." She headed over to Durante's bed and perched on the edge of it, reaching out and ruffling his hair.

"Come on, Kitten," she said, "we've got a big day."

The cursed alchemist grumbled but was easily swayed by Octavia. Peaking out from under the covers, he looked at her with those pink eyes and gave her a slow blink. "You look very nice," he said gently, reaching up to rub his eye.

"Thank you," she said with a smile, and laughed softly. "If I hadn't spent so much time getting dressed, I'd be tempted to climb in with you. You're adorable in the mornings." She climbed up onto the bed long enough to give him a kiss. "Come on, handsome, let's get going." One more kiss, then she climbed off the bed again.

"Mrf," he responded, but relented and slid out of bed. He was just in his breeches and padded over to where his clothes had been laid out after Comicha altered them.

Putting them on, he looked them over and tilted his head to the side. It seemed Octavia's little familiar may have gone a bit far, taking his ruffled shirt, removing the ruffles and the sleeves, and dropping the neckline far lower than anything Durante had ever worn. The pants didn't need much of a touchup, but somehow Comicha had made them tighter. "Um," was his only response.

"Looks like she got excited," Octavia said with a smile as she got up and walked over to Durante, adjusting his shirt and smoothing her hands over his chest before looking up at him. "Then again, given what I wear, I shouldn't be surprised. You can throw a jacket over it if you like, but it looks good. I promise we won't have the tailor cut anything else this low if it makes you uncomfortable."

"I mean, if you think it looks good," he said, but he did touch his stomach. While it was mostly under his shirt, he still had old stretch marks from before he was adventuring. They might show, but the cut wasn't quite low enough. "We'll have to get a jacket in the market, I don't think Comicha altered mine."

She set her hand over his, and cupped his face with her other hand, focusing his gaze on her. "You do look good. Better than you think you do." She kissed him again, with a little more heat this time. "Come on. We'll find a tailor, pick up some things, and find clothes you feel like yourself in. But first breakfast."

"Okay," he said. She did always have a way of making him feel better. He was so stuck in his previous image of himself. Taking a deep breath, he nodded and gently took her hand, walking to the door. "So, do you have an idea what I should be wearing?"

She nodded. "A bit, but I also want to see what you like." She held his hand as they headed out and down the stairs. "You and I both enjoy sumptuous things. While Rupaiyan fashions are good for that, their men's fashions aren't great for adventuring. We'll probably be looking for a mix, something that combines the sturdiness and tighter lines of, say, what's popular in Uroia with something softer from the very south of Ascherol."

As they made it downstairs and into the dining area, she signaled to the innkeeper for a table. While everything she wore was a little too sensuous for the position they were claiming she held, what she wore today at least looked like it was the right level of money. And people were used to Rupaiyan fashion showing a bit more skin on a woman.

The gazes towards Durante weren't nearly as severe, or noticeable, with his new cut. If anything, he fit in better with Octavia there. They got a table in due time, and it wasn't long before Alces and Sumner came down, looking like proper adventurers, and honestly a massive danger to any of the civilians in the dining hall. But they were all friendly smiles and no noticeable weapons, so there wasn't much uneasiness as they sat down. Octavia did catch Sumner baring teeth at someone who looked a little too long, then snickered as they darted their eyes away.

"The little plum did a number on your shirt, brother," Sumner said as they sat down next to them.

"You look well and in the style, chic Durante," Alces said with a broad smile.

"Thanks," Durante said, smoothing out his shirt again.

"Little plum," Octavia repeated, and giggled. "It fits. It's interesting being around people who are aware of Comicha. And now let's not mention her again before she decides that counts as a summoning."

"Oh, I dare not speak her name," Sumner said with a grin.

Breakfast was the same for everyone—the waiter, who looked to be related to the innkeeper though possibly not his son, brought out black and green olives, cucumbers, cured meats, dips and sauces, eggs, fresh cheeses, fresh tomatoes, fresh-baked bread, fruit preserves and jams, honey, pastries, and sweet butter. He also set down two pots of strong black tea. Octavia quietly asked for him to bring again as many eggs and nodded towards Alces as she said it. The man smiled at her, perhaps a little more charmingly, and assured her it would be done. Alces was considerate and didn't inhale everything that was available until everyone else had had their chance at seconds.

The plan was relatively simple: Durante and Octavia would go shopping for clothes and alchemical ingredients, plus whatever other travel items they deemed necessary. Sumner provided them with a coin purse that seemed generous but not exorbitant. Meanwhile, Alces and Sumner would go looking for work, whatever that may entail. They'd been living from town to town for many years, this would probably be old hat for them, and they'd meet back up in the evening.

"When you're ready, I've set aside the things I'd like you to try to sell for me," she said, looking at Sumner. "I know you've checked out a couple places already. It's all fairly pedestrian, nothing as unique as the triplets' collection."

"I figure we'll swing by the places I checked out yesterday, sell what I can while the big guy and I are looking for jobs," Sumner said with a nod.

Octavia nodded. "All right, then, before you leave, grab the black velvet pouch out of Matilda. It's right on top. And I already separated out the sapphires that I think Durante can use."

As breakfast wrapped up, the waiter brought out small cups of a rich, spiced coffee. He had another charming smile for Octavia. She smiled back, amused and unable to help herself, and hoped it wasn't too encouraging. It probably was.

Sumner gave her a little salute and stood up to get the bag in question and get moving. As he walked by, he put a hand on her shoulder and kissed her head. Alces stood as well, following behind to wait in the lobby, squeezing her shoulder as he went.

The coin purse tucked away, coffee finished, Octavia turned to Durante with a smile. "Ready for a fashion adventure?"

Durante gave her a half smile and nodded. "Adventure, huh," he said, glancing towards Alces' retreating back, "I'd be a pretty poor adventurer if I wasn't always ready for that."

"It takes a different kind of courage," Octavia said, standing up with a slightly mischievous look on her face. "Come on. This will take longer than you think."

Durante laughed and shook his head. "Alright, I am in your hands and at your mercy, Tavi," he said, brushing himself down, "let's do it."

"I promise you won't regret it," she said, taking his arm and leading him out of the inn and back through the market.

They went looking for a tailor first to alter the shirts, someone doing alterations and repairs, as opposed to the shops selling half-made items that could easily be taken in or let out a little for people who couldn't wait for a purely bespoke outfit. They found a little closet of a shop where a man in his 50s bustled them inside and got Durante up on the riser before Octavia had finished describing what they needed.

"So, we are taking it in," the tailor said as Durante traded his current shirt out for one of the ones in his satchel. "And what else? What are we doing with the neck? And the sleeves?"

Octavia looked to Durante. "What do you think? Let's start with the neck. The ruffles need to go. I know the neck on the other shirt ended up lower than we intended. Where are you comfortable?"

"I... I don't really know. I guess about here," he said, indicating his sternum. It was certainly more of a plunge than he'd ever worn, but it was higher than his current shirt. "I don't really know this fashion or style, so I'm open to whatever she thinks is good."

The tailor nodded. "Very good. The sleeves?"

"Take off the ruffled cuffs," Octavia said.

"Of course," the tailor said, almost rudely. "But how tight?"

Octavia looked back up at Durante. "Well? What would you like, what would feel good?"

Durante looked at his current top, which had no sleeves, but Comicha had done an admiral job hemming the arm holes. "This seems okay," he said looking over his arms, "whatever length." He twisted his arm, inadvertently flexing as he did. He'd gained some fair definition there.

"Okay, let's see," Octavia said, and they took a moment to pull the rest of Durante's shirts out of his bag. She divided them up by weight and turned back to the tailor.

"All right, let's take the sleeves entirely off these lighter ones, and keep them on the heavier fabrics. Let's leave them with some fabric for movement. Something a little flowing," she said, sorting things as she went. "Take the frills off everything, though these two," she grabbed his more winterweight shirts, "let's keep the high neck and just make it neater. Less fabric, clean lines."

The tailor nodded. "Very good."

The tailor had Durante try on a shirt of each weight so that it could be properly pinned and used as a guide for the others. It wasn't going to be cheap, but Octavia was as charming as her smile (and her magic) would allow her to be, and they managed to negotiate the tailor down a little given both the size and the ease of the job. The rush fee was not negotiable, but that was also understandable.

Once they were outside of the little shop, the order written up and a downpayment made, Octavia turned to Durante and took his hand.

"How are we doing so far?" she asked, looking up at him.

"Good, I think," he said, but he was standing a little straighter. There was something familiar about the process of working with a tailor and getting a wardrobe put together. "Although, you basically went through all my clothes. I'll have to get new ones if we go back to Ascherol."

"Why?" She grinned at him and took his arm. "Do you have a driving need to 'fit in' in Ascherol? I suppose if we attend an event of state or something." She paused and turned pink. "I mean, if you attend an event of state. That was… presumptuous. I'm not saying I would… um, anyway."

"I don't see a problem with 'we', Tavi," he said, squeezing her hand. "Can't think of anyone else I'd rather have with me at an event of state. But regardless, I don't know if we'll be going back there anytime soon."

She cleared her throat and began to lead him through the market again. "Ah, anyway! I want to say that I found a shop that did pants more in the style of Uroia yesterday. They were near one of the dress shops I was looking at. Let's find you something at the crossroads of function and fashion."

"Probably a good idea," he agreed, "then I won't have to keep asking Alces to mend up my clothes anytime we wander off-trail. Which is a lot."

Laughing, she nodded. "I'm going to be getting leathers as well while we're here, for the same reason. That and… well, maybe it's all in my head, but I swear my pants never feel the same after the mending spell."

"Between the spell and your, um, thing with clothes, it may just be psychosomatic," Durante said with a chuckle.

They wandered through the market, and Octavia reflected once again on how nice it felt to just be strolling arm in arm with someone, particularly a handsome someone whom she could confidently say was at least fond of her. The more she walked around with him, the more Durante eased and became casual with her. It seemed like he'd backslide a little each time they were in public or around the others, but also each time it seemed like he slid less and less. By the time they'd gotten to the leather shop he was talking to her about alchemical theory and how the phase of the moon affects reagent properties in certain mixtures.

They entered the shop, and she briefly left him in the hands of the leather workers long enough to pop next door. The neighboring clothier had been home to a handful of delightfully shameless dresses during the night market. She had a quick talk with the proprietress, who knew exactly what dress Octavia was referring to, and was happy to let her pay for it and arrange delivery. She assured the girl behind the counter that she had someone to take it in, and if they could please just deliver it to the inn Octavia's "girl" would see to everything.

Heading back into the leather shop, she sauntered back into the fitting area where Durante was back on a riser again and smiled up at him as they took his measurements and discussed what stain he would want on the pants.

Thinking about it for a moment, Durante turned to Octavia while addressing the leatherworker. "I think a good deep green would be complimentary, yes," he said, seeking validation.

She smiled. "That does sound lovely. I agree." She briefly considered what colors his shirts were and nodded to herself. Green would work well with his purples and reds and blacks, particularly if the shade was dark enough.

A young woman off to the side of the man taking measurements nodded and pulled out a pile of scrap pieces from the currently available leathers. Durante picked the green he liked best, and she jotted down some notes. The gentleman straightened up from where he had been stooped to measure Durante's calf and stepped back with a nod.

"I have what I need, sir," the leatherworker said, and turned to Octavia. "Are we making anything for you as well, miss?"

"You are, actually," she said and removed the shawl that was draped over her, setting it aside before taking Durante's place on the riser.

The leatherworker nodded and handed the measuring tape to the woman who had been taking notes, accepting the notebook. The young woman stepped up and looked Octavia over for a moment with an expression that was… not critical, per se, but a little judging. Octavia remained quiet and let her measurements be taken.

Another half an hour later and Octavia had been measured and an order put in for a pair of traveling pants in a charcoal gray. The shop tanned and tooled their leathers by hand, but used magic in the assembly stages, so they would have their pants when it was time to leave the city. The rush fee stung a bit, but there would never be a time they lingered anywhere long enough to avoid it. Best to pay it and move on.

"So, what do you think," Octavia asked as they left the leather shop, "should we grab a light lunch before we continue with supply shopping?"

"I think I'd like that very much," he said, walking a little closer to her, their arms still entwined.

They made their way towards the center of the market, where all the food stalls had been set up. Given the time of day, it was quite crowded, but the slingers here were very experienced and were able to get orders out quickly. Octavia got them both kebabs that used flat bread as a plate. Durante never really ate much, deriving most of his energy from his other hunger, but he could still eat food. And she had noticed that when he did eat, meat tended to go over better. She had no shame about eating his leftover bread if he decided he was done.

"I'd love to offer you something else," she murmured, teasingly, as they ate, "but I don't think we've accomplished quite enough today to justify sneaking back to the inn."

"I do so appreciate that you would offer that to me," he said, smiling at her. "It means a lot. I know this... thing that I've done to myself is an oddity and a burden. Also, I am a little done for the night after I feed off of you. I should make sure I don't make any important decisions after that." He nibbled daintily on the kabob and handed her the bread.

"I know, I remember," she said with a sigh, pouting a little. "I can't believe my bond to Kamvasana taints even my blood. The benefits still outweigh the annoyances, but there are a lot of annoyances." She bit into the bread far less daintily.

"I'm sorry that it makes me loopy and odd. Despite that, though, I'd agree. The benefits outweigh the annoyances," he said, bumping against her and smiling.

"Why are you apologizing? It's my stupid blood," she said with another pout. She finished the bread, and he leaned in to kiss her, smiling all the while.

"It's my stupid reaction to it," he said, taking an arm and wrapping it around her waist as they walked. "Your blood is delicious, if you don't mind me saying so."

That was more flattering than it probably should have been. "Okay," Octavia began, attempting to refocus, "do you know what else we're supposed to be getting today, or were we supposed to just see if anything jumped out at us?"

Durante considered and shook his head. "Whatever stands out. We're not sure where we're travelling to, but if there's something you've noticed we're lacking when we're on the road, we should pick it up."

"I don't think—oh! We need more dishes. Like bowls. If Alces is determined to do more cooking, we need the right things for it to be served in." She thought for a moment, then pulled him towards the side of the market she remembered seeing servingware.

A few hours and several more purchases, and Octavia and Durante were hauling back enough dishes for a service for four, with a couple different serving trays as well. They had put a dent in their purse, but hadn't exhausted it, and left the dishes in Octavia's room on the table so that Alces could go through them and declare if he thought they still needed anything. And so when Alces and Sumner returned, Octavia and Durante were enjoying a light wine downstairs and had returned to the conversation about how the phase of the moon affected reagents.

"Hail, friends," Alces said as they walked in. They looked exhausted, but it wouldn't put a damper in Alces' spirit. She'd seen him with a half-dozen arrows in him, and he still smiled. Clearly, they'd found something to do. "Did we have a successful excursion?"

"Do we have any money left," Sumner added, flopping himself into a chair and rolling his head back.

Octavia smirked. "Yes and yes," she said and slid the purse back across the table to Sumner. "What did you all find today?"

"Would you believe 'officiating a wedding'," Sumner said, lifting his head up to look her in the eye. Alces bellowed out a laugh, then cut himself off with a chuckling hiss as he held his side. As they sat there in the light, Octavia could now see the bits of - something - that still clung to the joins of his armor that might have gotten missed from an initial cleaning.

Her brows arched. "I hope you're going to elaborate on that."

Sumner rolled his head back and waved his hand dismissively towards Alces. Another laugh, although slightly more reserved, and the dragonkin turned towards Octavia and Durante. "Daring Sumner is not wrong. We came across a couple that was seeking an elder of the ancient spirits to lead their wedding. As a knight of the Spree Spirits, I am such a person."

"I do so love weddings," Alces said, looking off into the distance with a softening smile. "Proper ones, joinings of love and want, cherishing one another on a promise before the Spirits. Not these political exchanges that are nothing more than business transactions with souls as currency. No better than devils, they are."

"So, what happened," Durante said, trying to get Alces back on track.

"Oh, yes," Alces said, looking back at the table, "so we ventured out of the city to the place where the wedding would occur. A lovely grove to the north, on the other side of the river. It was high on a cliffside overlooking the lake. Friends and family in attendance, boughs of lavender and basil tied to the trees, rose petals on the path to the plinth."

"A wedding would not leave you in this state, Alces," Durante said, amused and clearly used to the dragonkin wandering off on tangents. "What happened to cause such a state?"

"Please, big guy, I want to eat and then sleep. Get to the point," Sumner groaned.

Alces looked over at the ex-circus performer and narrowed his eyes. His smile showed that he was not nearly as irritated as he was putting on. "Fine. I asked if there were signs or words that they should not be married, discovered that someone had cursed the wedding bands, fiends rose from the earth to attack the couple, and we fought them off. The short version. Happy with that tale?"

"I'll get the whole tale out of you back in the room," Octavia said, smiling fondly at Alces. "You can elaborate as much as you like, Ser Knight. I am glad you were there to defend the young couple."

"Wasn't just them," Sumner said, finally sitting up when the mention of food was made. "Whatever the curse was, it was meant for the whole congregation. On the plus side, we got paid a lot more than we had originally intended and have a place to stay should we come back this way. We also have a job for... well, hopefully just tomorrow. Anyway." He rested his head on his hand and closed his eyes, just giving himself a moment.

She looked over and gestured to the waiter that they were ready for food. Her gaze drifted to Durante, and with an amused expression she leaned in towards him and murmured, "I guess I won't be sneaking into your room this evening."

Glancing over, Durante raised a brow. "Because of Sumner?" he asked, a little unsure of where that was going.

"Because he's exhausted," Octavia answered, still looking amused. "I mean, I'm hardly bothered that he's there, and I would assume you both know how to play nice and share your toys." Her eyes sparkled, and she turned her attention back to the table as food started to arrive.

Durante was mentally stunned, or at least enough that he didn't have a response for Octavia's implications. There were many implications in that statement and look.

"I think we will check back in with the apothecary tomorrow," she said, speaking more clearly. "Though that won't be until the market turns over."

"The two of you are free to do as you wish, then. Sumner and I will be busy," Alces said, and Sumner groaned. "It sounds as though you were productive." With the food starting to be set down at the table, Alces made up a plate and set it before Sumner, tapping him as he did so that he'd noticed he'd been given food.

Octavia giggled. "We'll figure something out. I would say that I would finally get around to looking at the book we retrieved from Gravemont, but I'm not sure I want to do that within the city walls."

While Alces did give off the aura of the undefeatable spirit, his movements were clearly slowed as he went about dinner. After that, Octavia took over. She made sure they all got as much food as they needed, ordered a tartar for Durante because she thought he would like it more, and covertly switched Sumner to a lighter ale when his exhaustion really started to show. Dinner slowed, with Alces eating far more than the server had expected. He always ate a lot, but after a series of fights, it seemed his stomach was almost bottomless with the energy he needed to replace. He did call it, probably for the inn's sake. Many ales and ciders were had during the course of dinner and Sumner certainly looked ready to be put to bed.

With Sumner out of it, Octavia was the one to pay for dinner. A sweet young waitress marveled at how much Alces had eaten but was very happy at the coin Octavia handed her as well as the warlock's beguiling smile. It was a little funny—she was used to charming the staff at the inn or wherever she was staying. She'd coaxed many a barmaid and waiter into her bed in the past to satisfy the conditions of her pact. Now she didn't have to, and she was having a hard time not flirting with the staff.

Alces helped Sumner get off to bed with Durante and Octavia following them up. It didn't take long for Alces to put Sumner to bed, mostly just setting him in place and letting Durante take over from there. Coming back into the bedroom with Octavia, Alces sighed as he set himself down on the edge of his bed and started the process of stripping himself of his armor and cleaning it. Octavia bound back her hair and got to work helping Alces out of his armor without a word. It was easier this time—she was more familiar with how it all fit together, and she was learning where to press to create enough slack in the straps to undo the buckles.

"It sounds as if you won a noble victory today, my knight," she said with a smile as she fetched a cloth from the basin and began to wipe Alces down as they peeled the padding away.

"The first battle in a small war, dear Octavia," he said, rolling his shoulder around once the pauldron had been removed. "Tomorrow, we aim to break the curse on the bands so the couple can be married and find the scoundrel who placed it. The two of you had your own victory, it seems. Durante will be clothed agreeably and I think I spotted some new dishes over there?"

"A bit of a trifle in comparison," she said, and tsked as he moved his shoulder. She set down the cloth and darted to her chest to pull out a salve before coming back and rubbing it into the light bruising she could just barely see through his scales.

"If one does not have a comfort to return to, it weakens one's light in the fight," he said, unhooking the other pauldron and setting it down as she stepped away. "Your victories are no less important." The dragonkin smiled and nodded his head to her.

"So yes, dishes for the tent, so that we are prepared for whatever you wish to make," she finally said as she rubbed his shoulder as best she could. "I'll probably be able to fetch a couple of Durante's shirts tomorrow, and the rest should be done by the time we're ready to leave. Leather pants for the both of us, so we're better equipped for going off trail. And I think I'll pick up a leather fauld. I saw a pretty one in the shop today. And if you'd like to take Durante with you tomorrow, I can visit the apothecary on my own"

"I think Sumner and I can handle it, unless you need some alone time," he said, looking over to her as she worked on his wounds. "We're intimate with the curse itself, and on the off chance the person who cursed them seeks revenge on those that stopped their plan, I'd rather any of us not be alone. Not that I do not feel you could handle yourself."

"As you say," she said, setting the salve down, "though if either of you are gravely injured, I'll be very unhappy about it."

"I will keep Sumner safe, worry not," he assured her.

"Not just Sumner, you ridiculous dragon," she said, side-eyeing him and swatting his hip.

She left Alces to finish and went about preparing for bed. She made a note to see about getting her things laundered tomorrow—the cleaning spells didn't perfume the fabrics or fold them neatly or any of the other niceties just having something washed provided. With his armor off, he stood and stretched. Easing his muscles, he let out another sigh and dropped his arms before removing the padding and leaving himself in his under breeches. She eventually returned to Alces side, hair bound back but no longer up, and in a light chemise.

"Do you wish to sleep by yourself, or would you like me beside you?" She tipped her head to the side, regarding him curiously.

"I welcome your light whenever I may be blessed by it, sweet Octavia," he said, smiling warmly at her. "I will try my best not to wake you in the morning."

"It's all right if you wake me a little," she said, smiling again. "If you have to pull me off of you, then pull me off. If I'm sleepy enough, I will fall back asleep." She kissed his shoulder. "Hurry up and come to bed. I'll sing you a lullaby."

"As you wish, my Octavia," he said with a smile. As directed, he settled into bed and opened his arms to her so that she could snuggle up and get comfortable however she would like.

Climbing into the bed, she settled against him, a little higher so that she could stroke his horns as she sang to him. Closing his eyes, Alces settled in and softly caressed her hip and thigh as she sang. It was her favorite lullaby, about the courtyard at night and two lovers in repose. He had heard it before, but she assumed he wouldn't mind. The soft smile on his face proved that he, indeed, did not mind and that her voice was all he could want right then. There was nothing more he needed to say, as it was time to rest and sleep, and she was guiding him there expertly.

By the time the song was done, Alces breath was deep and even. Octavia gently stroked his horns for another moment, looking at his face in the moonlight and contemplating. The urge to care for Alces, the desire to play with Sumner, the want to guide and encourage Durante. The way they all made her feel cared for and wanted. She felt that flutter beneath her ribs again, and swell in her chest. Sighing, she kissed Alces on the shoulder and settled in against him. For all that it had been a less grueling day, sleep still came quickly.

FIVE

Octavia was gently woken up by Alces again. The cool breeze as he blew softly on her face interspersed with the deep but quiet sound of the dragonkin calling her name. "It's time to wake, adorable Octavia."

"Hmmm?" Her eyes fluttered open and she yawned, looking up at Alces. The quieter night meant that it was easier for her to wake up, pushing through the fog of sleep and focusing on the dragonkin.

"I was going to get up, but realized that I needed to put on armor and the like and would just make far too much noise. I felt this would be the better way to rouse you," Alces said, arm still cradling her and giving her a squeeze.

"It wouldn't have upset me if the sound of you woke me," she said, and yawned again. She stretched, then rolled towards Alces to kiss his chest and shoulder and climbed out of bed. "At least we're all well rested."

"That we are," he said, following suit and getting up to dress up and strap in. The little cat bath that Octavia gave him last night would be enough, but after today he'd probably need a real one. So would Sumner.

The morning was much the same: Alces needed Sumner to help him get armored up in due time and Durante needed woken up. Sumner was awake, although he still looked out of sorts. Better than last night, so maybe some food would help him out.

Octavia played with Sumner's hair, smoothing it back, and kissed him gently before sending him off to help Alces. She then climbed into bed with Durante and snuggled up against him, playfully biting his shoulder.

"Time to wake up, Kitten."

Groaning a little, Durante rolled over towards her and returned the bite on the shoulder. It was playful as well, and a tiny bit gentler because his teeth were sharp. Even the graze of his fangs made Octavia shiver a little.

"M'wake, I'm awake," he muttered but pulled her in closer.

"We should be good and not just come straight back to bed after breakfast, huh?" She nuzzled at him, kissing along his neck.

"You sure," he muttered and was rubbing his face into her arm and the side of her breast. It was a mirror to when she had woken up next to Alces yesterday, burrowing in for cuddles.

"I mean, I suppose we could see how we feel after breakfast," she said with a little giggle. After a minute, though, she sighed and pulled back gently. "Speaking of breakfast, we do need to get up. And I need to get back out of bed before I wrinkle what I'm wearing."

"Of course, yes," he said with a sigh, relenting his grasp on Octavia and sliding out of bed as well. He still just had the one outfit Comicha had altered for him, but they'd be picking up the rest of his outfits today. Or at least the majority of them. Dressing quickly, he joined her to head downstairs and have breakfast with the rest of the group before they split to go on their separate errands.

Breakfast was almost identical to the morning before, with the kitchen staff having traded out a few different pastries. The young man from the previous morning remembered them and brought a giant dish of eggs just for Alces. And he unsubtly paused to make sure Octavia knew he was happy to get her anything she needed before heading back off to the kitchens.

"This is your last chance to take Durante with you if you think you need him," Octavia said as they finished breakfast. She looked over at Sumner. "I told Alces yesterday that I will be very unhappy with the both of you if either of you come back gravely injured."

"I think it's alright for D to have a couple of days off," Sumner said around his pastry and Alces nodded in agreement. "Besides, if anything happens to us, we'll need someone to patch us up, and he's the next best thing to the big guy that we've got. We'll be fine. Only reason we came back so haggard was because it was a surprise. Now we know what's up. Going to take more than a dozen or so fiends to keep us down."

"Brave Sumner speaks true. For the average guard, much trouble. For us, no problem," Alces said, reassuring Octavia and Durante seemed to shrug in agreement.

Octavia eyed them both suspiciously but picked up her tea and drank it without further commentary. She knew they were both very competent. All three of them, really. If they wanted to make a name for themselves, they could have. They didn't, though, near as she could tell. Alces just wanted to help the world, and the rest of them—herself included—had been swept along for the ride. Yes, they had their own motivations, but the goal was not what kept them together.

"Fine," she said, setting her tea down. "Durante and I will occupy ourselves today until the market changes over. We have some things to pick up, and more that will be done tomorrow. How much longer are we staying here, do you think?"

"We could stay here for quite a while," Alces said, "but honestly, we will stay until wise Durante has what he needs. Big as this city is, however, I feel we will need to find some of the more rare items elsewhere, which is when we shall leave."

"So, depending on what the reagent dealer, ahem, shares with you," Durante said with a bit of a smirk, "we may be leaving as soon as tomorrow or day after."

Octavia laughed. "Ah, yes, there was her offer to 'negotiate.' We'll see how that goes, I suppose." She poured herself one more cup of tea.

Breakfast was relatively quick for Alces and Sumner, as they finished up their meal then headed out. Demonic curses waited for no one and Alces tended to get particularly agitated when it came to those fiends. As they left, Alces kissed Octavia on the forehead and squeezed Durante's shoulder. Sumner ruffled Durante's hair and kissed Octavia on her neck by her shoulder. Durante huffed slightly, more amused than irritated, as he attempted to right his hair.

Giggling, Octavia rose up on her toes and slid her fingers through Durante's hair, helping it to lay right but also just for an excuse to touch him. "Given he's barely taller than me, I'm surprised he had the reach for that," she said, commenting on Sumner.

"It's worse when he's trying to be sneaky about it," Durante said, smiling at her as she caressed him.

Hair fixed, she stepped back. "Ready to get a few more of your shirts back?"

Brushing himself down quickly, he nodded to her. "All yours, Tavi."

"I wish you'd said that in bed this morning," she said with a little pout.

"I, uh, well," he started to stammer then cleared his throat. "You can just assume as much in the future. But I'll try to say it more often." She smiled and took his arm, leading him back out to the market.

The Stone Cross was bustling as usual. The best part about the inn's location was avoiding the foot traffic just to get into the market. Beyond that, however, it was the usual throng of market goers, traders, and grifters. The Stone Cross was truly a haven for shoppers and people watchers, but it was expected that even it had its limitations.

Once out of the inn, Octavia focused on their task. They picked up Durante's shirts—all but the winterweight shirts were done—and checked in on the leather shop, where Octavia purchased a protective cincher style belt with faulds (they would adjust it and have it ready with their order in another day). It was in a deep reddish purple that would match well with the gray pants.

They returned to the inn long enough to drop things off, and Octavia took a moment to kiss Durante until they were both breathless—well, she was breathless, he could hold his breath indefinitely. They headed back out, though, without acting on her relentless teasing, and got lunch before combing the market again. By the time the market switched over, and it was time to find the alchemist, Sumner and Alces still weren't back, and Octavia was doing her best not to worry. While also trying to figure out why she was worried at all.

Durante was looking at Octavia and made a small noise of concern. Moving to her, he took her hand and squeezed it. "It's alright, they're dealing with the one thing Alces specializes in. It's an enemy he knows. They'll be okay," he said, smiling for her. "I'll wait here, make sure everything's alright and they're okay. You go negotiate." Giving her a slightly more amused grin, he squeezed her hand again. He didn't seem worried for them, just her and how anxious she looked.

Sighing, Octavia blushed a little and squeezed Durante's hands. "I don't know why I'm… ugh. Okay, I'll go negotiate, maybe it'll be a nice distraction." She smiled at him wryly. "Hopefully I'll have everything you need in short order."

One last lingering kiss, and she parted with Durante. She let out a sigh as she made her way to the alchemist's. Unpinning her hair, she let it bounce around her shoulders, framing her face, and popped one more button on her already low-cut shirt. If the alchemist was interested in what Octavia had to offer, as it were, might as well use it to her advantage.

Given the nature of her products, it probably wasn't surprising that the ork woman's stall was bare of customers. It did make one wonder how she stayed in business, but there was also a chance that a single sale of rare materials could warrant a month's worth of expenses to the average stall keeper.

Glancing up from her book, the woman absently slid the place marker ribbon onto her page and drank in Octavia's appearance. A smile graced her lips, and Octavia caught a glimpse of the small fangs that jutted up from her top and bottom teeth.

"She comes alone," the ork remarked, setting her book aside and tucking her reading classes into a fold of her robes. Leaning forward, she moved her eyes up and down Octavia's form. "I take it you've considered my proposal, glitzy eyes."

"I'm thinking about it," Octavia said with a smirk. "Although I think I'd like to know what you were able to find first. But I enjoy novelty, and I've never… negotiated with someone such as yourself before. And I have a weakness for avid readers."

Keeping up the smile, the woman leaned back, crossing her arms in front of her. "I'll admit, I have a bit of a weakness for those blessed with powers. Your eyes gave it away the moment I saw you," the ork said. "I was able to find some things, yes. Blood, I have a few vials of it. As a bonus, I also know of a source for organs. Little bit of a journey, and you'll have to discuss their terms for trade, I guarantee nothing on that end other than I know they have what you're looking for."

Octavia nodded slowly, listening carefully to everything the ork said. The blood might do it, but she suspected they would need to follow up with the organ source. Which they could certainly do.

Clearing her throat a little, the woman slid off her stool and stood up, now quite a bit taller than Octavia. "Formalities first. I'm Erash Wyrdsight," she said, offering her hand.

"Octavia Baudelaire," she returned, taking the other hand in her own. "Formerly of Driscoll's Rest, though the earth can swallow it for all I care. Bound in service to Kamvasana." While she normally didn't reveal her patron to people, the ork already knew she served someone, and it might be more fun if she recognized who.

"Long way from home," she remarked as they shook. "And Kamvasana? Now there's a name I haven't heard in a long time. Oh, I do hope you take me up on my offer, you'll be very fun." Erash's hands were a little rough, but not nearly as rough as an ork's probably would have been normally. Octavia also caught a whiff of something earthy and spicy with a hint of honeysuckle.

Ah, it is so good to be recognized. Not enough followers of the old ways in this modern era.

Octavia kept her smile and ignored her patron. "So where shall we go to begin negotiations?"

"Excellent, step right in," Erash said, opening a small passage gate on the side of the counter and offering her hand. The ork helped Octavia up the single step and then closed the gate behind her. It was very cramped in the little stall and Octavia found herself pressed against a pair of breasts that, while not as ample as her own, were still hefty while hidden in the folds of the robe.

Erash gave Octavia a wink and reached up, taking the window shutter off its hook and closing the booth up. As the shutter fell into place, the whole booth went dark, and Octavia felt a slight whoosh of air. As light started to come back in, Octavia saw that the back of the stall had disappeared, and they were standing in a much larger room that appeared to be a cozy living room.

There were a few doors leading off, but the current room was covered in drapes and pillows, some easily big enough to seat two or three people. There were a few more jars and containers sitting on shelves, but mostly it appeared to be herbs hanging to be dried and a few mounts on the wall of creatures Octavia couldn't recognize and weapons that had clearly seen better days.

"Not many get invited in here, believe it or not, so I hope you don't get the idea that I offer discounts to anybody," Erash said with a smirk and stepped into the room, presenting it to Octavia.

"Oh, don't worry, I was under the clear impression that any offer of a discount was just an excuse." Octavia considerately removed her boots before walking through the cozy lounge area. It looked like Erash had a good number of secrets. "This is lovely. Pocket dimension or portal?"

Erash put a hand on a hip and grinned at Octavia. "Pocket. As you can see, we're still attached to the stall," she said, motioning towards where they had just been standing, which still looked like the stall minus the back wall. "Used to live in a shitty apartment down on the other side of Ashtide Gate. Cost me quite a bit, but now I only pay for the stall rent, so it'll pay for itself in a few years."

Octavia nodded, smiling. "I have a tent like this. I wasn't made for camping, so it makes travel much more amenable." She looked around again, then moved back towards Erash. "I have to be back by dawn. I will worry my traveling companions if I am not. I do not say this to rush you, just to be transparent."

"Well, we wouldn't want that. Sounds like you have more than the dapper dhampir amongst your courtiers, then?" Erash asked.

"He is dapper, isn't he?" Octavia smiled fondly. "We travel with a dragonkin and a... you know, I'm not actually sure what Sumner is. He looks human, but he shifts a bit when he's fighting or excited. He's not a wer creature, though, but he's very catlike."

"You have quite the menagerie. Your friend probably has wer in his bloodline. I've heard of such but never seen one," Erash commented, intrigued.

"Yes, I occasionally feel very unremarkable in comparison," Octavia commented dryly. She tipped her head to the side and looked the orkish woman over. "So, shall we have something to drink and get to know each other a little? Or did you have something else in mind?"

"Oh, if you like, yes," Erash said as she moved towards one of the doors. "What's your flavor? After which, I'll give you my proposal."

"I love teas and sweet wines," Octavia said. "Shall I help, or shall I just sit?"

Erash opened a door, and Octavia could peek into a kitchen of sorts just beyond. From what she could see, it looked disorganized but not messy. "I can handle tea. I'll be right back."

There were a few moments where it was very quiet. Octavia could hear the noise of the market just beyond the shutter, but it was muffled and distant. She settled comfortably on one of the large pillows. Then came something a little more cacophonous from the kitchen and some growling in a language that was harsh and rumbling, followed by some more noise.

In due time, however, Erash returned with a tray, and a set of glasses half-filled with a red and amber swirling liquid, as well as a tea pot, gently steaming in the soft light of the room. "I think you'll like this. It's a more refined take on a drink from my home. So, Ms. Baudelaire, what would you like to share or ask?" Folding her legs underneath her, the ork woman placed the tray down on the coffee table and motioned for her to wait. Clearly the drink wasn't quite ready yet.

Octavia shifted her weight and did a little cat crawl over to the coffee table—it wasn't far enough to get up, in her opinion. Erash's eyes gleamed as she watched. Settling across from the other woman, Octavia looked over the table but folded her hands in her lap.

"Octavia or Tavi, please," she said, smiling again. "You needn't be that formal. I will admit, I'm curious as to how you got into this business, if you don't mind my asking?"

"Observation, mostly," Erash said, letting her robe slip off one shoulder as she slowly rolled onto one hip. "Had a few traders come to my town. Turns out our hunters were killing some very interesting beasts with parts that alchemists, mages, clerics of lost pantheons, and so on really like. They didn't think anyone saw their brows raise when our merchants were offering it as little more than offal. I noticed, however."

Lifting the lid to the pot, Erash took a sniff, tilted her head to the side, then nodded. Picking the pot up, she started to pour the tea into the glasses and the soft brown liquid mixed with the swirl that was already in there and started to turn purple. Not vibrant, but hard to miss. "So, I started collecting the bits and pieces, preserving them as best I could, and started mixing and testing them too. While I certainly can't create potions of great power, I do pretty well for myself. Made my way to the nearest dwarven and human settlements, made some pretty decent money. Enough to get myself a wagon, horse, and a route."

She took a set of spoons and mixed the drinks. The two glasses became a subtle swirl of purple and gold as she extracted the spoons and motioned towards the glass. "What about you? Gorgeous warlock of Kamvasana, traveling with quite a group. What's your play in this? I don't see you as the alchemist."

Smiling, Octavia shook her head. "I am not. I became a warlock because, well, I was raised to be a wife and didn't much like the idea but hadn't picked up a lot of marketable skills, either," she shrugged. "And being a governess was awful. These three found me in Gravemont, of all places. They needed someone who can read anything, so they hired me. I'm playing research assistant at the moment. They're more like a family than a mercenary group, though."

"That was a twist I was not expecting," Erash said with a smirk. "The two other thralls of Kamvasna that I have met did so out of power and desire. One simply wanting to escape is new."

Seeing Octavia not take a sip, Erash picked up her own glass and did so, swirling the liquid in her mouth before swallowing and smiled. "Before we go much farther, I need to present to you my offer. Spend the evening with me, giving power to your patron, and I'll give you a heavy discount on the blood and the information."

"However," she grinned, pulling a small vial out of a fold in her robe and holding it up, the light dancing in the pink liquid, "let me put this in your drink and then spend the evening with me, and you can have everything for free. It is completely safe, and it will only affect you tonight. I swear to the hunters of the sky and tillers of the land, I wish you no harm. Quite the opposite."

That certainly made the entire deal more interesting. Octavia considered, and took a sip of the drink, rolling it in her mouth for a moment to savor it. Sweet notes of peach and honey, bitter balance of the tea, and the faint tang of something mildly alcoholic. It also gave her a moment to wait for something from her patron. Kamvasana, for as much as they regularly let Octavia fall on her face, would not allow her to put herself in a situation where she was assaulted. More than one would-be rapist had found themselves immolated by what normally was a more minor spell. If it was possible to fight her way out, Kamvasana left Octavia to fix her own messes, but if she was alone, if there was no other way, Kami would intervene.

The Embodiment of Lust was silent. It seemed Erash was genuine. Octavis set her cup in front of the ork. "Do I get to know what to expect, or am I going in blind?"

The orkish woman all but giggled as she uncorked the vial and poured the contents into her drink. "Oh, this is going to be quite a night. I will tell you what I expect to happen, if you like, or you can just experience it. I have used this before, but not on someone gifted by Kamvasana, so I do not know how those gifts will affect the tincture. I apologize, I could not completely remove the taste, but I was able to mostly mask it with juice and alcohol."

"Will you be taking notes?" Octavia picked up her tea again and gave it a little swirl with her wrist. "Should I summon my familiar to take notes?"

"I hope to be far too involved to take notes, but if you're offering, yes," Erash said with a grin and took another sip of her tea.

Octavia reached out a hand, swirling her fingertips. "Comicha!"

The little imp popped into being. "Yes, Mis—," she stopped, looking around the room and at Erash. "Oooh, you did it! You agreed to the deal! Wait, why did you summon me?"

Octavia snickered. "You're here to take notes. I have agreed to take something that will affect my state of being. We don't know how my ties to Kamvasana will alter it. You're here to document the experience."

"Oooo, sexy research!" The imp disappeared, then popped back into being in the corner of the room with a notebook, a pen, and tiny glasses that perched on the end of her tiny nose and were attached by a chain to one of her horns. "Ready!"

"Blessed hunt, she is adorable," Erash said, crawling over to Comicha to look her over. "I don't know if I want the notes or to play with her too. Join in whenever you wish, cutie." Smirking, the ork woman booped Comicha on the nose, then returned to the table to finish her drink.

Comicha looked over at Octavia, excited. "Mistress, can I?"

Octavia sipped the tea and wrinkled her nose at the change in taste. "Only if you take very good notes."

"Yes, Mistress!"

"We can talk a little longer, it does take a few minutes to take effect," Erash added, leaning back against a pillow. Her robe was all but open at this point and Octavia could see dark green freckles dotting her skin along her chest and the tops of her breasts along with stronglegs that slowly rubbed against each other. "Your group takes care of your needs, huh?"

"Mmm, yes," Octavia commented, and drank off the rest of the tea. At the harsh medicinal tang, she made a face that made Comicha giggle. "Might I have another to wash that flavor away with?"

As Erash saw to that, Octavia unwound the shawl she had been wearing and set it aside. "I've been bedding the three of them for a month now, I think? Individually. They don't see each other in a sexual way, near as I can tell, and I have not yet tried to get them to work together, though I did bring it up recently. I think Kami wants it—I've been dreaming about it a lot."

"I could tell," the woman said as she went to fetch some more of the liquor that went into the glass. The tea was probably a bit stronger now but not so much as to be bitter. When Erash returned, the robe was hanging on by the barest bit of friction at the waist, giving the shopkeep an extremely plunging neckline. Given the planned events, modesty didn't seem high on Erash's concerns.

"Not so much the way you were carrying yourself with the gentleman the other day, but more of your current casualness," she said, sitting down at the table again and pouring the two bottles into Octavia's glass. The red and amber liquids swirled together as she filled it halfway, then purple returned when she poured in the tea and stirred it.

"The two I'd spent time with were nearly ravenous for affection by the time I laid with them."

"Ahhhh." Octavia nodded, thoughtful. "It does make us hungry. And I don't know about those you laid with before, but it's part of my pact with Kamvasana. That I experience and inspire pleasure, and they drink of that pleasure through me."

Accepting the cup, Octavia gave it another stir then sipped before looking back up at Erash. "I am looking forward to being with you. I have never been with an ork and never imagined I would want to based on my limited experience, but you are very different. Smart, pretty, and I'm going to trace a line between your freckles with my tongue." She grinned.

"I look forward to feeling what drawing you get out of it," Erash said with a grin. "I certainly can't say that I will be a good example of ork intimacy, but I do bring some flavor with it." Leaning back, Erash lounged out on a set of pillows and parted her robe entirely. While not shaved, she was neatly trimmed, and it matched the flow of dark hair that had been laid out around her, held together in locks by golden beads, the glittering color matching the woman's eyes.

Following suit, Octavia undid the remaining fastenings on her top and let it slip from her shoulders, freeing her breasts and exposing the creamy warm expanse of her skin, like tea with a little too much milk. She went ahead and slid out of her pants as well, setting them aside.

"I like to say I am an exemplary sample of human intimacy, but I might be fooling myself," Octavia said, picking up her tea again and laughing a little. "You'll remember me, though. I guarantee that."

"Of that I have no doubt," Erash said, beckoning Octavia closer. "From what I see, you are quite exemplary. and that view will be burned into my memory forever."

"Oh, which view? This one?" Octavia smiled impishly, then rather than crawl to Erash, stood back up and walked towards the other woman. When Octavia stood, she could feel her head swim a little. Not so much that she would lose her balance, but just that she felt lighter than she expected, and couldn't help but exaggerate her movements. It was a pleasant feeling, warm and encompassing. She stopped when the ork was not quite eye-level with Octavia's sex. "Or this one?"

"Both," Erash said, reaching up and placing a hand flat on Octavia's hip bone, teasing the soft spot where it met her thighs. Sliding it down, her touch became focused to a single fingertip that brushed against Octavia's hood and sent a shock through her body.

"Ah!" Octavia's legs wobbled just a little at the intensity of the sensation. "Oh, oh that's… striking."

"Could you describe it better?" Comicha asked from across the room, and Octavia laughed.

"Observe, don't ask questions," she shot back.

"A good reaction," Erash said, sliding both hands around Octavia's hips and pulling her closer. "And so quickly. Allow me to make sure you never forget me, either. Little imp, watch closely."

Erash blew softly on Octavia's sex, the cool air on her growing wetness sending a shivering chill through her body. It was quickly snuffed, however, when Erash's hot mouth met with her pussy, and the woman's tongue slid into her. It couldn't be helped, Erash's fangs and tusks pressed against the sensitive skin of Octavia's mons as she ate her out.

"Goddess of Mercy," Octavia gasped and grabbed at Erash's shoulders to keep herself steady. The feel of Erash's teeth were just heightening the shivering tension building in her pelvis. Erash's movements weren't hurried, but they were hungry in their own right. She wasn't gentle, but neither was she severe. While Octavia was sensitive by an anointed gift, whatever she had ingested earlier had spiked it even farther, and she could sense everything, right down to the soft exhalation of Comicha sitting several steps away.

"Gods, I'm about to come," she said, her shock clear even through the moan in her voice.

"Don't hold back," Erash said, kissing Octavia's hood between every other word. "Just feel everything. Let go, fall into the sensations." The ork went right back to what she had been doing, her grip tightening on her hips to also help with keeping her steady and, more importantly, directly against her mouth.

"Yes," Octavia moaned, legs quaking again, "YES!" The grip on Erash's shoulders tightened as she came. "I… I can't keep standing," she managed to get out as she caught her breath.

Dragging her tongue out of Octavia, Erash squeezed Octavia's hips and smiled. "You don't need to. Come, sit down. I'm going to keep playing with you for a bit. Feel free to touch me or do whatever you like," the ork said as she helped Octavia down off her feet.

Dropping down, Octavia kissed Erash warmly, sucking the taste of her climax off the ork's tongue. She started to sit down next to Erash but was instead guided into the ork's lap—Octavia's legs draped over one of Erash's, her back propped up by the other bent leg, and the ork had unfettered access to her body.

We should give you a dose of this and throw you at your boys, Kamvasana chimed in Octavia's head, sounding impressed. *Or better yet, a pleasure house.*

Octavia continued to ignore her patron and bit down gently on Erash's shoulder. Pulling her close, Erash resumed their previous kissing, as she started to caress Octavia's body. While her nails were hard, they had been filed down to soft curves, and they were quite good at tingling Octavia's skin. Octavia briefly wished she could do this with Durante - the way her blood affected him, he might appreciate her being under the influence of something that made her equally sensitized. One of her seeking hands found Erash's breast, cupping it and giving it a squeeze before sliding her thumb over the nipple.

Erash hissed pleasantly when Octavia teased her, seeming to be a little sensitive herself, but that didn't stop the ork's motions. Sliding her arm around Octavia's back, Erash cradled her while grasping one of her full breasts firmly. Erash's other hand traveled south and teased over her clit, gentle but insistent, knowing not to apply too much pressure.

"I'm going to turn you into a puddle, Tavi," the woman said breathily into her ear.

"Gods, I think you are," Octavia said, panting. There was a small part of her that was bothered that Erash wasn't getting a better performance, but Octavia suspected in the course of an hour she would be mindless and animalistic. She licked her lips and squirmed in Erash's arms. She just wanted more. And if Erash didn't stop, she would absolutely come again.

"Praise be to Kamvasana," Erash said cheekily and sunk a pair of fingers into Octavia's dripping pussy. Crying out, Octavia arched. Soft and beautiful and trembling, she quivered like a vibrating bowstring for a moment before falling back into Erash's arms. Given how wet she was, there was little resistance when the ork started to pump those fingers in and out of her while giving her breast a kneading squeeze. It seemed, for the moment while in the enthrallment of the concoction, Erash was quite happy just making Octavia her plaything.

Octavia's cries only drove Erash, and she pulled her closer so she could suckle at one of Octavia's tits, licking and teasing as she pumped her fingers into her. The ork wanted more, more of Octavia's cries, more of her soft body in her hands and mouth, more of her quivering and soaking her fingers. Octavia was losing herself. The room felt like it was breathing with her, a warm and attentive presence that wanted to see Erash turn her into a mewling, helpless toy. She writhed in the ork's arms, coming again as her sensitive tits were sucked and teased.

Delicious, Kamvasana purred as if in Octavia's ear, making her twitch and moan. *You always serve me so well.*

Her hands grabbed at Erash, anything they could reach, caressing and squeezing, clawing as the pleasure peaked. Removing her mouth off Octavia's breast with a pop, Erash lashed at her nipple with her tongue before turning to Comicha.

"Little imp, I have a task for you," the ork panted, a flush darkening the green on her chest and cheeks, "go through that door, chest at the foot of the bed. I need a toy, two ends. You'll know the one. Time to break your master's mind in the most wonderful of ways."

Comicha squealed happily and zipped away.

Turning back to Octavia, the ork leaned in and licked the warlock's lips. "Don't worry, I'll take care of you."

Still in a haze but not incapable of movement, Octavia reached up and took Erash's face in her hands, kissing her deeply.

SIX

S he feels so wonderful right now," Comicha said cheerfully as she came back into the room, holding the toy in question. "And I have so much energy! I understand how your potion is playing with Desire's magic, so I've taken very good notes for you! If you need anything let me know!"

Erash parted from the kiss to acknowledge Comicha's presence and the toy she brought. Eyes half lidded at this point, the ork took the toy from the imp and grabbed her by the waist, pulling her close and giving the purple plush demon's tit a lick and a nip. Comicha whimpered, and kissed Erash's face.

"You've done very well. Maybe you'll get more of a reward later," Erash said, releasing Comicha. "One more set of notes, then you are welcome to do as you wish."

"Thank you!" She then flitted away back to her little station.

Picking the toy up; which was a double phallus made of what looked like smooth glass, the ends near each other in a curved V-shape; Erash licked a length of it while returning her attention back to Octavia. "Want more, glitzy eyes?"

Moaning, Octavia blinked and gave her head a little shake, trying to come back to herself and not entirely succeeding. "More," she repeated, and leaned in, licking at Erash's neck. Ooo, that felt good. And she tasted spicy. "Yes, more..."

Grinning, Erash moved carefully. Reaching down, she inserted one end into herself, moaning as the length sunk into her. Taking just a moment to relish in it, she gave Octavia's breasts another squeeze then went back to work.

With a guiding touch, Erash got Octavia to rotate, facing her with her legs on either side of the ork's hips. Scooting close, Erash reached between them, guiding the other end of the toy into Octavia, then pulling her down onto it. It sank in, hard and unyielding and exquisite, nestling deep into Octavia's vessel as the women found themselves face to face, breasts mashed together and sending shivers into both of them.

"Move for me, Tavi. Show me what you can do," Erash said, leaning forward to bite at her shoulder. Octavia cried out as Erash bit down, coming again around that strange glass cock.

Move. A command. Easy to follow. A simple instruction that cut through the haze. Slowly at first, a careful and controlled twisting of her hips as she got used to the unyielding glass sliding into her pussy. The way her body rubbed against Erash was fantastic, and the want to feel more of the other woman brought strength back into her limbs, shaking off the lethargy of so many orgasms. Her hands slid eagerly over Erash as her hips found a good, steady ride that rocked the double ended dildo into Erash every time their hips met.

"Oh, krakth, that's good," Erash said, one hand behind her to keep her propped up against Octavia, the other holding on to her hip to keep them moving together. The ork woman was rolling her hips as well, making sure it speared into Octavia just as much. Erash's movements were growing more feverish - now that she was getting some physical attention, she was wanting more.

It was as if a switch had been flipped in Octavia. The soft, vulnerable woman from just minutes ago was replaced by something feral and voracious. She continued to ride Erash at a hard, steady pace as she kissed her then started to lick and bite down the ork's neck. One hand tangled in Erash's hair as the other seized her breast, squeezing it, teasing at the nipple.

"Yes," Erash hissed, her hand moving down to grab Octavia's ass in a firm hold, "fuck me, you thrall of lust. Make your mistress proud." Their bodies started to press against each other like waves in the ocean, crashing and sliding apart, their breasts sliding against each other as a thin sheen of sweat started to form. Erash's panting started to pick up, as did her movements as she bucked against Octavia. With a strained grunt, she leaned forward and bit a little harder into Octavia's shoulder, an orgasm rocking through the large, green woman as she clung to Octavia while still moving.

Another sharp cry echoed from Octavia, but she didn't stop, even as she came hard enough to gush over Erash. She pushed the ork back against the cushions and continued to ride her. Erash was a little surprised at the sudden shove from Octavia, but she moved with it and smiled, showing off her fangs and tusks. The potion in Octavia's system made everything feel good, even the ache in her thighs.

"Yes," Erash hissed again and moved both her hands to Octavia's hanging breasts, kneading them firmly as the woman rode her. The toy was made so they'd both feel the sensations as they bucked against each other, and Erash was starting to chuff with effort as she refused to lay back idly.

Years as a warlock of Kamvasana meant that Octavia had strong thighs and good muscle memory. It was easy, even in her state, to maintain her energetic pace as she braced herself with one hand and used the other to tease and touch Erash. Octavia's eyes seemed to grow a little brighter, something gleaming in that vibrant, unnatural blue. She didn't say anything, but her voice still filled Erash's ears.

Grinning wildly, Erash tightened her grip on Octavia's hips and started to thrust up into her, crashing them together. The sensations were building to a peak and despite her best efforts, Erash was not a warlock of Kamvasana, and keeping up was impossible. The build soared through her, still sensitive from the last orgasm, and she roared out as she arched her back and lifted Octavia with one final thrust before she collapsed underneath, quaking and making a noise like a growl and a whimper combined.

"Yield, yield," Erash said, playfully slapping Octavia's thigh. "Need a break. Too sensitive."

Octavia bounced one more time, then stopped herself, closing her eyes for a moment before lifting off of both Erash and the dildo and sitting back. Panting, she fell back and laughed. "It's… hard to think… " she said, panting, and reached between her legs, rubbing herself and moaning. "I just… just want to… oh, Gods…"

Comicha flew up, flushed and looking pleased. "Notes taken! And I have a suggestion. You had another toy in your chest. The one with the heavy base. I could bring it out, and my mistress could give you a show while you relax. And you could play with me, and when you were ready, I could go down on you while you watched! I can even get you a drink while you recover!"

Another shiver of pleasure and Erash moaned. Smiling up at

Comicha, she reached up and caressed the little imp's face. "Aren't you so eager to please? Alright, let's do it. After all, your mistress still needs to be a puddle before I'm satisfied," she said, making another sound of latent pleasure.

"Yes! I just want everyone to be happy!" Comicha beamed and then flew off. She came back with kind of a big toy, clearly meant for solo play. It had a large, flared base that would make it heavy enough to stand on its own, and two cocks pointing up from it, one slimmer than the other.

Octavia picked her head up, curious, and looked over with arched brows. "Naga, I think," she murmured, rolling over and crawling towards the toy. "For me?"

"Yes, Mistress," Comicha said in a quiet but excited voice. "Your new friend wants a show!"

Laughing, Octavia's eyes flicked from the toy to Erash and back. "I can do that."

As Comicha flitted about, bringing fresh tea to Erash and making sure the ork was comfortable with everything she needed, Octavia looked back to the toy before her. She slid her tongue over each of the cocks. They were made of a softer material than the glass, a little rubbery perhaps—some sort of hide that she didn't recognize. She sucked each one in turn, the idea being just to make sure they were slick enough, though she did get a little lost in the sensation. She wished Sumner was there. He loved to thrust down her throat, and she was pretty sure that would feel great right now.

Finally, Octavia pulled back and mounted the strange toy. The larger shaft in her slick, already well fucked pussy, and the slimmer in her tight ass. She eased herself down on the toy, moaning loudly as she took it. Erash also moaned as she watched, absently fondling Comicha.

This time, with no one else to be mindful of, Octavia let herself fall into a feral, rutting heat. The tincture in her system, the blessing of Kamvasana, and the fact that this set up was also just incredibly hot. She bounced herself on the twin shafts and moaned, coming again and again, wishing it was Sumner and Durante. Ooo, or it could be Durante and Alces, and Sumner could bury himself down her throat. She came again imagining it.

Octavia lost track of time. The room filled with moans. Erash at some point came to stand before her, grabbing her hair and making use of her mouth as Octavia kept riding that delightful toy. It seemed to just keep going until, finally, Octavia could feel her head start to clear. She lifted herself off the toy she'd been straddling for… an hour? More? Comicha had disappeared, back to her little den in the ether. Moaning again, Octavia fell over.

Carefully scooping up Octavia, Erash moved her over to a pile of pillows and handed her a cup of tea, just tea, and cuddled her while caressing her gently. "Well, thank you very much, Tavi. That was an excellent evening of experimentation," she said, petting Octavia's hair.

"Goddesses of Mercy and Magic, that was… an experience," Octavia said, panting still. "I will absolutely feel this in the morning." She got enough of her breath back to sip her tea. "I… wow. What was that?"

"A careful concoction of specific mushrooms, herbs, and just a hint of harpy milk," she said, still petting Octavia gently. "Since you were so good about it, and showed me such a lovely time, I'll give you a couple of vials, if you like."

A tired giggle bubbled out of Octavia. "You know, I did think about it. The dhampir I travel with, my blood does something like this to him, only he's more passive." She took another sip of tea. "Might try only half a dose, though. He's still getting used to me. A full dose experience might kill him." She snorted at her own joke, far too well-fucked and exhausted to maintain a sophisticated demeanor.

"What a way to go," Erash said, continuing to sooth Octavia with gentle touches and refills of tea if needed. "As promised, I will also give you the strix blood and directions to my organ source for free. Next time, you have to pay. Can't just be handing that stuff out to any sexy woman with a talented mouth."

"Thank you, though I defy you to find another woman of my talents." She sipped her tea, then snickered again. "And if you do, tell her where to find me."

"I will definitely do so, after I've had my turn," the ork woman said with a wink.

Octavia finished her tea, then turned and kissed Erash gently. "I did have a lovely time. Though I think I should dress, gather my prizes, and be on my way back before what little energy I have left leaves me."

Returning the kiss, Erash then stretched and helped Octavia up as she stood herself. "You are very kissy. I'm not complaining, but the others were more purely physical. Just a note of interest," she commented as she picked up her robe and went about wrapping and tying it so it looked more appropriate.

"I have a heart, apparently," Octavia noted dryly as she started pulling her clothes back on, briefly thankful to her past self that they were all in a neat stack. "I'm not sure Kamvasana always appreciates it. And… I used to be more purely physical. Between you and I, those three boys of mine are undermining my wild and free reputation."

"You're claiming ownership, so you may be right," the ork smirked as she walked towards one of the many racks inside her house proper and produced a small satchel. It seemed to already have something in it, but she added two extra vials as well.

"Shit, I am," Octavia muttered, pausing for a moment. She then sighed and drew her scarf around her again.

Waiting by the part that looked like her stall, Erash casually held out the satchel as she waited for Octavia. "I can walk you to where you're staying, if you'd like."

Accepting the satchel, Octavia made sure she had everything and nodded to herself before looking back up at Erash with a smile. "If you feel the need, I thank you, but if you'd rather not, I will be fine."

"Oh, it'll be fine," Erash said, pulling Octavia close and flipping the latch on the window shutter. Everything went dark once more and Erash pulled the shutter up, finding themselves once more in her tiny stall, middle of the night market, with a confused looking young man looking at the two of them.

Erash grinned. "Oh, hello Sarraf Temel, I didn't expect you," the ork woman said, letting go of Octavia and opening the side gate for her. "I was just seeing my friend off."

"I, uh, yes, I can see that," he said, trying to hide his obvious interest, "do you have my supplies prepared?"

Octavia smiled at the young man, in a manner that did not help the implications of what he had just witnessed.

"Of course, Sarraf, of course," Erash said, then turned and leaned down to Octavia, whispering, "terribly sorry, unless you want to wait, we'll have to have that walk some other time."

"Thank you again, Hanim Wyrdsight," Octavia said as she stepped down and smiled with understanding. "I will get out of your way. Enjoy the rest of your night."

She bowed her head to the sarraf, then headed back across the market to the inn, thanking every benevolent deity they had chosen one nearby. She kept her pace steady as she trekked back to the inn so that she didn't give the impression that she was an easy target. Once she crossed into the inn proper, however, she dropped the act and groaned as the muscles in her legs protested.

She headed briefly into the tavern area to ask for anything the kitchen could give her. Lucky for her, she found the young man who had been unsubtly flirting with her the last couple days. He got her some warm bread with cheese melting on it and a small bowl of berries. She thanked him and kissed him on the cheek.

Finally, food in hand, she dragged herself up to the floor where their rooms were. She paused for a moment, then knocked lightly at the door Sumner and Durante shared. Maybe Durante was still up.

There was a sound of shuffling and then the door opened, maybe a little quicker than expected but not in a panic. Durante stood in the doorway, peering past her for just a moment, then looking back at Octavia with a faint smile. "Tavi, you're alright. Well, at least I know where one person is," he said, playing with something shiny in his hands.

Her brows rose. "The others aren't back yet?" She looked over her shoulder, then sighed and looked back at Durante. "Kitten, I'm done for, can I come in and sit down? I need to eat something before I pass out."

"Of course, of course," he said, motioning back into the room. It was much like the one she shared with Alces, although a bit smaller and not quite as decoratively furnished. "Not yet, no. Not sure where they are either. I was just about to set Buzzy off to find them." Durante opened up his hand to show a metallic dragonfly, with delicate wire wings and big, emerald shining eyes.

"It's beautiful," she murmured, then smiled up at him, "like so many things you make." She was too tired not to be sentimental. Kissing his cheek, she sat down on one of the chairs and started to eat, albeit slowly. Even chewing was tiring right now.

"Thanks," he said, smiling gently and helping her sit with a free hand. Once she was settled, he moved to the window and opened it, letting the dragonfly out into the night air. "So, how was the... negotiation?"

"It was a surprisingly scientific evening," she said, snickering. She set down the bundle Erash had given her and pushed it towards him. "Strix blood, and a couple vials of an intriguing elixir. Don't drink it. Also, I have the name and location of her organ supplier. Or rather, it should be in the bag." She took another bite.

Durante brightened up and scooped up the bag, setting it on a desk and removing the items within. He set aside two smallish jars; which probably had the blood; the vials, and was able to pull out a folder piece of parchment. "Oh, this is very good. Still not what I need to start on an antidote, I think, but we're almost there," he said, smiling at Octavia. "Absolute godsend, you are."

"I guess Kamvasana is kind of a god," she said with another snicker. She took another bite. "Kami's not jealous like gods are, though. Not when it comes to reverence. Maybe they used to be. Sometimes when they're on a tear they go off about the "old days" when people had "proper respect." Or something."

She yawned and took another bite. Eating was getting harder. "But Sumner will be relieved to learn that none of this came out of the purse. Given for services rendered. Though she did warn me we'd have to pay next time."

"Oh, I could kiss you for all this," he said, spreading his hands over the spread. Smiling, he stood up and walked over to her. "In fact, I think I will." Leaning in, he gave Octavia a tender kiss, then looked at her. "Tavi, you're exhausted. Should I carry you back to your room?"

She caressed his face. "I… I am but, I don't… I want…" She was too tired to be anything but vulnerable. She stood up a bit shakily and wrapped her arms around him, nuzzling into his chest.

Chuckling, he scooped her up gently. "Tell you what, I'll take you back to bed, then bring your food, and feed you until you're ready to sleep."

She whined a little. It wasn't exactly what she wanted, but it would do. "Okay," she said, wrapping her arms around him again. She forgot sometimes that he was strong enough to lift her. It wasn't unfaltering, like with Alces, but whatever had been happening to him over the years did give him more strength than he appeared to have.

"If you want anything else, let me know, but you just seem wiped," he said as he carried her, carefully opening the door and moving past it.

"My Kitten," she murmured sleepily, and nuzzled into him again.

Her shawl slipped away as he set her down, and she yawned again. She wasn't entirely certain she'd stay awake long enough for him to make it back from the other room. Durante caressed her hair and leaned down to kiss her forehead. Another yawn, and Octavia slid out of her shoes and wiggled off her pants, leaving everything in a neat heap just to the side of her bed. The rest of her clothing swiftly followed. She had enough awareness to pull on a shift to sleep in, but it was lace and satin and clearly more the type of thing meant to be pulled off. By the time Durante came back, she was perched in bed with the covers pulled back wearing a rather short negligee.

Durante returned with her plate of nibbles and smiled as he gazed at her. "You're adorable. I, um, brought your food," he said, walking over and setting it down on the nightstand, then set himself down on the bed next to her.

As he sat down, she wrapped her arms around him again. "Come to bed with me," she said, a little plaintively. "Just until I fall asleep. Please?"

"Yeah, of course," he said after a pause. He was already wearing what could be described as nightclothes; a soft shirt and linen breeches. He moved as little as possible while sliding in next to her to keep her arms around her. "Whatever you want, Tavi."

She scooched back a little and slid up against him once he was far enough in the bed. "You're my favorite for cuddles," she said, hooking her leg around his and pulling herself closer. "You give the best ones."

"I am all too happy to be your favorite for something," he said quietly with a chuckle, holding her close and running a hand through her hair. Once he was settled, he was dead silent, the change making it so he didn't really need to breathe but his heart still beat, regularly and slowly.

She kissed him, slow and soft, and snuggled into him. "My kitten," she murmured again, eyes closing. Within moments she felt her body start to soften as she dropped into sleep, the long night catching up with her.

When Octavia finally regained consciousness, she noted that it was bright outside, the sound of birds and the marketplace steady with the trees outside muffling it to a dull roar. Her snacks from last night still rested on her nightstand and Durante was not next to her.

Blinking, Octavia sat up and looked around the room. She was still very sore. The memories from the previous night were a little fuzzy. She'd asked Durante to stay until she fell asleep. And… Alces and Sumner hadn't made it back yet. She popped out of bed and headed over to where Alces slept, looking for some evidence that he'd come back last night.

Alces was still in bed. He looked much like he had the first evening when he and Sumner had returned from their work, only worse. His scales and coloring made it difficult to single out bruises, but there were definitely nicks in various plates and something splattered on him in places it wasn't easy or obvious to wipe. No doubt Sumner was in a similar shape. It was also odd that it was well after daybreak, and he was still out.

Octavia's heart seized for a moment as she looked him over, but she matched her breath to the rise and fall of his chest until she calmed down. She moved back to her bed and got dressed in the most practical clothing she had, sturdy canvas pants and an old linen shirt that even Kamvasana couldn't make sexy (though it was still pretty low cut). She considered for a moment, then decided to check in with Durante first.

Stepping lightly out of the room, she moved to the next door and knocked. There was a slightly longer moment than she had anticipated, but Durante came to the door, looking a little tired. "Morning, Tavi. Is it still morning?" he asked, looking around for a clock and not seeing one. "You missed all the excitement."

"I'm sorry, I'll let you go back to bed in a minute," she said, keeping her voice soft. "Can you tell me what happened?"

He waved her off a little, he was a little more dressed than last night, but only by the addition of pants. "A little bit after you passed out, they got back. They're fine, just a little beaten up and very exhausted. What say we eat, get some food to take back to them, and then see if we can't patch them up," he offered as a distraction.

"Fine, but I'm going to punch them both once they've recovered," she said, narrowing her eyes a little and glancing towards Sumner's bed. Sumner looked in slightly better shape, but that wasn't surprising. The handful of skirmishes she'd had with them, she knew that Alces would always throw himself between danger and his friends. "Let's go get food, I guess."

"I think they will accept that punishment." Durante looked at her, amused. "I just want them to sleep a little bit more, and I figure this was a good enough excuse. I patched up the bad bits, they're fine."

"They are NOT—" she started and then checked herself. And her volume. Stepping back into the hall, she waited for Durante to follow her out and the door to close before she continued.

"They are not fine, as evidenced by the fact that Alces is very unconscious and the sun has been up for hours!"

"I know, I know," Durante said as he escorted her downstairs but keeping his volume down as well. "I can only imagine what they went through. Alces mentioned something about darkness, or a lack of light, something like that. Probably why he's still recharging. But they're breathing, they got here on their own, and no major injuries."

Grumbling, Octavia didn't quite stomp down the stairs. "Stupid, proud dragon. And Sumner's an even bigger idiot. Repeatedly, I told them to take you with them. That I would be fine. But nooooooo, they're seasoned, they know what they're doing."

"But if they had taken me with them, you would not have had your favorite snuggler to hold you until you slept," he said, giving her a smirk and taking her hand, holding it as they walked to the dining hall.

She still grumped, but she took his hand and leaned into him. Once they hit the dining hall, her mood lifted a bit simply from the smell of food. She was still hungry from the night before.

The dishes today were a little lighter, but plenty in quantity. A bean salad with lemon, spices, and soft-boiled eggs, a dish of chopped up vegetables cooked in olive oil, with healthy portions of stuffed leaves and fish. They were served with chilled juices to drink and soft flatbread. Octavia ate ravenously, her appetite coming back in full swing at the first bite.

"Honestly," Durante said, still only mostly drinking and taking the odd nibble of something, "I was surprised you didn't wake up. They weren't exactly quiet coming in."

"So, remember that elixir I told you not to drink?" She took another bite and followed it with more juice before she continued. "The deal I made with Erash was that I would take the elixir and spend the evening with her. She'd given it to people before, but never one bound to Kamvasana. I knew she meant me no harm, and she swore as much, so I agreed. It increased my sensitivity and my libido for, oh, the span of I think four or five hours. I was very tired. I'd also had a few drinks, and that probably didn't help."

"Your libido is, well, quite extensive to begin with," he said with a smile as his eyes widened. "So, were you tired just from that, or do you think the comedown contributed?" Durante perked up and sat up straight, taking another sip of his drink. Despite the subject, which he was already interested in, they were now talking science.

"I do think the comedown contributed. Once my head cleared, I was… done. Being physical, I mean." She had a few more bites. "I wasn't put off by my actions or anything, but I was just very tired and suddenly aware of the ache in my limbs. In the beginning, it reminded me a little of when you, ah, take from me. That hypersensitivity you seem to get. Though I was more, I dunno, I had more of my faculties. It seemed."

"Hm," he thought to himself, as he considered a few things. "I wonder if I could alter the formula." He took another sip and graced one of his fangs with his tongue as he pondered. She bit her lip as she watched him.

"She didn't tell you what it was by any chance, did she?"

"Huh?" She blinked, realizing he had asked her a question. "Oh, yeah, she did. Um, not precisely, though. It was "mushrooms, herbs, and just a hint of harpy milk," but she didn't tell me anything beyond that."

"I wonder if I could break it down," he said again, motioning for a waiter to swing by. He ordered four lunches for them to take up to the rooms - one for Sumner and three for Alces - then turned back to Octavia. "That is, if you're willing to let me play with one of the vials. They're yours, if you want to save them that's fine. I won't insist."

"Of course you can," she said with a smile. "Honestly, you're the reason I asked for it. Granted, that was because I thought you might enjoy having me be as lost in our joining as you for an evening, but when she said she'd give me more than one I figured you would want to study it."

"You're so thoughtful," he said with a smile and reached over to squeeze her hand. "Although, given how out of it I usually am due to your current nature... actually, you know what, no. It would be fun. When we're at another inn or something."

She found herself beaming at him, happy he approved. She also almost immediately blushed as she realized she must look like an idiot. Or maybe she didn't. Maybe she just looked happy. She hoped it was that second one.

"Ah, good, I'm glad you agree. And I would, ah, wait to take anything until after you… you know. So that we didn't make anything worse." She pushed her hair back with her free hand.

Durante smiled back and those pink eyes of his seemed to tinge with just a touch more color. They hadn't gone red, he wasn't hungry, but it was something else. Still, he seemed equally happy with her response.

"I'm not sure I do know, but we can discuss that later," he said, glancing about, "more privately."

"Who, ah, who do we start with, when we get back upstairs? I was going to do a better job of washing down Alces and making sure he wasn't still bleeding anywhere." She seemed to be over being grumpy, and now just looked concerned. "I imagine Sumner may need the same."

Octavia's question seemed to be one he asked himself a lot, or just instantly knew the answer to. "Sumner first. He's got a few bruises. Most of the cuts and scratches I cleaned and healed. He'll mostly be just exhausted and sore. We may need to drag them both to the bath house if for nothing else than to soak in hot water."

She nodded. "All right. They have nice baths here, Alces and I went down the other night. Shall we gather their food and head back up?"

"I think so," he said, gathering up his own lunch and tucking it away into a cloth. The waiter came by a short time later with a couple of baskets containing the ordered lunches. Durante made a remark about how mad Sumner was going to be when they checked out due to the food being put on the room's tab, but he laughed it off.

SEVEN

Getting back up to their floor, Octavia followed Durante into the room he shared with Sumner and started to get set up. She used a small spell to heat the water in the pitcher by the basin so that it wouldn't be cold when it hit his skin and got rags ready.

"Do you have a preferred salve?" she asked as she worked. "Any cuts will need to be redressed after a more thorough wipe down, and we may find new ones."

"I usually use this," he said, going to his bag and producing a strap with several small bottles sitting in pockets. "Make it myself. I gave them some yesterday. Some more today should help."

The commotion woke Sumner, who groaned and put a hand to his head. "Been fightin' demons all day, can't a guy fuckin' sleep?"

"It's lunch time," Octavia said, wringing out the cloth and walking up to Sumner's bedside. "We have food for you. Which you need to heal. And I'm going to finish cleaning you off and checking your cuts. And as a kindness, I won't punch you until you're feeling better." She set her knee down on the bed, cloth held ready. "All right?"

"So sweet," he said, sitting up and coughing. "Just, ever so kind, Tavi. Truly." Sumner stuck his tongue out at her, and Durante snickered as he prepared some clean wraps.

"I know, I should have become a healer," she said with a smirk, but leaned in and lightly kissed Sumner on an unbruised part of his forehead. "You can go back to sleep after we make sure you're not at risk for infection, though later tonight you and Alces should get down to the baths for a good soak." She settled behind him and started to clean his back. "Would you like me to feed you while I'm at it?"

"If you're going to play nurse, might as well go all the way," he said with a smirk and slight wince as she moved him around. All in all, Sumner was as lightly injured as someone that had spent the majority of the previous day hunting fiends could be. Mostly superficial cuts and bruises. He did have a sizable bruise on his left side, which was probably what caused the wince.

"I don't know, you were criticizing my bedside manner just moments ago," she said with a faint smile.

Despite the comment, though, her hands were soft, and she deftly cleaned him off, likely more delicately than Durante had the night before. The rag needed to be rinsed and wrung out again, but it was not so bad that the water needed to be changed. She got up and let Durante apply a new coating to the scratches and cuts while she made up a flatbread loaded with fish and the bean salad. Handing the flatbread to Sumner, she switched places with Durante again and began to gently and patiently work ointment onto the large bruise.

"That's everything I can do for right now," Durante said, picking up his apothecary strap and kit. "I'll go see if Alces is up and what he needs."

Nodding to Durante, she smiled. "I'll meet you over there in a bit."

"Between the two of ya, think I'll be good as new by nightfall," Sumner said with a sigh. His body moved in a way that he couldn't decide if he should sit up and eat or ease into Octavia's ministrations. She leaned forward and kissed his shoulder.

"Eat. I'll be around later if you feel the need for something soft to lean into." She didn't think Sumner "cuddled" (or at least didn't see himself as the type that cuddled) but she kind of suspected that if she sat behind him and brushed his hair later tonight, she could probably get him purring.

"You do have a fabulously cozy set of pillows," he said with that toothy grin.

"Keep that up and you're going to get smacked after all," Octavia said dryly. She finished carefully rubbing the ointment into the bruise and worked gently on the surrounding flesh, mostly to get the excess of her fingers. The bad joke didn't stop her from kissing his cheek before she wiped off her hands and emptied the basin.

"All right," she said, setting the lunch basket on the side table. "Here is more food if you have the energy for it, otherwise eat well and enjoy your nap." She lightly touched his shoulder, then headed next door to see how Durante was fairing with Alces.

Counter to Sumner, Alces looked significantly more abused. It looked like something rather large had tried to take a bite out of his thigh and, were it not for his scales, might have succeeded. He was awake, sitting on the edge of the bed, and smiled broadly when Octavia walked in.

"Hail, bright Octavia, how was your shopping day and night of negotiations," he said, completely ignoring his own state of affairs and just interested in hers. Durante was dabbing his healing solution on the deep scratches and the odd cut with his healing salve while rolling his eyes.

"Tiring, but fine. I'm sore but the evening went well enough." She said, walking over and doing the same she had for Sumner, pouring water into the basin and muttering a short spell to heat it.

"That was until I came back and learned that the both of you were still gone," she said sharply, "and that Durante was about to send one of his little creatures out to find you." She glared at Alces and set the basin down on the table with a thump, the water sloshing a bit. "You could have taken Durante with you! He's an excellent sniper, and clearly whatever you encountered was not just a walk in the park!"

"It's quite alright," Alces said, his eye barely twitching as Durante dabbed on a wound. "While I know Durante would have been useful, as he always is, the quarters were tight. No good places for him to set up. We do not know this city, best everyone travels with someone else."

Octavia continued to glare at Alces as she fetched a rag and went about cleaning him off a little better, careful to stay out of Durante's way. She worked silently, which didn't help.

"I am sorry we worried you," Alces said gently after a moment, gazing down a little, "I do not like splitting us anyway, but we each had jobs to do, and I knew we could do them. In the future, I will make sure all is included. Good, yes?"

Something in Octavia crumbled at Alces' apology. It was easy to maintain anger with Sumner; he was bitchy and unapologetic. Alces was repentant and meant it. The anger melted away, leaving the memory of the fear she'd felt this morning when she'd seen him, still asleep far past dawn, clearly injured. A tear fell, and then a second one, and she still didn't say anything, but she set the rag down and wrapped her arms around him, pressing her face against his uninjured shoulder.

"Oof," he said with a bit of a chuckle, it was clearly not painful just an expression. Reaching over with his other arm, he gave her a pat and a squeeze. "I wish never to give you a reason to shed a tear, dear Octavia."

"He's going to get hurt, though," Durante said, patching another spot. Alces was already starting to look better, the salve working its literal magic on him. "That can't be helped."

"Yes, I know, I was there when a tower fell on him," Octavia said, lifting her head to glare at Durante. The glare didn't last, though, and she sighed, letting go of Alces and sitting back. "Even injured, though, he wakes before I do. Usually. I just wasn't ready. I'll get used to it."

"Fiends," Alces attempted to reassure her. "Pure darkness, sometimes. It can be very draining. That is why I am pleased with your little imp friend. She has no darkness to her, it's very interesting."

Nodding, Octavia wiped her face and picked up the rag again. "She's technically not an imp. Not a proper one, at least. But warlocks are supposed to have imps, so that is the creature that warlocks of Kamvasana summon when they seek a familiar." She rinsed out the rag and went back to cleaning off Alces. "I've actually been trying to learn more about Comicha. Kami won't tell me. I'm hoping there might be something in that book I still haven't cracked open."

"I heard my name!" Comicha popped into existence, cheerful as always. "Oh, wow, big guy, you found something bigger than you, huh?"

The dragonkin laughed and reached over to ruffle her hair gently. "Several, in fact. One got lucky," he said with a nod. "But, the curse is broken, and the wizard punished. We were very successful."

"Yay!" Comicha was always a ray of sunshine. A strange, sex obsessed ray of sunshine. "How are we celebrating?"

Octavia rolled her eyes and rinsed the rag again. Those bloodstains on Alces' back still hadn't been dealt with and she had to scrub very gently to get it off the edge of his scales without pressing on any of his injuries.

"I think we celebrate this particular victory with a bath," Alces said. "The other kind of celebration will need to wait." The silver-scaled knight sat up straight so Octavia had a better look at his back and seemed to be enjoying the attention.

"Given how celebrations go with this group, I imagine everyone needs to finish healing first," she muttered as she continued gently scrubbing at Alces' back.

"No second try at a wedding reception?" Durante asked.

"Aye, there is, but not for a few weeks." Alces sighed. "Fun as it would be, I don't wish to stay here that long."

"In that case, let's take it easy for today," Durante said, "I'll spend tonight going through these goodies that Octavia graciously obtained for me, then make a plan for tomorrow."

"I'll head out in a bit and pick up the rest of Durante's shirts." Octavia rinsed the rag one last time and gave Alces a final wipe down, then got up to go empty the basin. "And I'll see if the leathersmith is done. They should be. You and Sumner should absolutely have a soak in the baths as soon as you feel up to it."

Glancing around, she saw the baskets of lunch and picked one up to drop in Alces' lap.

"Thank you, doting Octavia," Alces said, examining what was for lunch. "Do you want to take kind Durante with you? He is an excellent companion and shopping partner." The dragonkin gave her a wide, toothy grin to show he was playfully teasing her.

"It's true," Durante said, drying off his hands. "I am all those things."

"If he is not too busy, he is welcome to accompany me," she said as she wiped off her hands and cleaned up the side table. She took the basin and poured the blood–tinged water into the planters outside the windows. Comicha decided not enough fun was happening and popped off to wherever she popped off to.

Basin back in place, rags put away, Octavia pulled out a little pot of scented lotion and worked it into her hands, briefly filling the space with a spiced honey scent. She fished out her amulet of protection and slipped it on, then looked at the rest of her ensemble and decided she didn't care enough to change.

"Do you need anything else, Ser Knight?"

"I am better than I could hope to be, dear," he said with a nod, and slowly stretched out his sore muscles. "I shall devour this offering of food, then drag brave Sumner down to the baths. We shall be in much better moods when you return."

Alces probably didn't need it, but Octavia did make a point of balancing the remaining three lunches on the side table in easy reach. Much as she had with Sumner, she paused and set a hand on Alces shoulder before she stepped away. Alces patted her hand, then reached for the first lunch and went to work devouring it.

Durante smiled and moved towards the door. "I hope you don't mind spending a few more hours with me, Tavi?" he said. Before, that would have been an honest question. These days, though, he was starting to know better. Mostly.

"I'm looking forward to it," she said, smiling softly. She wasn't sure he was ready for her to tease him about these things. Not yet.

Durante opened the door for her. "We'll be back shortly."

Alces, mouth currently full, waved them off. Durante chuckled and closed the door behind them.

Sighing, Octavia ran a hand over her face as the door closed. "Gods, this was easier when I didn't care so much," she said, then blinked and looked over at Durante. "I'm not saying it's bad! These last two months have been some of my best! I just… I…" she blushed.

"It does change things a little, doesn't it?" Durante asked, taking her hand as he glanced over to her. "From just some people you're traveling with to some people you couldn't imagine not traveling with. At least, that's where I am. I wouldn't impress that upon you yet."

"More than a little," she murmured, squeezing his hand as they headed down the stairs and out of the inn. "I was on my own for so long. I thought I preferred it that way. I'd worked with people for jobs, but I never… no one welcomed me in the way you have." She sighed and looked away. "A lot of the time it went poorly. One of the last jobs I took before I headed to Gravemont was with a small group trying to clear out an old manor. The leader thought I was stupid, the cracksman tried to grope me regularly, and the leader's girlfriend almost got me killed twice because she was jealous. The person who had recruited me for the job ducked out at the last minute." She grumbled a little remembering it.

"Oh, shadows, Tavi, that's awful," Durante murmured, and squeezed her hand back. "Though it does sound like, perhaps, you haven't traveled with, well, heroes before." He glanced back at the room where Alces was recovering.

"Perhaps not," she mused. "It's been two months, but I already can't imagine leaving. I can't imagine wanting to." She grew more scarlet with every word. It was strange how she could tell him who she had sex with last night without batting an eyelash but couldn't say how she felt without becoming a bumbling child.

"Good, because I happen to know we're all quite fond of you and would be sad if you left," he responded, squeezing her hand back as they walked out of the inn and into the marketplace.

She giggled a little. "It's not just because of my tent? I suppose it might be for my body."

"I believe those are referred to as an added bonus," he said with a wink. "I assure you without the tent and, um... yes, we'd like you all the same. Or at least I would. Don't know about Sumner."

A loud, surprised laugh burst out of Octavia. "Goddess of Mercy, you may be right," she said, still giggling. She smiled her bright, enchanting smile at Durante, the tension from the night before finally gone.

By the time they made it to the tailors', they were the same adoring couple that had been there two days before. Possibly more so with the way Octavia was smiling. They gathered Durante's shirts, picked up the leathers, and Octavia hopped next door to make sure that the dress would be delivered that afternoon. They combed the food stalls for some treats, and Octavia used a little of her own money to buy a ham shank for Alces. Overall, however, they were back at the inn much earlier than their last time in the market, and a quick check revealed that the other two gentlemen had, in fact, made their way to the baths. Durante went off to study his reagents, and Octavia retired to her own room to review her notes and examine the volume from Gravemont. The exterior, at least. She wanted to make sure she knew which wards to look for.

Fishing the book out, as well as her journal, she paused. "Comicha?"

The little imp popped into the room. "Yes, boss?"

"Did you make copies of the notes you took from my night with Erash Wyrdsight?"

Comicha looked mildly offended. "Of course!"

"Take a copy to Durante," she said, the corner of her mouth quirking up, "and tell him they're observational notes for that potion I gave him."

"Yes, boss!" The notes appeared in Comicha's hands, and she gleefully flitted out the window.

"I'm a terrible person," Octavia said with a sigh and sat down to begin her study.

There could hardly be any question what pantheon the heavy book belonged to. The leather was supple to the touch, almost velveteen despite its age, and embossed with an odd combination of Kamvasana's ancient symbol and the coat of arms of House Venebore. Along the border were detailed embellishments of figures in various acts of congress, in so great a number that it alone would give someone pause. If one stared at them long enough, one would swear they moved.

Even the intricate, heavy, magical lock had a sensuousness to it. There was no keyhole—the book would open for the will of its master. Or someone with enough magical knowledge to convince the lock to come undone. Octavia knew she could unweave the magics that held the book shut. However, it was so interwoven with Kamvasana's magic that not only could she not immediately detect any sort of traps or wards, but it seemed to welcome her fingers and eyes, begging her to dive in and read.

Octavia smiled, amused. "It's a shame the Venebore triplets were awful people," she murmured to herself as she examined the book and took notes. "They probably threw amazing parties."

The lack of warding made her suspicious. Then again, the triplets' arrogance was well documented. Maybe they assumed no one would dare? Regardless, she would stick with her plan of waiting until they were out of the city to open it.

Octavia had a few moments of quiet before Comicha came back giggling then tugged on her shirt to make sure she was paying attention to the door. Not three seconds later, Alces walked in with a towel over his shoulders and his kilt on... and little else. He was also looking much better than he had this morning, the salve Durante had prepared seemed to have excellent healing properties. Octavia almost dropped the book but caught it at the last minute.

"Ah, good evening, radiant Octavia," he said with a grin. "How do we fair? Was the time in the market fruitful?"

She cleared her throat and stood up. "It was good. Everything we ordered has been retrieved. I'm very pleased to see you looking better."

He flexed a bit, subtly posing, not completely unaware of her reaction, before he wandered to his bed and sat at the foot of it. "I feel wonderful, thank you. It was a scuffle, nothing to be worried about. If I don't have any parts missing, then all is well."

She wrinkled up her nose and wrapped the book in silk before setting it back in Matilda. "If you lose a limb, I'm burning things to the ground." She walked over and set a hand on his shoulder. "I know I shouldn't worry so much. But this morning… it was just such a shock."

Reaching over, he rested a hand on her hip and gave it a squeeze. "I am sorry to have worried you, dear Octavia. It is a dangerous lifestyle, but I appreciate your sentiment," he said, and leaned in, placing his forehead against hers. "Should any danger come to you, trust me, the source's land would be razed and their line ended."

"Do I have your word, Ser Knight?" she asked with a faint smile, her hands coming up to caress his face.

"I swear upon my duty as Knight of the Spree Spirits, for any that should wish you harm is clearly not one that wishes joy, happiness, and light upon this world," he said with a smile. "Now, speaking of happiness, I think I should get dressed and we should get dinner. I am starving, and I heard Sumner's stomach roaring for prey while we bathed."

She laughed, and kissed him softly, but let him go and stepped away. "A pity, but your glory might be too much for the dining hall. I'll head down and warn them you're coming. Oh! And I got you something today. It's wrapped up on your side table."

"Should I open it now or after?" he asked, looking over at the table. It was fairly obvious that the package contained a ham.

"I mean, open it now if you're starving and don't want to terrify the innkeeper at dinner," she said with another soft smile.

"Now, now, if they don't understand the revelry behind a hearty meal after a refreshing bath, can they call themselves an inn?" he said with a grin, standing up. "I shall save it for later, so warn them fair. I'll dress and meet you down there."

Nodding, Octavia slipped out of the room and pulled the door closed behind her. She took a breath and leaned against the door with a sigh.

"You could drown a dwarf in my panties," she muttered to herself, reflecting that she could have found traveling companions that were less gorgeous, and it would have made her life much simpler. Another sigh, and she headed downstairs to secure a table and warn the wait staff.

When the group came down together a few minutes later, there were already drinks and plates of stuffed leaves and a richly flavored dip to go with the small mountain of flatbread. Sumner looked as refreshed as Alces had, with his hair brushed out and loose behind his head. He'd normally wear it up in a bun, but this was probably best for drying out as it fell past his shoulders. Durante, however, looked a little flustered.

"Hey there, sexy," Sumner said as they walked up. "Miss me?"

"My aim is improving every day," she said, but she couldn't keep a small smile from twitching up the corners of her lips. "I never see you with your hair down. You should let me braid it sometime."

"Whenever you want," he said, sitting down next to her while Alces and Durante took spots across from her, Durante directly, "always available for you."

Durante picked up his glass of juice and gave it a sip but was mostly quiet. Alces looked expectantly at the appetizers but waited, downing his glass of juice with aplomb and refilling it.

Setting her own glass down, Octavia glanced at Durante. "You read the notes, didn't you?"

"Of course I did," he said, and she got that feeling that he would blush if he could. "You sent them to me."

She managed not to giggle. "I'm sorry, I thought you'd look at them later." The other two seemed confused but didn't pry. She cleared her throat. "So do we get to hear about what brought the two of you back in distressing shape?" she asked as she got herself a stuffed leaf and a dollop of the dip along with some flatbread. "Or is it too unpleasant for dinner conversation?"

Sumner laughed and Durante even chuckled slightly, Alces grinned. "My beautiful flower," Sumner said, turning towards her with a beguiling smile. "No tale is too unpleasant for Ser Brightrain."

My beautiful flower. There was something about the easy sincerity of the compliment coupled with the fact that Sumner wasn't actually hitting on her that brought a faint, girlish glow to her cheeks. The smile didn't help.

Alces then cleared his throat, drawing her attention back to the matter at hand. With his typical pageantry, he raised his arms, and all eyes turned to him as he related their death-defying exploits for all to hear.

EIGHT

R ings of bonding," Alces began, "as the ways of the ancients request, are chosen by those to be bonded. They need not be fancy, but of deep importance. The material, the stones, if any are used, the shape. Each ring is different, but they are made together so the infusion of love is as strong in the rings as it is in the heart. One need only curse a singular ring to curse all involved, that is how close the connection is. However, it also makes that magic all the more singular, and easier to track."

He recounted how they began a strange hunt through the city, how he stalked their prey like a bloodhound with Sumner as his watcher. Octavia was a rapt audience, her dinner all but forgotten as she let herself be swept up in the tale. The rings had the "scent" of the magic and caster that they sought. Through the city they went, and masked as the magic had tried to be, the binding from the ancients was too strong to hide. In the shadow of the palace's southern tower, they found the sorceress' home. An estate of its own, but the lingering taint of the fiendish powers darkening the home.

"The woman was led astray," Alces continued, a sadness in his voice—regret for a lost soul. "She had longed for the groom, and the pain in her heart from being denied his adoration grew to call the notice of a demon. One who took advantage of her jealousy and anger. She was a sorceress, already touched by magic, and her heart already dark, so to sway her was a simple feat. With the fiend's power, they coerced the jeweler to add the shards of darkness that would enact the curse."

"Sadly, even discovered, her machinations brought to light, she would not turn away from the demon, nor release the curse she had cast. The dark spirit had its hold on her for too long, and too tightly." Alces paused for effect and stood. "The demon appeared, along with its cat-like minions, to stop our quest." He spread his arms wide. "A creature of the abyss, claws long and gnarled, wings tattered, a gaunt face that looked more like that of a vulture with its beastly cadre of emaciated six-legged panthera."

Alces went on to describe the battle not so much in detail, but in dramatics. By now most of the dining hall had gone quiet, captivated by the story and the larger–than-life dragonkin telling it. Alces had demanded a duel with the sorceress's dark patron, while Sumner prepared to deal with the strange, abyss tainted felines. The great fiend made a show of agreeing to the duel, but demons fought dirty, and they were set upon by the smaller fiends that would leap in and out of the shadows. Had it been a standup fight, Alces insisted—with acknowledgment from Sumner—they would have been flawlessly victorious.

The battle raged into the night, but such foes could never prevail against so mighty a warrior and so clever a rogue. The fiends were defeated. The sorceress' power was all but drained from her tether with the darkness. Her will broken, her magic depleted, the sorceress no longer posed any danger. With the demon dead and cleansed by the light, the curse diminished.

"But curses of passion and hatred clutch at life like sailors to a shipwreck," Alces cautioned, even amidst the applause that had begun, quieting the hall once more, "so a cleansing was needed. Brave and stalwart Sumner, even with his wounds, sought the couple as I found the proper ritual site to commence the purification. A curse of such darkness must be burned away by the light, a light ancient and steeped with magic. An ephemeral pool, its still waters reflecting the light of the moon, would be needed. Meeting back on the shore, Sumner had brought the bride and groom, and the ceremony could resume. Underneath the moonlight, in the cleansing waters of the pool, I recited the ancient words of love and devotion, of bonding and desire, of a oneness among spirits. The lovers spoke of their promises and vows to each other and sealed it with the blessing of the rings. The spirits will safeguard their union, and woe to anyone who attempts to stand in the way."

A cheer went up around the dining hall, and Alces smiled broadly as he returned to his chair. It has been quite a day. A few people came up to chat with Alces and Sumner, though they didn't linger, particularly since

Alces had begun to focus on his neglected dinner. Octavia sat there for a moment with a smile on her face, looking over the three of them with gentle admiration. She felt that warm swell in her chest again.

"Quite the adventure," Durante said, sipping on his second glass. He'd nibbled a bit at dinner as well, but he took little nourishment from it now.

"So, do you forgive us for coming back a little battered last night?" Sumner asked, squeezing her thigh under the table.

"Well, you're both fine, so yes," she said, looking a touch embarrassed. She refilled her own glass and took a healthy drink. "You did something noble and good. You helped someone in love. How could I be upset about that?"

"Your worry was warranted, sweet Octavia," Alces said after gulping down a well-seasoned and grilled haunch of boar. "I am sure we're all quite happy that you care so intensely." He smiled, and it got a round of nods from Sumner and Durante in agreement.

You care so intensely. A strange thread of panic flitted through her at those words that she didn't entirely understand. She took another drink and decided it was time to shift focus.

"Durante, were you able to figure out where we're going next?" She leaned forward and looked at him perhaps a bit more earnestly than she meant to.

"Uh, um, oh, yes," he said, snapping out of his own little daze and straightened up in his seat. "The supplier has a contact that lives on the coast near Boulcairn. It sounds like an unremarkable place. About a week's travel, give or take, to the west."

"Boulcairn?" Octavia furrowed her brow. "I don't know the name. Will we be crossing a border?"

"We will be. Into Algeleli. It's a neighboring beylik. The burg is, um, contested. Not actively, just politically," Durante explained, much quieter now. "So, we won't be able to charter anything all the way there. Which is unfortunate, because it's directly west as the roc flies."

"Huh." She gave her glass a little swirl and took another drink. "How volatile is it? Should we be concerned?" She also kept her voice lower.

"I don't know," he said with a shrug. "We could ask around. But, given what all is going on here, I think they have other things to worry about."

Nodding, Octavia leaned back with her drink. "So, when do we leave?" she asked, glancing over at Alces and Sumner.

"We've done our good deed here," Alces said. "Sadly, we'll miss out on the celebration, but sometimes there are more important things."

Sumner also gave a shrug. "This place really doesn't do it for me, so I'm game with taking off tomorrow."

Durante made a small, dismissive gesture with his hand.

Octavia smiled a little and nodded. "I like it here, but I'm happy to move on. How early tomorrow?"

"We shall find other cities," Alces said reassuringly. "Early to bed, and I'll wake you all up when I do?"

There was a collective groan from the guys, but it was so well timed that it felt practiced. It made Alces grin more broadly.

She sighed. She would always prefer a later morning, but she smiled and nodded. "Early to bed it is, then."

"I know none of you like mornings as much as myself, but I promise we will camp early," Alces said.

Durante chuckled and raised his finger to interject. "Actually, we'll need to see if we can charter a boat. We can't sail all the way there, but we can get much closer, and still within Yadeli," he informed, "so, get up early, find a good ship, then relax for a day or two?"

She arched her brow. "A ship? All right." She hoped she still had that potion for seasickness.

"Problem?" Alces asked sincerely.

"Ah, no," she said carefully, looking embarrassed again. "It's just, I've only been on a ship one other time, and I found the experience very picturesque but also nauseating."

"Ah," Alces said with a nod, "I have a technique for that."

"Should that not help, I think I can whip something up for you," Durante added.

"I could distract you," Sumner said with a smile.

Octavia spent a moment vacillating between feeling inconvenient and being touched and finally decided to stick with being touched. "I will do my best not to worry about it, then."

"It's alright, depending on how bad it is, Sumner will need a dose as well," Durante said with a grin and Sumner rolled his eyes.

"Nice to hear it's not just me." She snickered. "We can hold each other's hair back."

"Been a while since I had a fistful of yours," Sumner said with a toothy grin and another squeeze higher up on her thigh. It was Durante's turn to roll his eyes, and the corners of Alces' mouth turned up since he was still eating.

Octavia couldn't keep from smiling at him. It had been a little while. Shame it needed to be an early night.

"So, what, if anything, do we need to do tonight?" She tried to recenter the conversation on their departure, but also subconsciously spread her legs a little as she moved the one closer to Sumner.

"Pack," Sumner said. With her movements, his hand was getting dangerously higher up her inner thigh.

"I can think of nothing else," Alces added. "Our business is done."

"We picked up everything we ordered for me, right?" Durante asked.

She nodded, folding her arms on the table and leaning forward, her leg now rubbing up against Sumner. "All of your parcels are in my room right now; I can bring them over when we go upstairs."

Sumner took the invitation, and his hand now strayed to pet her over her clothing from time to time as he caressed her thigh. He was doing a very good job of looking casual and still drinking as they talked.

Oh, this was a problem. She didn't want him to stop but she was already frustrated. Thank the gods he was teasing her and not being more focused. Though she was sure they all knew that there was only so much they could get away with in a public area in this particular establishment.

"Then I don't think there's much else for us to do," Sumner said.

There were general sounds of assent. She picked up her drink again and sipped delicately. Alces caught up in his delayed eating and the dishes were taken away. Sumner's teasing had become more and more insistent, but he wasn't sliding his hand into her pants. Yet. Alces finished whatever was left and then stood to head upstairs and complete their preparations for the night. Surely they'd sleep well tonight, what with Alces and Sumner still recovering and relaxed from the long bath.

Stifling a groan, she finished off the last of her wine and stood. She could feel how wet she was, and suspected she was in for a very frustrating night while everyone else slept peacefully.

"All right, I'll sort through the parcels and bring your things over," she told Durante as they made their way up the stairs.

"Thanks," he said, moving towards his door, "I've got a lot of materials to sort and pack up. And clothes." Durante gave her a soft smile. It was gentle and happy, something that didn't appear on Durante too often, but more so with her. She smiled back at him and told the voice in her head that wanted her to revisit the conversation she had with Durante about sharing to please shove itself in the abyss.

"I'm going to take a bit of a walk," Sumner said, "relax myself before bed."

"I'll be up for a bit. My armor needs to be desperately cleaned," Alces said and gave them a nod before retiring to their room. She followed Alces, and went about quickly sorting through their clothing purchases, tucking hers away as she did. In truth, she really didn't have that much to pack. They hadn't been there long enough.

Durante opened the door for her and welcomed her in. His bed was covered in books and sheaves of vellum that she recognized as notes she'd taken in translating the materials from Drukankor's tower. Sumner was still gone. Perhaps on another quick patrol. He would have been too injured for one last night.

"Thank you," Durante said gently as he took the parcels from her hands and set them on a chair, "it means a lot to me that you helped me out with this and spent so much time with me these past few days. I had fun."

Smiling softly, she stepped up to him. "I was happy to," she said, putting a hand on his chest. "I enjoy spending time with you. I had fun, too."

She rocked up onto her toes to kiss him, which he returned happily. Durante was getting better at kissing. He had known how to kiss when they met, she hadn't been his first anything, but there had still been a stuttering hesitation. Now it was more adoringly tender instead of awkward.

"I don't see us having another shopping day anytime soon, but maybe we can figure something else out to have fun. Besides the obvious." The tall dhampir wrapped his arms around her to give her a squeeze.

She laughed. "I mean, I am always up for more of the obvious. But you and I both love to study, I wouldn't mind sitting around over tea and discussing your favorite arcane permutations." She liked this, him holding her, comfortable with her in his arms. Two months ago, she wouldn't have been sure it was possible.

"I would love to. It's nice having someone around to talk to about that sort of thing," he said, giving her another gentle kiss before releasing her to get back to packing. "I'm glad you joined us."

"I am, too," she said, and the heartfelt sincerity in her voice made her blush and clear her throat. "I suppose I'll go see if Alces needs assistance. Good night, Kitten. See you in the morning."

"Good night, Tavi," he said, watching her leave.

When the door closed behind her in the hall, she suddenly found her arm hooked by Sumner and she was being dragged away.

"Come here," he said, giving her a grin, "I've got something that I think you'll really want."

Her pulse quickened at his grin, and she followed with quick steps. "Are you going to make up for what your hand was doing at dinner? Because that's what I really want right now."

"Going to do a bit more than that," he said, and pulled her along until he brought her to a dark alcove along the wall. It was an off-set hallway, possibly used for inn staff or some other purpose if the building had ever been anything other than an inn. It was as private as one could get, but they'd still have to be quiet.

"Pants off," he demanded, undoing the lacing and straps of his own pair.

"Oh, yes, ser," she said, want heavy in her voice. She undid her pants but looked down for a second - she was still in her boots. "Off or just down?"

Still working on his pants, he smirked and looked into her eyes. "Down if you just want me to bend you over, off if you want me to fuck you against the wall."

"Tough call, but fuck it, off it is." It took her a minute longer to get out of her boots, but in short order her pants were around her ankles, and she was stepping out of them.

In the time it had taken her, Sumner's were off, and he was upon her. His hands gripped her ass firmly, fingers sinking into the plush flesh. Teeth grazed her neck as he kissed and nibbled upon it. She moaned and turned her face into his shoulder to stifle it, whimpering against him. Everything about this moment, from his want to the threat of being found, set her blood racing.

"It's been too fucking long," he growled, "I need you."

"Then take me," she murmured in his ear, wrapping her arms around him in preparation for the lift. "I'm yours."

Octavia heard a small, bestial growl rumble in the back of Sumner's throat. It was hard to see in the dark alcove he'd tucked them into, but she felt claws grip at her ass. They were similar heights, so she didn't get lifted much, just enough so that Sumner could push her against the wall and slide the length of his cock into her. If his words weren't enough, the solidness of the cock that speared into her proved how much he wanted her. She exhaled hard as he pushed into her. She was so incredibly wet from the teasing and her body's heightened desire from the last few days. Once he'd positioned her right, the angle of his cock pressing against the spot as he entered, the notch of her legs on his hips, he started to move. Firmly, insistently, and with no give from the wall. Her legs tightened around him, and she clenched her teeth to keep back a cry.

"You're so good," she let herself whisper. "I wanted you so bad!"

"As badly as I missed this tight pussy," he grunted in return, also keeping his voice down despite his efforts.

Leaning down, he bit upon her neck and held his teeth there, almost assuredly giving her a mark when he was done. She strangled another cry and clenched around him and didn't say another word as she panted and held tight. His movements didn't slow in the least and thanks to the firm stone structure of the inn, there was little noise save their bodies colliding, accentuated by her wetness.

Her hands gripped his shoulders, and her nails dug into him as he fucked her. Gods, he could do this any time he wanted. His uniquely studded cock was pressing against her in all the right ways. His teeth had her nerves sparking. The grip on his shoulders tightened as she came for him, whimpering as she tried hard not to cry out.

There was a sudden noise of a door opening down the hall followed by a couple of voices talking. To stifle her whimpers, Sumner suddenly shifted and kissed her firmly, his tongue dancing with hers while breathing deeply through his nose. The tension in Octavia disappeared, the combination of her climax and Sumner's kiss had her melting into him. He slowed his pace, but he did not stop moving. She couldn't stop a quiet moan as their tongues slid against each other, but it wouldn't travel down the hall.

His hips continued to thrust, pumping up hard into her where it was now little more than a pressed rocking motion. She could still feel him deep inside her, but now her body bounced slightly instead of his hips crashing into her. The conversation continued for a moment, as did Sumner despite the rush she felt inside her and the grunt that flowed into their kiss. It wasn't until the footsteps retreated and they knew they hadn't been caught that Sumner broke the kiss and held her in place. Buried to the hilt inside her, she could feel him pulse, and he shuddered with pleasure.

"By the moon, that was intense," he said with a grin, that same toothy grin when she knew he was being naughty.

"Yes," she said, panting, and let go of him with one hand so she could caress his face. "And amazing. I'm no good for your ego, I can't stop telling you how incredible you are."

"You make me want to make sure I maintain that level of performance," he said, panting gently.

She kissed him one more time, then gently pushed on his chest. "Let me down so I can pull my pants back on before I leave a mess for the staff to discover."

"Not if I had my druthers," he said with a smirk, but set her down on her feet and backed away enough to retrieve his pants and start pulling them back on. It seemed Sumner may have had a little experience getting dressed, and undressed, in a hurry. Well, that made sense, of the three of her companions, Octavia was fairly certain Sumner was the most experienced. And definitely the biggest rake.

She wiggled back into her pants fast enough, then started to pull on her boots. "Do you want to head back first, should anyone else be in the hall?"

"Since no one caught us, I really don't care," he said, offering her his arm, "I have no problem being seen with you."

She finished buckling herself back in, and straightened up, adjusting her shirt before smiling at him and taking the offered arm. "Good."

A quick check, and they stepped into the hallway, walking at a relaxed pace, as if they had just been looking around the property. "I'm very glad you grabbed me," she said quietly as they headed back towards their rooms. "I was anticipating a long, aggravating evening trying to sleep. I think it will be easier now."

"Happy to be of service," he said, bumping her gently with his hip. "I feel you should never have an evening alone, and I am always available to you."

"I don't know, I think you all sleep better when I spend an evening alone," she said with a grin.

"We may sleep longer, but is it as fulfilling or restful?" he quipped and leaned in to kiss her neck.

As they reached their doors, she let go of him with a sigh. "And speaking of sleep. I'll see you in the morning. And know that I'm up for exploring more dark alcoves with you in the future, should they be available."

"I'll be keeping my eye out for any convenient places to dash away to, count on it. Goodnight, my beautiful flower."

Clearly, Sumner had caught what the term had done to her, or at least her reaction. With a wink, he slipped into his room to pack and bed down.

When the door closed, Octavia sighed and ran a hand over her face. "I do not enjoy how you all seem to read me this damn easily," she muttered. Another moment, and she went back to her room to start getting ready for the evening. She did feel better, though.

Alces smiled at her, parts of his armor in his lap as he was wiping it down. He didn't have a lot to pack, considering most of what he owned he wore on his person. As she reflected, there seemed to be more to that smile than him being happy to see her.

Glancing over at Alces, she smiled sheepishly. "It's not my fault; he grabbed me in the hall. I was prepared to be good."

"I was not judging, dear Octavia," he said with a slight shake of his head. "Is it not good to revel with your partners, to enjoy each other mutually? You *were* good, as far as I am concerned."

She finished getting her boots off and sighed. "It is sometimes hard adjusting to the three of you," she said, and walked over to the dragonkin. She pulled her shirt off as she walked, and tossed it on her bed, but she still had a chemise beneath.

Sitting next to him, she leaned her head on his shoulder as he worked on his armor. "I worry at times that your… acceptance of our shared intimacy will wear thin. You're like brothers, but I've seen brothers fight over a woman. I'm not ashamed, but I sometimes wonder if I'm doing the right thing."

"I will never fight over happiness," he said, turning his head and kissing the top of hers. "Besides, you seem to care for us all equally. I will keep the other two in line if need be, but as long as you are true to yourself, and your feelings, and us the same, then there is no wrong in what you are doing."

"You are very distinct," she said, smiling. "In the same way my love of cherries doesn't diminish my love of peaches, it is easy to… to value you individually." She wished she had better words. She turned her head and nuzzled at Alces' shoulder. "I would feel awful if I ruined this," she murmured quietly, giving voice to a fear that had plagued her since they first took her in.

"While I cannot guarantee anything, know that I will be here for as long as you want me. I feel the other two will be as well, they are good pupils." Alces grinned again with his little joke and paused working on his armor to reach over and caress the side of her face. "You are a bright and true person, noble Octavia. Do not doubt."

She leaned into his touch and closed her eyes. As long as she wanted him? She couldn't imagine ever not wanting him. Not wanting any of them. Sure, his early mornings were aggravating, and there were times when she wished he knew how to be less bombastic. Sumner's arrogance and frequent thoughtlessness made her want to punch him on occasion. Durante needed a little more of a backbone, and a little more self-esteem, but he was getting there. None of that was enough to make her not want to be with them.

She kissed his shoulder and stood up. "All right, I'm going to climb into bed and try to convince myself to sleep if you're about done. Or I could wait until you're done and climb into bed with you, if you like. One more night before we're on bunks in a ship's hold."

"I will always prefer to have your warmth joined with mine," he said with a grin. "I should not be much longer. While messy, fiend blood tends to burn off in the sunlight. I'm just getting the fiddly bits out." Alces proceeded to do as he said, getting into the joints and clearing out the little bits.

Smiling again, Octavia nodded and went about preparing for bed. By the time she had undressed, bound her hair back, given herself a quick wash with the basin, and folded up her clothes for the day, it seemed Alces was ready for her to douse the lights and join him.

As she slid into bed next to him, she curled up against his side, under his arm, one of her legs hooked over his, her head on his chest. She felt delicate in a way she hadn't believed possible every time he held her. It was a novel sensation.

"Sleep well, my knight," she said softly.

"Sleep most sweet, dear Octavia," he responded, giving her a squeeze with the whole of his arm before settling in. The night was overall calm, with the gentle sound of music and the occasional distant voice of the market beyond the windows. Octavia found herself drifting off fairly quickly, sated in multiple ways.

When morning came, she found herself being gently caressed on her face and arm. "I'm sorry to say, dear Octavia, but it is time to wake. We have a busy morning ahead of us," Alces was saying, leaning towards her ever so slightly but still on his back in bed.

Grumbling, she tried to burrow into him for a moment but gave into his gentle insistence and pulled away enough to push herself into a sitting position. She yawned and ran a hand over her face, then pulled away the sheets. Only to see that there was blood on her thighs, and the bed beneath her.

"Oh, no," she groaned as she stared at the red stain on the white linen.

"Kamvasana does not protect you from the monthly cleanse?" Alces asked as he slid out of bed to see the problem. He wasn't disgusted or shocked, just questioning. "I thought maybe that was the case, as it had not happened in the time we've been travelling."

"No, um," Octavia said, blushing as she cast a quick spell to take the blood out of the sheets. "No, my cycle is longer due to my infertility charm." She held up her left hand and wiggled her fingers, indicating the thin ring on her forefinger that never came off. "I'm not sure why, but a side effect of the spell is a slowing of my cycle. It takes about two full cycles of the moon. I knew it would be soon, I just hoped it would be after the ship." Though that did confirm why she had been crawling the walls with want. This could not possibly bode well for the coming journey.

Alces noticed that he, too, had streaks of blood on him and shrugged it off, walking to the basin to wipe his thigh clean. "If you require anything before we leave, please let me know. I hear chocolate is something we should have on hand?"

She sighed as she followed Alces to the basin. "Chocolate is always appreciated. I'll have some pain today and tomorrow. Um, my moon time is short but intense. I'll bleed pretty heavily for three days, then it'll peter off and we're good for two more months." It felt a little awkward explaining it to someone, especially someone male. In her experience it wasn't a topic they enjoyed hearing about.

"I understand. Should you need anything, do not hesitate to ask. I will wake the others and tell Sumner to retrieve chocolate and whatever else you like," he said, getting his underclothes and padding on, giving her time to think of what else might be needed.

"Thank you." She cleaned herself off, then went and dug through her chest, pulling out the only pair of pants they hadn't seen her in yet. There was nothing exceptional about them from the outside, except that they were a beautifully saturated black. On the inside, however, were clever hooks for her to attach thick fabric pads that would keep her from leaving a mess everywhere she sat.

She braided her hair back in twin tails, found a darker shirt to compliment the pants, and otherwise got herself together as she usually did. The morning was a bit of a rush to make sure they procured last minute items and still kept on schedule. Sumner retrieved a selection of chocolates for Octavia, as well as a layered dessert made of thin, crispy dough, chopped nuts, and syrup. Durante and Alces paid for their stay, which was more than they had anticipated, but Alces made a show of standing at full height and looking... disappointed at the innkeeper, which brought the price back down to what they had initially agreed upon.

Once everyone was packed and ready, they headed to the docks to find a ship. It turned out the route to Anoba, a direct southwest route, was so calm and close to shore that it was practically a ferry ride. It would take the entire day, but they'd shorten the journey by nearly a week traveling by sea instead of land. They were able to procure a pair of rooms aboard a sloop called the "Rüzmek."

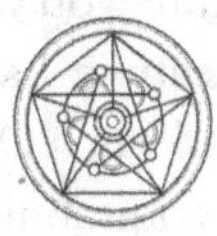

NINE

Durante was on edge, his eyes changing to red and his mood swinging slightly. He kept as much distance between himself and Octavia as their group allowed. Alces kept him calm until they got below deck.

By the time they got aboard the ship and got everything put away, the muscle cramps that Octavia had predicted were starting to hit. Alces separated the rooms with himself and Durante in one and Sumner and Octavia in the other. Given the time being spent, they were glorified sitting rooms with a single cot in case someone got tired. She was worried about Durante, and wanted to check on him, but by the time they were heading to their rooms the cot was welcome. She murmured an apology to Sumner and curled up on the cot without asking.

Sumner smiled and sat next to her, giving her head a pat. "No apology needed. I understand. Would you like anything?" he asked, pulling up his bag that contained the treats he got for her.

"I heard there might be chocolate," she said, looking up at him a little pitifully. "It won't be this bad tomorrow. The first day is always the worst. By day three it's just annoying."

"There is lots of chocolate," he chuckled, fetching the first of the little boxes. "It's alright. You think that's bad. Most of the women in the troupe had theirs at the same time. That was chaos. Just you? Easy."

She giggled a little as she opened the box and took out a square. "Do you miss it? The troupe?" She nibbled on the chocolate and looked up at him with her bright blue eyes.

"I do. It was really nice until the old man sold it. Things went sour real fast. Lost some good people, might have lost everyone eventually had Alces not showed up," he said, also eating a piece of her chocolate as he did. There was plenty, he'd followed instructions quite well.

She reached out and slid her hand along his leg, squeezing his thigh. "I'm sorry," she said. "Do you think you want something like that again?"

"Yeah," he said wistfully, leaning back in his seat. "I mean, I like travelling with Alces and D and you. Definitely pays a lot more. But settling down sometime with a community like that seems like the right thing to do."

"What if you build something together?" She continued to pet his leg and got herself another piece of chocolate. "The three of you do a lot of good, from what little I've seen. I suppose it would be hard to settle somewhere with Alces. But... I don't know. You're all... you're amazing. You have your faults, but you..." She sighed, and let go of him, rolling onto her back. "It seems there's potential for something there," she said as she looked at the ceiling of their little cabin.

"Don't you usually need a base of operations or something," Sumner said, reaching over and caressing her hair. "Alces can't be still for more than a few days. Also, thanks for hitting me with my faults. Appreciate that." Despite the snark, Sumner did smile and give her a subtle wink.

"That was a general "you" as in all three of you have your faults but you're still very effective and work well together." She stuck her tongue out at him but couldn't help a happy sigh as he played with her hair. "Maybe you have a base of operations. Maybe Alces roves out but has a safe place to come back and heal and even teach other people how to protect and spread joy as he does. Durante wants a base of operations; he needs somewhere to tinker to his heart's content. And you need a community." She turned pink. "Or maybe not. That's a lot of conjecture for someone who's only known you all for a couple months."

Sumner gave her a little shrug but continued to run fingers through her hair. "Maybe you're right. Maybe something to think about. But you know what's going to happen," he said, lowering his gaze at her a bit. "I'm going to end up running the damn thing."

"Maybe..." she looked up at him, a little shy. "Maybe I could help. I was raised being taught how to run a household. I don't use it much, but I know a lot about delegation and managing things."

"Sure, why not," he said with a small laugh. "As long as we're dreaming about stuff."

"Yeah." She closed her eyes with a sigh. She wasn't sure why it felt like rejection, but it did. They were all fond of her now, but as she pointed out, they'd been traveling together for a little over two months. They would get tired of her in time. Either tired of dealing with her or tired of sharing her or tired of the attention she garnered or something. Like everyone else did. Her current state was probably influencing this feeling, but that didn't make it go away.

Sumner continued to pet her for a while, letting her relax and nibble on chocolates. Alces came in some time later, looking over the two of them. "So, how's the patient?" he asked.

Sumner snickered. "She's going through it. Half the chocolate is gone," he exaggerated.

Octavia wrinkled up her nose. "One box of chocolate is gone."

"Can I try something?" Alces asked, kneeling next to the cot.

"If you wish," she said, "though I don't want to be any more inconvenient than I already am." She hoped that sounded polite and not pathetic. It was very strange having anyone attend to her during this time instead of finding an inn and hiding in it for a couple days until she felt human again.

"You're ridiculous," Sumner said with a roll of his eyes.

"Well, there, I have my faults, too," she said, briefly glaring at Sumner.

"Never," Alces said, putting his hand on her tummy and leaning in. "If any of us are injured, we tend to it. Would do it for anyone else." Alces softly blew on her abdomen right above her pelvis. He was very careful not to make it too cold, enough to numb it slightly and relax the area.

"Oh!" The initial chill startled her a little, but she relaxed quickly enough. Heat would have been better, but it did feel soothing. The ache didn't disappear but some relief was provided. "That does feel nice," she said, closing her eyes.

"Were my bloodline different, this might be more effective," Alces chuckled, "but I am glad it helps. I wasn't sure." He alternated between gently blowing on her and then massaging the area to let the cool ease.

Sumner continued to pet her and feed her an occasional chocolate. They doted on her for about an hour before Alces needed to breathe more normally. By then, Octavia was drifting off to sleep. When she woke the room was empty and a fresh bundle of chocolates had been left next to the cot. She yawned and sat up. She felt better physically, and less dour emotionally. She climbed to her feet and stretched, then went looking for the others.

Out in the hall, there were some heavy steps and a few subtle crashing noises from the room next door. Otherwise, it was empty. It was midday, so they were possibly in what passed for a galley or on the deck. She moved carefully through the ship, back towards where she remembered the public areas being. She could feel the rock of the ship, but it wasn't too bad. Yet.

The lunch was a spread of meats, cheeses, a variety of sauces, and flat bread for people to help themselves at. It was nice for a boat voyage but given the short voyage of the daily trade route, they never needed to worry about storing fresh food for long. Leaning back in a chair until he was pressed against the wall, Sumner sat with his plate of food. He gave her a little wave when she spied him.

Pausing long enough to get some cheese and flatbread, she wandered towards Sumner and sat next to him.

"Thank you for your kindness earlier," she said, sincerely. She knew objectively that he hadn't meant to hurt her feelings and probably didn't realize he had. What mattered was that he'd sat at her side for over an hour petting her head and feeding her chocolate.

"Think nothing of it," Sumner said with a wave of his hand, "I got an excuse to touch you and got you to lick chocolate off my fingers." He couldn't help but grin at her after that comment.

"I did do that a couple times, didn't I?" She smiled a little and folded her cheese into her bread. "Where are the others?"

"Big guy is up on deck, soaking in the 'light' and D is in his room working off some things. Best to leave him alone for right now. He'll be fine in another hour or so, I think," Sumner said before taking a bite and smiling at her.

"Is Durante all right?" She looked up, brow furrowed. "Did something happen to one of his samples or something?"

"He'll be okay," Sumner answered, pushing off the wall and sitting upright, the chair settled on all its legs. "But... okay, I want you to know this is not a problem, it happens, it's not your fault, alright? He smelled you and it triggered him. Alces fed him this morning, but the side effects of his blood make him, um, not angry but very prone to tossing furniture and punching walls. Great when we get into a fight or something, not so great any other time. Like, he's not going to hurt anyone, he's not berserk or anything."

"He smelled..." Her brows rose and she ran a hand over her face. "He's never travelled with a woman before. Right." She laughed softly.

"You should have left him in the room with me; my blood has rather the opposite effect on him. Of course, you probably would have had to carry him off the ship after."

Sumner chuckled and gave her a shrug. "You can certainly present the idea. However, you were in pain, and we weren't going to, as we thought, 'sacrifice' you to Durante. We know he wouldn't hurt you, but I'm not, and certainly Alces isn't, going to say 'well, it's your fault, you deal with it.' That's just shitty."

She nodded. "I wouldn't have seen it that way. In the same way I can't stop what is happening to me right now, he can't stop what he is. And I know he wouldn't hurt me." She said it with such surety.

"Then next time, he's all yours," Sumner laughed. "Or, tomorrow, depending on how the proximity is going to tweak him. New territory."

"Though that explains the crashing I heard when I left the room," she mused, and took a bite. She considered for a moment while she chewed. "We'll be reaching Anoba this evening, right? Are we getting a room there?"

"I would assume," he said, folding up a piece of meat and tucking it in with a bit of flat bread. "But nothing fancy. We're not sticking around."

She nodded. "OK, here's my proposal. If he is still on edge tomorrow, say at breakfast, we stay in the town one more day and you give him to me. We'll spend the day in the room, I will make sure he is saturated, and we will leave the following day."

"We're on his timetable," Sumner granted her another shrug, "tonight, tomorrow, whatever. Again, not sure how long he'll be like this. Usually it's a one and done, so Alces' dose should ease him, but we really don't know."

"Two more days and the smell will decrease significantly." She took a bite and was quiet for a moment. "I know the urges get triggered intermittently, but how long is he usually exposed to the things that trigger him? And does his connection to me affect it at all?" She shook her head. "I don't expect you to be able to answer those questions, just things to consider."

Sumner shook his head. "Beyond me, flower. His condition isn't exactly normal, and not something I'd come across before. Maybe ask Alces? If we have a particularly nasty fight, that's definitely a trigger. All the blood, what have you, but then we kinda look the other way while he does his thing."

She nodded. Sumner didn't really need her conjecture. Ironically,

Durante would be the most interested in discussing the theory behind it all. She finished her breakfast and absently petted Sumner's thigh. Once she was done, she stood and kissed his temple. "I'll go check on our dragon and make sure he knows I'm functional."

"If you get bored, let me know," he said with a grin and made another pile of meat on flatbread and waved her goodbye.

Alces was indeed on the deck of the ship, near the bow, one foot propped up on the railing. If she didn't know better, she'd swear he was striking a pose but that was how he was.

She smiled as she walked up, taking him in. He was such a heroic figure in so many ways, it often didn't feel real. "You're quite majestic, Ser Knight."

"Nonsense, radiant Octavia," he said, turning to her. "This is majestic." He waved a hand out, and it was a lovely view. Sun reflecting off the water of Lake Sizhou. It sparkled off the ripples of the water as they extended far out to the north. Lake was a misnomer; it was more of an inland sea. She could see land approaching to the south, land that they'd be skirting as they made their way to Anoba.

"Both can be true," she pointed out as she came to stand next to him. She leaned against the railing. "It is beautiful. Have you been to sea often?"

"A few times, indeed. Did you know my people are actually adept seafarers? One of the proudest navies in the Cobalt Domain," he said, offering her a hand so he could brace her next to him. The lake was large enough to have ocean-like waves and currents, but sailing so far had been relatively smooth.

She took the offered hand, settling against him. "I've only heard the vaguest of stories about your people. I look forward to learning more firsthand."

"That makes two of us," he said with a laugh. "So, how are you faring, dear Octavia? Between the cleansing time and the waves, after all, but you seem well. Have you eaten?"

She arched an eyebrow, curious about the implication that he didn't know much about his own people but let it go for the moment. "I'm feeling better, and the waves have been gentle." She looked out across the water again. "Sumner told me about Durante. How I've affected him."

"Unforeseen accident, but easily handled," he said, giving her hand a squeeze. "His hunger gets the best of him sometimes. It's not often, but we can control it. No terrible mishaps."

"I promise, I am unruffled." She said, squeezing back. "If it happens tomorrow, I've proposed that you leave him with me, and we rest for a day. My theory is that if he is… saturated it should remove the trigger. And we'll know for next time."

"If you feel that is best, I will trust you with that decision," Alces said with a nod.

"I appreciate your trust." She leaned into him, content to enjoy the view and his presence.

"You've more than earned it, dear Octavia," Alces said, putting his arm around her. The rest of the voyage was easy going, with the view of the expansive sea to the north and the lush green of the Yadeli shore to the south. They'd traveled down enough that the temperature was considerably warmer despite it being fall, and the lake breeze made for a very pleasant evening with only a hint of chill.

Durante stayed in his room while Alces checked on him and spent the evening repairing furniture and reassuring the flustered alchemist. Sumner made a little coin entertaining the other passengers with acrobatic acts and even trick knife-throwing.

Pulling into Anoba, it was a rather rushed affair to get the passengers off so the cargo offloading could begin. Anoba was considerably smaller than Limanyadeli but was still a bustling trade town. They couldn't get a real good look at it as it was quite late when they arrived, but there was enough noise and lights to get a feel for it.

One of the stevedores directed them to an inn in an area called the Starrise. It was an area of the town that was high up on a hill and furthest from the shore, which would help when they decided to continue their journey. It did make for a bit of a walk, though the hike up to the inn felt good after a day of rest. Octavia was drained from her cycle, but the walk up the hill wasn't bad. She wanted to check in with Durante but felt like maybe she needed to let him decide when and if he could be close to her.

As they started to crest the hill, she turned and looked back at the dock and the town below. One way or another, she knew they didn't want to linger here, so she wanted to take it in while she could.

Alces and Durante continued walking, but Sumner paused and moved up next to Octavia. "You're going to need to talk to him," he said softly. "He's doing better, but he's still sensitive about his, uh, condition. As such, not great about working out the kinks, as it were, without a little push. I think he'd appreciate it." Sumner gave her a wink and a playful pat on the rump. She smirked at Sumner but nodded and looked back at the town for a moment before turning back around and continuing up the hill.

"After dinner, then?" She arched an eyebrow at Sumner. "It's still a bit of a private conversation. And I don't think he'd appreciate us discussing it around the table."

"Yeah, that'd be good. Just saw your 'thinky' face and figured that's what you were worried about," he offered as they continued back up the hill.

She grinned. "My thinky face? I have a face?"

Reaching over, Sumner gently palmed her face and gave it a squeeze. "Yeah, pretty sure that's your face," he laughed.

She pushed him off. "Ass."

The district they entered was very nice, with buildings plaster and paint kept up. Like most of the town, it wasn't a big area, but it had its charm and hinted at the wealth of the burg from trade. The inn of the area, the Gazer's Peak, had the symbol of a star and a looking glass, and was darkly painted with stained glass windows of constellations glowing from the light within.

Inside the inn was quaint and unlike a common roadhouse. The décor was made up of star charts and various spy glasses, and a small collection of astrolabes. The keeper was a rail-thin man in his late to middle ages with a small set of round glasses on his nose. He seemed almost overwhelmed when they came in but was happy to be of service.

After a brief conversation, it turned out that the stevedore who directed them this way was his nephew, and their coming was probably the most business he'd seen in a week. As such, dinner wasn't ready immediately, but he disappeared into the kitchen and got to work as they sat around one of only two meal benches in the establishment. As the others settled, she found the inn's water closet so that she could cast a quick cleansing spell on everything and hopefully reduce the strength of her smell through dinner.

Coming back out, Octavia didn't sit down right away, but wandered around a little bit, looking at the star charts and other astronomical paraphernalia. She was quite charmed, and glad the stevedore had spoken up about his uncle's inn. She doubted anything closer to the docks would be this unique.

When she finally came to sit, however, she sat herself next to Durante. While she was prepared to give him his distance if he demanded it, Sumner said he needed to be poked, so poked he would be. As she sat, Alces was in the middle of telling Sumner a tale of one of the constellations in the closest window. Durante smiled as Octavia sat but otherwise seemed quiet, probably a little embarrassed.

Settling in place, she reached across and gently squeezed his leg.

"Sorry about today," he said softly, placing his hand upon hers. "I didn't know that would happen. Well, how could we, right?"

"You don't need to apologize," she said, smiling softly. "I didn't think about it either. A new situation for both of us."

"I know, but I don't like it. I don't like that I get these... urges and needs," he sighed. "Alces is always there to help, but that has its own problems. Given how his blood affects me, I'd be afraid of what would happen if I ever got some from a full dragon."

"Yeah, I wouldn't recommend it," she said wryly, and squeezed his leg again. "Let's talk after dinner, all right?"

"Oh, okay," he said and nodded.

Dinner was soon upon them, and the keeper would definitely need to make more for Alces. It was a nice, simple meal with red lentil soup, grilled and seasoned fish, and crusty bread.

"We usually only get visitors during the equinox, solstice, and certain celestial events," the keeper said, "but, happy to have you. Just wasn't expecting it."

"Your nephew was very persuasive, and you're in the right direction," Octavia said to the keeper with a charming smile. She also beckoned him closer and covertly passed him several coins. "We're going to need a lot more fish." Her eyes flicked to Alces, making it clear who they needed it for. The keeper was grateful and brought more fish, laughing about how he'd need to go to market the next day to get more.

As they ate, she frequently reached over and gave Durante's leg a squeeze. He needed to know she wasn't upset with him in any way, and for now that seemed the easiest means of conveying it. Durante seemed accepting, and Octavia felt very clear that he wasn't upset with her in any way. Perhaps himself, but not her. By the end of dinner, he was returning the squeezes and smiling a little more.

Given that the inn was empty, they each got a room to themselves and despite the long day of travel, it wasn't very exhausting as they sat in a ship for the day. As they ascended the stairs to their rooms, Octavia let the others go up first so she could see where they went. Once she had her chest safely tucked away in her own room, she headed over to Durante's and knocked lightly on the door.

"Come in," Durante said. When Octavia opened the door, Durante was sitting on his bed. The rooms were nice. Small, but neatly appointed and had large windows that were covered with a thick curtain.

Octavia closed the door behind her and walked over to Durante. "Hey, Kitten," she said, reaching up and running a hand through his hair. "I didn't mean to cut you off earlier, but… well, it's a sensitive subject, so I thought it would be better if we talked in private. Is that all right?"

"Always," he said, tilting his head to her touch and closing his eyes. He sighed again and patted the spot next to him on the bed.

Octavia paused and got her boots off, then climbed up onto the bed a little more closely than perhaps Durante had anticipated, one of her legs folded underneath her so she could face him. "I'm sorry I didn't think to warn you," she said, turning a little pink. "It's not something a woman talks about, right? Particularly to men. But it's still blood, and for three days there's a lot of it."

Durante chuckled a little and gave her a shrug. "I think Sumner already said so, but we assumed it wouldn't happen with your blessing and it being two months and all. But I didn't know I'd respond this way, either. I'm not usually so… close to women during this time."

She nodded and reached up to play with his hair again. "You've never travelled with a woman. And my cycle is long. I'm sure you've noticed this?" She held up the hand with her ring.

He nodded. "I can tell it's enchanted. Is that why?"

"Yes." She went back to playing with his hair. "It's an infertility charm. It slows my cycle in addition to keeping me from becoming gravid. But I wanted to say, you…" she considered for a moment, and bit her lip as she tried to find the words. "There's no reason you can't come to me when this happens."

Looking up at her, he had to tilt his head slightly in wonder. "Come to you… for what?"

"For my blood," she said frankly, an amused smile on her face. She dropped her hand to his shoulder and gently rubbed his back. "Either from my veins if you prefer, or you can go down on me until you're satiated if the idea doesn't horrify you. If you have your fill early enough, I imagine it may make the following days easier. Less… tempting."

"Really?" he asked, a reaction mixed with hope, doubt, and perhaps a touch of arousal. "I, um, I mean if you don't mind, or it doesn't disturb you." Chuckling, he rolled his eyes then shook his head. "No, why would it, you suggested it. I'm sorry." Despite the seriousness of the conversation, Octavia could already see a tinge of red on the rim of his pink eyes.

"Kitten," she murmured, and slid her fingertips inside the collar of his shirt. "I know that you know how much I like it when you bite me. And there is, maybe, something arousing about the idea that you might… crave me." She looked up into his eyes.

"In, um, more ways than one," he said with a little grin.

She felt that squeeze around her heart again. She wanted to tell him… she wasn't sure. Instead, she pulled his head down and kissed him, her lips light against his at first. She wasn't sure what he wanted, and she didn't want to push. Leaning into it, Durante slid a hand around her waist to caress her back. His kiss was gentle and tender as well, but not hesitant. They'd done this enough that he was comfortable and no longer unsure in his movements around her. At least not with this.

The kiss lingered for a while, until Octavia finally sat back and looked up into Durante's eyes again. "I told the others that if the hunger takes you again before we leave, that I would take you with me and we'd just stay an extra day here. Will that work for you?"

"As long as you're not only doing it for my sake," he said, reaching up to caress the side of her face. "If you want me to, then I'd happily stay with you, Tavi."

"Can't it be both?" She felt vulnerable again, but also like this needed to be said. "Can't I want you, and also want to be there for you?" She leaned into his hand.

"Well, yes, of course," he said, with an awkward laugh. "But it should be both, not just because you want to help me."

She smirked. "I told you before that I would never share myself with someone solely for their benefit." She leaned forward again, very much in kissing distance if he desired. "Of course I want you, Kitten. How could I not?"

"I could come up with an excuse, which I'm sure would get an impassioned argument from you that I could not logically refute," he said with a gentle smile, talking more quietly as he leaned in to get closer, "so I'm going to have to agree with you." Closing the last few millimeters, Durante kissed her softly once more, his hand cupping her face.

They spent a long time kissing. Part of Octavia marveled over the fact that it didn't seem to be building into anything and yet that was fine. This was lovely. This was all they needed from each other right now.

They finally parted and Octavia drew in a breath, looking up at him.

"Would you like me to stay tonight? Would you like to feed tonight?"

He looked at her for a long moment, then gently released her and shook his head. "While I would love to, it's probably not a good idea to mix blood in my system," he said reluctantly. "It's probably best if you head to bed. Sleep well, Tavi."

She giggled. "I can't even imagine what that combination would look like. You would become aggressively cuddly?"

She stood up but leaned in to kiss him one last time. "Good night, Durante." Her fingertips brushed his cheek, and her heart swelled again, but she pulled away and headed out, smiling back over her shoulder at him before closing the door.

Retreating to her own room, she closed the door and leaned back against it. "Why does my heart ache being around you?" she murmured to herself, brows furrowed. Why did it hurt so much when Sumner didn't understand that she was being vulnerable? Why did Alces' praise make her light up like a pyre on a festival night? Shaking her head, she pushed off the door and started to undress.

You could still go back... her patron purred in her head.

"Don't bug me when I'm bleeding, Kami."

Oh, very well. Octavia could hear the sulk in Kamvasana's tone, but she also felt their presence retreat. She got herself to bed before anyone else could pester her.

The inn was so quiet compared to the ever-present sound of the market she had fallen asleep to the past few days. Nothing but insects singing quietly and the distant call of wolves.

TEN

Morning came with a knock on the door as the curtains did a marvelous job of keeping the sunlight out.

"Dear Octavia, are you awake?" Alces asked, doing his best to be quiet but failing as he didn't have a volume that went down that far.

Startling awake, Octavia flailed in the covers and then almost rolled out of bed, catching herself with one foot against the floor. "I'm up!" She called out as she righted herself. "I'll be downstairs in a minute!"

"We shall see you down there," Alces said through the door with a bit of a laugh, then she heard the heavy steps down the stairs.

She stuck her tongue out at the door. "He had to be a morning person," she muttered as she stood and got her bearings.

A quick spell took care of the blood that had ended up on the sheets in the night. She cleaned herself up and cast the cleansing spell several times to remove any potential lingering traces on her clothes. She dressed in her stark black pants again and a soft shirt of brushed silk that was the same deep blue as the night sky. It felt appropriate in this quaint little inn they'd found. She also put on Sumner's necklace. The blue of the stones fell somewhere between the shirt and her eyes, tying the look together.

In a short while, she was heading downstairs to meet the others. It had been more than a minute, but not so long that she felt she'd given anyone reason to complain.

Breakfast looked to be a simple spread of bread, fruits, cheeses, and a bit of dried fish. This would do for most people, but Alces would need to go out to find more protein. The keeper was up and yawned as

Octavia came down the stairs.

"Oh, good morning, miss," he said gently. "I hope I got enough for you and your friends. Please let me know if you plan on staying longer. I hate to say so, but I may need an advance so I can buy more food."

"Ah, yes," she said and nodded sympathetically. "I do understand. You aren't accustomed to travelers this time of year, and particularly not ones with the appetite of a dragonkin." She smiled her most reassuring smile at the innkeeper. "We'll be on our way either today or tomorrow. As soon as we've determined which, either myself or the blond gentleman will be back to discuss payment with you."

"I appreciate it. I also warn you, I'm not much of a cook, so I hope you're okay with simple things," he said, smiling back and looking a little bit tired with a small hint of borderline smitten.

The rest were sitting and waiting for Octavia. The food hadn't been touched yet, but they'd been drinking some nice juice that had been offered in earthenware jugs. "There she is," Sumner said with a toothy grin. "Even D beat you downstairs this morning."

"I spent some extra time cleaning up and getting dressed," she said, and stuck her tongue out at him. She tossed her hair back over her shoulder and sat down, then reached for one of the jugs. "Everyone sleep well?"

Durante was sipping on juice and picked up a piece of cheese, examining it. Alces smiled and nodded. "The bed is a little small, but nice," he said.

"Surprisingly, actually," Sumner added after he swallowed his first bite of meat. "Although the quiet is a little odd, the beds are certainly comfy for an inn."

"I told you that you sleep better alone," she said with a playful smile.

"Didn't we already have a discussion about quality of sleep versus enjoyment of sleep," Sumner said, quirking an eyebrow at her.

She got herself some bread, cheese, and fruit. She made a small happy sound at the jar of sour cherry jam on the table. Since it seemed they had been waiting on her to eat, she made a point of getting started. She was also starving. That was consistent for the second day.

Thus far, Durante hadn't started to show signs of hunger, but he was also being quiet. He wasn't avoiding Octavia, but he wasn't making conversation either. Alces didn't seem bothered, however. Octavia focused on eating for the moment. She did glance at Durante, but she also didn't want him to feel like she was too focused on him. Well, if he seemed fine, then he seemed fine.

Everyone ate quickly. Alces declared that they should set up the tent, take inventory of their supplies, and make sure they had everything they needed for the trip ahead. It was still going to be anywhere from five days to over a week, depending on what they ran into along the way, so they had to be prepared.

She nodded. "All right, I'll go grab it. Are we still planning on leaving today? The innkeeper mentioned that he might need us to pay upfront if we're staying longer - it's the slow season and he wasn't ready to feed a group like ours."

"I think we will need to stay another day," Alces said with a nod, "make sure we have everything we need. Going into town proper to get what supplies we may be lacking will take too much time out of travel for the day. Besides, we should properly equip our fine inn keeper as well."

"Yeah, we need to get the big guy enough meat to run on," Sumner laughed. Durante smiled but didn't add to the conversation. It seemed he was trying to make himself as unobtrusive as possible.

She turned towards Durante and furrowed her brow, lowering her voice a little. "What's wrong?"

"Oh," he said, her words snapping him out of whatever he was thinking about, "nothing really. It just takes me a bit to feel comfortable after the hunger rises. In some ways Alces' blood makes it worse, the fury that comes with it."

"All right," she said, brows still furrowed, but she didn't push. She finished her juice and stood, placing a hand on Durante's shoulder and giving it a gentle squeeze. "I'll go get the tent. Be right back."

The rest finished eating and Alces went to talk to the innkeeper. Durante decided to head out to get fresh air while Sumner grabbed a few more pieces of food to munch on, and they were all waiting outside for Octavia when she returned. Unsure of what the day would entail, Octavia had her satchel and the tent. A quick survey and Sumner found the inn actually had a sizable field behind it. It was rather unkept and didn't appear to be used for farmland. There were a few fruiting trees that looked like they needed to be harvested, but otherwise it was bare.

Octavia found a clear spot where they wouldn't be trampling windfall fruit and set up the tent. It looked like a cube, but she tugged the little tag on one corner and it quickly unfolded into a night blue canvas tent that looked well-made if a bit small. Everyone was still suitably impressed by the magical construct of convenience, despite them living out of it for the past couple of months. It was so useful yet unassuming. Alces stepped up and held the front flap open for everyone.

"All, wise companions, check out your rooms and the main area, make note of anything you feel we need for the trip ahead."

Walking into the tent, the interior lights flared to life as they entered, illuminating a space that was much bigger on the inside. The tent had been Octavia's, and big enough, but once they began traveling together, she had used what she knew of the tent's properties to improve it. More space, separate rooms for everyone, a bed big enough for Alces. She headed to the room that was hers, doing a quick check. Everything was in place as she'd left it. They still needed to unpack the items they'd picked up in the market, but otherwise she didn't really see anything they were missing.

The morning was occupied by inventory and making sure everything had been put away properly. They had plenty of fresh foods and the makings for baked goods, which was all well and good when they were camping, but travel rations would help. More materials for snares and traps so Alces and Sumner could hunt would be good. As would a refresh of some of their medical supplies.

All in all, they were nearly set. A few more items and they'd have everything they'd need. A local map would be beneficial and may even show them a route they hadn't considered. Perhaps even their stargazing inn keeper might have an idea.

The first to leave was Durante, standing outside and jotting down items on a slate that he carried around for notes. They would need to go into town after all. Sumner did make Alces swear that he would not somehow find them an 'adventure' to go on while they were there. They were picking up travel supplies and that was it. Alces could only provide a non-committal shrug. It was not encouraging. A smile quirked the corner of Octavia's mouth as she followed them all out. It was fun to watch Sumner try to reign in Alces. It reminded her a little of a married couple. She hummed to herself as they headed down into town, happy in the peace of the moment.

Now in the daylight, they had a better look at Anoba. It was almost a smaller version of Limanyadeli, where it was a port town established next to a tributary river. The buildings were nowhere near as grand, with a much smaller marketplace in the old part of town which was down the hill from Starrise.

The keeper, who was named Najm, also recommended a place across the river that was the Spice Hall. It was mostly for the trading companies and ships that came through, but if they wanted to get something more interesting and felt like spending the money, that was the place to do it. There was also a fruit exchange closer to the water. Sumner didn't think they needed to spend any more money on frivolous things when they should be moving on. Octavia didn't contradict Sumner, but she was willing to ignore him. She did still have her own funds, which while they were less impressive on their own, were essentially now her fun money as the group pooled resources. At the same time, she was happy to refrain from shopping unless the fruit market had peaches or cherries.

The trip was relatively quick. They found a place selling easy rations, another selling hunting supplies, and a third with roasted meats for Alces as an addendum to his breakfast. Durante secured a shipment of fish, meat, and staples to the inn. They even had enough time for Alces to explore the Spice Hall, even with Sumner's iron grasp on the party's funds. Octavia got her peaches and ate one on the way back to the inn, making a slightly sticky mess of herself in the process. She was unapologetically teasing as she licked the juices from her hand. They grabbed various foods to try for lunch and were back at the inn early in the afternoon with the rest of the day to spend lazily preparing for the trip ahead.

Once they made it back, she put the rest in the tent for the trip. When the tent collapsed, time inside was frozen, so they would stay perfectly ripe for at least a few days. Aside from that, there wasn't much else for her to do, so she followed the guys and helped with whatever they needed. After a bit, Durante had to excuse himself and step back outside. The other two were finishing up; particularly Alces who was rearranging the kitchen area to make sure everything was to his liking. It made sense, he was the one who cooked the most unless he made someone else do it so they could learn.

Octavia was starting to get bored. She'd helped Alces as much as she could, but at this point it was really all up to him. She'd helped Sumner put things away, but he had shooed her off after a point. When Durante headed out, she shrugged and followed. At least it wasn't sitting around.

"Durante," she called out as she stepped back out of the tent, "need anything?"

"No," he said, breathing deeply. It was a change, as Durante didn't need to breathe, it was a habit from when he was human. He glanced over to her, and as his eyes were already darkening to a red, he tried to give her a reassuring smile. "Just needed a breeze."

"Oh." She smiled a little sheepishly but stopped where she was. Not for her safety, but for his comfort. "Are you sure I can't help? Like, maybe you go back to the inn, but you go to my room, and then I tell them that we're going back to the inn and they need to send up some food for me later or something?"

Durante smiled back gently at her and gave her a shy shrug. "If you're sure, then, I may very much like that."

She nodded. "Quite sure. Go on, I'll see you soon."

Turning about, she headed back into the tent. "Gentlemen? I'm afraid Durante is indisposed for the rest of the evening, as am I. Though I would really appreciate it if someone brought me some food in a couple hours." She smiled wryly. "We're going to see if my theory holds."

Alces looked up from what he was doing in the kitchen area, regarded her with curiosity, then nodded with approval. Sumner blinked. "Oh, we gotta get lots of juice," he laughed.

"Be careful," Alces added before she left. "I know uneasy Durante would never harm you, but you may not know your own limits."

She nodded. "I promise to be mindful." She paused for a moment, then smiled and darted up to each of them, pulling them in for a quick kiss. "Since you won't get good night kisses later," she said, laughing at herself a little. "And don't forget to bring me food!"

"Oh, you'll get your food," Sumner said with a smirk and Alces shook his head.

"As always, we will take care of you, as we would any of us," Alces said with a soft grin and a nod.

She smiled at them and headed back out of the tent towards the inn. She wasn't nervous. Durante would never hurt her, even driven by hunger, she was sure of that. But she might also be wrong about this. What if that much blood made him worse? What if it made him want more next time?

She shook her head. No, he'd been permitted to gorge himself after battles before, Sumner had said as much. While this may not solve the problem, it would not make it worse. Heading into the inn, she smiled and waved to Najm then headed to her room, opening the door and stepping inside.

Durante was sitting on her bed, his fists grabbing and balling up the ends of his shirt. When he looked up at her, his eyes were quite red, but not an angry red. It was softer, the color of salmon and coral but deeper.

"We've been together plenty before," he said, his sheepish smile exposing his elongated fangs, "but I feel nervous all over again."

"I don't know about plenty," she said with a soft smile. She walked up to him and ran a hand through his hair. She did love the feel of his hair. "I could always do with more. But I understand. This is new. For both of us."

He couldn't help but laugh a little. "It's been more than three times, that's a lot for me," he answered. "So, I've been trying to keep things calm, but you... smell... delicious and it's hard to calm the hunger. But I'm… I'm all right, and I want to know how you want to do this."

"It is probably ridiculous that hearing you say that excites me," she said, laughing at herself a little. She bent her head and kissed him. "I trust you, Kitten. If I can, I want to fill you. I know there will be a little bit of a mess, but I'm prepared for that. So why don't we start with getting undressed?"

Durante smiled a little more broadly this time, a little more genuinely. Standing up, he started to go through the process of unlacing his shirt and pants and stripping down. This part wasn't nervous; they'd done this before. Even when he was hungry, nothing changed in the body she'd seen a number of times before.

As Octavia stripped down, she set her clothes aside and cast the cleansing spell as she did. She didn't want additional scents in the room. She was still bleeding heavily—the thickness of her thighs was all that was keeping her from making a mess on the floor. She took off everything save for that ring around her left forefinger.

"So, Kitten," she said, moving back towards the bed. She could already feel a slickness on her upper thighs. "While I may eventually make demands of you, I'm going to let you lead for once." She paused to kiss him, deeply and with want. "Come to me when you're ready." She was grateful that the coverlet was the deep blue of the night sky. She would clean it, of course, but she wasn't sure if streaks of red on white sheets would be too much.

"I've been ready since yesterday," he said, crawling up onto the bed to join her, kneeling at her feet. He carefully picked up one of her legs and brought her foot up to his height. Softly, gently he began to kiss her ankle. She smiled at him, unable to help herself. She remembered the first night they had spent together, when she had instructed him to do exactly this, begin at her ankle and make his way up. Tenderly, he moved farther up her leg, lifting it until he got to her knee, then started bending down to follow it more. A faint thread of nervousness did pass through her then, simply because she'd never been with someone during her moon time. It had always been short and intense; it was easy enough to turn down potential lovers until it was over. Even in her service to Kamvasana, it wasn't seven days.

None of this stopped her from whimpering softly at the feel of his mouth against her skin, and she watched him with bright eyes. Durante's movements became more wanting, more insistent the closer he got to the apex of her legs. He somehow controlled himself enough after a pause to repeat his affections on her other leg, starting from her ankle. Savouring every inch of her skin, his fangs brushing against her skin with every kiss. Moving up her inner thigh, he couldn't hold himself back anymore. He wanted her, and what she was offering, too much. With her offering so openly, he was letting himself go. Parting her legs, he breathed in her scent, then descended upon her, licking up her claret and cleaning her with tender efficiency and gusto.

Moaning, Octavia twitched beneath him. It was different. He was feeding from her, his tongue desperate for every drop of red, and less focused on what would bring her to her peak. But he was still eagerly and hungrily licking at her, his fangs brushing so lightly against her most tender skin, and it was the most intense tease she had ever experienced. She grabbed the coverlet and did her best not to twist her hips. Right now, this was for him. She would take what she wanted before he was done. Her thighs cleaned, Durante moved to where it would satisfy both of them to an extent. His tongue, longer than she remembered, sought out and drove into her. Hands gripped her thighs, holding them apart while keeping her in place, as he explored her depths. The snaking tongue sought out every drop of the fine wine she exuded and he wanted more of.

"Ohhhhh, Gods, Kitten!" Her back arched as his tongue pushed into her. "I didn't… ohhhh, I didn't know you could do that!"

It was still different, but different was proving to be good. He'd never held her down before—he'd held onto her thighs, sure, but the grip wasn't the same, and there was a strength in his hands that she knew was always there but didn't often experience. She moaned and tossed her head and reached down with one hand to run her fingers through his hair.

As more of her blood filled his mouth and surged through his system, the more long and adoring his attentions became. Soon not only was he holding her in place, his hands were massaging her skin and caressing the softness of her. He tilted his head, so he was laying upon her thigh, a soft growl rumbling in his chest. Octavia was losing her mind. She lost track of how long he had been licking at her. She needed release. She was desperate for it. She was gripping the sheets above her head and almost vibrating with tension. Sliding his hands up her body, he had one of her thighs hooked in his arm with his hand across her tummy, keeping her in place and firmly against the bed. The other had gone up far enough to find her breast and start kneading it.

"Please," she whimpered, "Kitten, please! I need… oh, Gods! Please, kitten, let me come!"

For a moment Durante didn't respond, but then he shifted, and his mouth surrounded her sex. She felt his fangs start to pierce her mons, above and to either side of her clit. Octavia's eyes snapped open, and her body started to tremble. Lapping with an odd insistent laziness, his tongue would dip into her, then draw out and up, grazing its length against her clit before slipping back in again. Her orgasm struck her hard as her body spasmed, and she screamed out her pleasure. The scream ended, but she couldn't breathe in, she couldn't move, she couldn't do anything as electric jolts of pleasure ran through her. Drinking deep of her as she came, Durante was in a state of blissful daze.

And then her body went soft as she fell against the bed, drawing in a deep breath. She moaned and reached down again, sliding both of her hands into his hair.

"My Kitten," she murmured, "my darling… Gods, you're so incredible."

Extracting his fangs, he licked the wounds gently, and they healed from the supernatural nature of it. Laying his head upon her thigh, he dreamily kissed and licked upon her lips once more, gently and slowly in his brain-addling state. It sent small shivers through her.

"Sweet, wonderful Tavi," he muttered between ministrations. "Takes care of me. Lies with me. Is so sweet to me."

"Always, darling," she murmured. She caressed his hair but let her hands fall away as she basked in her afterglow. After a long moment, she lifted her head and looked down at him. "Kitten? Have you fed well enough to come hold me for a little bit? I promise to let you have more in a little while."

"Mmhmm," he muttered gently and started to drag his body up hers, kissing and nipping gently as he went. This was familiar, the languid almost drunken state that her blood put him in. Her softness attracted him utterly, his hands, body, and legs rubbing against her at every point he could. Once his head was more level with hers, he'd had his arms and a leg completely entangled with her, holding her close. With a small giggle, Octavia got a hand free long enough to cast the cleansing spell again—while Durante had been very thorough, he'd still gotten a bit on his face. She wiggled enough to pull the lighter blanket over the both of them, then settled in against him.

They cuddled and nuzzled into each other. Durante no longer needed to breathe, and so they would kiss until Octavia was lightheaded and had to pull back with a gasp. He blissfully caressed her as she told him how wonderful he was, how handsome, how sweet and thoughtful, how charming he could be.

Eventually there was a knock at the door, and Octavia gently extracted herself. A quick cleanup, and she pulled on her robe before going to answer. Sumner was on the other side of the door with a plate of fish, fruit, and bread. In his other hand was a large jug full of juice.

"Well, you're still standing, so it appears you have tamed the beast. How's D doing?" he asked, not bothering to look over her shoulder.

"Pretty out of it," she said with a smile, accepting first the pitcher, setting it on the closest table, and then coming back for the plate. "He's had his fill and is now experiencing the side effects of my blood." Her smile grew. "Like a kitten in catnip."

"Ah, kitten, is that why…?" Sumner said, lifting a brow and leaving the question hanging.

"Actually, it was his timidity," she said, leaning on the doorframe. "That first night at the tavern, after you got mad and then went off to seduce Mariah. He was so shy and uncertain. Like a kitten. The more we interacted, the more it became affectionate rather than an observation." She picked up a piece of melon and popped it into her mouth.

Sumner scowled a little, it almost looked like a pout. "I had my reasons."

Smirking, she held the plate out of the way and pulled him in closer. "I was just giving you a reference, my storm," she said, then kissed him lightly before letting go.

"Well, fine," he said, licking his lips after they parted. "At least you're helping him open up. Oh, curtains are thick, so you probably don't know it's past nightfall. We're heading out tomorrow so don't stay up too late or, well, Alces will wake you up regardless."

"Thank you for telling me," she said, picking up another piece of fruit. "I didn't realize it had gotten so late."

"Anyway, you've been warned. Avoid the wrath of the dragonkin." Clearing his throat, he grinned and gave her a little wave before turning to head back to his own room.

She ate another piece of fruit and watched him walk away, then stepped back inside and closed the door. "Still with me, kitten, or did you doze off?" she asked as she walked back over to the bed, setting the plate on the nightstand.

Durante smiled, his eyes half-closed as he reached out for her. "Here. Still here," he said happily. "C'mere."

She set down the plate and popped a berry in her mouth then slid back across the bed to him. "It's a little late," she said, kissing his forehead, then his cheek. "We shouldn't be up too much longer. Do you want to feed again before we go to sleep?"

"Ooo, you are so good to me," he said, his hands sliding over her and urging her to lay against him, or on top of him, or anything as long as she was pressed against him. "Been a while since I had so much dessert."

She let out a soft, breathy laugh and caressed his face. "I wonder if you're like this when you're drunk?" She kissed him lightly, a bare teasing of her tongue. She suddenly grinned—she had an idea. "Do you want to try something new?"

"New with you?" he asked with a grin, and his red eyes shimmering. "I love new with you. What are we experimenting with today?"

"You're going to scoot down the bed a bit, and roll onto your back," she said, still grinning. "And I'm going to climb up and straddle your face, my legs pinning down your shoulders. What do you think?"

"Sounds like we're both eating," he said with a laugh and released her.

She laughed again. "I suppose I could try, though based on last time it won't be long before you're very distracting."

Shimmying down, he got himself into position on the bed and rolled onto his back. "Like this?"

She smiled at him. "That's perfect." She picked up the plate and set it closer, then leaned in to kiss him. The kiss lasted for a while, drawing out as she fell into it, but then she pulled back with a grin and got herself in position, climbing up so that the tops of her ankles pressed down into his shoulders, and she was straddling his face. When she settled in, Durante's tongue immediately dove into her while his nose bumped against her clit. Hands came up to hold her ass, giving her even more of a seat to relax into.

"Oh, this is gonna be a challenge," she said softly to herself, laughing a little as she picked up her plate. Okay, eat as much as possible before it felt too good to keep going, finish the rest afterwards. Fish first. Everything that wouldn't keep. Fruit could wait.

She ate with her fingers, a bit messy and panting as they both had their dinners. Her seat's movements had become languid but no less insistent. He wanted to taste her, deep, but was taking his time with it, enjoying it. By the time she'd gotten through the fish and bread and licked her fingers clean and gotten any bits that fell on her breasts, her legs were trembling. She set the plate back down, pushing it as far out of the way as she could, and slid her hands through Durante's hair.

"Gods, kitten," she murmured, twisting his raven locks around her fingers. Now that she wasn't focused on trying to eat the sensations pulsing through her were even stronger. She closed her eyes as the tremble in her legs spread up through her pelvis. "Almost..."

His hands had come up and around caressing over her tummy and petting the soft underside of her breasts. Having just fed, Durante didn't feel the urge to bite her again, but his fangs did keep pressing against her skin. With her weight on his face, it was impossible not to. The slower build of her orgasm manifested in a soft, musical cry that rang out through the room as her head fell back, and she shuddered above him. It also seemed to linger, the pleasure unspooling through her leisurely rather than a sharp, quick climax that would have knocked her over. As her muscles went soft, and she actually sank down on him more—it would have smothered someone who needed to breathe.

Finally, legs still shaking a little, she lifted up off of him, falling forward onto her hands. "Are you satisfied, darling?" she managed after a long moment, still panting.

Dreamily, Durante moved his hands to her hips and started to gently persuade her to slide down. "In one way, yeeeeees," he said, drunk on her blood. "In one way, nooooo. May I have some more of you, Tavi? Sweet, sweet Tavi. Beautiful, soft, lovely Tavi?"

She giggled, but let him draw her down, sliding her legs off his shoulders and inching down until their eyes met. She reached up with one hand and wiped a smear of red from his lower lip, which he eagerly licked away.

"What more do you want, Kitten?" She smiled, fairly certain she knew the answer.

He wriggled a little underneath her. "You. Want to be with you," he nearly whimpered. Usually well spoken, his mind wonderfully addled with the fey touch of her blood, Durante lost his higher vocabulary. "Let me feel you, please?"

Tempting as it was to tease him further, that was enough. She kissed him, a languorous tangling of tongues, then inched herself down a little further until she could feel Durante's waiting erection. She knew from experience that intoxication could often impair a man's desire, but whatever else was in her blood, it also contained the touch of Kamvasana. Performance would not be an issue. She sank down slowly on his cock, moaning softly, until her hips came to rest against him.

"Is this what you wanted?"

"Yes," he hissed, arching his back a bit and pressing up into her. "Tavi, you feel so good. All of you is so good." He slowly bit at the air, fangs fully extended, but he did not lunge at her. Most likely it was sensations running through him. Durante's hands had come to knead upon her thighs and hips, pressing into her softly as he wanted to touch every inch of her.

"My Kitten," she murmured, and lowered herself against him, kissing across his chest and shoulder. "My darling." She started to move her hips, slow and easy. She bit gently at his chest.

Nails clawed at her back enough to send a shiver through her, sure to leave red marks but nothing deeper. Having her lay upon him pressed so much of her warm, soft flesh against him that Durante was left able to do little more than wriggle under her. Thankfully, this undulating motion did ensure that he met her hips movements in a slow, steady pace.

"Shadows beyond, Tavi, you feel so... so..." his voice trailed off into more groans and delicate noises of pleasure.

She pushed herself up a little bit, not enough to completely pull away from him, but enough to be able to ride him with a little more force and watch his face as she did. She felt that swelling warmth in her chest as she reached up with one hand to caress his face. He trusted her so much—he had to, to put himself in this position, drunk and drowning in pleasure and at her mercy.

"Will you come for me, Kitten?" She asked him, voice barely above a whisper.

"Yes," he hissed again, moving more wildly under her. "For you, always for you. All yours."

As the peak started to bring a sense of focus to his mind, temporary though it might have been, Durante grabbed her hips and started to thrust with purpose. Leaning up, he latched on to one of her heavy breasts that hung before his face when she arched up, sucking hungrily. When his orgasm hit, he bit down, fangs sending a shock through her in the sensitive nerves of her breast and sending the dual sensation of him sucking on her hard nipple and drawing another drink of blood out of her. Octavia's quiet moan spiraled up in shock. That was new, but today has been all about new. And the feel of his teeth still sent the same delicious tremor through her.

When his peak subsided, Durante set his hips to rest, his fangs pulling out of her and his tongue lazily dragging over the marks to seal them before he fell to the bed. Eyes closed, smiling in afterglow, and ever moving but with the subtlety of a lake's shore. As Durante calmed, so did she, falling against him and getting her breath back. Durante's grasp lessened and was replaced by gentle petting. "So perfect, Tavi. You're so perfect."

ELEVEN

If she was to travel with them, Octavia would either need to learn to wake up earlier, or get used to Alces' voice doing it for her. "Rise and shine, my friends," Alces called out, although it didn't seem as resounding as the day before, "breakfast will be ready soon. I will see you outside."

She cleaned up carefully, not wanting any extra blood left anywhere. She finished her fruit as she did and drank a little over half the pitcher of juice, leaving the rest on the nightstand for when she woke. Finally, she climbed back into bed, snuggling against Durante and kissing his shoulder. Durante's arms wrapped around her and pulled her close, still making happy noises.

"Ready to sleep, my darling?" she asked softly.

"Mmhmm." Kissing her softly, he nuzzled and squeezed her in his arms. It was only a few short moments before his body went still, and she could tell he was asleep. Settling in, Octavia felt adored and warm and… she didn't have the words for it, but it was wonderful. She hoped they could do this again in two months. Assuming she was still there in two months…

She gave her head a little shake. No, there was no reason to think she wouldn't be. Let that thought go. She kissed his shoulder, settling her head against him, and fell asleep.

Morning came to Octavia still wrapped in Durante's arms, one hand cupping her rump, the other resting on the small of her back. The nice thing about sleeping with the dhampir was that one wouldn't overheat; he was almost always cool to the touch. In the summer months, this would be a boon.

There was a gentle knock at the door, and Sumner's voice came through, which was far quieter than Alces'. "Wake up, kids. Time to head out."

Octavia rolled onto her back and called out, "Yes, Daddy," towards the door, then giggled to herself as she turned back to Durante.

"You can try calling me that later," Sumner laughed as he walked away from the door, his duty completed.

"Come on, darling, we need to get up," she said, kissing and nibbling at Durante's shoulder and collar.

Durante gave her a squeeze, then moved gently to raise his arms up and stretch, yawning. She noticed his fangs had shrunk back down to slightly larger than typical incisors. "Oh, I'm rather liking that," he said with a smile as he blinked his eyes open. The color was a rosy pink, much more subdued from the deep red that had been penetrating his irises yesterday.

She propped her head up on her hand and smiled down at him. "Feeling more yourself today?"

"Far better than normal," he said with a grin, reaching up and caressing her face. "I don't think I've felt this good in years. Thank you, Tavi."

"We can absolutely do it again in about two months, provided I haven't driven you all mad by then," she said, still smiling. "Thank you for indulging my idea."

"I think that is the opposite of what you will drive us," he chuckled. Giving her another squeeze, Durante relinquished her from his grasp and started to move out of bed. They were travelling that day, and many days after, so it was best to get going. "If you have any other ideas or experiments, I am happy to assist."

"I might have a few," she said, grinning, but also climbed out of bed and went about getting dressed quickly. Alces would never leave anyone behind, but they might disappoint him, and disappointing Alces seemed to be the greatest sin known to Durante or Sumner. Octavia was beginning to understand why.

The other two had made an effort to be ready to go so there was little need to wait around. Breakfast had been set and was a little more filling than the day before. Much of this had been the food they'd ordered from the market yesterday, padding out the inn's stores. As such, the keeper seemed to be in higher spirits, knowing he had enough to supply his guests and then some. It seemed Sumner could be rather loose with the coin if food was involved. Then again, food wasn't expensive, not compared to components for Durante or Alces's generosity or her taste in clothing. She did find she was thirsty and very hungry after her day with Durante, though even at her most ravenous she wouldn't hold a candle to Alces.

After breakfast, they were ready to go in short order. She thanked the keeper again for his patience and for being so accommodating on short notice, smiling her most charming smile. And then she was outside with Matilda close behind, ready for what would no doubt be a grueling day of walking.

Durante was definitely more awake than usual and started off the walk with a spring in his step. More than once, Octavia caught him smiling at her, and it took him a moment to look away. Octavia always smiled back. It was impossible not to. She reflected that he should certainly feed more often, but also wondered if maybe… well, maybe it wasn't just the blood that had him energized and smiling.

They'd found a map in town that showed Boulcairn was northwest of them, somewhat along the coastline, but there were no direct roads. They could go through the lush forests of Yadeli but there was no telling what they would find there or what the terrain was going to be like. They seemed to favor the road, but they'd travel through forests before so cutting through may not be a bad idea if they wanted to cut time.

The first night would be on the road, no matter their decision. The next town down the way would take two days at least, maybe three, and who knew how accommodating the roadside inns would be. Octavia's tent would more than suffice and keep them out of trouble. The part of the land they were in, the trees showed no sign of changing color. Still vibrant green and, if anything, the rainy season would be picking up soon. If they could make it to Boulcairn in time, they probably wouldn't be hit by it, but the weather was fickle like that.

As the evening was getting on, Alces called for them to make camp. Despite the thick forest, the road had plenty of clearings nearby that others had used for respite along their journeys. Sumner did a little scouting and found one near a river that was far enough from the road they wouldn't be spied on. Octavia tried not to be too obviously grateful when they stopped. The long days of walking weren't as hard as they used to be, but she didn't think she'd ever enjoy them. At least this had been a good bit downhill, and on easy terrain. She thought back to her first journey with the three of them up into the mountains. That had been significantly more miserable.

"How many days out are we?" she asked as she set down the tent and pulled the cord to let it unfold.

"Depends," Alces said, looking off into the distance. "By road, maybe another six to eight days. Through the forest... four? Impossible to say, given I have no idea what lives here. We are sure to find adventure, however."

"Woods would be fine with me," Sumner said, crouching down to bend and flex his legs. "Had enough of people for a bit."

"While it should be alright, we don't know this area, and the road might be wiser. We could get lost," Durante added, taking his rifle off his shoulder and massaging where the strap had laid.

"Was there anything on the map?" She directed Matilda to waddle into the tent. "Notes about the area, anything?"

While Alces seemed to be distracted by a cloud, Sumner slipped the map from off his belt and whipped it open. "Um, we're going up, so the trees are going to be different, according to the symbols, I think" he said, looking it over and shaking his head. "It's written in Devrekish, so I have no idea."

Smirking, Octavia held out her hand as she invoked her ability and shifting, sparkling violet runes filled her eyes. "Let me see."

"Oh, right, right," he laughed and handed it to her, "the whole reason we hired you originally."

"Yes, imagine that, I can be useful," she muttered as she examined the map. The comment wasn't directed at Sumner, but rather self-deprecating.

She'd seen plenty of Devrekish by now, as it was the language of the Beyliks and even Rupaiya. She could actually read it fairly well on her own after her year or so in Rupaiya, but the spell helped fill in the gaps in her vocabulary. The map was very local, mostly the central southern coastline of Sizhou Lake. It wasn't the most detailed, as it was primarily a trade map, but it at least gave her a lay of the land. Two main reasons they couldn't take a ship to Boulcairn was the high coastal cliff it sat away from, and that it was in another country whose relationship with Yadeli was rocky. Not to a point they wouldn't be able to cross, but to a point where trade ships would most likely only be welcome in major ports without serious scrutiny.

She could easily see that they were approaching a curve in the road, following the terrain, and would head back south and west towards the town of Uzeki. From there, they would go north to Akayol and then wind back north and east to Boulcairn. If they went straight north from the curve, trekking through the forest, they'd head right into the road to Boulcairn from Akayol as it, too, curved. Dense trees, mostly uphill, and no noted dangers aside from that. But it would definitely shave days off their travel barring catastrophe.

"It doesn't say anything about animals or monsters in the wood, just dense trees and mostly uphill." Lovely, more climbing. She managed not to sigh. "It does seem we could take days off the journey."

"Perhaps a shortcut would be best," Alces said, holding the flap open for the rest of them. "While we're not in a rush, we should also not keep inquisitive Durante's contact waiting. Promptness pleases such people often." Durante simply nodded.

She rolled the map up and handed it back to Sumner. "Into the woods, then. At the next bend." Yawning, she stretched. "Tomorrow. Let's head inside, I want to clean up."

"We camp early to make sure we are rested and happy," Alces said with a nod, following them in.

The tent was all prepared for them; with a stock of meats, bread, cheese, and fruit to make sure they were well fed and weren't surviving on rations alone. Alces and Sumner wouldn't need to hunt for many days. Alces asked Durante to follow him so that he could doff his armor faster and start dinner cooking. Sumner kicked off his boots and fell onto the couch, rather enjoying the comfort of actual cushions out in the wilderness.

Octavia headed into her room and let the curtain fall with a sigh. She was still moody. She hated that. It would settle out in a couple more days, though. She changed into more comfortable clothing, her softly billowing pants and short top from Rupaiya, and undid her hair, shaking loose her curls. She would take a bath later that night. The cleansing spell did the job, sure, but it never felt as clean as when she actually washed herself. She headed back into the main area, teased the back of Sumner's neck with her fingertips as she walked by, and then settled in one of the chairs, curling up and tucking her legs in.

"How was the hike?" he asked, smiling up at her and watching her sit. "It seems cramps haven't been bothering you too much, or you're good at hiding it."

"It's getting easier," she said, and shrugged. "Still not my favorite mode of transportation. And no, the cramps aren't so bad. The first day or two is always the worst." She shifted herself around in the chair so that she could rub her feet a little. "I'm probably going to summon Comicha for foot rubs in a minute like the baby I am."

"If I had a cute masseuse at my beck and call, I'd take advantage of it too," he said, giving her a shrug of his own. "Alces can always call Nutmeg for you. Probably should when we stray from the road and into the woods."

She wiggled her feet. "I can't be too delicate, or you'll all get sick of catering to me." That probably wasn't fair, she didn't demand much, and she did her best. She sighed and leaned back in the chair.

Durante came out and found himself a seat. He smiled over at Octavia. "It appears I need to get used to road travel again. I was rather enjoying having a plush inn to stay in."

"You would," Sumner said with a laugh.

"The inn back in Limanyadeli was nice," she said, smiling at Durante. "The nicest inn I've stayed at in a while, now that I think of it. I'm sure I'll miss it in the next few days." She wrinkled up her nose, her expression playful. Talking about missed luxuries didn't make her feel defensive with Durante. He understood.

"Maybe we'll have a nice manor of our own again," he said with a laugh, then blinked, as if realizing what he had implied.

Octavia did manage to keep herself from looking straight at Durante when he said that, but she wasn't able to keep the blush from her cheeks or stop the way her lips parted slightly in surprise. She wasn't a green girl, she knew those words did not mean much in of themselves, but the fact that he seemed to be thinking it at all made that flutter beneath her ribs stronger.

"As long as you got room for the rest of us," Sumner said, tossing a knife in the air and catching it on the return, pausing occasionally to balance the tip on his finger.

Sumner's comment got a more relaxed grin. "That is what manor implies," she said. "That there would be room enough for everyone."

Alces returned from his room wearing a loose tunic and his casual kilt. He smiled at the lot of them then walked towards the kitchen area. "First day back on the roads. I'll make something special," he said.

She looked over at Alces, curious. What little of his cooking she had experienced had all been very good, but she knew that his talent had been hampered by their supplies. Now that they had everything he needed, she was very curious as to what he would produce.

Alces started by pulling out some of the meat they'd purchased and began carefully cutting it and seasoning it. Adding a bed of root vegetables underneath it in the cooking tray, he paused to stare at what was effectively the stove.

"Spirits bless my mind, how does this work again?" he asked everyone.

"I remember," Durante volunteered and got up to help Alces set the magical cooking device.

"Manors come with big plots, right? Lots of land?" Sumner asked, catching his knife before looking over at her, brows raised.

"They can, yeah." Octavia leaned back into her chair again, giving Sumner her full attention since the others were busy. "Not so much the ones they build near cities, but manors do tend to have a lot of land. They can be almost like a tiny town in their own way."

"We'll need that, then," he said, smirking at her. "Room to run, roam, expand. All that good stuff. Can't have a proper round top without expansive land."

She smiled at him, a softer smile. "So, we need a country manor. But close to the trade roads, I would think."

"Well, sure, that goes without saying," Sumner said with a shrug.

Durante returned to his seat as Alces started in on something that looked to involve flour and fruit. It was a good thing they had started up camp in the afternoon, as it would probably be a bit before Alces' dinner was made.

"Near a port or river as well," Durante jumped in. "Oh, or if we could find one of those tidal caves, we could hide a ship in."

Sumner sat up and laughed. "Better be sure to find a place that has a good number of storms as well, so when you're working in your lab, you can have lightning crashing, lighting up the tower against the sky."

Octavia giggled, then glanced over at Alces working in the kitchen area. "It needs orchards, I think. A place to raise animals. We could trade with farms for vegetables, but probably still an herb garden. Defensible, but not hard to get to. Somewhere that can be easily found."

"We're gonna need a bigger map," Sumner added with another laugh.

Looking back to Sumner, Octavia smiled again. This was nice. And she knew they were dreaming, but there was something touching and sweet about the fact that the dream didn't involve anyone going off on their own. They would run this fantasy manor together: Durante would have his lab, Sumner would remake the circus he missed so much or something better, and they would have everything Alces wanted when he came home.

And she… her gaze drifted, and her brows furrowed a little. What would she do in this place? Like she had told Sumner the other day, she could help him run it. She'd been trained to, she knew how. But what did she want? What would her corner of the manor look like? Did she even know?

As if guided by her thoughts, Durante looked over at her. "What was your place like, Tavi? I know you didn't like your, um, situation as it were, but surely you lived in a nice place," he said, trying to be positive about it. "Anything you really miss?"

"It was nice." Octavia looked up and smiled, but she couldn't keep the old sorrow out of her voice. "We lived in the city, with a view of the river. I would sit on the terrace and read and look at the boats coming in and out of the port. We had a library. It was small, we mostly had one because it fit my father's idea of something a noble family would have, but I loved it. My mother would find most any book I was interested in. It was important to appear educated, you see. Nobles in Driscoll's Rest valued what school you went to, what you could talk about, things like that." She sighed and leaned back in the chair again, letting her head drop back. "You know, I spent my life being raised to make other people happy. And then when I left, all I knew was that I had to find a way to be independent. To be able to be more than someone's wife. And I succeeded, but…"

"But you're not sure what will make you happy?" Durante asked, leaning in a little.

She looked up at Durante, and she turned faintly pink again. They made her happy. Happier than she had been in her whole life. Yes, she would enjoy books and art and being a woman of leisure, but she had found what made her happy. The moment of clarity struck her dumb for a moment, and her lips parted as she tried to find the words.

"You know, now that we have someone who wants to read more than anatomical charts and alchemy manuals, we'll have to make sure we actually grab some of those ancient books that nobody can read," Sumner said, laughing again. She gave her head a little shake before looking back over at the rogue with an easier smile.

"Yes, collect all the strange books for me," she said, and turned her smile to Alces as he sat down, the mystery baked good set aside to proof while the scent of roast filled the tent. "Whatever you have been up to smells amazing."

"I certainly hope so," he grinned. "Spices we found in Limanyadeli. A bit of an experiment, but I feel we're in that sort of mood."

"We were just talking about what sort of place we would want to have. Such as a big manor or the like," Sumner said. "What would you want?"

Alces needed a moment to think, tilting his head to the side. Then he grinned. "Fellowship. And maybe a kitchen and comfy bed," Alces laughed, "but I do not think I could stay. The world draws me out, so many dark corners that need the light brought to them."

"But what about a home to come back to?" Octavia leaned forward, a little earnestly. The emotions from her revelation were still roiling within her. "Where that large kitchen and bed that's actually big enough for you are waiting when you need rest? With people who care?"

"That would probably be very nice," Alces said with a nod. "Never really had a home to come back to. Always found home in those that I was with, that joined me in my travels such as your wonderful selves. Would certainly be a change."

Octavia nodded. She was a little afraid of saying anything else, certain she would say something awkward or too… presumptuous. She felt like she should tell them what she realized, but also like it was too much. Two months felt like too short a time for what she wanted to say.

Sumner laid back and reverted back to tossing his knife in the air and catching it. "Makes sense. Getting Alces to settle down is like trying to contain a storm. Slightly less destructive," he said, smirking at the large dragonkin. "Slightly."

"I am not averse to the idea of a place to return to," Alces said, gesturing towards Octavia in solidarity.

She smiled softly at Alces, appreciating what he was trying to do. She never doubted his sincerity, though it could be hard to determine what things meant to him. Everyone was wonderful, he praised and appreciated everything in the Light. She fought back a sigh. Oh well. It was who he was.

The rest of the afternoon went on as Durante, Octavia, and Sumner talked about all the things the manor should have, which got more and more fantastical as they went. This included Durante's lab being not merely a tower, but a floating tower, and Sumner having a menagerie of wild creatures from various realms of mystery to tame and put on display—humanely, of course.

Alces got up multiple times to check on dinner, finally trading out the roast for the baked treat he had been prepping. Sumner and Durante set out dishes and got the table ready while the roast rested. Once Alces determined dinner was ready, he set the baked goods off to the side to cool while he brought the roast and vegetables to the table.

The dish in question was a beef roast, heavily seasoned with a spice rub that made the outside a vibrant reddish-brown and smelled slightly sweet and earthy. It was tender and juicy, and the flavor matched the smell with a layer of garlic, pepperiness, and a bit of smoke despite not being grilled over a wood fire. The vegetables shared a similar flavor, considering the meat was cooked on top of them and they'd soaked in the jus. The dinner was surprisingly rich, and easily something that would have been far more difficult out over a campfire.

Octavia quietly stewed through dinner but had the sense to still praise Alces for producing a succulent and flavorful meal. She hid her quiet behind eating, which wasn't hard—she ate more than Durante and almost as much as Sumner on a typical day. Alces did make notes of her appetite and smiled, taking it as further sign that she was enjoying his cooking. Sumner glanced around the table, then back at Octavia.

"I have to congratulate you. Whatever you two did," he said, wiggling his finger between pointing at her and Durante with a fairly knowing smirk, "worked. D hasn't flared up at all. I figured, while we're walking, there's a breeze and all that. But here, in the tent, not much wind. But there he is, calm and eyes pink as can be."

She blinked and then glanced over at Durante who smiled and shrugged before looking back at Sumner. "Saturation. I would guess, given Durante resents his current state—sorry, Kitten, but you do—that he's never been, well, full before." She looked back to Durante. "So, we know what to do next time. We just need to… take a day." The corner of her mouth quirked up a little. "Kind of looking forward to it."

Sumner held back a laugh but gave her an acknowledging shrug. Durante looked over at her with a brighter, less sheepish smile.

"Excellent," Alces said as he stood up. "Solutions that make everyone happy, light flows through you all." Turning away, he retrieved the pastries and came back to the table, setting them down. "Don't shy away. Eat them all, I can always make more. Later." What Alces presented looked like square tarts, the edges folded in, containing the macerated fruit generously drizzled over a baked, soft cheese.

"Oh, Gods, Alces, I'm going to get so fat." She took a bite. "Mmm, but I don't care."

"No, no," Alces said with a grin, "not with us, not while adventuring. Enjoy yourself, you have, and will, earn it many times over."

"Seriously, I mean, look at me," Durante said with a smile. "I'm not as strong as Alces or as cutting as Sumner, but I think I've done a little bit better since I joined them."

"Brother, you're half the man you used to be, and I mean that as a compliment," Sumner added.

Octavia arched an eyebrow at Durante and took another pastry. "Have you seen your shoulders? 'Done a little bit better,' Goddess of Mercy preserve me. You're not kind enough to yourself."

Durante gave a half shrug. It was hard to say if he would ever be kind to himself, even with all the progress he'd made to his own goal, setbacks aside. Sumner scoffed and threw a leftover bit of carrot at him and rolled his eyes. Alces billowed out a laugh and clapped Durante on the back.

"You handle yourself with bravery and fortitude regardless of the situation we find ourselves in, reserved Durante," the dragonkin said. "Stand tall and straight, you have done yourself proud, even if you do not realize it."

Grinning back at Octavia, Alces continued. "So, voracious Octavia, enjoy what this life offers you. Worry not, we will keep you well in shape."

Octavia almost choked on the pastry. She knew what Alces meant, but given the type of relationship she had with each of them, there were a lot of ways to take that statement. She managed to chew and keep herself together.

Dinner wrapped up, and the company cleaned and started making their way to their individual rooms for the evening. All but Sumner got a goodnight kiss, as he planned on getting a little more that evening. Not a wild night, as they had been walking all day long after several days of rest, but enough excitement to put them to bed properly. For all that Sumner made jokes about how being her only partner might be the death of him, he could be a little insatiable. She was pretty sure that fear of being judged by Alces was the only reason Sumner wasn't in her bed every night she wasn't planning on being with someone else.

As they settled in to sleep, Octavia played with his hair until he was purring. She was warm and humming, and he'd definitely left a bite mark on her shoulder. He usually did. She had joked with Durante about how Sumner wouldn't want her anymore if she wasn't beautiful, but she wondered if it really was true. It might be. Though he would hardly have the chance to prove it, even if she left Kamvasana's service, she would still look the same. The changes were permanent; it had been part of the pact.

She sighed and settled into sleep. It wasn't worth agonizing over, and she was pretty sure it only bothered her because she was at the tail end of her moon time. She kissed his neck, murmured sleepily into his ear, and drifted off.

Another early morning as Alces called to wake everyone up. Sumner was still happily pressed against her when he started to wake. A large yawn that ended with him playfully biting her neck.

"Oh, right, didn't have to go hunting," he muttered. "S'why I'm still... mmmm." Sumner purred again and gave Octavia squeezes and caressed her.

"Come, friends. Breakfast is ready, and we have a long walk ahead of us," Alces called out.

The smell of spiced meat was drifting into her bedroom to further entice her. She yawned and rolled onto her back to look at Sumner. "You're usually up out of bed the moment you wake," she said quietly, but he hadn't moved yet, so she didn't see a reason to either. She reached up and ran a hand through his hair. He never wore it down, but it was a beautiful golden color. It was thick, but soft, and fell straight. She curled it around her finger.

"Was comfy," he said with a smile, then nipped her shoulder and made his way out of bed. He stretched then started to get dressed. "Probably shouldn't laze too long. Don't want a cold breakfast, after all."

Octavia sighed. The moment was over. Oh well. She rolled out of bed and started getting dressed. "It would be a shame to leave breakfast to get cold after Alces put work in," she commented as she pulled her pants on. Clothes went on quickly, but then she had to deal with her hair, which always took a minute. She occasionally thought about cutting it off, but she also loved how long and voluminous it was. Well, most of the time.

Sumner waited around for her to finish getting dressed so they could head out together. As they walked into the main room, Durante was already seated and waiting as Alces carried a couple of trays to the odd low table the seats surrounded.

Upon them was a collection of breads, jams, and cheeses that

Octavia recognized from the markets they'd been too. Additionally, there was a dish of sliced and cooked spiced sausage and individual dishes of an egg, baked with cream and sprinkled with herbs.

"Good morning," Alces said with a smile. "Just in time. We have a forest to conquer."

"Gods of Harvest," Octavia said as she looked over the spread before them. "Alces, we need to make sure you always have supplies."

"Food is a celebration all on its own," Alces said as he sat down near the table. "I will say, most of this was just purchased at the market, but I experimented with the eggs and cooked up the sausage. I need to work out the cooking muscles a little more to make sure you all are happy and well fed."

"I second that, though," Sumner said, "we need to make sure you can always cook whatever you want, big guy."

Octavia gleefully ate her egg, and some sausage, and bread with jam and some of the soft cheese, and then a bit more cheese, and a little more bread. With cheese. Durante still didn't eat much, mostly having his egg and a touch of sausage. Sumner had everything that was given to him.

After they were done eating, she gave Durante a brief good morning snuggle—a kiss on the cheek, a nuzzle at his neck, and a hand playing briefly in his gorgeous hair. Durante made a slightly surprised but happy noise, and reached up to run a hand through her hair and caress her neck. When she pulled back, he was smiling softly. She then went to help clean up.

It was relatively quick, as the dishes mostly needed wiped down and Alces ate anything that was leftover. Within half an hour, they had packed up the tent and were making their way down the last bit of road they'd see for a couple of days.

TWELVE

Drifting to the north as the road curved, they headed into the forest. Sumner would dart ahead now and then to scout for the best route, then come back to lead them through. Walking behind Alces ensured that any branches, roots, or vines that might trip them up were folded or cut out of the way.

Even in the fall, the southern forest was very jungle-like, with lush green all around them. As they started to gain altitude and head north, the trees started to thin slightly and the bark became rougher.

When they finally settled on camp, everyone was tired. There had been no path, no road, not even a goat trail. Following in Alces' wake had made the path easier, but it was still more work than the road would have been, and it was entirely uphill. The clearing they had found was caused by a heavy canopy above creating continuous shade. Timing was good, as they could hear thunder in the distance and no one really felt like hoofing it in the rain. Too easy to get lost or injured.

Octavia got the tent set up and everyone ushered inside as the rain started to fall. She stood in the opening of the tent for a moment, watching the rain, enjoying the smell that came with the first drops. There was no worry about the tent washing away, no matter how heavy the rainfall. She didn't linger long, though, and came back inside, ready to help with dinner and also a bath. Her cycle was ending, and she felt overdue for a good scrub.

The rough hike and the dark clouds forced them to make camp earlier than they'd planned. Given the extra time, Alces started to chop up some of the meat and vegetables they'd gotten and began making a stew. Since he had ample time to cook, he decided to make bread for this evening's meal. Octavia watched as he fished around his bottomless bag and retrieved a jar that had a bit of raw dough in it. He folded it in with the dough he was already making before setting it aside to proof.

Sumner took the time to go through his own gear and find his more waterproof set. This was mostly a long coat made from waxed canvas that had ties at the wrist and was split with ties that went around his ankles to keep it close to him and not impede movement. Durante rummaged in his room for a moment, then sat in one of the couches with a book. They'd retrieved so many from the tower, and his own handful that he kept with him, that it was impossible to tell what he was reading now.

Octavia helped Alces as much as she could and then headed into the bath. She took her time, even if the tub wasn't really big enough for a good soak. She washed her hair, squeezed the water out, and bound it carefully in a scarf to dry. Her pact with Kamvasana kept her from ever looking too mussed or too frumpy, but nothing beat actual effort.

She finished up, wrapped up in her robe and darted back across the tent to her room. She decided to take pity on the others and finished applying lotion and adding a little oil to her hair in her room, coming back into the main area fully dressed in her lounge clothing.

It was early evening when she sauntered back into the main room. Her appearance got an appreciative whistle from Sumner, a warm smile from Durante, and a question from Alces. "Do you like anything in your bread, lovely Octavia? Cheese or herbs? I'm just about to start the first knead."

"I love cheese in almost anything," she said with a smile, walking around to give both Durante and Sumner a kiss on the cheek. "Herbs are also welcome. I love all breads, really." She walked up and offered one to Alces as well.

"As there is no cheese in the stew, in the bread it goes," Alces laughed then leaned down to accept the kiss. Turning back to the small cooking area, he began taking some of the firmer cheese that they had purchased and started crumbling it gently into the dough.

"How are you faring after the hike today?" Durante asked, making room for her on the couch.

"Sore, but it's not awful," she said with a smile as she sat down. "It is getting easier, though I'm sure I'll be making sad eyes at Alces to summon Nutmeg by the time we're out of the forest."

"The terrain is rough," Alces said. The dough didn't need that much working, so he placed it back into its proofing bowl and set it aside. The tent was beginning to fill with the smell of the stew. "Nutmeg is at your beck and call, sweet Octavia."

"None of us will mind if you need the big elk," Sumner added. He'd also changed into loose garments and was going through a series of stretches, some of which clearly showed off his flexibility.

"I'm not ready to fall over yet," she said with a little shrug. "And as someone pointed out the other day, I won't build up endurance if I don't walk."

"Road, sure," Sumner said, "but this is shitty unbroken forest that'll be wet tomorrow. Just saying, we won't blame you. Now, if we were walking on a nice road, different story. I'd probably tease you then." He grinned at her to show her he was kidding.

Octavia stuck her tongue out at him. And then curled it.

She got up long enough to go fetch her journal from her room, then came back to the couch. She stuck her feet in Durante's lap with a little smile—she had ended up with her feet in his lap accidentally once, but their relationship had changed quite a bit since then.

"Once we're out of the forest, but still on the road, I'm going to try to open that tome we got in Gravemont," she said as she flipped through her journal to where her notes on the book were. "I'm sure it's warded, though I'm having a hard time seeing it because of the sympathetic magic. I should be able to get past the wards. In case I trip them, though, I want to be away from any towns."

"Any idea how it might be warded?" Durante asked, absently rubbing one of her feet as he held his book in his other hand. "Anything we should protect ourselves from?"

"Given what we know of your benefactor, I don't think I could protect us from any of her magics," Alces added, taking a seat amongst the group. "You are the expert."

Finding the right spot in her notes, Octavia absently nodded. "Well, the lock is magical, though I suspect there's a variation on a charm spell woven into it. I should be able to unravel that easily enough. The lock looks sophisticated, but it's—" she paused for a moment and considered. "Um, okay, it's technically divine magic. The Venebore triplets were devoted to Kamvasana, they worshipped them, none of them had a pact. And there's a… straightforwardness to divine magic. The spells on the tome are layered, but each one should have a single purpose."

She pondered for another moment, then looked up with a reassuring smile. "If something happens, and I trip any of the wards, it should only affect me. You may need to pin me down until it wears off or something like that, but there's nothing volatile there."

"Oh, we'll pin you down, don't worry about that," Sumner laughed. Alces shook his head but smiled.

"Regardless, should something happen, we will take care of you and the problem, no matter what," Alces reassured her.

"Whatever it might be, I don't think it'll be that bad," Durante said.

"I don't think it will be either," Octavia said, and stuck her tongue out at Sumner again. "What very little I know about clerics of Kamvasana, back when there were any, is that their magic abilities are never destructive."

"I have no worry," Alces said, "you are wise in your magics and learned."

"I sure don't know anything about it," Durante added with a shrug, still pressing his fingers into the arch of her foot. "I'd love to learn sometime, but I don't think you have a primer on ancient powers or anything."

"There's a lot I can teach you, but honestly, this is part of the reason I wanted this book so badly," she said, folding up her journal. "There was a time when Kamvasana and the other primordials were as revered as any deity, at least in the right parts of the world. Then religion and politics shifted and that worship fell off. I..." she considered for a moment, then laughed softly. "I am hoping to find something that will give me the leverage I need to renegotiate my contract."

"Shrewd," Sumner said with a smirk. "Though, for the most part, you have a pretty sweet deal already."

Idle chitchat floated around as the evening went on, and the stew bubbled. At one time, Alces got up to put the bread in the oven. When he proclaimed the stew as completed, he presented it along with the now-crusty loaf of bread.

The stew was rich and hearty, easily something that they may have leftovers with. The bread was soft on the inside, chewy, and a touch sour which complimented the gooey bits of cheese that were sprinkled about. Octavia praised Alces for the stew, and again for the bread. She ate entirely too much of it, loving the melty, cheesy pockets and the distinctive tang. Durante didn't move her feet all through dinner, and once he'd finished picking at his food he went right back to absently rubbing her feet. They all chatted and laughed, and Octavia felt that warmth fill her chest again.

This. This was what made her happy. They made her happy. She would find a way to tell them. Eventually.

After dinner was cleaned up and put away, Octavia kissed each of them and headed to bed alone. The hike through the woods hadn't been too bad, but it had still been exhausting, and tomorrow wouldn't be better. A night of actual rest would be good for all of them. Even though part of her wished she could curl up with all three of them like a pile of puppies. Full, content, and exhausted, even without a bed partner, Octavia fell quickly into sleep.

Another morning woken by an enthusiastic Alces as he called forth the party for breakfast. More cheese, fruit, the remainder of last night's bread, and fried sausages. No one seemed particularly eager to go out trudging in the wet forest, but most were even less enthused about staying in the forest, no matter how comfy the tent was.

Outside, the storm had drifted, leaving behind a gentle, light shower and rainbows where the sun started to penetrate the canopy.

"Let's hope we have enough ground coverage to avoid mud," Sumner said, stretching and yawning.

Octavia had a brief mental image of herself falling face first into the largest puddle of mud imaginable and shuddered. That was really the only problem with adventuring. She didn't much like dirt. She wasn't afraid of it like her mother had been, but she didn't relish getting dirty. She would have to get over it.

"Worry not. Mud is only a temporary thing, but the fresh air and peace of the forest will rejuvenate us on the walk," Alces said with a grin.

"We'll have to clean off before going back into the tent tonight," she said as they cleaned up after breakfast and prepared to head out.

"I have plenty," Durante said, drawing out one of his bottles of solvent that cleaned anything.

Another nice feature of the tent was when it folded up into its little box, it didn't have much surface area to clean and was spotless in less than a moment before it got tucked away.

Grateful for her leather boots, Octavia tucked the tent away and headed up the slope, wanting to be ahead of Alces for once instead of behind - she was confident he would kick up mud on merit of the shape of his feet. The forest was starting to lighten a little, the trees becoming more spaced and the canopy falling away to sky breaks above them. It had lightened up enough and was on enough of a slope that they could see the lake off in the distance. It was a beautiful walk, and she had to admit he had been right. The forest after the rain, with a slight mist still hanging in the air in the late morning, was peaceful and restorative.

"Something's here," Sumner said, pointing out how a flattened path was starting to form and some of the green was broken and pushed aside.

"Beast?" Alces asked, unstrapping his shield from his back and readying it.

"No. This was padded out. Cleared on purpose," Sumner said, crouching down to look at the start of the trail. Durante moved a little closer to Alces and unslung his rifle. They all paused for a moment, looking and listening.

Octavia stopped and looked from Sumner to the cleared path. "Odd that it begins in the middle of the forest," she commented, a little more quietly.

Sumner nodded and looked around, then pointed downhill. Just a little ways down, the undergrowth was quite a bit heavier and they could make out a pond. Without the mist, it would have been a lot easier to see.

"Fishing or water source," he commented, a little quieter.

"Let us continue," Alces said, looking around and sniffing the air. "They'll be friendly, or they won't, we must progress regardless."

"But who's 'they'?" Durante asked.

Sumner shrugged. Impossible to tell at the moment. Octavia nodded and moved closer to Alces as they continued forward. She hoped it was nothing to be concerned about. It had been such a lovely, quiet morning so far.

They moved carefully down the path, continuing to head vaguely north. Rain had made the path muddy and a little slick, which made Sumner move off the path and slink through the grass to the side. Alces had no problem, as his clawed feet could easily grip into the earth.

Then, there was a sudden flurry of activity. Alces twitched, Sumner whistled, and Alces spread himself out so his shield protected Octavia, his arm in front of Durante, and a sudden burst of arrows came out of the woods. They clattered harmlessly off of the shield and Alces' armor.

Octavia darted back behind Alces, though the mud made the movement less graceful and she had to scramble a little. From the corner of her eye, Octavia spotted Sumner scrambling up a tree and hiding in the shadow of the leaves. Alces remained unmoved, Durante using his outstretched arm as a brace to steady his rifle. Blue energy started to crackle in her hand as she looked about, trying to see where the arrows had come from.

"Show yourselves," Alces said with a loud authority. "We don't want to hurt you, but we will defend ourselves."

A half-dozen or so hairy creatures came into the light. They were humanoid, with molted brown fur that blended with the tree bark, long pointed ears, sharp teeth, and beady yellow eyes. The fur around the face was black, giving the impression of a beard. Their armor was patchwork of cured bark and, where they may have stolen or salvaged, leather and metal.

Snarling and hooting, they moved in and out of the trees, but they didn't seem to approach. A stray arrow came out of the woods and tinged against Alces' armor. He was completely unfazed.

"You walk on our land," came a deep voice from the forest. Following it was a larger version of the other creatures, wearing far more armor than the smaller ones and holding a morningstar that had clearly seen better days. "Your bodies will feed our land."

Alces straightened up but kept his arms where they were. "Forgive us, it was not our intention to trespass," Alces said. "Allow us passage and we'll never return."

"No," the larger creature shouted. "No leave. Die!"

"Well, I tried," Alces said with a sigh. "Volley!"

On command, Durante fired his rifle, striking one of the smaller ones and sending it into a spin before falling wetly to the ground. Two arrows fired down in quick succession from where Sumner had hid, downing two more of the forest brigands. Octavia was a beat behind, but caught on quick enough, dropping to one knee in the mud so that the arcs of blue energy that shot from her hands went out below Alces' shield into two of the smaller attackers. She thought they were bugbears—she'd never seen one in person, but she'd read about them.

Seeing a handful of his compatriots killed or disabled sent the chieftain into a fury. He dashed forward, spiked mace raised as he ran towards Durante.

"You face me," Alces said, and Octavia could feel the power in his words. The bugbear immediately turned towards Alces and ran up, swinging with all his might. The dragonkin held up his shield and the impact rang through the woods, the knight unmoved.

"Get the chaff, we have more coming in," Sumner yelled from the trees as he sent another arrow into the arm of one of the archers, taking it out of the fight. More were pouring out of the woods now, like a kicked nest.

"Oh, shit," Octavia muttered and got up. She wanted to give Alces some distance so that he wasn't tripping over her. She stumbled into the grass to get off the slick path and sent two more bolts of crackling blue energy into the hooting horde.

More were coming out, and Sumner's attacks had been put on hold as arrows started to fly his way, and he needed to use his tree as cover. Durante had moved to the side as well, ducking behind a felled tree and popping up to fire when he could.

"Dragon fire out," Durante yelled, pulling a glowing orange ball of glass from his coat and chucking it towards the horde. It hit one of the trees and erupted into a burst of fire, sending several of them into the mud and one of them running off, screaming as its flaming body disappeared into the woods.

Another electric blue blast as Octavia looked about for cover that wasn't the massive dragonkin. As she moved, she reached into her bag, digging for one of her vials. She would have to be more careful in the future, more at the ready.

Alces and the chieftain were locked in but the dragonkin knight was holding his own easily. From the outside, it was a one-sided fight; each of the bugbear's blows were intercepted by his shield or parried by his own mace while Alces struck into the creature's shoulders, arms, and legs; wearing it down.

"Relent," Alces said, but thus far the beast seemed undeterred.

Sumner dropped down from the tree perch he was on and slipped into the woods, the creatures currently unaware of his change of position as more arrows hit the trunk and branches where he'd been hiding.

Octavia's hands closed on the vial she was after, and she started to run, the scrub and rock of the forest floor giving her a sure footing. Moving closer to the line of archers, she poured out the vial, casting the spell as the last grain of sand left the glass. Heavy dark blue fog rose, engulfing a wide swath of the forest and all the little bugbears inside. Searing heat and shrieks of pain, as well as strange, chilling whispers emanated from the fog. She didn't stop moving, though the arrows died off significantly. She headed towards another tree. Cover was still a good idea.

Alces slammed his mace into the chieftain's hip, dropping him to the ground on one knee. The beast looked up at him, fangs bared. "You strong," he said, spitting blood onto the dirt at Alces' feet. "You strong enough, send us to Kovrakkish!" The chieftain then let out a bellow that echoed through the trees. He grinned up at Alces, which the dragonkin simply tilted his head to the side, curious what that was supposed to do.

"Oh, deepest shadows," Durante muttered as he looked down the trail. Something was coming, something big.

Alces wretched the rusty morningstar from the chieftain's hands and tossed it into the underbrush, far away. Considering the creature with the broken hip out of the fight, Alces stepped forward to consider the new threat.

Crashing noises and more hooting filled their part of the woods until a vile looking giant pushed its way through into the light. The monstrosity was green of skin and wore nothing, its rubbery skin covered in blisters that oozed purple. Horrid claws tipped its fingers and pointed teeth lined its mouth.

Octavia's step slowed for a moment as she looked back to see the monster crashing towards them. "Goddess of Mercy," she whispered, eyes wide. The shock only lasted a moment, and then she was running again, ducking behind a cluster of bushes. It wasn't great cover, but it would give her a minute to find something better.

"Troll problems," Alces called out, and Durante ducked back behind his log, rummaging through his bag.

"Tavi," Durante called out, pulling out a clip of red-coated bullets, "do you have any fire magic?"

Alces tsked slightly, not having fire of his own, but he'd hold fast so the others could work on it. The other bugbears stopped attacking, instead chanting from the forest and banging their weapons against the trees. Sumner moved towards the bugbears in the trees, drawing his sword and cutting them down until they started to run away.

"Yes!" Octavia called back, "but only—" She cut off and looked up over the bush. The weapon enchantment was the only true magical fire she had. She could probably enchant Alces' mace, but she had to get closer.

The vile troll suddenly burst forward, roaring out at Alces and raking down on him. The knight blocked the blow but could do little more at the moment than deflect against the assault.

"Gods guide me," she muttered and darted back out of her cover. She didn't have to be right next to Alces, but she did need to be a lot closer to him. She did her best to move between the trees as she ran. She hit the path again and slid, falling onto her hip but keeping stable enough to use her fall to get her close enough.

"Alces, fire incoming!" She threw up her hand, blue flame sparking at her fingertips and arcing to engulf the head of the mace.

"Ideal, Octavia," Alces grunted as he deflected a claw but took the other on his shoulder. The armor took the majority of the blow but it did bite and Alces hissed.

Looking to create a distraction, Durante moved to flank and fired off shots at the troll. The bullets burst into flames as they traveled, sizzling as they struck into the monster's flesh. More of the oozing purple splashed out from the hits and Alces raised his shield to guard against it as well.

The distraction worked, however, and Alces swung his mace, smashing it into the side of the troll. It roared out in pain, boils near the impact bursting and more of its purple ooze splashing out onto Alces. He had to glance away so none of it hit his face, but that gave the troll an opening. The monster backhanded Alces, knocking him off his feet and sending him to the ground.

"NO!" Octavia's eyes grew wide, and the void of fog she had raised earlier fell, revealing a lot of crispy bugbears but a surprisingly unmolested forest. She spun on her knees, facing the troll, and brought up her hands to cast. An ear-splitting scream erupted from behind the troll, rippling out in a wave of force that stopped short of Alces, splintering the smaller trees too close to the path. The creature spun around, holding its ear, eyes wild as it looked about.

"How ya doing, big guy," Sumner said, climbing up another tree to get to higher ground.

"I will live," Alces grunted, rising to a knee before standing back up. "My thanks." The dragonkin needed to shake his head to release the daze. Reaching into his bag, he pulled out a helmet he rarely wore, but this battle seemed to warrant it. It slid down over his triad of horns and covered his face. It looked to be an intertangling of several clusters of elk antlers.

Landing its gaze on Octavia, the troll snarled, figuring her scream had caused the noise that rang in its ears. Holding up an arm, it cut a gash into it with its opposite claw and flailed it at Octavia. A spurt of the purple ichor splashed over her.

"Ah!" Octavia flinched back, the ichor falling over her shoulder and down her arm and the front of her pants, though blessedly missing her face and cleavage. It felt like someone had rubbed sumac all over her, itching and burning. She had the sense to pull her small dagger and cut off the sleeve it was soaking into, using the cloth to try to wipe it from her forearm, even as the burning intensified.

"Tavi," Sumner roared out, his arms and legs elongating as his face drew back and his ears and teeth grew, taking on a slightly more animal appearance. Leaping from the branch he'd been perched on, he took to the air, firing several shots into the troll before landing on its shoulders. Tossing his bow, he drew his sword, but before he could fatally strike the creature, it swatted at him, forcing him to tumble off.

Durante rolled over his log and crouched to brace his rifle, firing shot after shot into the monster. Alces slammed his mace into its calf, causing it to roar out and start to stumble. A gap presented, Alces ran to Octavia and slid to a stop next to her, planting his shield and setting a hand on her. "Octavia, are you alright?"

"It hurts," she said through clenched teeth. Really, "hurt" was an understatement. The oiled canvas of her pants protected her leg, but her arm itched like mad and also felt like it was on fire. She had wiped it off as much as she could, but her skin was already starting to blister, worse where she hadn't been able to clean it well.

"It spews a vile venom," Alces said. His scales and spiritual gifts had mostly protected him. "I can ease it, but we will need to wait to purge it entirely." Closing his eyes, Alces set a hand down on her arm, gripping it gently. It started to tingle as the power of the Spree Spirits flowed through their paladin and began to ease the pain. A cooling sensation coating her arm and while it still stung, the burning and itching had started to subside.

"Thank you," Octavia said, unable to completely keep a quaver out of her voice. The touch of relief somehow made the initial pain worse.

"It's not dead yet," Sumner yelled, dashing in to take a swipe at its leg, then moving out of the way before it could retaliate. "Kill this giant fucker!"

"I'm working on it," Durante said, sending another volley of burning bullets its way. "Keep it busy." Rolling behind a tree, Durante started to rummage in his bag again.

"Oh, I could do this all day," Sumner said, baring his teeth, easily sidestepping the troll's next attack and stabbing its arm with a dagger he produced suddenly in his off hand.

The monster tried desperately to hit Sumner, but the acrobatic expert easily moved out of the creature's way, making it pay for each attack with another gash. So far, he was lucky enough not to get hit by the poison spilling out, and the wounds he was giving it were slowly starting to heal. Looking up across at Sumner, Octavia braced herself against Alces and cast again. Lifting her arm sent a shock of pain through her, but not so much that she couldn't still do it. Fire leapt from her hand to Sumner's blade, and then she fell into Alces.

Alces held her close, still shielding her to ensure no more of the splatting hit her from Sumner's attack. Holding his free hand out, Alces narrowed his eyes. "Blessed Spirits, bind the will of this forest, aid your servant to fell this monster." he chanted. Ethereal vines uncoiled from the muddy earth and lashed out towards the troll, grappling its arms and neck, pulling it to the ground.

The beast fell to its knees, its back arched as the vines pulled its head back, its arms struggling against the holy tendrils. Sumner took the opening and made two fiery gashes in its chest, dodging away from the poison. This time, his cuts did not heal thanks to Octavia's enchantment.

"Sumner, catch," Durante shouted, tossing something from his bag at the rogue. Sumner caught it, leaping up and driving the device into the creature's skull. The acid within the injector Durante provided started to eat away at the troll's skull and brain, coursing through it and starting to weaken its flesh.

His blade still dancing with fire, Sumner spun around and drove his sword down, lopping the troll's head off. Between the acid and the fire that burned from several wounds, the monster could not regenerate and fell lifeless to the ground, the vines dissipating into mist. A cry of relief escaped from Octavia as the creature began to burn. But then she looked back to the rest of the forest, remembering the veritable army of bugbears that had come to witness the battle. They had killed so many of them, but were there more?

Durante stood up and started to look around, changing out the clip of ammunition and averting his gaze from the mess that used to be a troll. Sumner hadn't cooled down, and he started to walk towards the chieftain who had been crawling off the path.

"Oh, we're not done yet," Sumner growled, a vicious grin on his face. The chieftain started to back away, holding up a hand and muttering.

"Fukav, fukav, fukav," the chieftain said in a panic, his confidence gone when the troll's head left its neck.

"Oh, fuck off," Sumner said, and gave the chieftain the same fate as the troll.

"Easy, we have a moment," Alces said, cradling Octavia and placing a hand on her chest. Closing his eyes, he started to chant softly, and she could feel more of a radiating warmth as the blisters subsided and the fog that was starting to form in her mind cleared.

The flames left Sumner's and Alces' blades as Octavia swooned in Alces' arms. "Goddess of Mercy bless you, my knight," she murmured as she began to come back to herself. Her arm still ached, but the ache was nothing compared to the burning that had been before.

Sumner whipped the blood off his blade and turned back towards where the bugbears had come from and started stomping in that direction. Alces helped Octavia to her feet and kissed her forehead. "I will always be your shield, my sweet Octavia," Alces said.

She put a hand to her head, still a little unsteady. "Please tell me they're going to give up and leave."

"I think they ran away," Durante said, looking into the distance as he walked.

"I'm gonna kill 'em all," Sumner said, crouching as he got ready to run in that direction. Alces stepped in and grabbed Sumner before he got far.

"Calm, my friend," the dragonkin said, resting a hand on his back. "They are defeated. They will bother us no more with their champion and chieftain dead. It is done."

Sumner struggled a bit, but Alces' grasp was iron. "They hurt Tavi, they're going to die," Sumner said. Shocked, Octavia looked up at Sumner. The rage in him surprised her, but even more so that it was on her behalf.

"The troll hurt Tavi, and you felled it quite handily," Alces said, his voice even. "Calm."

She stumbled up to the two of them, and stepped in front of Sumner, setting a hand on his chest. "Sumner," she murmured, "my storm, I'm all right. The troll and the chieftain are dead. Let's just go."

"I... mmf... fine," he muttered, finally settling. The length in his appendages diminished, the fur on his arms and legs disappeared, and his face returned back to his normal human self.

Durante caught up to them, slinging his rifle again. "Bugbears, yeah? If I remember correctly, the strongest leads, and we dropped him, so they'll be too afraid to come after us until a new chieftain is chosen, which will be a while," he said, looking everyone over.

Mostly they were okay. Sumner was untouched, Octavia was out of danger, and it would be unknown how hurt Alces was as he would shrug anything off, so they wouldn't be able to tell until they got his armor off.

"The trail will help. We'll take it as far as we can until night falls, let it buy us some time," Alces said. "Octavia, do you wish to have Nutmeg while you heal?"

"I—" she started, turning towards Alces, determined to tell him that she would be fine, when exhaustion hit her hard enough to make her swoon again. She put one hand to her head and the other reached for Sumner again to steady herself, then nodded. "Yes, perhaps I should. Durante, can I get some cleansing solution? Alces needs it for his armor as well, that puss from the troll is nasty business."

"Sure, sure," Durante said, pulling out one of the vials and handing it to her.

Alces made a motion with his hand, and the proud great elk stepped out from behind a tree and trotted towards Octavia. Stepping up, he snuffled her face and nibbled her shoulder with his lips.

"Easy," she said softly, the skin of her exposed shoulder healed but still tender.

"I'm sure she did," Alces said to Nutmeg as he picked up Octavia and settled her on the elk's back. "But now, please carry our fair girl as she heals." The elk chuffed once more and turned its head to give her leg another little soft nibble.

Sumner still needed a moment to pace, but he took that moment gathering his spent arrows from the corpses of bugbears. The sun was reaching its zenith in the sky; they still had a lot of walking to do.

Durante splashed a little of his solvent on Alces' armor as he wasn't really paying attention, then stepped up near Nutmeg, placing a hand on Octavia's leg. "Let me know if anything else is bothering you, I'll whip something up," he said gently.

Smiling, Octavia reached out and ran a hand through Durante's hair. "I'm all right. Really, I am. Alces did a good job. I ache, and I'm surprised at how tired I am, but I'm okay."

Sumner finished gathering his arrows and cooling down and rejoined the group as they started to move along. The trail helped them make up time considerably, and while they could hear movement and see the occasional pair of eyes on them, nothing dared venture out of the woods towards them.

As they walked, Octavia found it impossible to stay awake. Nutmeg was very comfortable, and his steady gait seemed to rock her. She slowly dropped down until she was laying across his broad back, loosely holding his neck, and drifted off to sleep.

THIRTEEN

She woke to Alces carefully removing her from Nutmeg's back and carrying her into the tent. He passed through the main area, straight to her room, and set her down gently on her bed. Brushing her hair off her face, he leaned down and kissed her forehead.

Blinking, Octavia looked up and blushed. "Oh, my knight. I'm sorry I fell asleep. Did we make it out of the forest?"

"No need to apologize, dear Octavia" he said, crouching down next to her bed. "You were poisoned. I purged the last of it out of your system as you slept. The road is just over a rise; we'll stay within cover for the evening."

"Cover is good. Is Sumner all right?" She asked, trying to understand his rage. They had been in fights before, but... well, she really hadn't gotten hurt before. Not more than superficially.

"Fiery Sumner is fine. He has an anger in him that sometimes needs to come out. I can send him in, if you'd like," he said. "Are you hungry? I was about to make dinner. Is there something you'd like?"

"Whatever you make will be good, though I hope you see to your shoulder first," she said, remembering the blow he took. "And yes, send Sumner in. He can help me change."

"You can examine it all you like later," he said with a smile. Standing up, he caressed her hair gently. "Take your time, good food takes a moment to cook."

She was left alone for barely a moment before Sumner came back in, sitting down next to her on the bed.

"Hello, my beautiful flower, how're you feeling? Alces said you wanted me? I mean, you should always want me," he grinned, giving her a wink.

"Hello, my storm," she said, pushing herself up carefully. "Feeling much better. The dullest of aches still in my arm, but I'm clear headed again, and the sense of illness and lethargy are gone." She looked down at her missing sleeve and sighed. "I liked this shirt. I don't have a lot in dark purple. Oh well."

"We'll get you a whole wardrobe in dark purple," he said with a grin and fluffed her pillow behind her back.

She looked back up at Sumner. "I was a little worried about you. I've seen your temper, but never like that."

He shrugged. "They hurt you. I don't care much for you being hurt, that's all."

She smiled a little and tipped her head to the side. "Didn't you and Durante tell me that people were going to get hurt, and I needed to learn to deal with it? Maybe that was Durante." She reached out and took his hand. "I don't think anyone has been that upset about me being injured in my life."

"Just because you might get hurt doesn't mean I have to accept it," he said with a half-smile, squeezing her hand. "And they should be upset if you get hurt. You're too... good to be hurt."

She snickered. "I don't know about good. I do know that I broke my arm on my last job with a group, when a priceless bust fell on me and broke. I was screamed at for almost half an hour before anyone was willing to hear that my arm had been broken." She shook her head. "I wasn't even the one who knocked it over."

"You tell me who they are, and I'll break their arms and yell at them for wasting my time," he grumbled, but then gave her another smile.

She looked at Sumner for a moment, wanting to press further, but decided not to. "If you are all right, then I won't worry. I was hoping you could help me change."

"I do enjoy undressing you. I suppose I can be convinced to put clothes back on you," he said, offering his help.

"You'll still have to undress me first," she said with a smile, taking his hand and getting up on her feet. "The problem is mostly the shirt, I feel like raising my arms is going to be unpleasant."

"Keep the one arm down, and we'll slide it off that way," he said, leaning in to kiss her softly before doing as asked. Unsurprisingly, Sumner was very adept with his hands and was able to slip the material off one arm and up over her head before coming down the sore arm. Tossing it aside, he turned her around and slid his hands around her sides to the front of her bra. He unlaced it as he leaned in to kiss her neck and shoulder.

She murmured softly, leaning into him. As the lacings came undone and the bustier fell away, she turned again, wrapping her good arm around him as she drew her tongue up the side of his neck before biting softly just below his ear.

"Have I told you that it's incredible to watch you fight," she murmured before catching his earlobe between her teeth and sucking at it lightly. She let go and nuzzled at him. "You're so fast and graceful."

Sumner purred gently as she teased him. His hands came up to caress along her back, tracing the soft curves. "Tavi, I'd fight for you anytime," he murmured.

She stepped back with a little grin. "Ah, the velvet top is right over there."

He sighed dramatically and slumped, walking over and picking up the blouse in question. "Tease," he said, coming back and gently moving her arm to help her pull it on.

She leaned in and kissed him again once the top was on, before turning around so that he could fasten it in the back. "Give me a day for the arm to get better, and then I'll make good on my teasing. All right?"

"I suppose that's fair," he said with a chuckle and tied her velvet top. "Which pants do you want? Or is it skirt time?"

"I think a skirt will be good for the night," she said with another little smile, sitting down to start taking off her boots. "Can you grab me the pink one? Unless you wanted to undress the rest of me. I can probably get it myself, but you did say you liked it."

"Oh, full service," he smiled, looking around and finding the pink one before coming back to kneel before her. Smiling, he placed the skirt on the bed and helped her finish removing her boots, then went through the process of unlacing her pants and working them off her hips. Octavia needed to bounce a few times to get them down off her curves, but once they were down to her thighs, he slid them off.

As he did so, however, he followed behind with his mouth, kissing down her leg as the pants exposed more and more flesh. She moaned softly as he traveled over her skin. He gave her foot a playful nip, which made her giggle, then tossed her pants to join her tattered shirt.

Biting her lip, she shifted towards the edge of the bed. "The panties, too. I don't tend to wear any underskirts."

With a lascivious smirk, Sumner grabbed her ankles in one hand and carefully lifted her legs up until they were nearly vertical. His other hand worked the panties off until they were on her thighs. Her legs still together from the way he held them and the panties, he leaned in and took a swipe at her pussy with his tongue. She clenched her teeth around another moan.

Satisfied with teasing her, he set her legs back down and pulled the panties all the way off, discarding it with the rest. Clearing his throat, he grabbed her skirt and slid it up her legs. As he inched the skirt up, she stood up in front of him to make it easier. This also put her sex at the level of his eyes, the evidence of arousal shining on her skin even in the dim light.

"I hope we're not too worn out tomorrow night," she said, her breath a little faster than it had been.

"Just a little walking," he said, giving her another swipe of his tongue before standing. Smiling, his fingers somehow graced her sex as he lifted her skirt up and rested it on her hips.

"There, all dressed," he said with a grin.

"You're an utter rake," she said with a matching grin, and pulled him in again for a kiss before letting him go. "Thank you, my storm. Let's see how dinner's going."

"Happy to," he said, escorting her out of her room. "Any time."

Durante was posted on a couch again, this time cleaning his rifle as opposed to reading. Alces was working on dinner, which was a collection of ingredients for the moment, but she could already smell cooking berries.

"You feeling okay, Tavi?" Durante asked as he picked his head up and smiled at her.

Drifting over to the couch, Octavia ran a hand through Durante's hair. "I am, yes. The arm is sore, but I suspect I'll barely notice by tomorrow." She bent to kiss his cheek, then came around and sat down next to him, tucking her feet up beside her, but leaving them out of his lap while he worked.

Once dinner was ready, everyone had finished their tasks and were dressed more comfortably. "I tried to copy some of the food the stalls were selling in Limanyadeli. Let me know what you think," he said, setting down a couple of trays.

The first was piled with soft, fresh flat bread. The second had a lamb shank that he had seasoned and sliced thin, accompanied by various peppers and chopped cucumbers. Lastly, there was a red sauce that had a strong tomato and garlic flavor with a bright lemon and mint accompaniment.

He demonstrated by taking a piece of flat bread, smearing the sauce on it, then layering some of the lamb with the vegetables, then finally rolling it up to make it easy to pick up. In his large hands, and with his mouth, it disappeared in an instant, but he grinned and waited for everyone else to eat afterwards. Octavia smiled but followed Alces's instruction, layering sauce, meat, and vegetables before sitting back and eating significantly more slowly. The spice of the meat was accentuated by the sauce, and the whole experience was intensely more flavorful than one might expect from camp cooking.

"Ser Knight, you're going to ruin tavern food for me," she said with a grin between bites.

"Nonsense," he said with a laugh as the others nodded in agreement with Octavia's statement. "I was inspired, and I wanted to make something special. We'll run out of the more interesting spices, and we'll be back to stews and roasted forage in no time."

Once dinner was complete, Alces pulled out the dessert he'd been letting sit in the oven. Setting the heavy pot down on the table, he gave everyone spoons. It appeared to be a collection of biscuits with a slight caramelized sugar crust, resting on top of a layer of stewed berries.

"I used the last of our berries with this, but it seemed like a good time to do it," Alces said.

Sumner prodded with his spoon enough to break off a piece of biscuit with some of the berries and blew on it gently. When he was finally able to take a bite, he grinned again. "I don't know if you'll ever retire, big guy, but if you do, run an inn. Fame and fortune will follow."

Octavia leaned forward and scooped out a bite, holding her hand under it to catch any drips and blowing on it gently before trying it. The berries were sweet with a touch of tartness, there was some cinnamon and something else in there, and the biscuit was soft and beautifully crumbly.

"Oh, Gods," she murmured and slid off the couch onto her knees to get closer to the pot.

Alces couldn't help but laugh, and she swore his violet eyes glowed a little as he watched them eat. Even Durante got a taste of it, but his hunger for food always lacked in comparison. The knight had a few sizable bites himself, but as usual he waited until everyone else had their fill.

Octavia ate Durante's portion and then crawled back into the couch overfull. "I may have made a grave error, but it was worth it." She sighed contently and stretched out, rubbing her feet against Durante's leg before sliding them into his lap. He had set the rifle aside for dinner, so surely this was all right for a moment.

"A good meal can cure what magic and medicine cannot," Alces said as he tucked away the leftovers into the cold box. While he would destroy leftover meats, the desserts he seemed well enough to save for later.

"So, how much longer we got?" Sumner asked Durante, settling in. He'd almost eaten as much as Octavia had. They'd even dueled spoons for a few bites, but the rogue had relented.

"A day, depending, until we get to Boulcairn. Note says the person we're looking for is beyond the town, near the cliffside," Durante answered, pulling out the map to look it over.

"Damn," Octavia murmured, pulling her feet out of the way so that Durante could spread the map out. "I suppose we'll see how far we get tomorrow. I really want to get a look at that book, but I don't want to breach wards in a town."

"Maybe we should camp out before the border, then," Durante said, pointing to the map. The city was only a couple of miles from the border between the beyliks of Yadeli and Algeleli. "That way, anything happens, it's far from anyone and doesn't cause people to think we're starting something between states."

"Would you mind?" she asked, looking over at him. "I could wait. I don't want to impact your timing or anything. But if it will take us most of the day anyway, I suppose it wouldn't be that big of a deal to stop outside of town."

"We saved so much time going through the forest, I don't think it's a problem," Durante said, looking hopeful towards the rest. Sumner shrugged. Alces grinned.

She smiled. "Thank you. I really only need one night. Like I said yesterday, it's some sort of charm spell. Just, you know, hold me down if I try to wander off or something. We should be able to go into town the next morning just fine."

"We shall keep you safe regardless," Alces said as everyone started to put things away and get ready for bedding down. "Restraining you will not be a problem."

"Think you'll need someone to watch you? Make sure nothing weird is going on," Sumner said with a raised brow.

She considered for a moment as she helped clean up. "Maybe. I plan on casting a protection circle regardless. Stay out of the circle, and you should be fine, but if something goes wrong, you'll know immediately."

"I think I should watch over her," Durante said as he cleaned up around the table. "I'll be able to tell when the magic starts to bend and might notice if powers from the embodiment of lust are affecting her and it's not just... Tavi."

"Oh, you think so," Sumner said, a little surprised but still smirking.

"I do, yes," Durante said, standing up.

She looked between the two, brows arched, not entirely certain what was happening. Perhaps it was Durante's sudden confidence that had thrown Sumner. The artificer was often the quieter one.

"I can promise nothing will breach the circle," she said. "Whomever is out there will be safe. Mostly safe."

"Best idea," Alces said, turning around as he wiped his hands. "We're a team. You make the circle here, in the main room, and we all make sure you're safe. No worry about guessing, no worry about helping in time if something happens." The other two had to relent. It did make the most sense.

She blinked. "Um, we'll have to clean up the circle after, but okay. That should be fine. Magic gets absorbed into the tent if it's collapsed, but while it's up it all seems to be fine."

"Also, this way your bedroom doesn't need to be messed up," Alces grinned and nodded.

She laughed a little. "Sure, make snacks, you can all watch me perform magic badly tomorrow. No heckling, though, I need to concentrate."

"I have just the idea for the snack," Alces said. The others laughed, but it seemed they were determined to watch and make sure all went well. There was also a general agreement about not heckling, but Sumner made no promises for afterwards. Octavia stuck her tongue out at him.

They all stayed up for a short while longer chatting. She got the impression they were all sort of making sure she was okay. It struck her that she never expected them to become protective of her. She had once feared they might fight over her, but she never considered that the three of them together would be devoted to her safety. She wasn't sure what it meant.

Eventually she headed to bed alone, a little reluctantly. Not that she had the energy to pay Sumner back for his teasing earlier—she was wiped out, and her arm was still sore—but something about the fight made her want to be next to one or all of them. She shook her head and climbed into bed, sleep stealing up on her as her head settled on the pillow.

Another early morning, but this time she was woken gently by Alces, coaxing her awake with a soft touch and calling her name quietly, or at least as quietly as he could.

"Dear Octavia, time to wake. We have breakfast cooking," he said.

She yawned and looked up at Alces, blinking in surprise. He'd never come into her room to wake her before, usually calling through the curtain. She had to say this was far more pleasant than the usual startled flailing.

"Thank you, my knight," she mumbled sleepily, yawning again. She stretched and could still fill a dull ache in her arm, but it was already much better than the day before.

"How are you feeling?" he asked, helping her to a sitting position with a hand on her back. "I wanted to check you over once more before we left. I was sure I had purged the poison from your system, but I am unfamiliar with it."

"I think I'm doing good," she said, pushing her mane of curls back out of her face. "There's still a faint ache, but I think I'll be fine today."

Alces moved his hands to her arm and caressed it with his fingers, examining it. "Very well," he said after a moment. "As long as you only feel an ache, and it doesn't get worse. Let me know if anything changes." He leaned forward, pressing his forehead to hers, then stood.

There was something very touching about that gesture. He was the only partner she'd ever had who did it. It was like a kiss, but somehow more? It was hard to explain.

"I shall let you dress. Breakfast will be ready after, then we walk," he smiled.

"I'll be out soon, I promise," she said with a smile. She waited until he stepped out of the room and climbed out of bed. She'd slept naked and didn't feel like teasing him before their long day on the road.

In short order she was dressed, hair up, and heading into the main room. At least her moon cycle was over. One less thing to worry about.

It seemed Durante had not awoken yet, but Sumner and Alces were finishing up breakfast. It was the most straightforward of cooked meals Alces had made so far since they restocked. Slices of fried ham, a fresh fruit compote, and fluffy biscuits.

"There she is," Sumner said, looking over his shoulder. "All good today?"

"Arm's still a little sore, but much better," she said as she walked up. "Nothing that will keep me from keeping up. Is Durante getting up or does he need poking?"

"Might as well fetch him. He'll certainly like it more coming from you," he laughed.

"Be quick, though. Time to eat," Alces added as he put the last of the biscuits on the table.

"Oh, I'll hurry for fresh biscuits," she said with a grin and darted to Durante's curtain. "Hey, Kitten," she called out before stepping inside. "Are you up?"

Sitting in his breeches on the side of his bed, Durante nodded and smiled up at her. "I'm awake, Tavi," he said with a yawn. "Think things are running their course. Just a little sluggish this morning."

"Gods, you're so cute in the mornings," she murmured and walked up to give him a warm kiss. "I'm sorry I can't be your late-night snack more often."

"I could never ask—" he started to protest, then sighed and gave her a half smile. "Right, you're fine with it. Probably for the best, or I might get addicted." Standing up, he stretched and looked for his clothes.

"Would that be so bad?" she asked with a teasing grin. She gave him a hug and kissed his chest, then let him go about getting dressed. "I'll see you out there."

"I'll be out in a minute. Thanks."

Popping back out into the main area, she headed to the table. "See? Super quick. Reward me with biscuits."

Laughing, Alces pushed the plate towards her. "You've earned yourself biscuits."

Breakfast was a simple affair. Durante did arrive in due time and ate a little more than he normally did, but still far less than someone his size would. Cleaned up and ready to go, the group exited the tent. Alces called Nutmeg again and insisted that Octavia ride for at least half the day to ensure she was mended. Octavia didn't fight and took the opportunity to review her notes for the evening, digging out the book and giving it another examination. She was pretty sure it would be fine. She could see how the runes were structured, and they clearly weren't made to keep out anyone who knew actual magic. She didn't have the experience that, say, a wizard had, but she'd studied a lot these past seven years. It should be okay.

The day's journey was uneventful. The combination of moving further north and the increase in elevation meant it was growing swiftly colder, and they were getting some wind off the lake. They reached a point where they could see the border wall a few miles ahead as it was getting into the afternoon, so the day had been a relatively short one, as this is where they'd camp for the night.

Cover was light, as the forest had given way to more shrubs around the road, and certainly open near the border wall, but they were able to find a cluster of trees a few hundred yards off the road. Someone would have to be looking to find their tent in the shade that far out.

She felt a little guilty that they were ending their day so early, but Durante had said it was fine, and he was the one setting the pace right now. She was more than a little excited as they got the tent set up and made camp. She had only been after the book for a few months when the three of them had found her back in Gravemont, but she had gone after the tome the minute she learned of its existence. The journals and teachings of the last priests of Kamvasana. Three centuries or more ago, Kamvasana had been revered across Ascherol and Rupaiya, and likely neighboring kingdoms as well.

Then something happened. There were still shrines and small sects dedicated to Kamvasana in Rupaiya, but worship had disappeared in Ascherol. Not only of Kamvasana, but all the Primordials. Kamvasana wouldn't speak to Octavia of it, but she suspected that if she could figure out how to get people to honor the Essence of Desire once more, she'd be in a position to renegotiate her contract. She didn't want a lot, mostly little things. Like shirts that didn't immediately become scandalously revealing. Or being able to go more than seven days without sex. Well, that last part was less important than it used to be.

Alces went to work on something easy for dinner. Tonight looks like it was going to be another stew night, mostly of leftover meat and vegetables from previous dinners, with another fresh loaf of bread since he had time to make it. The other two went about following Octavia's directions on how to set up the main room so that she had enough space for the ritual.

"So, I just need room for a containment circle," she said, looking at the furniture. "Um, let's push the couch over by the chairs and get the table a little closer to it, and then I can draw the circle here, in front of the bedroom curtains."

While they moved furniture, she got a pouch out of her trunk that contained chalk, salt, and some other items she would need. She wasn't planning on getting started before dinner, but she could at least get everything set up. If she unraveled the wards fast enough, it wouldn't impact their sleep at all and they could still be headed out early the next day.

Most of preparing for dinner involved getting things started and waiting, so Alces joined Sumner in moving the furniture. Durante went back to his room to find any books he might have had on primordial magicks and any curatives that could cover any range of magical debilitations. Unfortunately, he was woefully short on books.

Once the furniture was out of the way, Octavia started to draw the circle. The magically taut fabric of the floor was a very easy surface to draw on, and she briefly wondered why she'd never done this in the past. Probably because this type of process could be messy, and she didn't enjoy the clean-up. Much less of a concern with sand circles on the forest floor.

This part took a little longer, as the circle had to be large enough for her to comfortably sit in the middle with the book in front of her. Technically it was two circles encased in a larger one - one for Octavia, one for the book, each with its own ring of protective symbols, and then even more around the larger circle to keep anything from escaping should something go horribly wrong. Octavia could still walk out of the circle, though, which was part of why it didn't hurt to have the three keeping an eye on her. If the spell confused her or made her try to wander, the circle wouldn't stop her, but they could.

Dinner was relatively quick, as everyone was interested in what was going to happen. Sumner seemed the most expectant for something flashy, like all of Octavia's clothes bursting off or something ridiculously Kamvasana-like in that vein. Durante was the most serious, his tinctures for various things lined up and ready for administration. Alces seemed the most calm, having utmost confidence in Octavia and also having never felt an 'evil' presence from Kamvasana that fateful night when they'd visited the group when Octavia had not fulfilled her pact.

FOURTEEN

O kay, here we go," Octavia said as she slid out of her house slippers before stepping into the circle and using a bit of chalk to complete it, "locking" the energies inside. She laid the book out before her and set down a bowl filled with white sand that seemed to shimmer softly in the light. She knelt in her own circle. Alces held up a hand before him, in front of his chest, like he was cupping something and closed his eyes. He muttered a chant, softly as he could to not interrupt what she was doing, and the room felt a little warmer, but the climate had not changed.

She closed her eyes for a moment, breathing deeply, feeling the ebb and flow of all the spells around her before focusing on the book. She passed her hand over the bowl, and blue flames rose up from the sand, releasing a waft of some sort of incense, rich and spicy. Sensual. She let it burn for a moment before extinguishing the flame with her palm. She used a fingertip to stir the sand and ash, then sprinkled some in a circle around the book.

Durante was watching intently, even taking a few notes as he did so. He hadn't seen an actual ritual before, not a magical one at least, and undoubtedly wanted to know everything. He'd have questions after this was over. Sumner was lounging in one of the chairs, one leg over the arm, and chewed quietly on a piece of bread. He was interested in the subject, not the process.

Words forgotten centuries ago began to pour from Octavia's lips as she reached towards the book. She didn't touch it, not yet, her hands hovering outside the smaller circle. She could feel the protections falling into place. Everything was as it should be.

As she continued to chant, the sand and ash from the circle suddenly moved, drawn by an invisible force to the book, forming the runes that built the wards. She started to smile, and there was a slight catch in her breath—rituals were arousing, not only because this kind of magic was exciting, but because Kamvasana's magic always had a particular side effect. It wasn't overwhelming, a pleasant hum in her body.

Alces raised a brow ridge when the first tingles went through her body. The protective bond he had cast on her let him share her pain, take her wounds should something have happened. It seemed something else was also transferring through the bond. Much of the energies of Kamvasana and the Spree Spirits shared properties, origins, and etherics, and he was feeling that now.

The runes on the book began to glow fiery blue, and Octavia's smile grew wider as they lifted off the book, rotating in the air. The lock on the book popped audibly. The ritual wasn't complete, the wards still needed to be dispelled.

She started to unravel the wards, but the moment she began she understood that something was wrong. Her eyes grew wide, and her smile fell as she understood what was happening mere seconds before it happened. Her protective spells recognized the wards as sympathetic magic—her magic wasn't divine, but it still came from Kamvasana. Rather than grounding out in the ash as they should have, the wards followed the lines of her power, and she triggered every single one.

"Oh, no—" was all she made out before her body rocked with the power coursing into it. The wards had held up shockingly well over the centuries. She let out a cry as it coursed through her, but it wasn't pain. She fell forward onto her hands, panting, knocking over the bowl of sand and incense and smudging the chalk circle. It didn't matter. The magic was spent, and she had received it.

Durante and Sumner startled and reached for her. Alces held up a hand.

"I think she's fine," he said, though his words came a little slowly. "Give her a moment."

"I… the…" she panted and pushed herself up from the floor. A haze was settling over her, and it wanted only one thing. It was getting hard to think. "Same magic, the spell didn't… didn't stop it." She staggered forward. "I… I can't think. I need… I need…"

Durante had gotten to his feet in his concern, and so Octavia reached him first. Her hands slid over his chest to grab him by the collar, pulling him in to kiss him and kiss him hard. She moaned into it, lightheaded with want, and when she let him go to catch her breath she stumbled back and fell into Sumner's lap. Alces had a slightly better understanding of what was going on—the protective bond shared Octavia's state of arousal, though not the compulsion that was overwhelming her.

Sumner smirked slightly with the sudden package in his lap and grabbed her hips, "I knew it would do something like this," he said, looking her over, "but I expected more, I dunno, flash?"

"Yeah, uh huh," Durante said, licking his lips, tasting Octavia on them. "Are you alright, Tavi? Do you need something?"

"Need, yes," she murmured. Her skin tingled, sensitive like it typically only was after orgasm. She turned her head and licked at Sumner's neck.

"I need you," she murmured into Sumner's ear, then turned her head again and looked up at Durante, sitting up enough to grab him by the waist of his pants and pull him closer. "And I need you." She looked over at Alces as her hands slid over Durante's thighs. "And you."

"Well, I'm not going to argue with that," Sumner said, suddenly finding his pants painfully tight. Durante was having a similar issue, but his mind was racing.

"How do we, um," Durante started and Alces laughed. Not his usual boisterous bellow, but more of an affectionate chuckle.

"Lad, when a woman says she wants you, you don't ask how," he said, giving Octavia a hand up so she could stand, and so Sumner could do something about his pants. "You give her what she wants."

She accepted the hand up and looked up at Alces with a mix of hunger and adoration. Durante hadn't really stepped back, so she leaned into him, letting go of Alces so she could touch him. Skill and experience made it easy for her to get his pants undone and pull his shirt loose.

"Kitten," she murmured as her slender fingers undid his buttons. "It's… it's hard to focus, I just… I want you, and I can't choose, I could never—" She cut off as her mouth encountered his skin, leaving wet kisses before biting softly. She still felt lightheaded and set her forehead against his chest as she tried to focus enough to speak.

"You have me, Tavi," Durante said, quite taken in the moment at this point, focusing solely on her as his hands moved to cup her face, fingers entangling in her hair as he leaned down to kiss her. It was tender, but it was deep and longing.

"Gods, I'm on fire," she whimpered as the kiss broke. "Sumner, my blouse." It would be enough. He would understand. She shifted a little, rubbing her legs together. It felt like a river was running between her thighs, the light fabric of her lounge pants sticking to her skin as it was already wet.

Sumner had, in fact, understood and was behind her, reaching around to undo her blouse and slide it off her shoulders. Stepping up behind her, she could note he'd definitely already taken care of his own clothes and could feel his hardness nestling between her cheeks.

Certainly more forward than Durante, Sumner slid his hands around her as well, cupping her breasts and kneading them slowly as she kissed Durante. She was now sandwiched between them. Alces stepped back, knowing his presence would require someone to move out of the way. He sat in a chair, smiling faintly. If he could feel Octavia's desire he surely knew it was only a matter of time.

She moaned blissfully into the kiss. Magical accident or not, she had wanted this for a long time, to feel the two of them touching her. She knew distantly that her fantasy of all three of them was in reach, but she also knew they had all night.

They kissed until she had to breathe, breaking away with the gasp, swooning back into Sumner. She looked up at Durante starry eyed. "I adore you," she whispered. Somewhere in the back of her head her brain told her she needed to still be careful with what she said, but that voice was drowned out by desire and sensation.

Durante looked at her softly, affectionately as his hands slid from her hair and drifted along her neck until they parted slightly. "Oh, Tavi," he murmured, at a loss for words.

She reached back with one hand and slid her fingertips up into Sumner's hair, still gazing up at Durante. "Kitten, my pants." Nodding, he knelt before her.

"Take your time," Sumner said with a grin, leaning in to kiss and nibble at Octavia's neck. His hands never stopped and, with Durante out of the way, became more overt. Octavia was a chorus of whimpers and cries. She was loud. She always expressed herself in her pleasure, but there was nothing in her head telling her to keep quiet or try not to show how much she reveled in their touch. Teasing and pinching her nipples, squeezing her heavy breasts with the whole of his hands, trying to cradle as much of them as he could.

Durante finished with the fasteners and slid her pants off her hips and down towards the floor. Leaning in, he kissed her softly upon her tummy and moved his way down. Shyness in his movements was still present, but it wasn't enough to stop him from kissing over her pelvis, running his tongue across her clit, and dipping his tongue between her nether lips as he pooled her pants to the floor. The hand in Sumner's hair suddenly gripped the back of his neck. Her other hand slid through Durante's hair as he leaned in, letting out a musical cry as his tongue parted her.

"Oh, you like that? Sounds like you like that," Sumner said, giving her nipples a little twist. It wasn't hard, but it was certainly more firm than the others might do to her. That's how he was: a little more firm of hand, a little more demanding. With her pants now gone, Durante lifted one of her legs, setting her foot upon his knee, and started to kiss and nibble on her calf and thigh. His hands ran up her legs, over her hips, and over her ass and back to her sex. Touching, exploring, and wanting to please her.

Alces smiled and got up, heading back into the kitchen. Octavia's eyes drifted across the room and watched as Alces stepped back into the kitchen. She felt... guilty? But she couldn't think clearly enough to know what to do about it. Maybe it didn't matter right now. Maybe what mattered was that Sumner was holding her, and if she turned her head maybe he would kiss her. She wanted that.

At the turn of her head, Sumner took the cue and kissed her deeply, his grip a little more firmly on her breasts. She moaned against his mouth, sucking his tongue. She could feel his shaft nestled up between her cheeks, already smearing her with want. Her hand never stopped playing with Durante's hair, though it was harder to reach as he pulled back a little to tease her. She wanted the cock pressing against her, and wanted it badly, but not enough to interrupt her darling Kitten as he excited her skin and increased the intensity of her spell fueled desire.

She wondered, briefly, if Durante would be shocked by how she was wet enough that it painted her thighs, then wondered why it mattered. It was like being drunk, the way her mind drifted, unable to focus on a line of thought. The one thing she could focus on was how she felt. And she could feel how wet she was, feel it almost streaming down her legs. Durante didn't seem to be shocked, if anything, it excited him as well. At least, that's what the tongue that was sliding up her inner thighs then diving into her dripping pussy was indicating. His hands continued to massage and rub her thighs, squeezing her and touching her. She was growing lightheaded again, and had to break from her kiss with Sumner, gasping as she did.

"My storm," she breathed, looking up into his eyes with that same enchanted expression she'd favored Durante with a moment ago.

Sumner was panting gently, and she could see the spots starting to form around his face and arms as she excited him. He growled playfully in her ear and bit her lobe. "Do you want us," he asked, remembering her request, "right now?"

"Please." The word was a desperate whimper as her legs started to tremble. The hand in Durante's hair tightened, as did the one on Sumner's neck as she let out a cry that spiraled up into a musical note while she orgasmed. She drew in a sharp breath as she softened in Sumner's arms, moaning softly.

"Alright," Sumner said with a grin. Grabbing Octavia around the waist, he dragged her back as he sat down on the couch, seating her directly onto his lap. A little bit of maneuvering, and he was able to sink into her, Octavia saddled against him. She lost focus again as Sumner entered her, moaning. It felt exquisite. It always did, but it was like she couldn't properly appreciate it before. He gave her a love bite on her shoulder, then pushed her gently forward. Unable to think, only able to experience, she felt like she could count those strange nubs on Sumner's cock as he hilted within her.

Motioning to Durante, he gestured for him to stand before her. The dhampir got the hint and stood, walking and standing before Octavia. Sliding his hand up Octavia's back, Sumner grabbed a fist full of her hair and pulled her head back, putting her face-to-cock with Durante's shaft. The hand in her hair brought her back to the present, and she let out a gasp as he moved her where she needed to be.

"There you go, Flower. Both of us," he said, slowly rolling his hips beneath her.

"Gods, yes," she breathed, looking up at Durante with her luminous blue eyes.

She slid her tongue eagerly up the length of his shaft. She had never done this for him. She directed so many of their exchanges, but it had never unfolded this way.

"Take hold," Sumner said, smirking up to Durante, "I have work to do down here." Octavia felt Sumner move his hands back down, gripping her hips, and holding her in place as well as he could while thrusting up into her. It was steady but deep, not wanting to jostle her too much.

Durante stammered for a moment, then ran his fingers through her hair and gripped it gently. It was easy to feel the difference, his grip was more tender, less demanding, and his fingers moved. She let out another moan as she reached the head of his cock, swirling her tongue around it while Sumner started to fuck her. She had enough clarity to know she would make this the best cocksucking Durante had ever experienced. She had a reputation to uphold. She grabbed Durante's thighs and pulled him closer as she took him into her mouth, working her way down a little at a time, her tongue rubbing against the prominent vein. Her hands took turns, one holding onto him for stability while the other caressed his hips, his thighs, squeezed his ass. The moans stated Octavia's reputation was well placed. The twitching throb in his cock was a pretty strong indicator as well.

She was making a mess in Sumner's lap, gushing wet as he thrust into her. She was also coming again, though it seemed impossible. Maybe it was part of the spell. Maybe it didn't matter. Her nose hit Durante's pelvis as she clenched around Sumner.

"Oh, Tavi," Durante moaned, his grip in her hair more pronounced. In the suddenness of everything, he hadn't come yet, but feeling her throat him was getting him there. Already she could feel him swelling in anticipation, pre leaking onto her tongue.

"Fuck, she's wet," Sumner growled happily and used that to move her even more, friction not an issue. With her grip solid on Durante's thighs, Sumner was able to bounce her more roughly in his lap, using his grip on her hips to slam her down onto him with each thrust. With all the practice they'd had together, Sumner's stamina had certainly increased, and hard as he was, he wasn't on his peak yet either.

She pulled back from Durante enough to breathe and then let the rhythm of Sumner's thrusts set the pace for guiding Durante into her mouth. She was swallowing him again and again, hands massaging his thighs. Durante's grip tightened as he held on for dear life. All the while Sumner kept pounding into her, pleasure radiating from each thrust. She would tell him, after Durante came, how good it was. How she loved it. How she'd dreamed of this.

Octavia looked up at Durante, his cock fully engulfed in her mouth, her doe eyes glowing up at him, and he lost all possible resolve. "Tavi, I'm... I'm going to," was all he could whimper out before her efforts were rewarded. This was the first time she'd tasted him, and it was different. Given she was his last actual meal, the tingling on her tongue might have been an after effect from the fey touch.

"Mmmm!" She slid her hands around to grasp the cheeks of his ass and buried him in her throat again. She wanted all of it, every drop. She pulled back slowly, letting it sit on her tongue, noting the difference. She finally released him, falling back against Sumner as she swallowed and licked her lips.

"Darling, that was perfect," she said, panting heavily as Sumner kept up his pace. She turned in and nuzzled at the man still relentlessly fucking her. "Gods, you're so good at this...I've been dreaming about this since we met, did you know that?" She licked at his ear, moaning.

"We've done it a lot since we met," Sumner chuckled then nipped at her neck again. Durante was catching his breath, but it seemed this wave of lust she was spilling out was affecting the rest of them, as he didn't shrink in the least. If anything, he was harder.

"No, I mean with both of you," she said, laughing a little and still panting. "Though also just you. I'd play with myself almost every night thinking about it—" No, stop, that was too much again.

"My storm," she said, reaching up behind herself again to run her hands through his hair. "My beautiful storm. Fuck I want to feel you cum in me."

"You'll feel it soon, but first, I have an idea," Sumner said. With some notable restraint, he stopped and guided her to stand. She whimpered and turned her head to pout at him as he pushed her up. Big eyes, full lip, kicked-puppy pout.

"I know, but trust me." He nuzzled her neck and nibbled her ear, whispering into it, and she moaned in response. "You're going to love this."

Reaching down, he grabbed behind her knees and lifted her up, his chest holding up her back, and spread her wide. She let out a little surprised shriek as he lifted her. If there was one thing Octavia could note, all three of her boys were surely in shape.

"I'm going to fuck your ass now," he whispered, wiggling her around the tip of his cock. She was tight, he'd need some guidance. "And while I'm doing that, D's going to fuck your pussy. You'd like that, wouldn't you, Flower?"

Her eyes got wide, and a shudder passed through her at the promise in his words. "Yes! Yes, please, I would love it so much—"

Love. She loved. Would love. She... the haze took her mind again, she couldn't concentrate, especially not with Sumner gently pressing into her ass.

"D, get over here and grab her legs a second," Sumner said, needing a hand free to make sure his cock, which had been thoroughly lubed up from all the slick she was producing, went right where it was needed. Durante snapped out of it and moved forward, taking her legs by the crook of her knee and holding her there while Sumner eased himself in.

That telling purr came out of Sumner as he pressed into her ass, slowly stretching her as every inch sank into her. His hands moved to her ass, holding her stable while Durante kept her legs up and secure.

"Take her, brother," Sumner said and Durante blinked for a moment, but only a moment before lining himself up and sinking his shaft deep into her.

This was it; she now had both of them completely inside her, and they both moaned at how much tighter she had become. Her voice spiraled up again. It was like her dreams. Better than her dreams. She came again from the feel of them inside her. Had she always been like this? This easy to get off? She didn't think so… she didn't think…

She didn't think. She reached out to Durante, sliding a hand over his chest, up his neck to cup his face. "Amazing," she moaned, "you're both so amazing! You feel… ohhhh, Gods…"

"We're just getting started," Sumner said, starting to bounce her against the two of them. Everything felt doubled. Both cocks sliding out of her, then thrusting deep inside of her. Her body pressed against by two others, touching her, nuzzling against her neck and gazing into her eyes. The room seemed to spin, and the heat was building. She felt her body burning up with all the sensations.

"A little something to cool down," she heard Alces' voice cut through the haze. The dragonkin was towering over them, and in his hand he held a bowl with a spoon. Smiling, he glanced at her and Durante. "A treat for you both, I think."

Taking the spoon from the bowl, there was a white and purple swirled pudding in it. Carefully, he tilted the spoon over her breast, and what she thought was pudding fell onto her hot skin and a rushing sensation of cold radiated from it. She let out another startled cry at the drop of cold against her skin. The creamy concoction was just shy of frozen, and it dripped down the healthy curve and around her hard nipple.

With the grin remaining, Alces hefted her breast up and Durante wasted no time dipping his head down and latching his mouth onto her breast, engulfing her nipple and the frozen treat. The clashing sensations of the chilled cream and Durante's warm mouth was yet another pleasure on top of so many others.

The flood of sensation was overwhelming. It was even more intense than her night with Erash. And better in every way because it was with them. Her boys. She looked up at Alces with that same look of adoration and desire, lips parting as if to speak, but then the sensations overwhelmed her again, and her head fell back with another resounding cry.

Carefully, Alces dribbled a little more on her other breast, which Durante dutifully licked and sucked off her skin, paying particular attention to her nipple. His fangs brushed against her, making her shiver. She wanted him to bite, to feed, but she also knew what her blood did to him on a day when she wasn't bespelled. Alces took another scoop and placed it on his tongue, a tongue Octavia had felt but never quite seen this long, and caressed her face, presenting it to her.

Opening her eyes again, she looked up at Alces offering and opened her mouth for it. The cold, creamy vanilla and sweet, tart berry flavor was a delightful treat, the sugar of it making her salivate as she eagerly sucked all of it from Alces's tongue. Strangely, the flash of something cool allowed her another moment of clarity, even as Sumner and Durante continued to piston into her. They were all so magnificent. She wanted to tell them that. Wanted to tell them that she would dream of this night for years and wake up smiling. But she'd have to let go of Alces tongue.

But then she was coming again, whimpering, nails digging into Durante's shoulder. She didn't want it to end, but she also wasn't certain how much more she could take.

Sumner had reached his wall. Between already fucking her pussy, and now the tightness of her ass, he could hold out no longer. She could feel the rumble of the purr in his chest rise to growl as he panted. Just as he reached his peak, while she didn't get Durante's fangs she did get Sumner's teeth in her shoulder, holding onto her as he came hard inside her.

Durante was in his own rhythm, and Sumner's movements hadn't thrown him off, especially with his attention so focused on her breasts. Sumner gave a valiant effort, but when he was spent, he could hold her up no more. Stumbling back, he fell back onto the seat and sighed in contentment.

The sudden shift with Sumner no longer helping to hold her up, Durante wavered and over compensated, lifting her up suddenly and stumbling back as well. Without upsetting things too far, Alces could only slow Durante's fall and Octavia fell with him, landing firmly atop him, the alchemist still buried inside her. Alces, sure no one had actually been hurt, could only laugh. It was an amused laugh, not a guffaw at an embarrassing situation.

Durante looked up at Octavia with a touch of horror. "Oh, shadows, Tavi, I'm sorry," he stammered. "Are you okay?"

Giggling, Octavia pushed herself up enough to kiss Durante firmly before lifting her head and grinning at him. "Yes, darling." She then pushed all the way up into a sitting position with a devilish grin. "You can make it up to me by coming for me," she said as she started to ride him enthusiastically.

"Oh," he said carefully, then moaned. "Ooooooh." Durante's head rolled back but his hands moved to her hips, with one trailing up to caress and squeeze one of her breasts. It seemed like he'd be making it up to her soon.

Alces chuckled and handed Sumner the bowl of ice cream, who took it happily and held the bottom of it to his forehead for a minute as he panted, cooling off. The large dragonkin took up residence in the large armchair, watching the two of them, not wanting to interrupt this moment.

She let out a delighted laugh, a sound of joy that quickly turned into a moan. She'd had Durante beneath her many times, she knew how to ride him, how to make it exactly what both of them needed. She tossed her hair back and looked over at Alces, eyes sparkling. It would be his turn soon. Right now, though, she had a partner, and he was about to give her what she wanted.

"Tavi," Durante whimpered gently, smiling up at her. She was perfectly merged with him, and he was building up quickly. Both his hands now held her breasts, squeezing with each bounce of her body, getting tighter as he got close. "Tavi, I'm... you're so good. So amazing. So," he said, then cut himself off as his back arched, and he pressed up into her, buried to the hilt when he came.

Durante's eyes turned a richer pink for a moment, when his climax peaked, and his body froze. She came with him—she would have to look that up later, see why the wards enhanced her pleasure. If she remembered. She let her body drop against his, kissing him deeply as they both relaxed into each other. That familiar rush as she coaxed his essence out of him, sending shivering pleasure through his body before he relaxed onto the floor, smiling up at her once more, still caressing her gently. "You're amazing," he repeated, reaching up to caress her face.

"My Kitten," she murmured, smiling back at him. "You're so good to me."

Another kiss, and she gently climbed off of him. She didn't want to, and she couldn't completely suppress the whine as she lifted her hips and he fell out of her. She wanted more. But she also needed one minute. She knelt on the rug beside him, still panting softly. She could feel their cum dripping from her, and somehow that made her even more aroused.

"A momentary break?" Alces asked, appearing beside her with another bowl of the sweet, cold vanilla cream swirled with berries. He also held out his hand to her.

"Mm-hm." She accepted the bowl, and the hand up. "Um, could I—a towel, maybe? I'm sticky and I can't focus enough to cast." She did blush a little at that, embarrassed at her inability. She stood awkwardly for a moment and ate some of her dessert. She had enough sense not to sit on anything in her current state.

Durante was spent for the moment, and Sumner was nursing his bowl of ice cream but seemed to be recovering nicely. Bare as he was now, Alces offered her his shirt. It could be cleaned off easily enough later, and it was the only convenient cloth that he was comfortable volunteering. As she cleaned up, he handed waterskins to both Sumner and Durante, letting them refresh as well.

Despite him not making a scene about it, it was impossible for Octavia not to notice that Alces was hard as steel. After she cleaned, he scooped her up in his arms and settled into the chair once more. He was letting her take a break, as offered, but it would take very little effort to position her for a round.

FIFTEEN

About halfway through her bowl, Octavia repositioned herself, straddling Alces' lap, facing him. She rested against his massive cock, letting it nestle between the cheeks of her ass.

"You cast a spell earlier," she said, and took another bite. It was strange how the cold helped her think. Maybe the contrast startled her enough for her mind to function properly. "I think you were trying to protect me, but… I think it backfired a little, right?"

As she talked, she couldn't keep herself from rubbing back against him. She was very ready for him, but it could wait one more minute. A little longer of a rest. Alces was an intense experience on a normal day.

"A protective bond," he said, his claws gently dancing over her thighs. Alces wasn't one to be stoic or still, but he was controlling himself as well as he could at the moment. "Should you be hurt, I would take your pain. I did not think it would bind... this," he said, one hand's claws softly rising up her tummy and circling around her breast. "I am not complaining."

Her eyes grew wide, and she felt both that squeeze around her heart and a warmth flush through her sex. She took two more bites, then set the bowl aside, rising up on her knees to wrap her arms around his neck. "My Knight," she murmured before kissing him softly, then pressing her forehead to his as he so often did with her. "My heart."

It looked like Alces' scales shimmered a little at her words. He smiled, softly this time, and kissed her back. It was warm and playful, teasing her tongue with his own as his hands caressed over her hips and around her ass and back to her thighs.

She nuzzled at him, and bit softly. "I'm ready for you. How shall we do this?"

"I rather like you where you are," he said. "Where I can see you and touch you. Will you have me like this?"

She giggled. "I'll have you any way I can."

"We will have to explore all those ways," he commented as she rose up on her knees again, and reached between her legs, pulling his cock forward.

She didn't immediately start to mount him, though, but rather trapped his cock between them. Leaning forward again, she kissed him as she rubbed her very wet pussy up and down the length of him. Hands on her ass, he moved her against him, helping her grind and add to the wetness she was spreading over him.

His pinned cock was jumping with his pulse, finally giving in a little to the needs that were flushing through him. Alces' grip was a little tighter, his kiss hungrier, his movements a little more exaggerated as he pressed against her. She moaned into his kisses. He was always so careful with her, there was something very exciting about feeling that tremor in his self-control.

She pulled back gently, rising up on her knees again, and reaching down to position him at her entrance. She hoped that seeing her take something so large wouldn't traumatize the other two.

She exhaled sharply as she started to sink down on Alces. "Gods, you are so big," she whispered. She didn't think she would ever get used to it. Sumner whistled, clearly watching. It seemed he was not intimidated.

"Beautiful, astounding, desirous Octavia," Alces muttered, head rolling around as she sank down on him. He wanted to lean back, relish in the feel of her wrapping around him, but he also wanted to remain close, to touch and kiss her. "You flatter and spoil me. You fill me with light."

"You overwhelm me, my knight," she said, hands against his chest. "Will you move me, my heart? Will you show me what the spell did to you?"

"Just keep touching me," he said, then wrapped his hands around her hips and started to lift her. Slowly at first, then began rolling his hips as well. He leaned in, kissing her neck, running his tongue along her clavicle, and tracing the rim of her ear. "Do you feel what the magic has done? How our connection brightens us both?"

Closing her eyes, Octavia fought to focus, though she honored

Alces' request and made sure her hands continued to move over him, sliding up over his shoulder, caressing the sides of his neck and face, and finally sliding over his horns as he leaned into her. There was definitely something there, a strange feedback. If she concentrated on it, it was almost like she could feel what he felt compounded on top of what she was already experiencing. Not the sensations, but the derived pleasure and ache. The want and need.

"I… yes!" Her eyes opened again, and she smiled, excited. "I can… I can feel your want! I…" She looked at him, surprised by the depth of his longing. "Do you really… do you desire me so much?" And what did he feel in return? Could he sense how much the three of them had consumed her?

"How could I not," he said, moving with more intensity, but only by rolling his hips and grinding hers. He wanted her right where she was, where they could look at each other and hold in this moment. "You brim with light. You are wise and prominent, giving and caring, joyous and voracious. How could I not?"

Another heated kiss, and he parted, sitting back to gaze upon her. The soft curves of her body bounced and moved with their joining in enticing ways, and there was so much admiration in his gaze as he took her in.

"I… I'm so sensitive. I'm not… not sure why the spell is doing that," she panted, trying to stay clear for a moment. "I've come so many times, and it's so hard to think, but…" Her words drifted away as sensation overtook her once more, and she gripped Alces' shoulders as she started to shake. She let out a soaring, musical cry as she came again, clenching around the shaft that had her so impossibly stretched.

She fell, soft, against him as her climax ebbed, nuzzling into his neck. She hoped she remembered every moment, every thrilling touch, every shuddering peak. She hoped they all remembered this night with the same joy she felt. She licked at Alces' neck and reached up to rub his horns again. She knew he liked it. She'd have to ask what felt good about it some time. Later. Much later.

Alces held her for a long moment, caressing her back with a gentle scratch of his claws and kissing her forehead. She could feel him throbbing deep inside her. Feel how he was close, not on the edge, but a little bit more, and she'd be full once again. "But you want more," he said softly, coaxingly. "You want more of all of us, don't you?"

She blushed. She had no idea why, after everything that had already passed between them that night. Perhaps it was the potential double meaning in those words.

"So much more," she whispered, more to herself than him, but he would certainly hear it. She nuzzled at him again, still petting his horns, then moved enough to be able to look him in the eyes. He rolled his head to her touch, the caress of his horns guiding him. She could feel the tingling joy it sent through him.

"I…," she began, her voice bedroom soft but no longer whispering. She moaned softly as she moved, which caused him to shift within her. "Tomorrow I will hopefully wake up, having come back to my senses, and possibly never have the courage to demand this of you all again. So yes." She smiled sheepishly at Alces.

"Hardly a demand," he chuckled, "concerning we all enjoy you, being with you, bringing the light with you. Speaking of, my friends, come join us. She is not fulfilled yet, and we must assist."

The rallying call, as quiet as it was, still filled the room and the other two started to move off their respective seats. Excited but tired, they moved closer.

"I'm still alive, so I'm still down to play with Tavi," Sumner said, moving to the side of the chair. "Think it's my turn for some head."

Alces cleared his throat and looked at Sumner.

"Please, Tavi," Sumner corrected himself. "You're so good."

She laughed softly, and reached across, caressing Sumner's thigh. "I think Alces might not approve of some of the things you say to me when it's just the two of us," she said, sliding her hand up, across his hip, teasingly close to his eager erection, and up his chest.

"I do know that if he said anything you didn't like, my resolute Octavia, I'd be healing him in the morning," Alces said with a smirk.

"It'll be easier if I'm…" She considered for a moment, and looked back to Alces. "My knight? Would you be willing to move to the floor? I think… I think that will be best."

Upon her request, he held on tight to Octavia's ass and eased off the chair to stand. He'd carried her like this on many occasions, and rather enjoyed doing so, but for now it was to move to the floor as requested. He settled them down and stretched out below her. Sumner followed suit, standing at the ready for her direction while Durante wasn't quite sure what he was to do. For now he was looking at Octavia and probably would have been blushing if that were possible.

Octavia caught Alces before he settled, kissing him deeply—she wouldn't be able to reach his mouth once he stretched out, even if she weren't intending to pleasure Sumner. "Thank you, my heart," she murmured to him, then let him lay back. She wasn't sure if he knew what all she was thanking him for.

Once Alces was down completely, his hands and claws resting on her hips and holding her in place, she sat up and back as much as she could, letting out a moan as she did. She panted for a moment, awash in sensation, then lifted her head and looked back at Durante. "Will you indulge me, Kitten? You don't have to if you don't want to, but..." she bit her lip and looked at him with pleading eyes.

Durante looked up, snapping out of his little daze, and smiled at Octavia. "Anything, Tavi," he said, maybe a little too eagerly. Or he just wanted her that much. "What can I do?"

"Kneel behind me," she said, "and start slow. You're going to take me from behind, and I'm guessing this will be a first for you." She was a slick mess, he wouldn't need to get more lube. Had there been a lube spell in the wards? Maybe there was. Why?

"Oh," he said, his mind whirling for a minute, but it quickly relented. "Yes. Of course, yes." His voice picked up as he spoke, getting more into the idea. As he moved into position, Alces helped by grabbing her cheeks and spreading her open, making it easy for Durante as he knelt behind her.

"Yeah, D, get some of that foxy ass," Sumner encouraged. Alces glared at him again, but Sumner just smirked at the dragonkin. Alces relented, as Octavia hadn't protested and they were all in the moment.

Durante steadied himself, then slowly sank into Octavia's ass, moaning softly as the tightness gripped around him.

"Oh, Gods!" Octavia was lost for a breath, a shudder running through her body as Durante sank into her. It was even more intense than it had been earlier given the sheer enormity of Alces. They might break her tonight.

Another slight adjustment of his footing, and he was able to slowly move his hips. In this position, Alces wouldn't be setting the pace, Durante and Octavia would be.

Panting, she finally looked back at Sumner. "Come here, my prince," she said, reaching a hand out to him, her head swimming. "Let me pleasure you."

"Oh, fuck yes," Sumner said, seeming to rather like the pet name and attitude. He stood before her, clearly ready for her attentions, and ran his fingers through her hair, gripping it gently.

When she finally had all three of them inside her, she felt Alces swell in her depths. Whatever he was feeling, the swimming fullness was affecting him in some manner, and she heard a deep groan roll through him. The euphoria that overtook Octavia was like nothing she had ever experienced. She gazed up at Sumner in adulation as he grabbed her hair and took more control of her actions. Durante was getting into it now. Every time he bottomed out, he pushed her a little forward, which made Alces' cock glide a little out of her pussy and Sumner go a little deeper into her throat, before she settled back down against the two of them that were below her. She had grasped Sumner's thigh for balance and support, the other hand against Alces' muscled abdomen. Her eyes glazed as she came again, cries muffled. This moment, the fulfillment of the dream she'd had since they met. She hoped Kamvasana was proud.

She sucked eagerly at Sumner and clenched around Alces and Durante. She could feel exhaustion creeping into her limbs but also so much pleasure. She wanted them to fill her. Needed it in a way that seemed impossible. The joining of all four of them seemed to trigger something in the magic, or maybe it was the atmosphere, the sensations, or Octavia's pleasure–filled whimpers. Either way, there was a sudden build all around her. Durante was behind her, fucking her ass faster, deeper, and making grunts of effort. Sumner was gripping her hair a little tighter, even pumping his hips as he started to pant while vulgarly complimenting her skills. Alces was thrusting his hips slightly to surge into her each time she came back down. All of them were getting closer, and she could feel it. She could feel every inch, every vein, every nub of her three boys.

Once the peak was in sight, there was a sudden rush for the end, as if they were all matching her need. She was being deliciously used as she took all they offered to her. In a sudden burst, all three of them climaxed at the same time. Sumner grabbed her hair and came down her throat as she was forced down onto Durante and Alces' cocks, the two of them flooding her body with their cum as they all cried out. It seemed to last an eternity, as the sensations swam through their heads and the moment of all of them together held frozen. Then, whether relieved or reluctant, it was over.

Durante pulled out, stumbling back a little and falling to the floor, sprawling out at Alces' feet, dazed. Sumner released his grip on her and also stepped back, catching himself on the arm of a chair and half-stood against it, panting. Alces was the only one to remain, as he had nowhere to go but to be her pillow, the place for her to land and release.

With no one holding her, Octavia did fall onto Alces, rubbing her face against his chest like a tired child. She was panting hard and could barely move. She felt incredible, sated beyond reason, and... loved.

She loved them. She had to, didn't she? Or was this the spell? But the spell didn't account for the swelling warmth that filled her heart every day she was with them. She was too tired to say anything, and grateful for it. The night had already been enough.

Connected as they were, Alces wrapped his arms around her and kissed her forehead. "I think the spell has passed," he said gently. She moaned quietly and nuzzled at Alces again. She would need to move soon before she fell asleep.

"Oh good," Sumner muttered. "I mean, I'm up for another round, but that was... wow, and I'm going to need a bit to recover."

Alces laughed at Sumner's bravado. "Should I take you to bed, dearest Octavia?"

"Mm-hmm." Octavia nodded but didn't lift her head. She couldn't, and she didn't want to.

"Readied Durante, we'll need your cleansing potion," Alces said as he cradled Octavia and moved to a seated position, then rolled onto his knees and stood, never letting her go in the slightest.

"Yeah, okay," Durante said, still sprawled on the floor below. "Be there in a second."

Holding her close, Alces carried her back to her room and to her bed. They'd been together enough that he knew where she had a towel and placed it on her bed. Then, with much reluctance, he set her down, finally pulling out of her. Kneeling beside the bed, he gently cleaned her off, wiping away the combined fluids and sweat that made her body glisten in the low light. Her head was still swimmy as Alces wiped her down, but she murmured happily, enjoying the feel of him taking care of her. She managed to lift a hand enough to gently caress his side as he worked on her. She couldn't speak, though. Exhaustion and... something else kept her thoughts muddled. Alces had said that the spell had passed, but that wasn't completely true. The raging desire had passed. She still felt drunk and unfocused.

Moments later Durante arrived, having re-found his breeches, and assisted in cleaning up Octavia. He smiled softly at her and brushed her hair back from her face as Alces took the solution and continued seeing her cleaned and tended to. Alces also cast a light healing spell—no one had been that rough, and Octavia was an experienced lover, but that was a lot for a human body to take.

Once they were done, Alces lifted Octavia so that Durante could ease the towel out from under her and then tucked her in as Durante picked up the dirty clothes and tidied around them. They both kissed her goodnight, and even Sumner stuck his head in long enough for a kiss and a last little love bite before they took themselves to their rooms.

Octavia fell into sleep almost immediately, a sleep full of strange dreams. Not the carnal fantasies she would have expected after such a night.

She dreamt she had shrunk and was running through the magic circle she had drawn on the tent floor. It rose around her as if it were a hedge maze. She wasn't running towards anything; she was running away from a pink mist that was steadily filling the maze. Each time she thought she was near the exit, her path was blocked by the strange mist. She finally found her way to the center of the labyrinth, but the mist had followed, swooshing in on all sides. It touched her skin and suddenly she was reliving the pleasure of the night before, each orgasm flashing through her mind as she dropped to her knees. They were like strange bursts in her body, racking through her with a pleasure so intense it was becoming painful. She collapsed, spasming, as the mist consumed her.

She woke with a start, gasping, as the dream ended. She could tell the sun was up, and she could smell that Alces was awake and cooking. That made sense, after a night like they all had Alces probably slept just long enough for his body to reset before the energy of the "light" they had created woke him again. Her body was sore where she expected it to be sore, but not nearly as sore as she'd feared. She stretched and smiled. While she could barely remember the strange, disquieting dream she could absolutely remember the night before. She reached up to push her hair back from her face and paused.

Her hand was violet, her nails almost clawlike and decidedly purple. She stretched her arm away from her face. The violet came up the hand and a little up the forearm and then became pink. A soft pink, like cherry blossoms. She lifted her other arm. It was the same.

Heart pounding, Octavia scrambled out of bed and ran to her mirror. She was the only one with a full-length mirror, purchased years before she'd met her companions—a testament to her vanity, perhaps. She stared at her reflection for a long moment and screamed.

She was entirely pink.

From her nose to her toes, save where her skin shaded to violet at her hands and the purple claws on her feet. Her hair was no longer blond, but instead white, shot through with streaks of pale rose and lilac, though it still curled as wildly as it had before. Her eyes were the same blue they'd always been. And speaking of her eyes, there was a small heart shaped beauty mark under the corner of her left eye where her skin had once been clear.

The worst part, though, was that in addition to the color changes, she had little horns parting her hair on both sides, and behind her a whippy tail with a heart shaped spade on the end was snapping back and forth in her agitation. She looked a little like a shaytani, one of the fiendblooded, but not exactly. A little like a demon, but much like Comicha, she was too soft and smooth.

Heavy stomping preceded Alces pulling the curtain aside and peering into Octavia's room. "Octavia, are you—" he started, then his eyes fell on her, and he had to pause.

Standing up straight, he tilted his head to the side. "It seems there was more to the spell than I had thought," he said, apologetically. "I wish I were an expert on such things. Are you... alright?"

"I should have known there was more to it," Octavia said, still looking in the mirror, heart beating harder as panic overtook her. "I should've known anyone as petty as Baris Venebore would leave a greater punishment than making me unthinkably horny for the night. But I couldn't think! I couldn't do anything, but–" she reached out and touched the glass, her demi-claws clicking against it as she did. Something between a frustrated shriek and a desperate sob welled out of her.

Alces stepped up behind her and placed a hand on her shoulder. Leaning down, he looked at the figure in the mirror and smiled gently. "You're still you, though, dear Octavia. You're still lovely, just... different," he said, looking her over. "Is there anything you need? I do not wish to burn breakfast, now that it's not an emergency, but I want to be here for you if you need something."

The urge to demand to know how this wasn't an emergency was very strong, but instead she slowly shook her head and looked up at Alces' reflection. "Go ahead."

Alces saw the disappointment and nodded. "Let me ensure everything is safe, and I will come back. Whatever you need," he said, kissed the top of her head, then exited back out of the room. There was some muttering beyond, and she recognized Durante's voice first, then Sumner's, who seemed like he had come in from outside.

Octavia stared at her reflection for another minute, taking deep breaths, trying to calm down. "Okay, this is I think a purely cosmetic transformation." She held out her hand and summoned magic and felt the wave of relief as the telltale blue crackle swirled in her palm and a little up her arm. "Oh, Goddess of Mercy! Okay. I need… the book. I need the book."

She grabbed her robe and darted into the main room, eyes falling on the circle from last night, where the book still sat. She rushed forward and grabbed it, then remembered that the others were also in the room. She looked up slowly, a little afraid of what she would see.

The three of them all held different expressions, and it was quite the spectrum. Alces was slightly concerned but more for her emotions than her appearance. Durante appeared taken aback, after all it was a very sudden change from what she looked like last night, but he also appeared to be the farthest from horrified. Sumner, however, didn't look happy. There was the first look over, then something made him wince and turn away in disgust. Octavia felt like she had been stabbed. She held the book to her chest as she watched Sumner stalk out of the tent without a word. The look on his face made her feel like some grotesque monster and cut even deeper after the night before.

"Sumner," Alces said, watching him leave, but his ask went unanswered.

"What happened?" Durante asked, intrigued and not noticing Sumner's departure.

Tears had never come so quickly. They were rolling down her cheeks as she looked back to Durante and shook her head before darting back into her room. She couldn't speak. She could only sob into her pillow, overwhelmed by a sense of dread that everything that had been building between them all was ruined. It seemed like a horribly cruel trick of fate to open her heart only to break it.

SIXTEEN

Octavia cried until the sobs became sniffles, until her head ached. Then she picked herself up and wiped her face. There had to be a way to reverse this.

"Comicha?" She called, shaky and uncertain. Would her familiar still come?

A heartbeat later, the imp appeared in the room with an audible pop. "Mistress! Boy, you—" The imp stopped and stared at Octavia for a long moment, then squealed. "Oh! Oh, you look so cute! You look like a bigger version of me! Kind of. No wings. And look at that tail!"

Octavia stared at Comicha in disbelief for a moment as the imp zipped excitedly around the room, gushing about her mistress's "new look."

"Now is really not the time," Octavia said at last, and Comicha pulled up short, hovering in front of her.

"But why? You're so cute! You—" She flew a little closer. "You're crying. You didn't do this on purpose. Oh." The imp wilted a little. "Oh, I'm sorry."

Octavia sighed. "It… it's all right. I mean, it's all right that you got excited, you didn't know." She stood up and pulled Comicha in, giving her familiar a hug. "I need to talk to Kamvasana."

Nuzzling into Octavia's still ample cleavage, Comicha responded with a muffled, "Yes, Mistress," then flew back a bit. Octavia dropped her robe and approached the mirror again, taking a deep breath and trying to ignore how *wrong* her reflection felt. She reached out and drew a glyph on the glass with her fingertip.

"Kami, we need to talk."

A mist formed over the mirror, then cleared to reveal Kamvasana in all their glory. They wore a masculine face that day, their strangely floating hair billowing out behind their bare shoulders, the upper body a muscled physique that would rival Alces, though there was still a curve to the hips and they wore a split skirt that sat low.

"Well, this is a new look for you!" The Essence of Desire grinned broadly. "How delightful! Do a little spin, dearest."

Octavia glared. "No."

Kamvasana smirked and narrowed their eyes. "I said, 'Spin'."

Octavia's body obeyed before her mind caught up, and she let out a frustrated growl. "Happy now?"

"Absolutely. Loving it." The primordial smiled and lounged back on a cushion that appeared behind them. "And last night! Oh, dearest, it was everything I'd been hoping for! I wish it hadn't taken so long. You're an awful tease."

Anger was more manageable than heartbreak, so Octavia clung to it. "Can we please focus? Your magic made this happen. I need you to change me back."

Kamvasana blinked. "What? No."

There was a moment of stunned silence. "What do you mean, no?" Octavia finally managed to ask.

"You're adorable! Look at you, you're like a summoner's first succubus. I don't think I could have crafted a better object of desire if I'd tried."

Panic started to sink in again. "You can't be serious."

"Dearest, I'm always serious." Kamvasana looked Octavia over again. "Yes, you will inspire so many more fantasies now. I'm not sure I could change you back even if I wanted to. How could I injure my own Word by making you less sexy?"

"Goddess of Mercy," Octavia whimpered, and ran a hand over her face. "How do I fix it?"

"It's primordial magic. Find a primordial artifact." Kamvasana shrugged. "Well, if that's all, I'm off."

"No, wait—" Octavia reached towards the mirror, but the Essence of Desire was already gone. And she knew them well enough to know they wouldn't come back.

Octavia let out another frustrated screech and threw her robe at the mirror. She held her hands to her face for a moment as she fought the urge to collapse into tears once more. She couldn't. They needed to get moving. She'd promised to help Durante. Even if this might be their last journey together.

"Comicha?"

The little imp fluttered over. "Yes, Mistress?"

Octavia took a deep breath. "Help me alter my pants. The gray ones. I need a spot for this tail."

As Comicha cut and stitched an opening for the tail in Octavia's pants, Octavia filed her demi-claws into a softer, more blunt edge that wouldn't accidentally scar anyone (including herself). It had taken far longer than usual, but she came back out into the main area fully dressed, holding a short cloak, Matilda packed up and ready to go, with the Venebore book in her hand. Comicha hovered behind her.

As soon as she appeared, Durante walked up and grabbed her in a hug, holding her close. "Oh!" She froze for a second, then relaxed into him, leaning her head against his chest. He stayed there a moment, then pulled back to look at her.

"Are you okay, Tavi?" he asked in that way someone knows the answer, but they don't know what else to say.

Her eyes shone with unshed tears as he looked at her, and her heart twisted. He still cared. Alces still cared. But she couldn't stay with them if Sumner hated her. And he had kinda looked like he did.

"No," she said softly and simply. "And I don't think there's an easy solution."

"We'll find it," he said, smiling gently and brushing some hair out of her face. He bit his lip in thought, then gave her another half-smile. "Would it help if I told you I thought you looked really good like this?"

She laughed a little, incredulous. "Do you really? Kami says they won't turn me back. They won't or they can't."

"I really do," he said, looking her over once more. "I would be happy to prove it to you later."

"Breakfast and travel first," Alces said with a chuckle, indicating the spread that had been left on the table. Griddle cakes, fried meats, scones, clotted cream, surely this had to be the last of the berries made into a compote, and some seasoned vegetables for color and variety. Alces most certainly didn't sleep last night, nor would he have needed to.

At first Octavia feared she was too upset to eat, putting Alces' efforts to waste. After a few tentative bites, however, that proved incorrect. She was hungry from the night before, and also possibly from the transformation spell. She ate plenty. More than once, she caught Durante looking at her, then he'd look away and slowly eat whatever he was nibbling on.

Sumner's absence, though, continued to be a knife in her heart.

Once they'd finished, Alces sighed and stood up. "We can keep the food here, it'll remain as it is when we close the tent, yes?" he asked, looking towards the exit.

"Yeah, when the tent is closed, everything here is sort of frozen in time," Durante answered. Alces turned back to Octavia and pressed his forehead to hers.

"I am sorry this has happened. We will fix it, so don't worry. But you are still you, and we... we will care for you, always," he said, then kissed her forehead.

Tears coursed down her cheeks again. *I can't stay if he hates me*, she wanted to say, but she nodded. It had been so much easier when she didn't care. But they'd made her care, and now...

She held onto Alces for a moment longer, then let him go and gathered her things. She normally would have helped clean up, but if Alces wanted to leave everything that was fine. She headed out of the tent to wait for the rest of them. Alces and Durante weren't far behind, as they had mostly gotten ready when she was collecting herself. Nutmeg stepped out from behind the trees and trotted over to Octavia. He paused and sniffed at her, snuffling against her chest and neck, then chuffed.

"Yes, it is still our sweet Octavia," Alces said, patting the great elk on its hindquarters. Nutmeg bugled quietly and shook his head.

"No, you may not. Be a gentleman, she's had a rough morning," Alces gently scolded. Nutmeg nickered and lay down before Octavia, waiting for her to climb on. Alces also offered a hand, to give some stability, which she accepted.

Sitting astride Nutmeg was a little odd, as she had to accommodate the tail. She found herself shifting her hips a bit forward. It made her sit up a little straighter and lifted her chest. There was a crispness to the air, and she threw her cloak around her shoulders, pulling the hood up carefully over her horns and trying not to think about it too much. She would spend the day reading the book and figuring out what in the hells had happened to her. Durante walked next to her and smiled up at her every now and then. Sumner still seemed to be missing late in the morning, but Alces didn't say anything about it.

"It takes a bit to get used to when your body isn't, well, what you've lived in," Durante said after they'd been walking for a while. He looked up at Octavia with a soft smile. "I understand that. I'm here for you, whenever you want to talk about it."

She looked over and smiled a little. "I suppose you would, wouldn't you? I hope… I hope it gets easier."

"Maybe," he said, looking down a bit. "Maybe I'm not the best to ask about that, as it's been three years and I'm definitely not used to it, but we can commiserate together."

Sighing, she looked down at the book in her hands. "I understand a little more of what happened to me. The warding spell was more sophisticated than I had thought. The haze, the desire, is designed to make it easy to catch whomever tries to open the book. The triplets would have enjoyed an easy plaything. But here's where it gets devious."

Durante waited, curious, as Octavia flipped through the book and tapped on one of the pages. "There were layered spells in the warding which were triggered by the wards being breached. The overwhelming desire. The increase in sensitivity. And then, the banking of mana."

"Wait, what?" He looked confused. "The spell was accumulating magical energy?"

Sighing, she nodded. "Yes. In my body, in fact. Every orgasm created a charge of mana." She looked back at Durante, closing the book and smiling ruefully. "That mana is then used to fuel the transformation spell. Basically, my change was this severe because I enjoyed myself so much." She grumbled to herself, looking at the book again. "I'd go back and kill him if he wasn't already long dead."

"That is devious," Durante said, his tone careful. "The trespasser, presumably an acolyte, would be punished relative to how much they indulged themselves. At the same time, however, the initial spell leaves you in a state where you are unable to clearly consider your actions or take steps to prevent the transformation." He tapped his fingers on his screwshot expression, thoughtful. "Is there anything in the book about reversing it?"

"No," she said sourly. "Not that I've found yet, at least. It seems they were not very concerned about turning the afflicted person back."

Quiet descended for a little while as they walked. Nutmeg chuffed and snorted about something but otherwise kept at his easy pace. Durante looked like he was trying to come up with something reassuring to say but falling short.

Closing the book, Octavia looked away. "Do we... do we at least know that Sumner is all right? Wherever he sulked off to?"

Durante looked around and shrugged. Alces looked over his shoulder as he'd been leading them so far. "He's cooling off. He should be back soon. Definitely before we reach the border, which is right there," Alces said motioning ahead.

They were less than a mile from the wall. For a border station, it appeared pretty casual. Yes, there was a wall, but it could be easily scaled, and there weren't too many towers. There were two guards visible, and they barely moved as they approached. She did her best not to draw into herself. That would look suspicious, and rumors had been that there was some trouble with Yadeli's neighbors. She stayed put atop Nutmeg and let Alces take the lead, as he tended to.

In the time walking, Sumner did appear as Alces had predicted. He glanced at Octavia, and his eyes hinted at sadness and frustration, but it wasn't aimed at her. Or didn't feel that way. Like a puppy who had gotten into trouble. He remained quiet, though, as they approached and stood beside Alces.

"Greetings. I am Ser Alces Brightrain, Knight of the Spree Spirits. My companions and I wish to travel to the keep," he started and the guard on the right waved at him.

"Go on through," he said, and both the guards stepped aside.

"Aren't you inter-."

"No," the guard retorted, cutting Alces off. "You're not a merchant so I don't need to check your wares. You're not dignitaries, so I don't need to escort you. You're bigger than the both of us combined, your... beast horse is massive, you travel with a shaytani, a... vampire? and who knows what sneaky boy here is. None of my business, I'll tell you that. Have a good day."

"Oh," Alces said, a touch crestfallen. "Well, a good morning to you gentleman. I hope your watch is peaceful and pleasant."

"Most excitement in years," the guard on the left spoke up. "Welcome to the Beylik of Algeleli."

"Thank you," Alces said with a nod and continued on their way. Durante gave them a nod as well but otherwise hurried along with the rest of them.

Nutmeg snorted, and Alces simply responded, "No, and it wouldn't."

As they walked past, Octavia examined the two guards. She didn't imagine it made them feel any more comfortable. So, she *did* look like a shaytani—she had met a pair of shaytani before, but they had both been darkly blue with much sharper features. Well, better they assume she was shaytani than think she was some type of fiend.

"How much further to the keep?" she asked once they were far enough beyond the guards.

"A couple of hours," Durante said. "We can go through Boulcairn, get lunch maybe?"

"Best to be rested and fed before meeting new people," Alces agreed.

Octavia nodded and opened the book again, continuing her so far fruitless quest for a solution. The small consolation was that the book did, at least, seem to have all the other information she had been hoping for. Ancient rituals, prayers, everything you would expect to find in a priest's personal holy book.

Once they were out of earshot of the guards, or anyone else, Sumner fell back in the marching order to walk next to Octavia. He was quiet for a long moment, then sighed and looked up at her.

"Tavi, I'm sorry," he said, reaching up to set a hand on her thigh but hesitated, drawing it back. "I shouldn't have reacted like that. It was... it was stupid, frankly."

She glanced over at him and closed the book with a snap. "You know, just the other week, when Durante and I were at the markets and you and Alces were off being heroes, he'd teasingly said that he couldn't promise you'd still care about me if I didn't... look the way I looked. And I laughed, but I never actually thought you'd prove him right." She was trying to be mad, but it wasn't working, and tears started to streak down her face again.

Sumner winced, but he didn't turn away. The others stayed quiet, this was their conversation, and Durante walked up to join Alces to give them a touch of privacy.

"It... it wasn't you. Part of me reacted before I thought about what was happening. Just—"

"I saw your face before you stormed out." She said, looking down. "I felt like a monster. It..." she closed her eyes completely and whispered. "It broke my heart. That you could be done with me so quickly."

"I'm so, so fucking sorry, Tavi. I would never mean to break your heart." He paused, taking a moment to gather himself. "It wasn't fair to you. You didn't do anything wrong. You're still sweet, wonderful, fun you. But something in my head screamed at me about the past, and it was so loud it overtook everything else."

"The circus," she said, opening her eyes again and looking over at him. She remembered what he had told her, of how he and Alces had met. "The shaytani who almost destroyed your family. That's what you see now when you look at me." In some ways that was worse. She still had this pain, but understanding was taking away the anger.

"That was what the loud part saw, yes," he said, looking physically uncomfortable. "The shaytani who fucked over my life, got half my, well, my family killed. But you don't even look like him, or any of the others that worked with him. He was red. Like, a dirty red. You're not even the same color. Horns were bigger. You're fuckin' pink, because of course you are." Sumner laughed a little and shook his head.

"Yes, I am fucking pink," she said acerbically, and held up her hand. "Also, slightly purple. And I had to file down my nails this morning to make sure I didn't gouge myself pulling my hair back."

"I'm over it," Sumner said, though by his tone she wasn't completely sure who he was trying to convince. "It's... still you."

She dropped her hand back onto the book and sighed, looking over at Sumner. "I am sorry. I mean, it's not like I did this on purpose, but I am sorry it brought up old hurt." She looked back down at the book in her hands. "So where do we go from here? Kamvasana won't change me back. I don't know how long I'll be like this. I need a primordial relic to fix it, I don't even know where to begin."

"First, you don't apologize," Sumner said, finally building up the courage to set his hand on her thigh. "It's not your fault. You've done nothing wrong, that was all me. We go the same we've been going." He gave her a squeeze and looked up into her eyes, smiling a bit. "Your eyes are the same."

She started to smile in return, just a little. "Other than the color, my face is mostly unchanged. Just this damn thing," she pointed to the heart shaped mark.

"See," he said with a small laugh, letting her watch him trace his eyes over her, "all the important parts are the same."

"Oh, and these." She tilted her head towards him a little and opened her mouth wide. Her incisors were a little longer than they had been, enough to be pronounced, much like Sumner's were. "I almost bit my tongue five times during breakfast."

"Guess you can bite me back. Oh, shit, breakfast. Shadows, I'm an idiot."

"You are."

He sighed once more and squeezed her thigh again. "Okay, I'd like for us to be okay now, but I'm the one who fucked up, so you tell me what I can do to make it up to you."

She arched an eyebrow. "Getting over yourself is a good first step." She sighed and looked forward. "I want us to be okay as well, but that… Gods, Sumner, it hurt so much! Especially after last night! I thought… I thought you hated me. I thought I was going to have to leave at the next town, and I spent the morning panicking and crying over the possibility!" She wrinkled up her nose, irritated, but she wasn't crying anymore. It felt like she was blushing—could she still blush with pink skin?

"I'm working on it," he said, sincerely. "I could never hate you. I'm sorry, I will always be sorry for making you feel that way. I will say it every morning when you get up and every night before bed if I have to."

"Oh, do not, that would become so tedious so quickly," she said, wrinkling up her nose again. Her expression softened. "But I'm glad you don't hate me. I'm glad I don't have to leave. I would miss you all madly."

"Why would you have to leave?" he asked, a little confused. "You didn't do anything wrong. It's my shit I need to deal with. No, you're staying until you decide we're not worth the trouble." He looked at her for a minute, then smiled a little. "Also, last night was amazing."

She sighed a little wistfully. "It really was amazing. Maybe I can get you all to do it again for my birthday or something. If you're willing to be with me like this."

"Oh, my beautiful camellia," Sumner said with a soft laugh, "my body and spirit are willing. My mind will catch up soon."

She looked at him with a soft, hopeful smile, then looked back to Durante and Alces. "Do you want to go tell them it's fine, and I won't be running away or murdering you in your sleep?"

"I don't think that was a concern of theirs, but sure." he said, and moved up to tell them everything was alright. Alces nodded, and Durante made an exasperated noise, possibly because Sumner had caused all this in the first place.

After that, they fell back into their regular order, with Alces at the lead, Durante pacing Octavia, and Sumner moving back and forth as he scouted a head and then returned to check their tail. It was almost normal. The tension was still there, but it was no longer palpable and beginning to unwind.

SEVENTEEN

The sun had passed its zenith by the time they entered the town of Boulcairn. It seemed pleasant enough. It appeared to be an agricultural and lumber town, with a few cartwrights and at least two ranches raising horses. Looking around, Octavia felt like she must be missing something. It was odd that this quiet place was separated from the rest of the country by a wall and gate. It was a pleasant enough town, but unremarkable. Why the wall? And what was someone who brokered in fiend parts doing out here?

"There's something about this place that seems familiar," Alces said as they looked around, walking through the town square. "Not that I've been here, just that I feel it fits something I've heard."

That got Durante thinking, but Sumner just shrugged. "Looks like a green town like any other. Maybe some decent trade, being on a border. They don't even have a port, though, due to the cliffs," Sumner said.

"I can't think of anything," Durante said. "But I don't really know the history of the beyliks."

"I'll admit my knowledge of the continent is lacking," Octavia said a little sheepishly. "I can give you great stories and sordid details from Ascherol or Rupaiya, but that's about it." Her stomach chose that moment to growl. She rolled her eyes, and felt the heat of a blush rise, but again wondered if it actually showed. "I'm still starving. Lunch?"

Durante smiled at her. "You're... adorable," he said cheerfully.

"The new look is becoming on you, lovely Octavia," Alces said, with all his trademark sincerity. Sumner didn't have a comment, but he didn't argue either. "I heartily agree. Lunch should be had."

One of the key things that could definitely be found, given the nature of the town, was meat. Plentiful and presented in a variety of ways. Alces was temporarily lost as he smelled his way through the marketplace. The keeps all seemed to be rather pleased to see new people, new customers. Especially ones as colorful as themselves, which was remarked on more than once.

As they wandered, Octavia was struck by the realization that she no longer appeared human. Which seemed obvious, but for some reason she hadn't yet made the leap from "my appearance has changed" to "strangers will not think I'm human." Was she still human? She was fairly certain that the spell was cosmetic, but there wasn't a simple way to test it.

She was polite but quiet as they wandered the markets. She did fish out a few coins to buy some of the local tea and add it to her backup supply. When they finally sat down to a lunch of a variety of meats and sausages, flatbreads, sauces, and a refreshing salad made of tomatoes, cucumbers, peppers, and onions, Octavia was ready to eat half the table.

It was perhaps the first time a serving house didn't flinch at Alces' appetite, instead more than happy to throw more meat on the fire and bring out more food. Given the way things were politically, there was a chance trade had been reduced, and they had an overabundance of crops and vittles. When lunch had finally ended, Alces had eaten half a lamb.

"We must remember this town," he said with a laugh. "Come here every feasting holiday."

"That's a lot of travel," Durante noted. "Maybe keep an eye out for other green towns?"

"I dunno," Sumner said, finishing off a heavily sauced sausage, "they know how to cook out this way."

"The food is very good," Octavia admitted, and paused to burp daintily before taking another bite of flatbread. "Though I wouldn't mind a place that made pastries like you get in the Peninsula." The Peninsula was a strange little strip of Ascherol that was detached from the rest of the country, and she was inordinately fond of their baking prowess. "Though I also miss Rupaiyan chai. Oh, and those cookies they make out of the cheese, but it doesn't taste like cheese." Her eyes narrowed a little. "Maybe I like food too much." She took another bite of flatbread and contemplated.

Alces laughed and reached over to gently pat her face. "No such thing, my gourmand Octavia. Food is light made manifest; it brings joy to our hearts and stomachs. To love it is to love life," he said.

"I do love life," she murmured quietly around her bread.

"I rather liked it back when it was more, um, necessary," Durante said. As usual, he'd focused more on a cup of juice he'd had and nibbled a little on the rarer pieces of meat.

"I can't fault you, Tavi. This is pretty fucking good," Sumner said, reaching for one more sausage. They lingered over lunch, but not too long, and after picking up a few more things for Alces to experiment with in the kitchen, they were back on the road.

It was another hour or so before they actually saw the keep. The building was old, with high towers in crumbling shambles. Parts of the outer walls were so damaged they could see right through to the lake beyond. It was dilapidated and, from what they could see, abandoned. Yet this was where the instructions Erash had given them told them to be.

Upon venturing closer, they realized there was a far more functional-looking permanent camp set up in the field that would have once been the inner bailey, beyond the crumbling remains of the castle proper. Smoke rose from an impressive earthen forge as well as a large camp kitchen, and there appeared to be people moving about. Twin banners hung that flew a crest of an axe and sword crossed with a knight's helmet above them. It looked like a military encampment, but the numbers were low, and it lacked the rigidity Octavia associated with the military.

Octavia tilted even further forward on Nutmeg to try to get a better look at the camp ahead through the missing chunks of the walls. She couldn't see much. The symbols on the flag tickled something in the back of her brain. She'd seen it before, but she couldn't remember what it was in reference to.

"I know this tale," Alces said as they walked up. "I've heard it before, but I can't quite remember what it is."

"So, we're about to meet some famous people," Durante mused.

"Or someone running a scam," Sumner said cynically.

"It's larger than the operation Erash described," Octavia said, sitting back again. "Though I suppose we also didn't ask a lot of questions along those lines. Let's introduce ourselves and hope they're reasonable."

Nutmeg nickered and shook his head. "I'm quite aware," Alces responded.

They continued moving towards the camp. They were met relatively quickly by a young woman, dressed in rider's leathers, who ran up before they got too close. She couldn't have been more than 19 but stood straight and confident.

"Hail, travelers. Do you have business up this way? This area is very dangerous, and while you look capable, I would still advise caution, and turn back," she said.

"We're not lost," Octavia commented lightly. "Do people often end up this way by accident?"

"Not normally, but better to err on the side of caution," she answered Octavia, although her brows rose a little when she looked upon her. Octavia suppressed a sigh at the raised brows. Something told her it wasn't her daring neckline that got that reaction.

"Fear not, young lady, we are quite adept in both travel and combat," Alces said, giving her a bow. "We appreciate the warning, however, and take our safety into our own hands."

The woman took a longer glance at the four of them and seemed to do a mental calculation. Coming to a decision, she nodded. "Very well, but I would advise you to return to Boulcairn before nightfall."

"Thank you very much, uh, miss…?" Durante looked at the woman curiously.

"Tyro Yaren," she responded. Octavia recognized the title; a tyro was a squire of sorts.

"Thank you, Miss Yaren." Durante took a small step forward. "We're looking for someone who trades in alchemical reagents?"

She regarded him for a breath, then nodded. "I think you'd want to talk to Ser Ursile or Ser Aislin. I'll direct you."

The camp didn't appear to be terribly large. Maybe a dozen people or so, warriors in armor and a support staff. Octavia also noticed they were all female, save the cook, who was preparing gourmet meals if he cooked as good as he looked.

There wasn't enough time to contemplate the feminine nature of the camp, nor the surprisingly chiseled physique of the cook, as the young tyro was bringing them before an elf. An actual elf. It was a little unusual to see them outside of their own kingdoms. She was a southern elf, by her coloring—pale green skin, and a mane of white hair lightly highlighted with streaks of burgundy. Black-stained armor covered most of her figure and she was attacking a large training dummy with a jagged sword the color of a new moon.

"Ser Ursile, I have some outsiders here looking for reagents," Tyro

Yaren said.

The elf stopped and turned towards them, eyes that were also burgundy sweeping over their group. When she gazed upon Octavia, she held up hand and fired off a spell so quickly that not even Sumner had his blade out in time.

"What—" Octavia raised her hands, startled, then blinked as nothing happened and realization dawned. "You tried to banish me, didn't you!?"

Alces held his mace at the ready and positioned himself rather imposingly in front of the elf. "I do not wish to raze your camp, Ser, but you have very little time to explain yourself."

The elven woman looked simultaneously relieved and embarrassed and took a step back, falling to one knee. "A thousand apologies to you all," she spoke quickly, a soft lilt to her voice, her clear sincerity easing Alces and Sumner. "We are on edge this evening and your companion's appearance startled me. Any other night, and it would not have happened. I beg forgiveness of you all, and mostly of you, my lady."

Sighing, Octavia ran a hand over her face. "Yeah, I'm loving this so far," she muttered to herself, then straightened up and pitched her voice to carry. "It's a curse, and it's cosmetic." She pulled her hood back and shook out her hair. "And recent. And a sore subject. What happens when night falls, Ser Ursile?"

"Apologies once more," the elf said, standing up and sheathing her sword. Alces returned his mace to his belt and tentatively stood to the side. "This night brings the full moon, and the Dire Gate opens."

"Not an auspicious start, Ser Ursile," the dragonkin said and the elf nodded in agreement.

"Once more, any other night, I would never attempt such things against a woman of such beauty," she flattered in an attempt to ease the situation. "It was a spell against evil. Unaffected, I can see my mistake."

Durante took one little step and raised his hand slightly. "Reagents?" he asked.

"Oh, yes, of course," Ursile said, directing her attention to Durante. "We have many preserved. Depending on what you seek."

Sighing, Octavia patted Nutmeg. "Let me down, please," she said quietly. "So, I can hide behind Alces and be less of a target." Nutmeg knelt down and let out a little bugle and nickered.

Alces' eyes suddenly went wide, and he laughed. It was a big one, too. Ursile, and everyone standing nearby, looked at him in surprise.

"By the Spirits, that's it!" He was boisterous in his excitement. "You are the Sisters of the Moon Watch! That was the tale that I could not remember!" Turning to his companions he grinned wide. "The Dire Gate is told to be a way into the underworld that opens every full moon, as the great Sister Ser Ursile explained. When that happens, fiends and demons can find their way to our world. They are the guardians who protect us from the fiends!"

Alces turned to the elf, still smiling. "We shall earn our trade. Let us help you to turn back the tide of darkness this night. The light of the moon shall shine upon our victory!"

Ursile was taken aback, not only by being recognized and Alces volunteering, but by the sheer volume of his speech. The whole camp had heard it. In fact, they'd drawn a little crowd by now, including two other women in similar armor. One was of fair size, with ghostly pale hair and glowing ice blue eyes. The other was massive, nearly as tall and broad as Alces, with a bundle of raven black braids and skin the color of cinnamon bark.

"Do you know what you ask to participate in?" the ethereal knight asked, her voice sounded like it had a breathy echo all on its own.

"Oh, I think he does," the giantess said with a broad grin. "Let's let them."

Durante looked around a little lost, not entirely on board for what they'd been thrown into. Sumner also didn't look quite as enthused, but he'd follow Alces, so there was that.

Octvia snickered, hiding it behind her hand. "I don't know how we expected any other result," she said softly to Durante, then walked over to stand next to Alces before the Sisters of the Moon Watch. "You've convinced Alces, so you've got the rest of us. Though please tell everyone not to shoot at the pink one."

Ursile stepped up to Octavia and gently took her hands, lifting them to kiss the top of one. Octavia was surprised by Ursile's directness, and also grateful she'd filed her claws that morning.

"My lady," the elf began earnestly, "I apologize once more. No one will mistake you for an enemy, I was merely on edge. I promise upon my honor." Octavia nodded and gently took her hands back.

"Looks like we missed the initial excitement," the giantess commented as she walked up to Alces and offered him her hand. "Ser Magnia. And you are?"

Alces took her hand and kissed the top of it, which seemed to surprise and tickle the giantess. "Dear lady knight, I am Ser Alces Brightrain, Knight of the Spree Spirits. These are my companions; Sumner Taery, Master of the Guiled Shadows; Durante Calabria, Inventor Extraordinaire; and last but certainly not least, Lady Octavia Baudelaire, Paramour of Sorcery."

"Paramour of Sorcery," Octavia repeated quietly, arching a brow at Alces. He hadn't introduced her before, not formally. She remembered the others' titles from the day they met. Alces' flair for the dramatic was one of his more charming traits.

The woman with the glowing eyes looked at them all in turn, smirking slightly when it came to Octavia and gave her a little nod of the head. "Well met, adventurers. Quite the titles. Nothing fancy here, unfortunately. I am Ser Aislin, commander of the Moon Watch."

"Oh, give it the night, Alces will come up with something for you," Octavia said with a soft, amused smile. She nodded to Ser Aislin. "Well met. So, what did my knight volunteer us for, exactly?"

"*Your* knight?" Ser Magnia echoed quietly with a smirk. Octavia ignored the giantess. She had an answer, but she wasn't quite ready to say it. She needed to talk to them first. She needed to tell them what she'd realized, how they'd all found a place in her heart. She suspected taking out a demon horde would be easier.

"When the moonlight hits the circle in the keep's catacombs, things will come out. We have no way of knowing their number or their strength," Aislin started, walking towards the ruined castle. Everyone else followed. "Some nights, it's a few imps. Some nights, great red Molochs. Those are the nights we dread."

"We've left them in pieces every night, though," Magnia added with a grin. "Just, you know, some are harder than others." The giantess removed her gorget, exposing a large scar that started where her neck and shoulder met and disappeared under her armor. "That was a close call."

"But worry not," Aislin added, turning to the group. "We have enough to stand in the way of the beasts. If you can offer your spells whatever else you have, we would be most appreciative."

"I don't think we were worried," Octavia commented as they followed along. "It's just good to know as much as we can about what we're going into."

"Any chance you have some nice arrows?" Sumner asked. "I have good hunting heads, but I don't know if they're demon quality."

"Absolutely. Miyana, our smith, should have some ready. It is nice we get a moon cycle between attacks. Plenty of time to prepare," Aislin said.

While it was clear the circle had been made in the catacombs, the keep had been so ravaged that it was open to the sky. There was plenty of rubble, broken floors, and stepped walls to use for cover.

"I'm sure you've tried this, but why do you not seal the circle? Build over it?" Durante asked, looking around for where he would perch himself.

"The magicks that power it destroy any buildings in the way to ensure the light shines. It's how this keep ended up the way it is," Ursile explained. "We've tried to block it many ways, with many materials, but it always ends up in dust."

"That's… fascinating," Octavia murmured, brows knit as she looked over the circle. "Wow, that is… it's almost artistry. The skill this would have taken. Though I'm back to wondering why we can't find a wizardly wonder that wasn't built for evil." Her tone soured a bit towards the end as she remembered the tower that had brought their little group together.

"Oh, there are plenty of those," Aislin cheerfully answered, which was almost haunting given her voice. "They don't have orders of knights protecting them or adventurers sent to destroy them."

"I'll believe it when I see it," Octavia muttered. She looked over to Aislin again. "How long before moonrise? We should prepare, but I don't imagine it will take too long. Is there a place we could set up our tent? It isn't very big."

Aislin looked up to the sky and sighed. "It was nice when it rained the other day. It never rains on a full moon here. Never overcast. So, we have a few hours. Winter approaches, so the days are shorter." Another sigh, and she shook her head, then set her shoulders. "Yaren, be a dear and show them where they can set up, then guide them to the blacksmith."

The young woman bowed. "Right away, Komutan." Yaren turned to the others and motioned. "Please follow me."

"Thank you, Ser Aislin," Octavia said, nodding to the woman. "I hope we can make one evening easier for you."

As they followed Yaren, Octavia looked at the younger woman speculatively. "So, given what we have learned, I assume your reaction to me when we arrived came from a similar place as Ser Ursile's?"

"A little, yes, But only for a moment," Yaren said as she walked them to an empty practice field. Practice would obviously not be needed tonight. "The other part, well, you're quite an eccentric group, and we don't get much company out here. So, two oddities in one. I do hope you understand."

"Yeah, they get stares all the time," Sumner said with a smirk. Which was true, he was the one who could pass through a crowd the easiest. "But they're alright."

"I'd say I didn't used to, but I'm sure you'd tell me I was wrong," Octavia muttered. Of course, she objectively knew that was inaccurate. People stared at her all the time. It used to be for different reasons.

"I stare all the time," Sumner muttered, raising his eyebrows at her.

"Before it got weird, right?" She favored Sumner with a wry smirk.

Sumner stuck his tongue out at her. He then glanced purposefully at Durante, who was actually staring at Octavia, then quickly found something else to focus on. Glancing over at Durante, she smiled softly at him, a little surprised. She otherwise remained quiet and fished out the tent. Alces could engage their slightly taciturn guide if he so wished.

Alces laughed and nodded to Yaren. "We do tend to make an entrance. But we are more than show, as you will see this evening, brave Tyro. We will make the Sisters of the Moon Watch proud."

Yaren cracked enough to give Alces a smile and bowed in return. "I certainly hope you do, Ser Alces. They could always use more help."

The dragonkin nodded. "I am satisfied with my gear. Nimble Sumner, would you like to go with Tyro Yaren to the smith, see if they have anything to suit you better?" Alces asked.

"Yeah, sure." Sumner looked back to Octavia. "Tavi, want me to look out for anything for you?"

She shook her head. "No, I'm going to pull out my gear and see if I have time to make more dust." She set down the tent and pulled the tab, stepping back as it unfolded. "I'll be at the table in the main area if anyone needs me."

Nodding, Sumner turned to Yaren to make their way to the blacksmith. Alces walked to the tent and opened the flap for them. Durante turned and headed inside. Octavia followed, and took off her cloak as they came inside, waiting for Matilda to lumber in after them. Rather than head to her room, she rifled through the chest and pulled out her satchel, some of her own reagents, the fauld she'd purchased back at the town, and the leather pants. She'd change in a minute. It'd be easier to make spell dust in her softer traveling clothes.

Alces looked over the spread they'd left on the table. He tsked, looking back out the tent. "I wanted to show him the breakfast he'd missed, but I feel like it's better if we save what we can," he said, going to work starting on cleaning up.

Durante took a step towards his room. "I'm going to make sure I have all of my ammunition and gear ready. Oh, and Tavi, I have a gift for you," he added shyly.

She looked up from her rummaging, surprised again. "Oh?"

"Yeah, one moment," Durante started, moving quickly into his room. Alces smiled and continued cleaning.

"I know Durante and Sumner are used to it, following me as they do," Alces stated as he continued putting things away, "but I apologize now that I think of it. Brave Octavia, are you okay with joining us in this fight? I did not wish to speak for you."

"Better than waiting in the tent for you to come back beaten up and then having a fit over it," she said a little sharply, then looked over at Alces, her expression softening. "Yes, my Knight. I will follow you into the fight."

"At a safe distance," he said with a broad grin.

"Here it is," Durante exclaimed as he stepped back into the main room. Walking over to Octavia, he handed her a ring. It looked to be made of a silvery metal that shined blue in the light, with a series of three small gems that looked like scuffed black pearls, but they reflected a rainbow of colors as he moved the ring before her.

"Oh!" She stared at it for a moment, then gently accepted it. "It's beautiful." She tested a couple fingers and found that it sat perfectly on her right middle finger.

"I remember you having issues with spells. This ring helps you tap into those energies. You should find yourself able to cast more than you're used to," he noted, glancing past her towards the tent exit. "Figured this might be a good time for you to have it."

Looking up at him, she smiled again, then bit her lower lip for a moment as she considered. After a breath, she stepped a little closer and slid her hands up his chest to catch his lapels, pulling him in gently for a kiss. Durante kissed her back happily, placing a hand on her hip.

"Thank you, darling," she murmured as they parted.

He smiled, keeping his hand on her hip. "My pleasure. I wish I had more for you," he

"Perhaps you can have more for me later," she said, the words playful but also shy. She still wasn't sure of this form, but she was sure that Durante still seemed enchanted with her.

"Anything you want, Tavi," he grinned happily and squeezed her hip.

Alces chose to ignore them. He had little to prepare for, so making sure the tent was comfortable for their return of a weary night was the best he could do right now. She kissed Durante once more, then reluctantly pulled away.

"I should get back to work," she said, a touch sheepishly. "Thank you again for the ring. I'm sure it will be helpful."

"Of course. Right, ammunition and gear, I should do that too," Durante said, giving her one more squeeze before removing himself to his room.

"Do you need help with anything, Octavia?" Alces asked as he was cleaning dishes.

She pulled out a lump of pale sandstone from her bag on components. "I don't suppose you could crush this in your hand, could you?"

"I suppose I could," Alces responded, taking the sandstone from her. With a hint of effort, Alces squeezed it, and the rock powdered. He gently dumped it into her bowl and dusted his hand off.

She watched as the dusty sand fell into the bowl. "Well, that saved me about an hour or more of effort," she said, picking up her pestle to grind down any larger pieces left. "I don't think I will ever not be impressed by your strength, my Knight."

"I will always be your shield and your muscle, if needed, my dear Octavia," he reassured and stood. "If there is nothing else, I think I shall walk the camp, meet the Sisters."

She nodded. "As you will, my knight. I promise to be ready before moonrise."

EIGHTEEN

She got to work, crushing the remaining pebbles, adding other powders from various bottles and vials she had tucked away. When she was almost done, she set the bowl down and ran the pestle around the edge. The bowl "sang" for a moment as she did, a sustained note that continued for as long as she ran the pestle over the edge. Then she pulled it away and began to move the sand into the smaller vials she used during casting.

Once she had cleaned up from crafting, she changed into the leather pants and the new fauld. It was a little tight in the waist, and she noted with some irony that it further accentuated her figure and gave her breasts a little boost. She didn't remember it fitting like that in the shop, and suspected her patron was to blame.

She pulled her voluminous hair up and twisted it up into twin buns to keep it out of the way, before sliding on her bracers and her protective amulet. She reflected sourly that remembering the bracers against the troll might have been helpful. Or not. She wasn't sure what they did for poison. All in all, she was ready for the impending battle with time to spare.

Durante was still tinkering with something in his room and hadn't reappeared yet. Sumner came in with a quiver full of arrows made of a similar dark metal that the other Sisters had been using. He was examining one of the arrows then looked up at Octavia.

"Alright, Tavi, you ready for this mess?" he asked with his trademark grin. "Don't worry, I'll keep an eye out for you. No monster's touching you again."

She smiled a little. "Ready as I can be. Even if I do look absurd." She drummed her fingertips on the corset-like fauld. "It seems Kamvasana's 'gifts' even extend to my armor."

"And bless them for that," Sumner laughed. "Distraction is a powerful tool in combat. You might have a rival with their mage."

"Well, I look forward to meeting their mage," she said with a grin. "Though not nearly as much as I imagine you look forward to burying your face in my cleavage after the fight." She stuck her tongue out at him and realized with a start that it was slightly longer than it used to be.

"That is one of my favorite things to do. I feel I haven't done that enough," Sumner said wistfully.

Clearing her throat, she recovered and picked up her satchel, slinging the strap across her chest and let it settle on her hip. "Maybe I should get one of those bandoliers for my sands and dusts like Durante has for his screwshot vials. I could strap it to my thigh or something."

"I highly recommend them for keeping things at the ready," Durante said as he appeared from his room. He was a little more plated up than usual as well, but nowhere near as armored as Alces or even Sumner in his leathers. "I've also created a treatment for the leather, which is far superior, if I do say so myself."

She looked at Durante with a smile. "We can look into it next time we're at a big enough market. Ready?"

"Ready as I'll ever be, I suppose," he said, checking his rifle once more and running a hand over his bandolier to make sure he packed it correctly. On top of all of that, he also had a toolkit strapped to his hip that contained a myriad of inventions that he wanted to have at the ready. "Lead the way."

"I assume we'll just follow the sound of Alces' voice," she said wryly and headed out of the tent, walking back towards the tower and listening for their draconic companion.

There were certainly loud enough proclamations of bravery and daring coming from the entrance to the ruin. Alces was speaking to the Sisters, who were responding in a much more conversational tone. Aislin and Ursile were standing across from him, amused but nodding along. Magnia was standing beside him with her elbow on his shoulder, arm draped.

There was the fourth that Sumner had hinted at, which must be the mage. Bright blond hair surrounded a freckled and tanned face with a waterfall braid. She was shockingly beautiful and seemed to hail from the south of Ascherol or even Fontenia. Unlike the others, she was wearing a deep blue dress that sparkled like a night sky and was slit dangerously high on both hips. Underneath, however, she wore knee-high boots that were plated in the same dark metal as the others. The neckline plunged to nearly her navel and generously showed off why Octavia would have competition in the distraction department. There was an ornate pauldron on her left side that looked like a raven's head, with the beak running along and down her arm, ending before her elbow. The other hand had dark metal clawed armor affixed to each of her fingers. She was casually leaning against a dark staff with a top that resembled a bird's talons clutching a glacier-blue crystal.

As they walked up to conversational range, the mage turned to Octavia and smiled broadly. "Oh, thank Sihirizha you've arrived, darling," she said with a noticeable accent. The woman winked and Octavia heard her voice continue in her mind. **It's been forever since I had someone of our caliber to speak to. Us goddesses must stick together.**

Octavia was surprised, but smiled back, brightly and happily. A beautiful woman who was confident enough not to see other beautiful women as competition was Octavia's favorite kind. She strode up to the mage and greeted her like a friend, kissing her cheeks before standing next to her.

"Delighted to run into you, dearest. This is stunning, what you've done here," she said, gesturing to the pauldron. "I feel a touch underdressed."

The mage waved her hand and looked Octavia over. "Darling, when you walk in, you set the dress. You look fantastic and ready for this sortie," she said, and reached out for Octavia's hands, giving them a squeeze. "Tiphanie LaPorte. The pleasure is ours."

"Octavia Baudelaire. Enchanted." This was the last place she'd expected to find a friend, but she would not turn one down. She glanced over at the rest of the gathering and beyond to the portal, then back to Tiphanie. "So how did a paragon of magic and glamour such as yourself find your way here?"

"Calling, you could say. Felt compelled to be here, like I was needed. Not exactly my scene, but I would never leave these lovely ladies in need," she said, looking back at the other three Sisters. "And yourself? While I would never doubt your ability to lead such fine men at a whim, I have a feeling this also wasn't quite your choice."

"Oh, these three found me in a backwater town trying to breach a mausoleum," she said candidly and cheerfully. "Ancient tomes, you know, they're never in convenient locations. They hired me to raid an old wizard's tower, and along the way we found ourselves to be... sympathetic souls."

Durante seemed at a loss and stuck near Octavia while trying to be respectful of his gaze. Sumner patted him on the shoulder then went to talk to Alces.

She glanced at the three of her companions, and then back to Tiphanie with a sigh. "I'm afraid I'm too attached to return to civilization without them."

"I can certainly understand why. They are quite lucky," Tiphanie commented, looking them over once more. She glanced over to Durante and smiled. "Are you her noble guard? You dress yourself like a chevalier."

"Ah, hee, no," Durante conceded. "D–Durante Calabria. Inventor and chemist."

The mage continued to smile and held out her hand, waiting. When Durante snapped out of it and carefully took her hand, she curtsied slightly. "Pleasure, Durante Calabria. Of the Montes Calabria?"

Durante had a mix of shock and embarrassment and carefully released Tiphanie's hand. "Was, yes."

"Their loss," she said, adding a quick wink and keeping her gentle smile. She turned back to Octavia, gesturing out with her hand. "So, my darling, what are your thoughts for tonight? I specialize in a lot of ice and lightning, so it's going to get a touch cold and quite loud."

"Durante has a fascinating weapon, like a crossbow but more powerful," Octavia commented. "He calls it a screwshot. It's also quite loud, but he's a remarkable shot." She glanced at him with a fond smile, then looked back to the mage.

"Now, personally, my specialty is being the right kind of charming, which I don't think will work for this particular scenario." She spread a hand in a bit of a helpless gesture. "However, I do have a few quick strikes that I can cast as many times as I need to, and some particularly searing spells if they aren't all immune to fire."

Tiphanie moved to look towards the proposed battleground. "Not all of them. Most still burn just as easily. I feel like the three of us will be quite away from the majority of the clash. That's what the three of them are for, plus your mighty knight. I'm going to assume he's as imposing as he appears?" Octavia could almost feel the quiet double entendre in her question.

"Oh, entirely," Octavia agreed, shifting to stand next to Tiphanie and look over the battlefield again and the other warriors. "He is a force unto himself. And Sumner is the fastest duelist I've ever seen." A small giggled bubbled out, and she dropped her voice. "Though only on the battlefield."

"Naturally," Tiphanie smirked with a glance over to her. "I assumed they are all of high quality, given their company."

By this point, the rest of the group had returned, and Sumner gave Tiphanie a smile of his own, but before he could say anything, Alces spoke up.

"My fellow champions," the dragonkin's voice rang clear through the camp, "I believe we have a strategy. One mastered by the veteran Aislin."

"Yes, thank you, Ser Alces," Aislin said, seeming amused. "Given our rather healthy reinforcements, we'll have a clear path for blocking any insurgency. At cardinal points we'll have myself, Ser Magnia, Ser Ursile, and Ser Alces beside the circle as vanguard. We've noted fairly decent perch points there, there, there, and there." The pale commander motioned to said locations. Two were a higher floor that had mostly broken away but still left a viable platform, one was the remains of a spiral staircase, and the last was the remains of a gatehouse tower that had a broken main door serving as a ramp.

"Lady LaPorte, Lady Baudelaire, I recommend you two on opposite sides while the gentleman can take the two broken floors. This way the center can be attacked, and we all have each other covered. Questions?"

"There is no indication at all what will come through?" Octavia asked, her voice clear and curious. She wasn't nervous about the potential numbers.

"Never," Aislin sighed. "It's the hardest part about this. We never know if it's going to be an easy night or a bloody nightmare. But, we stick together, we don't relent, and we'll win the day. We have learned three things, though. The gate closes when either the dawn comes, enough devil's blood has spilled on the circle to hide it from the moon, or a large enough fiend comes through that it renders the gate."

"The best nights, Lady Baudelaire, are when something large comes through immediately," Ursile said. "The worst is when nothing comes. The waiting can be unbearable."

"The most fun is when they swarm," Magnia said with a grin. "So many of the little bastards to squish."

"Alright, so kill as many of them as fast and as terribly as you can," Sumner noted. "Gate closes, and we're safe for a lunar cycle, yeah?"

"That is the gist of it, Mr. Taery," Aislin concluded.

Octavia nodded and looked back to the sky. "I suppose we should get in position, then." She flexed her hand and felt her power crackle at her fingertips. After the other night, even with the strangeness of Baris's curse, she was feeling very energized. Kamvasana always did reward her when she indulged more than usual.

There was certainly a tension in the air, but the Sisters looked ready. Before they set themselves to their positions, Ursile said a prayer in a language Octavia did not recognize, presumably Elvish. When the words were done, she felt a rush of power that emanated from Ursile. Given the looks of the others, everyone had felt the blessing as well.

"The sun has set," Aislin said, drawing the twin swords she had been carrying on her hips. The blades were broad and curved, and the whole thing resembled a wave. They, too, were made of the same dark metal. It was difficult to tell if they were stained from battle or forged from some foreign material. "Let us go to our positions. For the living, my Sisters."

"For the living," the other three responded back, Magnia with the most gusto.

Alces joined them as they walked towards the circle, mace and shield in hand. Durante came over and kissed Octavia before quickly running to his position. She smiled in surprise and watched with amusement as he walked up the wall as if it weren't vertical and set himself on the perch, unslinging his rifles and setting a few items down on the ground at his feet, at the ready.

Not to be shown up, Sumner also gave Octavia a kiss and headed up to his spot. Sumner's kiss got a softer smile than usual in response. It was a reassuring bit of physical proof that he was coming around. While he could have climbed, he was a showman and exhibited his acrobatic expertise as he ran up one wall, flipped off of it, bounced a second time, and hooked his heel on the platform, curling and rolling himself up into position. Readying his bow, he gave the girls a wink and waited.

"That is our cue, Darling," Tiphanie stated, leaning in and kissing Octavia's cheek. "We shall chat again during the victory. Do let me know if I may borrow one of your charming boys, I would deign not touch them if you objected."

Nodding, she kissed Tiphanie's cheek in return. "Absolutely, dearest. I would never restrict any of them after a victory, but I do appreciate you asking. Of course, I wouldn't expect anything less from a peer." She winked at the mage and made her way to her post.

"Lovely, darling. You're magnificent," the mage said, then disappeared in a cloud of dark sparkles. Across the battleground, Octavia saw her reappear on the top of the broken staircase and appeared to lord over the space.

The broken gatehouse was an easy walk, as the broken door led to nicely even brick despite its disarray. From the top, however, Octavia had a decent view into where the warriors were staging. Both Magnia and Alces were the heavies, armed with shields and heavy armor. It appeared that Ursile and Aislin were more the agile types, their armor a little lighter and layered in flexible scales.

Right as the darkness of night was to take hold, Yaren came running up to the gatehouse and scrambled up to join Octavia. "Apologies, my lady. I was meant to join you this evening, but I had an issue with my gear," she panted, dusting herself off. She was still in her riding leathers, but now she was armed with a longsword at her hip and a crossbow in her hands. "Komutan Aislin said I would be able to join as there were so many helping. Do you mind?"

Glancing over at Yaren, Octavia arched an eyebrow. "I hope nothing comes close enough to use the sword, but you are welcome. If I say to stay back, please do so. I am not so skilled a spellcaster that I can protect you if you step into my line of fire."

"Of course, my lady. I will give you ample distance," she said, moving to a far point of the rubble. She readied her crossbow, which seemed to have a healthy draw weight as it required her to use the foot loop and both her hands.

Aislin wasn't kidding, with the disappearance of the sun also came the vanishing of every small cloud in the sky. It was a perfectly clear night and a beautiful view of the stars, so much that Octavia could see the purplish swirl of the heavens. As the moonlight came to rest upon the courtyard, swirling energy filled in the glyphs and patterns that had been so intricately carved into the stone. The air turned warm, and the crackling energy fluctuated between shades of reds and blues, bolts seeming to arc over the ground and the warriors below, though the bolts did not seem to *do* anything to those gathered.

She could feel the very energies in the area around them get pulled in, like it was draining the essence of the land, and the lights got brighter. When it seemed it could hold no more there was a sudden silence and darkness, then a rip in the universe appeared in the center of the circle. It was a swirling mass of energy in which the center was perfectly black. No light escaped, and the edge seethed with a pulsing red. A rush of fowl air spilled forth, heavy with sulfur and death.

"Amazing," Octavia breathed. She had never seen anything like it. It was so much more than a summoning spell, even more than a portal spell. She wondered what on earth the purpose had been, what the original caster hoped to accomplish.

As they watched carefully, the warriors braced for the first wave. It was as if the world held its breath, tense and anticipating. Octavia understood what Ursile meant about the waiting. Then a small imp popped out near Magnia, ruddy skin and a body covered in small spines, a far cry from the soft and delicate appearance of Comicha. Magnia unceremoniously dropped her axe on it. The double-bladed head cleaved the creature in half and the giantess snorted. Octavia tipped her head to the side, looking at the smear where the imp had been. It would be ironic if so little came through on a night where they had back up. Alces would undoubtedly be disappointed.

There was a sudden screech of activity and fiends started to pour out of the gate. They ranged in size anywhere from the tiny imps about the size of a medium dog to devils with snake bodies as long as a wagon. The sheer number startled Octavia at first. She had never seen anything like it.

Alces let out a roar of a battle cry and began laying into the group. Octavia hadn't really seen Alces fight from such a vantage point before. Typically, she was too involved in the actual battle, but he was a powerhouse. Between his mace smashing demons into crumbled piles, or his shield knocking them a dozen feet into the blades of one of the others, none of the fiends stood a chance.

Magnia was relishing the battle, her axe rending bodies and appendages alike, leaving a mess. Aislin proved to be a skilled and precise swordswoman, every swing and thrust measured and practiced to perfection. Who knew how long it took her to hone these skills, but not a movement was wasted as she whipped the twin blades around, her eyes bright amongst the darkness down below. Ursile was a little clumsier, but the power of her sword was unquestionable. Beyond the damage it brought to devilish flesh, there was a burst of holy light with each strike, causing the beastly enemies to screech in pain.

Octavia crouched down, contemplating what she could do without hurting anyone else or getting in the way. When flying creatures started to join the mass, throwing themselves into the air to avoid the reach of those around the circle, it was the spell caster's and sharpshooter's turns. There were targets a plenty to go around, and they were darting right towards them.

"That's what I get for thinking about ironies," Octavia commented quietly to herself, then raised her hands and began to shoot fiends out of the sky. She focused on the smaller fliers, the winged imps that her bolts could take down in a single shot. Crackling blue energy burst from her hands, illuminating the gatehouse as she cast. Her targets twitched from the magical jolts before falling to the hard ground, quite dead. It was a good thing she could keep this up, as there were plenty more where they had come from.

Durante was aiming for the larger ones, their bodies twisting in the air as they're struck from his bullets and splatting onto the ground. Tiphanie was currently tossing lightning into the air, the crackling boom following as it jumped from creature to creature. The only one that wasn't making themselves a target was Sumner, who silently fired arrows in the shadow of his shattered wall.

Despite the warriors unmatched prowess, there were too many, and they were starting to get past them. A small pack of demons, resembling slavering wolves that had been shaved bare and then disfigured, started to rush the others. A trio rushed up the stones and started scrambling up the fallen door towards Octavia and Yaren.

Yaren dropped the first one but was hurriedly trying to reload the crossbow as the other two advanced. Octavia's blast of energy dropped the other one to the ground, twitching and unable to move. The third lunged, snapping at Octavia, then fell to a thump at her feet, its body skewered by a pair of arrows.

Looking up, she could see Sumner's bright jade eyes reflected in the moonlight, looking in her direction. She met his gaze for a moment, panting a little from the battle rush. She remembered his promise that no monster would touch her again. She nodded to him and looked back to the circle. She wanted to say more, but it would have to wait.

The horde was relentless. Octavia reached into her satchel and pulled out a vial of sand. "Alces!" She called out, certain he would hear her even despite the fight in his blood. "Tell them to step back! Don't step into the fog!"

"Powerful Octavia has cast a spell. Step back from the portal," Alces called out, his voice cutting through the melee in a way hers simply could not. The others were wise enough not to question it.

She poured the vial of sand into her hand and chanted softly before blowing the sand at the portal. A breath later that strange deeply blue fog rose up past the casting ring, filled with strangely thrashing tentacles and that searing heat. Her spell was a stopgap, forcing the beasts to come through the hellish trial. Many did not live through it, fire and caustic burns lancing their bodies and leaving them in a pile. Tiphanie assisted, forming a freezing vortex above the portal, catching the remaining flyers, effectively stopping the flow.

A hellish centipede nearly a dozen feet long skittered through the fog relatively unharmed and darted past Magnia who had been admiring the magic's work. Aislin spun around and caught it with one of her blades, pinning it to the ground. It squirmed for a moment, then a boom rang out from Durante's perch, and the insect's head exploded.

There was a rumble, like thunder but the sky was still cloudless. Something had changed. With her back turned, Aislin didn't notice the large scythe that had come out of the portal, followed by the massive demon that was carrying it, swinging it out as it forced its way through the portal. It caught Aislin in the neck, the fearsome strength decapitating her. The roiling fog fell, and Octavia watched with horror as Aislin's head flew into the rubble. She then gave her own head a shake and pulled another vial from her pack. She could be horrified later; the fight wasn't done. Poor Yaren wasn't able to shake it off and collapsed to the ground next to Octavia, curling into a ball and holding her head in her hands.

The demon, a fearsome creature clad in charred bone, standing over ten feet tall, with five narrow eyes in an arch over its face, a pair of slits for a nose, and a vicious maw filled with jagged teeth that split into a grin extending from ear to ear, yanked itself through the portal. As it drew itself to its full height, there was a large crashing noise as the energies erupted outwards and the door was rendered inert, the runes and markings fading out.

Alces roared out and charged the fiend, slamming his mace into its leg with terrifying force. The beast stumbled but wheeled around, bringing the serrated scythe down on the dragonkin knight. Alces held his shield up and took the blow, dropping to one knee but otherwise unharmed.

Magnia cursed to the heavens and swung her axe wide, burying it in the creature's armor. It barely penetrated the exoskeleton. Ursile stumbled back, holding the hilt of her sword up and screaming curses in Elvish. The upper half of a gleaming knight made of pure energy appeared, raising its sword and slashed at the demon's back, also tearing into the beast's armor. Pouring more of the casting sand into her hand, Octavia made a fist and then cast it down. An intense ringing filled the air around the demon. Cracks formed all through the demon's armor and the creature reared back, bits of the jagged bone falling onto the ground as he sloughed it off. Magnia ripped her axe out and gave it another swing, more of the fossilized armor shattering upon the impact. Ursile's spiritual warrior struck again, and the demon was losing its protection.

Alces used his shield to throw the monster off balance, its weapon falling to the ground. It roared out as Alces held up his free hand. "Let the light burn you to your core and banish you from this world," he roared. A beam of silvery light descended from the sky, enveloping the demon, and it raged, thrashing wildly.

Durante stood up abruptly, as if inspired. "Lady Tiphanie, can you create ice? Above its head," he yelled.

"Of course, handsome," she said, swirling her staff in a dramatic spin. It seemed the movement built up energy, and when she thrust it forward, a burst of blue light emanated outward and formed a block of ice half the size of a man.

Durante smirked and held up a rod that had been at his feet. With the flip of a switch, there was a popping noise and the block of it wavered in the air for a moment, before increasing in size tenfold. Unable to handle the extreme change in weight, Tiphanie released it, and the massive block smashed into the demon, crushing its skull and flattening it to the ground.

There was a pause as everyone readied themselves in case the demon rose again. Octavia took a deep breath and then dropped down next to the girl at her feet.

"Yaren, dove, come back to me," she said softly, brushing a hand through the girl's hair. "I know it hurts, dove, but we have to get back up. We have to make sure the battle is done."

Yaren sniffed and crawled over to Octavia, hugging her close and burying her face in her chest. Octavia held her and petted her hair. Down below, there was a sudden rush in activity.

"Where's her head?" Magnia called out. "Find Aislin's head!"

Oddly, Aislin's body was still walking around. It stumbled slightly, then brushed itself off. Where a bloody stump of a neck should be was a wisp of ghostly blue smoke. The rest of Octavia's group were equally as confused.

"Down here," came a muffled sound from some of the rubble and corpses. Ursile dashed over and carefully fished out Aislin's head. It seemed Aislin hadn't realized she was dead yet, as she sneezed then sighed.

"What the fuck!?" yelled Sumner, still on his perch.

Octavia watched the scene unfold for a moment, then let out a startled laugh. "Goddess of Mercy," she said, then called out to Sumner. "She's a dullahan!"

"Could have been worse," Aislin said as Ursile carried her head back to her body, which reached out and stuck her back on her neck. "Yaren, dear, it's fine. I'm alright."

Shifting her weight, Octavia started to rise and bring Yeren with her. "Come on, dove. Your Komutan didn't fall. Not today."

Yaren's eyes were still full of tears, but she was recovering because, in the face of it, what else could she do? She let go of Octavia, scampered down the door, and ran to Aislin, throwing her arms around her. "Oh, my Komutan, I feared the worst!"

Octavia dusted herself off and adjusted her shirt, casting a quick spell to remove the tears and accompanying evidence of grief from her clothing.

Aislin laughed softly and hugged her girl back, kissing the top of her head. "Was really hoping you wouldn't need to find out."

Alces was still in awe, whether from confusion or the suddenness of it. "Mighty Ser Aislin, how are you still alive?"

"Spite, mostly," she said, massaging her neck as the other arm continued to hug Yaren. "They killed me once. I'm not going to give them the satisfaction of it happening again."

Durante and Sumner hopped down from their spots to join the rest of the group while Octavia found Tiphanie appearing right next to her. "You put up a marvelous fight, darling. Your boys are, indeed, quite adept," she said, standing next to her and looking down at them.

"They do me proud," she said with a smile, looking down at them as she adjusted her hair. "And thank you, dearest. You were also a delight to behold. Your spellwork is as stunning as the rest of you."

"Oh, thank you, darling," Tiphanie said. "I could compliment you all day on your ability to control a crowd."

Octavia turned back to Tiphanie and arched a brow. "So how do evenings go after the battle here? Alces is very big on victory celebrations and will undoubtedly attempt one."

"Oh, undoubtedly it will be a far better celebration than normal with you and your boys here." Tiphanie grinned playfully. "While there is plenty of drink and people stumbling into each others' beds. I do fear for Kieth. You probably saw him, he's our cook and, politely, our morale officer." Octavia snickered quietly, and Tiphanie also giggled.

It seemed the question was starting to answer itself, as Alces and Magnia were already both calling for drink and a feast. Aislin, unsurprisingly, seemed worn out, and Ursile was praying quietly. Sumner and Durante, already used to the ways of the Spree Spirits, were joining right in.

"Best while the spirits are still high and before the thrill has worn off. Shall we, darling?" Tiphanie asked, offering Octavia her arm.

"Indeed we shall," Octavia answered, and took the proffered arm, sauntering down towards the rest of their enthusiastic band. Compared to the last fight they all got in, Octavia was doing quite well. A little low on magic, but otherwise completely unharmed.

NINETEEN

When they got closer, Octavia could see the warriors had definitely taken the brunt of the attack. All of them had various cuts and bruises from the horde. Alces even had a large claw, and the arm attached to it, caught in one of his shoulder plates. It looked as though Ursile was already healing them, though, as Alces was too excited to think of it yet.

"Formidable Octavia and skillful Tiphanie, your assistance was invaluable," Alces said, reaching out to Octavia. He then noticed the amount of demon goo he had on his hands and thought better of it for the moment. "We are victorious. No fiend could take this night from us. We showed them that light will always banish the darkness!"

"That's what we do," she said, smiling at her knight. "Just call us the Lightbringers." It was a little flippant, but she assumed that Alces would forgive her.

A slight giggle from Aislin as she gently maneuvered Yaren to her side and nodded. "I can't thank you all enough. Without the four of you, this night would have been much, much worse."

"We still could have taken them," Magnia boasted with a wink.

"And this is every month for you?" Durante asked.

Aislin merely nodded while Sumner examined her neck from a distance. "Come, let us make sure Kieth is readying the victory feast and a few barrels are cracked," she continued, directing them back to the camp.

Octavia let go of Tiphanie and bit back a laugh as she rose up on her tiptoes to remove the claw from Alces' paldron and cast the cleansing spell on him. "Trophy, my knight, or toss it on the pile?"

"Oh," Alces said, noticing the relief he didn't realize he needed and turned around. "A minor scrap. To the pile. That does remind me, though. Honorable Ser Aislin, we came here for fiend parts for our wise Durante for his alchemy. May I request that he has first choice among those we've slain."

"Knight Brightrain, you can have whatever you want. You helped when you didn't need to, and you helped admirably," Aislin stated, turning to Durante. "Please, help yourself, and if you can't find what you're looking for, let us know."

"Although, I must ask, how did you know to come here at all?" Ursile looked over curiously as she was healing Magnia.

"We met Erash in Limanyadeli," Octavia said as she tossed away the arm. "And I was very persuasive." Her mouth quirked as she fought not to giggle. "We purchased what reagents she had, but she did not have all we needed, and after some consideration she agreed to send us in your direction."

Magnia snorted and grinned. "Oh, that whore. Glad she did. How is that emerald minx?"

This time the laugh made it out. "She's fine," Octavia said, turning to Magnia and casting the cleansing spell again after a good look at the giantess. "She talked me into trying one of her experiments, which made for a fascinating evening. But she seems to be doing well."

"Oh, thank you," Magnia said, looking over her armor. "I need a day of rest after one of those 'experiments'. Well, she knows quality people."

"I will have to send her a thank you," Aislin added as they started to walk back to the camp.

Durante took a moment, thought about it, then sighed. "I'll catch up," he said, "if I can harvest it now, it will be in the best possible condition."

"Allow me to help, handsome," Tiphanie said with a smile towards Octavia, "I'm quite versed in demonology. We can find the pieces you seek faster, then we can join the party."

Octavia smiled back, and nodded to Tiphanie, then looked towards Durante. "We'll see you when you're free," she said, then turned and followed after the others. Tiphanie and a very shy looking Durante went back into the ruins to find what he sought while the others headed up.

As they walked, Octavia cast the cleansing spell on Ursile and Aislin. Might as well, it wouldn't hurt, and she'd already taken care of the others.

She fell into step next to Sumner and smiled at him as they walked.

"I told you nothing would touch you," Sumner grinned as he looked over to her.

There were rounds of people complimenting the others about attacks they'd seen, some boasting about other maneuvers that maybe people hadn't caught. It seemed very true that camaraderie was found easily in shared conflict. Even Yaren had found the power to detach herself from Aislin and smile with them.

Reaching the camp, the Sisters excused themselves so that they could change out of their armor and freshen up a bit. Yaren ran to make sure Kieth had the celebratory meal ready, or at least cooking.

"You know, I had a dress made back in Limanyadeli that I've been saving for something," she said to Sumner as they walked back to the tent to change their own clothes and shed their armor. "Do you think I should wear it tonight? It might hide the tail a little if nothing else."

Sumner started to say something, then sighed and smiled. "Tavi, wear whatever you want. However you look, I need to get used to it. It's my problem, not yours," he said earnestly, taking her hands and kissing them.

"I mean, it is my problem. Not your reaction, but..." she sighed, and looked up into his eyes. "My storm." She looked at him for a moment, then gave her head a little shake. "I think I'll wear the dress anyway. You all have seen everything else already." She squeezed his hands and let go, heading into her room to change.

She pulled the dress out of Matilda, still packaged in the original wrap from the shop. Thankfully the deep blues and indigos would still look complimentary with her pink and violet skin. Stripping down, she looked in the mirror again and sighed.

"A relic from another primordial," she murmured to herself. "Where on earth am I going to find that?"

Or you could not worry about it! Kamvasana chimed blithely. *You're positively delectable like this! And there's so much desire in this camp right now! Ohhhh, I'm beyond excited for your evening.*

Octavia rolled her eyes and started to get dressed. There wasn't much to go beneath the dress. It dipped low in front, the fabric of the bodice overlapping before tucking into a wide waist that was tight from under her breasts to her hips, where the skirt flared a bit but was also split. All the way up. She couldn't wear smallclothes under this dress. It was perfect for an evening slated to end in debauchery. She undid her hair as she headed back out, letting it bounce down her back.

It looked like Alces had been waiting for her. Clad in little more than his casual kilt and a vest, he bowed gently to Octavia. "Gorgeous as always, radiant Octavia. The dress is lucky to be worn by such as you," he said, offering his hand.

She smiled softly and took Alces' hand. "Thank you, my heart," she said, looking up at him. "You always look resplendent. I don't think you can help it." She brought his hand up and kissed it gently.

"If I do, it is because of your influence and your eye, my wondrous Octavia. Now we celebrate, as is our tradition." He looked down at her, head tilted to the side. "Do you have eyes on anyone this night? Or desires?"

"I think… I'm not sure," she said, still smiling. "Tiphanie asked if I would permit her to chase one of you. I think Magnia has designs on you specifically." She giggled.

Alces laughed. "She is indeed a hardy woman, is she not?" Taking her hand with his, he walked her out of the tent.

Octavia laughed again and leaned into him. "She certainly is. I hope you don't find me too delicate afterwards," she said, teasingly.

Alces stopped Octavia and turned to her, leaning in to place his head against hers. "You are unique and desirous for your own qualities. I will find you so always," he smiled and kissed her forehead. "I am sure you already knew this."

"I do," she said, with a comfortable surety that radiated through her. "I think I'm content to see where the night takes me, and if you all find a partner before I make up my mind, I will not be upset. But thank you for asking me."

Nodding, Alces began to walk once more. "It would seem to me Tiphanie has already chosen to beguile Durante. She also seems taken with you as well, but I could be wishing things upon you."

"Tiphanie and I see ourselves in each other," she said, and shrugged. "While I would most certainly not turn her down, I think it's a sympathy more than an attraction. I think I have made a friend."

He smiled. "I certainly know she could provide a friendship that we could not, so I am glad for you."

Before they approached the table where most had gathered, Octavia brought Alces's hand up for one more kiss. "I hope you enjoy your evening, my knight."

The party had started to a certain degree. Kegs had been tapped, and there was an impressive spread on the large yet simple table they had near the bonfire. Roasts, skewers of smaller game birds, root vegetables in various sauces. Octavia knew enough about cooking to know that the roasts would have had to be started hours ago. This was clearly the normal meal at the end of this grisly monthly ritual.

Everyone was there, save Durante and Tiphanie. Kieth was talking to Sumner about something, which got a loud laugh from the rogue. Yaren was in a much better mood and no longer clinging to Aislin. There were two others Octavia hadn't yet met. One was a woman, perhaps of similar age and height to herself, but with a build of muscle that made her arms and shoulders prominent. She was all smiles with a dusky complexion and dark hair pulled back in a simple tail. She appeared to be from the area, as her features were similar to those Octavia had seen in Limanyadeli, with thicker eyebrows, smoky eyes, and high cheekbones.

The other seemed the youngest. A slight girl, the most casually dressed, with light pants and a shirt. She was adorable with a bright smile, sun kissed with reddish brown hair. Nothing about her suggested that she was a fighter, nor did she hold herself with the air of someone of the magical persuasion.

As Alces and Octavia approached, cheers went up, and Octavia got a number of looks from the group. Evidently, her dress was doing good work. She even got an encouraging whistle from Sumner. Kieth appeared slightly gobsmacked. As did Ursile. Aislin moved slightly and patted the seat next to her and Ursile.

"Come, Lady Baudelaire. Relax and bless us with your company."

"Oh! Um, of course." Octavia pushed a curl behind her ear and walked over to the stool in question. She briefly regretted the choice of the dress when she realized that in order to not sit on her tail, she couldn't sit on the skirt. Her bare bottom would be on that stool. The cleaning spell was getting a lot of use this evening.

Sitting down, she adjusted her skirts as much as she could, though nothing would keep them from exposing her legs all the way up to the curve of her ass. "Thank you, Ser."

"Of course. You and your group were invaluable today, you've earned. it." This close, it was impossible not to notice that it hadn't been a trick of the light or something else, Aislin's eyes really did glow. Constantly. Her hair had an etherealness to it that made it impossible to think she wasn't supernatural in some way. Of course, now they knew why.

"I don't think you've been introduced to some other members of our camp. This is Dilara," Aislin started, motioning towards the woman with the impressive arms, then to the younger woman, "and Safa."

"Nice to meet you, beautiful," Dilara said with a wink. "I like the horns."

"Hi," Safa said with a little wave and a soft smile.

Octavia laughed a little. "Thank you, I'm still getting used to them. Are you the smith?" She smiled and nodded to Safa as well.

"That would be me. Someone's got to keep everyone's gear in check with this war. I can certainly see why you don't need any of my services. Well, smithing services, anyway," Dilara grinned.

Octavia grinned back. "Not a lot in the way of gear, no. Gallivanting with these three finally got me to start investing in reinforced leather." She held up her hand and wiggled her fingers, blue flames briefly dancing at her fingertips. "I mostly stand back and throw things, so to speak."

"Your hair's very pretty," Safa included.

Looking at Safa, Octavia smiled. "Is it? I—"

"It's all of her," Ursile said, leaning in maybe a touch too close. "Look at her. Such a beautiful pink and those bright blue eyes. Like the commander's, but, well, they don't glow." Ursile giggled, it was clear she either started early or was a lightweight.

Blinking, Octavia glanced at Ursile in surprise, and did her very best not to laugh, but couldn't stop the smile.

"Lady Baudelaire, I'm so, so sorry for thinking you were anything other than wonderful. I have shamed myself," Ursile continued. Yes, she appeared to be quite tipsy. This was causing no small bit of amusement from Dilara and Aislin.

"It's all right, Ser Ursile, really," she said, and meant it. While she was struggling with her emotions over her appearance, she didn't blame the elf for her initial reaction. Understanding what they fought every cycle, how could she?

"You are not the first person to be… startled by my appearance," she continued, her eyes flitting briefly to Sumner before focusing on the elf once more. "Let us remember our shared victory rather than a brief misunderstanding."

"No, it's not alright," Ursile said, impassioned, looking Octavia right in the eyes. "It is not the way an abbess of Jistifèt should act, and I must make amends!"

"Just go along with it," Aislin whispered in Octavia's ear as she leaned over. "She invoked her god's name; she's not going to let it go. It's okay."

"Um..." Octavia glanced from Aislin to Ursile, "Would you accept it if I said I forgave you? What amends do you need to make? Also, I may need a drink for this."

"No," Ursile said, slapping the table and nearly knocking herself over in the process. "I have committed a great injustice, and it must be remedied." Octavia couldn't hold back a small snort at Ursile's passionate protestation.

"Here you are, my lady," Safa said, a mug appearing in her hand. "I'll make you a plate as well."

Picking up the mug, Octavia looked up at Safa with a smile. "Thank you, bunny. I do appreciate it."

Safa smiled brightly and nodded. The drink was definitely flowing at this point. Sumner has started to chat with Yaren, and they seemed to be hitting it off, comparing bows and crossbows. Magnia already had an arm around Alces and was trying to get him to drink. Alces was happily providing his favorite party trick of cooling off drinks. Octavia took a sip, and discovered it to be ale, after which she rose up enough to push it across the table to Alces. "Ser Knight, if you would."

As Octavia settled once more, Aislin turned towards her. "I know you were rather pushed into this, and we haven't gotten to speak casually," she said. "What can you tell me about the charming Lady Octavia Baudelaire?"

Octavia arched an eyebrow, a little amused. While she'd known from her exchanges with Tiphanie and Alces what the likely activity was this evening, she was actually surprised that the ghostly knight was interested. She had made assumptions about her and Yaren's relationship. Then again, it's possible those assumptions were correct, but much like Octavia and her boys, the Sisters weren't against an entertaining evening with new friends.

"I can tell you a great many things," Octavia said, turning a little to make it easier to talk to Aislin. "For starters, I am technically not a lady. My parents were merchants, and while they very much hoped to marry me to royalty, I have since been disowned and remain unwed." She grinned—she was still a little amused by that part of her history, and she wanted to be sure Aislin knew it wasn't a sensitive subject. "I'm also a warlock. But bound to a Power, not a fiend," she added quickly, given the night's activities.

"Both you and Mr. Calabria, abandoned by your families. Sounds like both of them can't recognize talent or valor," Aislin said, shaking her head. "Fear not, I've heard of many warlocks bound to all sorts of things. I once knew an elf that was bound to a spirit of the ocean."

"You are royalty, how dare they," Ursile proclaimed, leaning her head on Octavia now. "I will serve you, my Lady. This very night, to prove my oath and your status."

Aislin couldn't help but smirk and raised her eyebrows at Octavia. "We may need to get some food in her."

Subtly pointing to Ursile, Octavia asked, "How many?"

"Two or three," Aislin responded with a smirk. "She'll be fine."

Giggling, Octavia nodded and cleared her throat, returning to the previous conversation. "Are you familiar with Kamvasana? That is my patron. They are mostly easy to serve, only demanding about one or two particular things." She shrugged. "I'm not sure I was all that suited to being a wife anyway."

"Kamvasana, you say," Tiphanie said as she walked up with Durante. Her hair and dress were still immaculate. "Darling, I knew I liked you. It makes so much sense as well."

"Hi," Durante said, his hands covered in gore, "I'm going to go wash up. Um, don't wait up."

"Prudent Durante, did you find what you were looking for?" Alces asked.

"Uh, yeah, yeah I did," he said, cheering up a bit and standing straighter. "A number of things, actually. But I really should do something about this." Holding up his hands, it dripped a little with blood and ichor.

"Please do," Aislin said with a giggle, "and thank you for respecting the feasting table."

Octavia almost got up to go help him, set her hands on the table ready to do so, but paused and let him wander off. She didn't want to disappear, and if he and Tiphanie had already made arrangements, she didn't want to potentially derail their plans. Instead, she pouted at Alces until he chilled her drink and passed it back. Ale wasn't her favorite, but it was always better cold.

Alces chuckled and took her mug, bowing in apology. With a gentle blow, he cooled her ale until the wood started to frost, then handed it back. "Caught in the excitement. Forgive me, dear Octavia," he smiled. Octavia accepted her mug and sat back again, sipping carefully at first, then less so when she found the drink to be cold enough.

Tiphanie took a mug herself and walked past Kieth, running a hand along his shoulders before seating herself down at an available stool. Taking a sip, she glanced over the table. *You have quite the caliber of men around you, my dear,* Octavia heard through a tingle of magic. *I'm a touch envious.*

Glancing over at Tiphanie, she tipped her head to the side. She was fairly certain she could respond to this spell. *I suspect you would be able to gather a delightful menagerie if you weren't bound by duty,* Octavia returned, focusing her thoughts while she still felt the tremor of magic. *Though I promise that if I find someone worthy of you, I will compel them to come join the fight and add a little more variety to your camp.*

Oh, my sweet berry blossom, you are too kind. I'm only here three nights, for the sortie. Otherwise, I still travel and relax. You must visit me at my villa sometime. Tiphanie gave her a wink, then turned to talk to Dilara about jewelry or some such.

Oh, Goddess of Mercy! Good! I was at a loss for how you'd managed not to languish out here, but I understand now. Octavia hid a little giggle in her mug and took another drink.

The meal was delicious, many of the dishes similar to what they had been enjoying in the area. The last addition to the table was stacks of flatbread to accompany the heavily sauced dishes. It was finished up by a dessert of thin layered dough, syrup, and nuts. Octavia ate with a healthy appetite and made sure to get up and introduce herself to Kieth and compliment him on the food. Kieth thanked her for the compliment and responded in kind with some rather tasteful flattery about her dress and how it hugged her body perfectly. He was surprisingly smooth, but Octavia imagined that as the only man in a camp of women, some of which certainly found men attractive, he had a bit of practice.

Ale was flowing freely, though Octavia only had a couple mugs. She walked past Sumner and Yaren and raised an eyebrow at him. He grinned at her and shrugged, then returned to the conversation. Yaren was a little young and idealistic for Octavia's tastes, but she hoped they enjoyed each other. It did suddenly occur to her that she actually had no idea how old Sumner was. Safa had decided to turn in early, as she was no doubt going to be running into town early the next morning to inform them it was safe for another month and to get some supplies for an increased breakfast.

Returning to her seat between Ursile and Aislin, Ursile almost immediately cuddled up against Octavia, gently petting her leg since there was skin to touch. It was a struggle not to be too amused at Ursile's antics. With dinner, Ursile had sobered up a bit, but that did not seem to stop her from fawning over Octavia.

Aislin had also kept her focus on Octavia, mostly chatting about their histories and adventures. Talking with Aislin was fascinating. The woman was much older than she looked. She hadn't been lying, spite was keeping Aislin alive. She had been the first to fight back the demons when the gate opened and paid for it with her life, but her vow kept her here and placed her head neatly back where it belonged. She went on to found the Sisterhood, calling like-minded women to her side to deal with the gate. It was admirable, and impressive.

She had a couple more mugs of ale. She wasn't as easy to inebriate as Ser Ursile, but she was getting warm and flirty and relaxing more. By the fourth drink she had managed to stop focusing on the strangeness of her new body and was acting more herself. Alces and Magnia were singing drinking songs from the northern region, and what Alces lacked in tone he made up for with enthusiasm. It also appeared that Magnia may have a constitution to match Alces, as the rounds they were going through would have knocked out anyone else at the table. Still, the evening was starting to move in a direction. Sumner and Yaren had already disappeared. Kieth was being pulled away by Dilara towards the darker tents.

"So, as I am never one to assume," Aisil said gently, "what is your take on the evening?"

"I assume you mean where the evening is going," Octavia said, amused, "and not asking for my tactical summary of the battle." She giggled again and drank off the rest of her ale before setting the mug down with a thud.

"Well then!" She tossed her hair back and looked at Aislin. "Sumner and Alces were a little, oh, whorish before I met them, and have only continued to be so. Durante is shy, but capable of seeing to his needs if he so wishes. Alces was gentlemanly enough to check in with me before we came to dinner and has been informed that I don't expect his or the others' company this evening, and they are free to find their own entertainment. As am I."

"So," Aislin persisted, smirking and leaning on her elbow as she turned to Octavia fully, "would you like to find some entertainment? I think I know a couple of places." Ursile reached out, wrapped her arm around Octavia's and scowled at Aislin. This elicited a haunting yet cheerful laugh from Aislin.

"Now, ladies, you're both pretty," Octavia said with a giggle. She looked back to Aislin with a playful grin. "And I may not be a warrior, but for the right activity my stamina is legendary."

"First, sweet Ursile, I would never get between you and your duty, you know that," Aislin giggled, reaching out and petting Ursile's cheek. "Second, given Tiphanie's reaction to your sovereign, I would certainly like to test that."

Tiphanie appeared to be listening, because she giggled and raised her eyebrows at Octavia. She had been enjoying drink and food and teasing Kieth before he was dragged off, but had not left, quite delighted with the antics thus far.

"For whatever it's worth, I wore out Erash," Octavia said with a little laugh. She let herself lean into Ursile a bit, because it made it easier to turn towards Aislin. "Granted, I was under the influence at the time." She reached out and set her hand on Aislin's. "What do you think, Ser Ursile?"

"I will earn back my honor through your pleasure, my lady," Ursile said, still not letting go of her arm. Octavia couldn't keep herself from laughing. Aislin giggled again and turned her hand around, taking Octavia's.

"Magnia would never believe it, so as commander of the Sisters, I clearly need to test this claim," the dullahan smiled. "Do you require anything? More food and drink?"

"I think I've had enough to drink, and I can get a snack later. Have someone save me some of the flatbread and the red sauce." She pulled Aislin's hand towards her and kissed the back of it. Aislin smiled and returned the gesture. Her lips left a tingly sensation on her skin, which elicited thoughts of what the rest of her would feel like.

Not wanting to leave Ursile neglected, Octavia deftly slid her hand around the other woman's to turn her palm upward and kissed that as well, with the barest hint of her tongue. Ursile swooned slightly, then shivered at the touch of her tongue. The night was already feeling a touch warmer.

"Shall we take to my tent or yours?" Aislin asked as she rose, offering Octavia a hand.

"To be courteous to my companions, and because I haven't seen Durante come back yet, let's head to yours," Octavia said, accepting the hand up, careful of her skirt as she rose. She glanced back at Tiphanie with a smile. "We'll catch up in the morning, dearest."

"I do so hope to chat with you then," Tiphanie responded, blowing her a kiss. *Don't take too long. And, because I like you so much: Aislin's tummy and the back of Ursile's knees and the webbing of her fingers. You're welcome. Bless you.*

TWENTY

This way, then," Aislin said, turning to lead them back to her tent. Ursile released Octavia's arm long enough to stand, then reattached herself to walking beside her.

"I am at your whim, my lady, until my duty is fulfilled."

"Ursile, love, you're allowed to have fun." Aislin rolled her eyes a little.

"I will enjoy myself more if you're also enjoying yourself," Octavia said to Ursile with a smile. Not that she had a problem ordering the elfin knight around, but Ursile didn't feel like the type of woman who took particular joy in that.

"Of course I will," Ursile insisted. "How could I not?" Her hands had drifted slightly, one taking Octavia's hand and the other holding her upper arm. It was surprisingly adorable given the battle Octavia had witnessed not hours before.

Aislin seemed satisfied and escorted them to her tent. Unsurprisingly, it was the largest. The other Sisters may come and go, but this is where Aislin would probably remain for the rest of her days, so she might as well enjoy her home. It was more than a tent, the heavy canvas walls draped on a sturdy, more permanent wooden frame. The floor was also wood instead of canvas or packed dirt and layered with carpets beginning a little past the entryway. As they stepped in, Aislin motioned for them to remove their boots before continuing.

The interior was well furnished, with plenty of furs for when winter came, couches and chairs. Aislin had a surprising array of weapons, neatly displayed on racks and stands, as well as two full suits of armor that clearly were not made for her.

She continued guiding them to the bedroom. It was surprisingly cozy and feminine, with a massive bed that had to have been built on site, four-poster with gauze drapes, pillows a plenty, and a fur blanket that was so soft it could have passed for mink. There was a full-length mirror, an armoire, and a bed bench that spanned the complete width, no doubt made to match the bed exactly.

"Welcome to my room, Lady Baudelaire," Aislin said, smiling. "Ursile has been here before, of course. May I call you Octavia?"

"It's lovely," Octavia said genuinely. She was envious of the four-poster bed. "And please do. Octavia or Tavi if you prefer."

"Tavi. I like it, it's cute," Aislin said and took a moment to stretch, rolling out her shoulders.

She turned towards Ursile, still on her arm, and kissed her softly. "Am I allowed to drop your titles for the evening? Or is there something you'd prefer me to call you?"

Either Ursile was still drunk, or truly taken by Octavia, because she melted into the gentle kiss and leaned into it. "Um, just Ursile is fine. Or Ulla, if you like."

"Lin for me if you're feeling very familiar," Aislin added, taking off her shirt with a sigh and tossing it onto a rack for laundry. Aislin's skin was like marble, white with slight discolorations where scars were. They were faint, but her body was covered in them. With a content noise, she flopped onto the bench which, watching its give, was very plush.

"I highly suspect that we will all be feeling very familiar by the time we're done," Octavia commented, drawing Ursile with her as she moved closer to Aislin.

It was a little odd in that she didn't have a good feel for either of them. Well, Ursile was drunk or smitten, and seemed like she would be fairly pliable, but Octavia wasn't sure what Aislin wanted. Which was a bit of a shame as, though she'd never admit it to the lovely women she was with, Aislin was the one Octavia was interested in. Ursile was sweet, and they would have a fun evening as the knight "made amends," but Aislin was who made Octavia want to be there.

"Let's get you out of this, precious," Octavia said to Ursile in a low, caressing voice, her hands gently and insistently pulling up the elf's shirt.

"Please," Ursile said softly and lifted her arms to help. Neither Ursile nor Aislin were wearing much, probably in anticipation of the night's activities.

Ursile was a willowy woman out of her armor, fit and subtle of curve. She had a figure typical of an elf, and Octavia thought for a moment that it would be lovely to watch her dance. She imagined Ursile moved with the grace of a reed in the wind outside of battle. Aislin was certainly more built than Ursile, broader shoulders and a little more muscular, but also wide in the hip. And she seemed to be quite content, for the moment, with watching Octavia and Ursile.

"Shall I remove your dress?" Ursile asked after she'd been relieved of her shirt. She ran her hands over the material, over Octavia's plentiful curves, pleased with its smoothness and seeking out any ties, buttons, or clasps. Octavia was soft in a way neither Aislin nor Ursile was, a little heavier in comparison. From her spanning hips and lush backside to her weighty breasts and the soft curve of her tummy. The muscles in her legs had gotten more developed in the last few months as she travelled with her coterie.

"Here," Octavia said with a smile, and gently guided Ursile's hands to the cleverly hidden stays on either side of her dress. Once they were undone, the fabric easily slipped from her shoulders, leaving the dress to pool around her feet. Her tail swished a bit, happy to be free from the fabric.

"It is one thing to see you clothed, but another entirely to see you bare," Aislin said, her eyes eagerly taking in all of the warlock before her. "Glorious."

"May I?" Ursile asked, reaching towards Octavia, a little more conscientious at this point. It was kind of cute how the elf that was slaying demons with aplomb not long ago was now blushing.

"May you what?" Octavia asked, even as she reached towards Ursile again, quickly undoing the ties on the elf's pants. She kind of loved teasing the shy ones. "Tell me what you want, precious." Her hands slid up to Urslie's hips, leaving her pants undone but not pushing them down yet. Her thumbs brushed over the crease at the elf's hips.

Ursile pouted a little, then sighed and gave Octavia a very convincing pair of puppy eyes. "May I touch you, my lady? May I bring you pleasure?" she asked, whimpering softly as Octavia's fingers played right around the edge of her pants.

Octavia smiled. "You may." She cast her eyes to Aislin, curious if she was still content to simply sit. Aislin seemed to be enjoying the show.

"Thank you," Ursile said softly and took a step closer to Octavia, nearly pressing up against her.

Leaning forward, she began with soft kissing upon Octavia's breasts, a hand holding them up for easier access and softly kneading them. Octavia made gentle appreciative noises as she reached a hand up to play with Ursile's hair. The elf was making a very interesting noise that sounded like a cross between a soft purr and a field bird's chirp. She was worshipping Octavia's breasts with her touches and ministrations with her lips, only encouraged by Octavia's caressing. It was sweet and felt good, but it occurred to her that between Sumner's aggressive approach, Alces being… an experience, and Durante often not knowing his own strength, that this might be a little too soft. And why had Tiphanie told her not to take too long? At this rate, she would be in this room all night. Things needed to progress.

Careful not to actually disrupt the elf laying affection on her, Octavia gently ran a hand down Ursile's arm and carefully caught her wrist. The elf had reached Octavia's nipple, taking it into her mouth and sucking tenderly, her tongue playing over it. She kissed Ursile's wrist, then her palm, then ran her tongue across to the webbing between her thumb and forefinger and watched the elf's reaction as she sucked at the skin. She trilled and bit down a little out of surprise but leaned her body into Octavia and made up for the bite with more active licking. She was also squirming slightly.

"Oh, good guess," Aislin said, tossing off her pants and stretching out on the couch, now naked. "Perhaps secrets given by your patron?"

Octavia released Ursile's hand with a gasp and looked to Aislin with a smile. "Kamvasana tells me nothing," she said, a little breathy now. "Says that's cheating. But I've been in their service for many years. You learn some things." As she spoke, she switched hands, one gently sliding down Ursile's other arm as the other slid into her hair. She let her heavier blunted nails graze the back of Ursile's neck as she did.

"I think I'll have to get more acquainted with this Power at some point," Aislin pondered as her hands started to slowly explore herself.

Ursile went back to the softer, more gentle noises as she switched breasts to suckle at Octavia. Her hands released Octavia's breasts and slid down her body, going down her tummy and over her hips to grab her ass, firmly but deliberately. She alternated between squeezing her cheeks and spreading her open.

"Anything in particular you'd like your abbess to attend to, or are you happy with her services so far?" Aislin asked with a teasing smile.

"She's very lovely," Octavia said, sincerely, running both of her hands through Ursile's hair now, pausing to trace patterns on the back of her neck with her nails. Glancing over at Aislin, she wet her lips. "And what of you? I—ah! yes, just like that—I would have thought you'd prefer something more active?"

"I, um... I'd like to, but touching me tends to unsettle others. It's an effect of my nature," Aislin explained, a little embarrassed, but that didn't stop her from starting to please herself at the sight of the other two's actions.

Ursile smiled against Octavia's skin and started kissing her way down, moving to her knees before Octavia. Still gripping her ass firmly, she pulled Octavia close and leaned up, dragging her tongue over her slit before moving in. She ate Octavia out slowly and purposefully, praising her body with her motions. Octavia moaned, gently gripping Ursile's hair. She wasn't able to respond for a moment.

"I... ohhh yes... I touched you earlier," she managed at last.

"It's a bit more, mmm, intense intimately," Aislin explained. "I'm used to watching. Ah... I like seeing my Sisters happy."

That gave Octavia a bit of an idea. She looked down at Ursile. "You're doing so good, precious," she praised the elf, caressing her ear teasingly with her fingertips—elf ears tended to be sensitive. The odd cooing sound came out of Ursile picked up in pitch when her ears were teased. "Make me come, and then I have a task for you."

Upon Octavia's command, Ursile increased her attentions with gusto, her grip on Octavia's ass firm, with all the strength that allowed her to wield her massive, jagged sword. She kept Octavia in place as her tongue slid out to flick rapidly over Octavia's clit before diving back into her pussy. A motion she repeated many, many times.

"Ahhh, yes!" It seemed Ursile needed the right encouragement. Octavia gripped her hair again as she felt her peak racing up on her and let out a soft cry as her legs tensed, and she came on Ursile's eager tongue. Ursile guided Octavia through her orgasm, her tongue working wonders while she held Octavia's legs apart, making sure she couldn't close her legs and deprive her.

Panting, coming back to herself, Octavia released her grip on Ursile's hair and ran her fingers through it. "Good girl," she murmured. "Easy now. We have more to do."

Hearing Octavia praise her, Ursile released her grip and rocked back onto her heels. She kissed her way back up Octavia's body, briefly stopping at her breasts and neck, until finally sharing a kiss then standing before her.

"I am at your will, my lady," she said, biting her lip gently.

"Did you enjoy that?" Octavia asked as she slid her hands over Ursile's body, then reached into her open pants, sliding her fingers against her sex to see if those soft sounds of delight had been genuine.

"The important question," she started to say, before trilling as Octavia's fingers danced over her, "is have I pleeeeeased you, my lady?" Ursile's hands grasped Octavia's shoulders, keeping her up slightly. She was drenched and rocking her hips to press against Octavia's fingers.

"Oh, precious," Octavia murmured with a smile as she leaned in and kissed at Ursile's neck, sliding her fingers into the elf and teasing her. "You enjoyed that very much." She fingered Ursile for a minute, fluttered her tongue over her delicate, perky nipples and glanced back at Aislin.

"Lin, you've got toys, don't you?" Octavia grinned, continuing to finger Ursile. "I would be shocked if you didn't."

Ursile had a mix of purring song and whimpers as Octavia continued to finger her. She pressed her body up against Octavia where she could, her arms moving down to wrap around her waist and keep herself upright as her legs started to shake.

"Oh, plenty," Aislin sighed, pausing her self-pleasuring to slide gracefully off her couch. "Anything you're looking for?" She stepped over to her armoire and opened the left side of it. Inside was a plethora of sexual implements of various sizes, colors, and materials. Everything from artificial phalluses for manual stimulation, to strap-ons, a series of floggers, and even a sizable metal bar with padded braces on either side.

"Ohhh, that's quite a collection," Octavia said with open admiration, even as she continued to finger Ursile, shifting her hand so that her thumb pressed against the elf's clit as her fingers continued to move in and out of her. "Mmmm..." she left a sucking kiss on Ursile's neck, then looked back at Aislin. "Something double ended if you have it, and also whichever one's your favorite."

Ursile had a hard time keeping up, seeming to really enjoy Octavia's fingers. As Octavia looked back to Aislin, Ursile leaned down and bit down on Octavia's shoulder, stiffening against her as her first orgasm hit. The bite made Octavia moan, loudly. She did love being bit. Ursile shuddered but stayed in place, letting Octavia tease her more, use her as she wished. As the elf calmed, Octavia's hand slowed.

"I have an idea what you're looking for," Aislin smirked and reached in, pulling out a fairly good sized, double-ended toy with a strap a third of the way down to keep it in place. The other she removed looked remarkably like Alces' cock, although it was smaller overall and more bulbous in shape.

"That looks excellent," Octavia said, then kissed at Ursile again, gently extracting her fingers and pulling away from the elf. Glancing up at Ursile, she licked her fingertips. "Delicious." Ursile smiled dreamily at Octavia. "You are pleasing me, precious. Now get those pants off."

Ursile snapped at Octavia's command and quickly lost her pants, and any other clothing that might have still been left on her body. Turning around Octavia accepted the toys from Aislin and set them on the bench, then before the ethereal woman could react, grabbed her by the waist and pulled her in against Octavia's very warm and soft body. Aislin was taken by surprise and squealed slightly as the plushness of Octavia's body squished against her. She was about to protest, worried about ruining the evening that had gone so well so far, but instead moaned loudly and pressed back, unable to help herself.

Octavia felt what Aislin had meant. The tingling sensation from touching her earlier was amplified. It was like she was being cooled and warmed at the same time while her body was on pins and needles. It was a sensation that would be overwhelming and otherworldly had Octavia's sensitivity and ability to derive pleasure for nearly everything not been so keyed up. Instead, it was like a thousand tongues, half of which had been sucking an ice cube, were slathering her body.

"Oh, that's amazing!" Octavia squirmed against Aislin, nuzzling into her, and eagerly slid her hands over her pale skin, squeezing her ass, stroking her sides, teasing the edges of her tummy to see if it was as sensitive as Tiphanie had claimed.

"You... you like it!" Aislin gasped, still a little surprised, but very much enjoying Octavia's body. She was softly moaning until Octavia's fingers graced the edges of her tummy, then she shuddered in Octavia's arms and giggled slightly. Aislin wriggled in Octavia's arms a little but found it very pleasing. In return, she grabbed Octavia's ass and sent more of that ethereal sensation over her skin. Octavia smiled and slid her tongue over Aislin's breast, catching the nipple in her mouth and sucking gently. The ethereal knight let out the most beautiful, plaintive moan.

Octavia pulled back after a minute and looked up at Aislin. "So, I was thinking you should sit back down, and I'll kneel in front of you. I will touch you, kiss you, lick your poor neglected cunt, and use your favorite toy on you." She glanced back at Ursile. "While our lovely abbess gets behind me with the double toy."

"I like your plan," Aislin said, panting, "with one little caveat. I think we may need to utilize the bed." She wriggled out of Octavia's arms and picked up her toy, then crawled over the bench and scooted up on her bed, setting herself high up on it. "Get your lovely attendant ready and then come up here. I'm really looking forward to this."

Ursile recovered and held out her hands to take the larger toy. "How forceful would you like me to be, my lady," she questioned.

There was no reason to be utilitarian about this. Octavia took the longer dildo and the strap and stepped up to Ursile. She reached up and grasped the back of Ursile's neck, pulling her in for a kiss. As they kissed, Octavia eased the toy into Ursile gently until it was deep enough to get the straps in place. Ursile moaned loudly, her hands cupping Octavia's face.

The kiss broke, and Octavia started cinching everything in place. "You can be as forceful as you like, my precious," she said softly, smiling. "Though not so rough that you make it impossible for me to pleasure our captain. Is that all right?"

"I think I know just what to do, my lady," she said, panting, but with the same eager sincerity she'd displayed all night.

Aislin beckoned Octavia over while setting the toy down beside her leg. Within reach, but not in the way. As Octavia crawled over, Aislin reached up and with a slight easing twist, popped her head off. Continuing to smile, she held her head out to her.

"Since you seem to like how my magic feels, I'd like to lick you at the same time, if you're game for resting on my face." Aislin's grin was broad, clearly interested in doing so but also humored by what Octavia's reaction might be.

Octavia blinked and laughed. "As you wish. Though give me a moment to get into place." She slid herself up Aislin's body, pressing herself against the other woman once more, careful of the strange flame that flickered from her neck, and then slowly kissed her way down. She teased Aislin's nipples with her tongue, left sucking kisses and gentle bites along her belly. Aislin made a number of hauntingly delightful noises, especially when she kissed and nibbled on her tummy. When she had finally made her way far enough down, Octavia rose up on her knees to make sure everything was in place.

"Saints, it's been too long," Aislin cooed, a light shudder running through her.

"We'll make up for lost time," Octavia said with a grin, and held out her hand for the head. "Let's try this."

Aislin handed off her head to Octavia, making a kissy face at her as she did. Giggling, Octavia brought Aislin's head up to her own and kissed her, deeply, while the other woman moaned with a want that seemed to be growing more desperate. The strange tingling was even more intense as their tongues slid across each other. In a way, it reminded her of Alces. Not that they felt anything alike, but the intensity. Being with Aislin would be a memorable experience.

After the kiss broke, Octavia set the head carefully on the bed and spent a moment positioning herself against Aislin's mouth. "Ursile, precious, I think I need you to get into position to make sure I'm doing this right," she said with another giggle.

"You focus on my Sister, my lady. I'll handle everything back here," Ursile said, crawling up onto the bed on her knees. One hand holding Aislin, the other Octavia's hip, she positioned the three of them. Aislin's head was tilted just right, and Octavia felt that tingly tongue immediately start dancing over her clit and pussy.

Settling herself into position, Ursile paused Aislin's affections long enough to ease the other end of the toy into her mouth, letting her saliva coat the head. Satisfied, she set Aislin back in position, then pushed the toy into Octavia's pussy. It gave slightly, but otherwise filled her with a nice, hard shaft. Aislin's saliva brought a touch of the tingles, making the sensitive walls of Octavia's sex quiver. Octavia was panting now and needed a moment to take in the sensations.

"Is everyone good?" Ursile asked, and there was a loud, moaning sound of agreement from between Octavia's legs as Aislin went back to work on Octavia's clit.

"Yes, good," Octavia said breathily, then bent to her task.

She knew, objectively, that Ursile and Aislin together would have no trouble getting her to come. The tingling from Aislin's hungry mouth was already spreading through Octavia's sex, and she had no doubt she was going to come soon. But Aislin had presented her with an unexpected challenge, and she needed to make sure she gave the captain a night that would sustain her until someone else who could take her strange touch arrived.

Leaning in, she kissed at Aislin's thighs, wet kisses with a hint of tongue, and sucked hard at one side. She wasn't sure if she could leave a mark on the enchanted woman's skin, but she gave it her best try. There was a bright purple mark on Aislin's thigh as she let go, but it was already starting to fade when Octavia dove in. She then slid her tongue eagerly up Aislin's slit. Again, the sensations were intense, particularly against something as sensitive as the tongue, but Octavia moaned and focused, parting Aislin's lips and seeking her clit, swirling her tongue around it. Aislin's body reacted perfectly, squirming a bit, wriggling to Octavia's touch, and yet twisting and pressing in for more.

"That's so good," Aislin panted between licks. "Ah, eeee. Gods, you are talented." As payment for Octavia's efforts, she found her clit latched onto it, reverberations from Aislin's moans and cries transferring into Octavia's bundle of nerves.

Octavia found that Ursile was adept with the strap. The abbess's strong grip was a boon, as it meant Octavia didn't need to brace herself as fully as she might have. Ursile held her in place, and down to make sure Aislin was able to reach what she needed to. This also forced Octavia's back to bow and legs to spread farther. Moving into the bow of her back, she dropped her upper body against Aislin's thighs, which left her hands free to stroke over the captain's hips and stomach.

Braced in her position, Octavia felt Ursile start to move, gliding the toy in and out of her with full, solid strokes that would have shaken her had Ursile not pulled Octavia back at the same measure she was being pushed forward by the stroke. As she thought she would, Octavia came quickly. She shuddered and moaned, and in return curled her tongue around Aislin's clit as she suckled it. She wanted to see if she could get the captain to come once before she reached for the toy. Aislin wasn't far behind at all.

There was a tremor under Octavia's hands as Aislin tensed, and her hips bucked a little. She moaned loud against Octavia's pussy, then panted as she licked at her like ice cream. "So... so good," she whimpered.

The steady rhythm of Ursile's thrusting never wavered. This was her task now, and she was going to fuck Octavia until she told her to stop. It was impressive, as Octavia clearly heard the elf orgasm again, but aside from her trilling cry the only other indication was a tightening of her grip on her hip.

"That feels so good, Ulla," Octavia said, pitching her voice to make sure Ursile heard her. And it did. It would feel better if she wasn't so focused on Aislin, but she was still loving it and needed to make sure Ursile was properly praised.

"Thank you, my lady," Ursile panted. The elf shifted slightly, still holding her in place but able to run one hand up Octavia's back, gently raking her nails back down. She stumbled a little, but quickly moved back into rhythm, as another orgasm flowed through her.

Octavia bent her head and lapped at Aislin's flushed pussy then pulled back enough to see where the toy had landed. Reaching over, she shifted enough to grab it and begin to carefully work it into Aislin. Another loud moan came from between Octavia's legs as the knight lost her ability to focus for a moment. Octavia had no doubt the woman had played with it many times, but it had been a while without a partner, and that was always a little different.

Once Octavia found how much of the toy Aislin could take, she began to work it in and out of Aislin. Octavia's elbows were still supporting the weight of her upper body, which let her other hand slide back down over Aislin's tummy until her fingertips found her clit again. No one could see the somewhat feral quality to Octavia's smile as she began to move her fingertips in a circle, first around Aislin's glistening bead and then slowly inward, all while fucking her with that hefty toy.

"Oh, fuck, oh, fuck," Aislin started chanting again and again, building in volume as she did. She may have wanted this to last longer, but it was a lot suddenly, and she had been so keyed up once Octavia had suggested including her. Aislin nearly screamed, her voice sounding like a banshee, then had to back away from Octavia. Scooting up the bed until she was forced to sit upright, panting and playfully swatting away any of Octavia's advances. As Aislin pulled back abruptly, Octavia suddenly lost her bracing and face planted into the bed.

"No... no more. Too sensitive, Tavi. Saints, that was... oh, that was amazing," She whimpered, giggling slightly as her head rolled around unassisted on the bed.

Ursile took it upon herself to reach down and grab Octavia's left leg, lifting it so Aislin's head could be retrieved, but also to give her angle to push the fake cock in even deeper into Octavia. "My lady, mmmm, do you wish me to keep going like this," Ursile whimpered, "or change positions?"

Octavia laughed into the fur for a moment, then picked herself up. "Ulla, precious, stop for a second," she said, giggling. "Let's change positions. Lay down. I'll ride you and Aislin can watch."

"Mmm, of... of course," Ursile said, gently setting Octavia's leg down and sliding out of her. She took a moment to compose herself before crawling up next to Aislin and laying down, purring gently.

"Little help," Aislin giggled with a slight moan in her voice. Her head was still rolling around as they moved amongst the bed. Her body was reaching out, waiting to be handed her pate. Still giggling, Octavia picked up Aislin's head, gave her another exploring kiss, then handed it back.

"This is a delightfully memorable evening," Octavia said, still smiling as she climbed up across Ursile, kissing her as well before sliding herself back down on the dildo.

Aislin licked her lips and placed her head back into place. She was quite content to relax and watch the two of them have at each other. "I've certainly enjoyed myself," she commented.

"As have I," Ursile said, smiling up at Octavia after the kiss, running her hands up her body, squeezing as she went before resting her hands on her breasts.

"Are you ready, precious?" Octavia smiled her most beautiful smile at the elf beneath her.

"Ready for anything, my lady," she breathed.

"Anything?" Octavia giggled yet again and started to ride Ursile. Slowly at first to make sure they were both comfortable, but working up to a steady bounce fairly quickly, And, honestly, one she could maintain indefinitely. Aside from years of experience, and currently having three very regular partners, all the hiking here and there had done wonders for her leg muscles.

Ursile happily took Octavia's weight and movements, thrusting up her hips to match. She was certainly getting into it when Octavia set a rhythm, and she was moving with her. The shape of the toy and the nature of the strap meant they both felt the movements and the penetration, and Ursile was getting into it.

As she bounced on Ursile, Octavia caught her other wrist, the one she hadn't played with earlier, and brought it up to her mouth with a sparkle in her eye. She kissed up Ursile's wrist, peppered her fingertips with more kisses, and then sucked a little hard on that spot between the thumb and forefinger. Ursile cried out and arched her back. It was indeed a weak spot, and her hips lost the cadence. Instead, she squirmed and shuddered, thrusting up at varying times but with intensity.

Octavia shifted her hips back a little bit, still sucking at Ursile's hand, and slid her free hand down Ursile's belly to thumb carefully at the woman's clit. She'd already outlasted Aislin, the idea of leaving Ursile an equal mess was a tantalizing goal. Ursile squirmed again and moaned even louder, that off sing-songy trill filling the tent.

"Bondye, my lady, that's so sublime," she moaned, her voice catching as another orgasm shook through her. Octavia was indeed turning her into a shambling puddle.

Almost there. Octavia pulled off of Ursile's hand with a gasp, letting it go so that she could switch sides, knowing that too much sensation in the same spot would dull it. She changed which hand was teasing Ursile's swollen clit and then grasped the hand on her hip, bringing it up for a gentle bite at the wrist before glomping onto the known weak spot. Ursile was starting to lose it. Octavia was hitting every spot, constantly keeping her stimulated as she pummeled her deliciously with the toy. She let out another cry and then something snapped. Her sense of duty kicked in, and that purr turned into a growl. She carefully wrestled her hand away from Octavia, grabbed her hips firmly and started to thrust up hard into Octavia.

Octavia let out a surprised laugh but didn't fight Ursile for control. She relaxed into it, understanding the goal and slid her hands up her own body to play with her breasts as Ursile thrust into her. She was lifting Octavia's body with every pump of her hips. She needed to hear Octavia cum once more, she needed to be praised, she needed that sense of accomplishment before she could release.

"Yesss," Octavia hissed, eyes closed, head falling back. "Oh Gods… yes!" Octavia's legs locked as she came, resisting Ursile motions for a moment, then released. She fell forward, catching herself with her hands on either side of the abbess's head, panting.

It was at that point Ursile relented, slowing to a stop and panting underneath Octavia. She purred softly underneath her and reached up to caress Octavia's face, run fingers through her hair, and pull her down to kiss her. Now snuggly, she was lavishing in the afterglow of countless peaks of pleasure and the satisfaction of seeing Octavia cum by her own hand.

"Have I pleased my lady?" she asked softly. "Upheld my duty to you?"

"You did beautifully, precious," Octavia said with a smile, and another soft kiss. "You have more than upheld your duty."

"Thank you, my lady," Ursile said, returning the kiss and holding Octavia close against her before letting go.

Catching her breath, Octavia eased off of Ursile and helped the satiated elf remove the strap, gently withdrawing the toy and setting it aside next to the other dildo to be cleaned later. She gave Ursile a soft kiss, then came around the bed to give Aislin one more as well, then retrieved her dress.

"If I have satisfied you both, I believe I will find my way back to my bed," Octavia said with a smile, the dress over one arm, waiting to hear their answer.

"Oh, I'm very satisfied," Aislin said, sighing and stretching out on the bed. "You have done more for me this night than I could have hoped for. You're always welcome back."

Ursile moved to slide off the bed and stood, then needed to catch herself before she fell over. Exhausted and still a little drunk with nothing to focus on made her unsteady, and she giggled gently. "Oh, oh yes," she said, attempting to stand again. "I need to away back to my tent. Get there before I fall asleep."

Octavia slipped back into her dress, fastened the stays and found her slippers. "Do you require an escort, Ser Ursile, or do you think you'll make it?"

"I'll, mm, I'll be okay," she said, standing up straight and sighing. "It'll just take a moment. Thank you, my lady. Enjoy your night. I hope to see you in the morning."

She smiled. "Alces will undoubtedly wake me. I'll see you in the morning, my lovelies." She gave a little bow and slipped out of the tent.

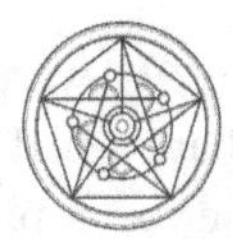

TWENTY ONE

Standing in the cooler night air, she took a breath and smoothed her hair back, then looked for the moon. It was late, but not too. Ursile's drunkenness and Aislin's sensitivity had made for a somewhat shorter evening. She made her way back towards her own tent at a leisurely pace.

Noises were softly emanating through the camp. Clearly, people were having a similar night as herself. The main table still had some abandoned mugs and plates, but otherwise the camp was cleared, everyone in their own places. Someone was causing a ruckus down in the keep ruins, and judging by the sounds, it was most likely Alces and Magnia. Probably safer that way.

The tent was quiet when she came in. It seemed the frivolities of the evening hadn't led anyone this way. Standing there, taking in the moment of calm, she heard some noise coming from Durante's room. It did not sound like activities on par with the rest of the camp. Something closer to glasses shuddering and objects being moved.

Slipping off her shoes, Octavia drifted over to the curtain that served as Durante's door. "Kitten? Everything all right?"

There was a shuffling of items, possibly a stumble, and then the curtain was drawn back. Durante was in a state, mostly one of being a general mess. He'd probably been sorting demon and fiend parts, given the spots of red and yellow on his hands, sleeves, and shirt.

"Oh, h-hi, Tavi," he said, with surprising shyness. "Yeah, I'm okay. I was just cataloging and preserving the parts I got tonight. How're you? Didn't really expect you back tonight."

She tipped her head to the side, curious. He didn't really get shy with her anymore. Certainly not when they were alone. She looked him over and laughed a little before casting the cleansing spell for what she hoped would be a final time that night. He smiled as her spell lifted the gunk off his hands and clothing.

"I'm fine," she said, smiling. "We were done early, and unless I'm too tired to move I don't tend to share a bed with someone without… well, more of a connection, I suppose you could say." She tossed her hair back over her shoulder. "Am I interrupting? I can leave you be if you're busy."

"Oh, no, not at all," he insisted, "I wanted to make sure this was done so I didn't worry about it later. You can come in, if you like." He started to step back to make room, then looked back at the mess behind him. "Actually, no. Main room?"

She giggled. "We need to build you a little construct that flits around and cleans up after you while you're working. Like a little fox or something." She stepped back, drifting towards the seating area.

"Oh, I could do that," he realized, "I hadn't thought of it." Durante followed behind her and waited for her to choose a seat so he could sit next to her.

She sank down on the couch and turned a little as she did. "Have you been here all evening? I had expected Tiphanie to request your attention for a little while."

Durante took up his seat and looked a little embarrassed. "Yes, just me," he said, fiddling a little with his fingers. "She, um, she did. But, you know, these reagents need to be handled carefully and preserved right away for full potency. Just wasn't time."

She smiled at him softly, turning a little more, her knee pressing against his leg as she leaned on the back of the couch. "Poor Tiphanie. And poor you."

"It's fine. I mean, she's pretty and nice and all, but didn't seem… like it wasn't… I didn't really want to," he said with a shrug. "Nothing against her. She seems great."

"Oh! Oh, of course, I mean," Octavia squirmed a little and tucked a curl behind her ear, "I had assumed, particularly after the last celebration, and I think Tiphanie is delightful so… I'm sorry. But no, if you don't wish to, I was not trying to imply you should have."

"No, don't apologize," he said, reaching out and taking one of her hands, giving it a squeeze. "Nothing's wrong, you didn't do anything wrong, I'm just… thinking about things."

She squeezed his hand back. 'What are you thinking about?"

Durante thought for a long moment, caressing her hand with his thumb, and looked back at her. "Okay, Tavi, I can trust you, right? Of course I can, silly thing to ask. But, you won't laugh at me or disregard me, right?"

"Of course you can trust me," she said, brow furrowed. She sat up straight and looked him in the eyes. "And I will not laugh at you, and certainly not disregard you. What is it?"

Durante had another thoughtful sigh and looked up and into her eyes. His had changed to a soft pink, a calming color of his if he had one. "I hope this isn't weird for you, or I'm reading things wrong, but the reason I didn't want to do anything with Tiphanie is because, well... I love you. And I wanted to... only be with you."

There was a moment of quiet as Octavia looked into Durante's eyes, cheeks flushed, lips slightly parted. "I... Kitten... darling..." She felt that flutter under her ribs, stronger than perhaps it ever had been, but she understood it now.

He spoke rapidly, as if he needed to finish his thoughts before she answered. "Not that I want you to change or anything about us or the others to change. But for me, I didn't want to go off with anyone else because all I could think about was you. Tiphanie's nice, she's pretty and all that, but she wasn't you. And... and yeah. That's what's going on in my head."

There was one more breath of quiet, then she slid into his lap and wrapped her arms around him as she kissed him until she had to pull back for air. While a little surprised, Durante had no qualms about pulling her in close and holding her there as they kissed. When she pulled back, he was a little dazed but smiled softly.

"Do you remember the other day," she said, caressing his cheek, "when you asked me what would make me happy, and I couldn't answer?"

"Yeah," he replied expectantly.

"It... it was because I realized I did know what made me happy, but I didn't know how to tell you, or if it was too much," she said, sliding her fingers through his hair. "You make me happy. I could spend the rest of my life like this, the four of us. I don't need anything else."

Smiling more broadly, Durante sniffed and dots of tears formed in the corners of his eyes. "Really? I wasn't sure, with your patron and everything, I didn't want to say anything and make it all weird," he said, overanalyzing. "But really? You're happy with us? With me?"

"Yes, really." She kissed him softly, and murmured, "I love you, Durante Calabria."

His smile at that moment was the most beautiful thing she had ever seen. She felt her own emotions rise, her eyes shiny with unshed tears. She laughed softly and caressed his face again.

"I'm happy with you, your inquisitive mind, your gentle heart, the way you look at me sometimes like I'm a gift you're still shocked you received. And with Alces' bombasity and Sumner's passions. I..." She laughed again, and one tear slid down her cheek. "I love you."

Durante wrapped his arms tightly around Octavia and leaned in, hugging her close and kissing on her neck and up to the side of her face. "I love you, too," he whispered. "I'm... you're so wonderful. Thank you."

She giggled, nuzzling into him. "Why are you thanking me?"

"Why shouldn't I be?" he asked, running a hand up into her hair. "You're beautiful and wonderful and smart and you want to be with me. Why shouldn't I be thankful for that?"

She kissed his cheek and giggled again. She didn't know what else to do with this strange, bubbling joy inside her. She kissed all over the side of his face and down his neck, nuzzling into him and breathing him in as if this was their first time together.

"I love you," she said again. "And I do want to be with you. You're clever, you're capable, you're so handsome. I... I didn't know how to tell you. I was afraid I'd gotten ahead of myself. I was afraid it was strange because of how I have feelings for all of you." She pulled back so she could look at him and smiled. "My Kitten. My darling." She caressed his face and drew her thumb over his lower lip. "My love."

Durante was still smiling, although his eyes were dewy and his cheeks a little wet from the tears of joy. "Yes, my sweetest Tavi," he softly said as he kissed her thumb.

She giggled again, and slid out of his lap to stand up, holding her hand out to him. "Come to bed with me. You've done enough tonight, and you've already said it's a mess in there. Come with me."

He took her hand and rose, keeping a hold of her hand and squeezing it. "I would love to. Always," he said, following close behind.

The adventure concludes in...

Saved by Desire

Coming in 2026!

ABOUT THE AUTHORS

Clea Salar (she/her) is a bi, sassy freelance writer who spends most of her days glaring at her computer in between bouts of actually writing. She's a specialist in all things fantastic, with an impressive resume that includes such skills as spending recess and lunch in the library reading folklore and mythology books all through school, a familiarity with a variety of role-playing games, and regular attendance at every convention and Renaissance festival within driving distance. Clea loves bubble tea, tiny desserts, and the Oxford comma.

Tallis Salar (he/him) is a Jack of All (IT) Trades who would rather be diving, at least until "space viking" becomes a viable career path. He loves a good sci-fi, and is happy to explain why "Aliens" is the greatest film ever made. His creative background includes a staggering number of role-playing games, particularly as the GM. Tallis can be bought with video games, sour candies, and frozen drinks (this is a joke, he can't actually be bought, but he welcomes you to try).